# CHAIN DANCE
## The Books of Joy – Volume Three

# Alexis Brooks de Vita

## CHAIN DANCE
## The Books of Joy – Volume Three

DOUBLE DRAGON

# DEDICATION

For My Children and My Readers

# Table of Tales

John the Conquer and the Devil's Daughter: Rhea, born
1778
The Warmth Between: Ella, born 1800
Something Like God: Myra, born 1790
Who: Layla, born 1788
To Feel Everything: Rose Red, born 1787
Now What Do You Believe: Vivian, born 1766
Only Angels: Baby Joy, born 1821
Fall off the World: Sister, born 1752
Lost Tale: Hope, born 1811

# Plantation Record of the Women's Births

Winged Daughter, born 1740
Sister, born 1752
Daughter, who becomes Mother Magdalen, born 1753
Mammy Water, born 1756
Vivian, born 1766
Angel, born 1767
Angel Girl, born 1769
Rhea, born 1778
Heaven, born 1786
Rose Red & Rose White, born 1787
Layla, born 1788
Myra, born 1790
Ella, born 1800
Solace, born 1804
Hope, born 1811
Baby Joy, born 1821

# CHAPTER ONE

JOHN THE CONQUER AND THE DEVIL'S
DAUGHTER: RHEA, BORN 1778

My man used to have a real name and a title, too. His
name used to be John and his title used to be Conquer
because he killed more drivers than any other man in the
Quarters.

Maybe I sound proud of my man. He was a good
man, while he was alive. Now that he's dead, he still tries.

I can't fault him. John never went out to stud even
when Mr. Dennis offered him money. Mr. Dennis said,
"John, look here. You go do up these young women for
me, get them big with babies all strong-armed like
yourself, and I might just give you something for it."

But my John said, "No, sir," because we made
promises to one another.

Promises in the dark. Folks talk down about promises
between people who ain't even free. They say what kind
of fool takes a notion in your head to break your own
heart, swearing to be true? "You are both a fool to believe
in anything your owner never signed his name to."

But my John said, "If we can't have each other, we
don't want nobody." And we promised to live together till
we die.

And we did, too. I have gone beyond our promise and
been with John long after he's dead. And I never held it
against him, either.

That is, not until the devil's daughter showed her face
around here.

That Mr. Dennis is the very devil. Folks on his farm
had no religion, no knowledge of good and evil between

11

the earth and sky and us trapped, running scared, in the middle.

But I come from a ma'am who taught me how to pray. Can't say my prayers turn out much like I want them to, though.

Like how I prayed to get rid of that Mr. Peter, the meanest overseer who ever clapped eyes on a woman.

I told you my John has killed many a driver. But I was scared to think what might happen if John up and killed this overseer, Mr. Peter. Because an overseer ain't no driver. And Mr. Dennis might not take it kindly if his overseer turned up a mass of rot and moss in the woods, like his drivers steady be doing.

But that Mr. Peter had his eye on me like I ain't never seen no man do no woman. Nasty man, that Mr. Peter. Brought disease and pestilence to the plantation and went around killing folks like a walking plague till we feared to farm the land for digging up dead bodies. The burying pit wasn't so far off that we didn't have to worry about where the wild animals dragged the body parts off to.

So I ain't told John nothing about this Mr. Peter and his mean old nasty eye on me. I figured, if Mr. Peter is so deadly he ain't even got to lay a finger on folks to kill them, I sure didn't want him to lay hands on my John.

But neither did I want his hands on me. So I up and said my prayers. "Powers that be, get this nasty Mr. Peter away from me," because spirits like it if you kind of sing to them.

And I said, "Powers in the sky, don't let my John the Conquer die," because what if Mr. Peter dragged my man off to the grave with him some way I didn't figure out when I said that first prayer?

The spirits must have been listening good. But sometimes what you fear is go'n creep up on you, no matter what prayers you say.

So that devil's daughter came on out from the spirit world, where she must have been hiding. She came out of the woods where her and her brother grew up wild as beasts and bloodthirsty as the bogeyman.

They wasn't free for one day before her brother committed to murder the man who stole them from their devil daddy. And only once he had blood on his hands rich and thick did the devil's boy come back on home.

But now that wild devil boy had got him a taste for murder. Couldn't stop killing up on folks. Wasn't home a minute, standing to wed one of the prettiest gals from out the cotton fields, and the devil's boy jumps up and blasts a hole straight through that walking disease, Mr. Peter.

His devil daddy don't say nothing but, "If you have finished with that business, son, let's get on with this wedding."

And Mr. Peter feeds the vultures.

So I'm watching the wedding and say to myself, "Ain't half bad, them prayers I done said." But still. Something just ain't right around here. I can feel it.

And sure enough. Three days. The devil's boy and his brand-new bride have hightailed it to the woods to honeymoon up and get acquainted with each other. Either they liked each other something fierce or ain't had much taste for each other's company because they're already making their way back to the plantation.

And here she comes, holding hands and skipping through the forest with them. The devil's daughter. On her way to rend my life and take my John from me.

Her first evil sign: her devil pap comes up to my shack and says, "Where's John?"

John hoists his big self off our pallet and comes out the rag door, squinting. He can't half see because the sun ain't even up yet.

I got a bad feeling.

Mr. Dennis says, "John, I need me a new overseer. My boy done killed the last one, and I'm tired of hunting up stray wight mens to do this job. Besides, I got a notion they keep secrets. Scares me when I sleep."

My John says, "Mr. Dennis, I know just how you feel, sir. Lot of folks can't sleep when it's overseers prowling the Quarters."

Mr. Dennis says, "So, John, guess what? It's you I done picked to be my new overseer. Driver, too. Everything. You're big enough. Here. Take this whip I brought you."

John says, "Sir, no disrespect. But I can't do no such thing."

Mr. Dennis blinked. Stepped back like he needed to think about this a little minute. Said, "Say what, John?"

My John didn't miss a beat. "I done spent my whole life, sir, keeping your drivers and your overseers off my people's back. How can I take that whip in my hand and turn driver my own self? It'd be like I turned traitor."

Mr. Dennis reared back and peered at John like maybe he'd never got a good look at him before.

Then Mr. Dennis shook his head like he must not have heard right. Tilted his head to one side and kind of studied up on John.

I held my breath, thinking fast of what to say before Mr. Dennis decided to ply that whip his own self.

14

But then Mr. Dennis looked like he made up his mind to laugh it off. He said, "John," chuckle, chuckle, "boy, I'd best give you a minute to wake up. We ain't out here before sunup playing no games, now."

John didn't take that minute Mr. Dennis gave him. "Sir, I been sitting up here wide awake since sundown, waiting on you. I already knew what you was coming here to ask me."

Mr. Dennis bust right on out and laughed. "John, John. You know me better than that! Don't you? I didn't come here to ask you nothing."

John looked confused. "But, sir-"

Mr. Dennis clicked his tongue like a woman who ain't got no more time for nonsense. "I've done my asking, John. I have dragged around these Quarters for two or three days now asking who the men respect and the women trust. And I ain't got but one name. Yours." Mr. Dennis squared his shoulders back. "So I have done my asking. I ain't standing here asking you *nothing*. I'm *telling* you, John. Take this here now whip in your hand. And put a gag in your sass." Mr. Dennis held out his own hand to show John a whip looped around the palm like a snake coiled to strike.

John didn't flinch. And he didn't say nothing more but, "Sir, I can't do no such craven thing."

Mr. Dennis lost what patience he never had. "Oh yes, John. You most certainly can do what I say. And more to the point, you *better*. You are going to take this whip in your hand or on your back. It's all the same to me."

"Sir, it ain't the same to me. I ain't never go'n take that whip in my hand."

I said, "John. *Please*."

John said, "Woman. Hush."

15

And Mr. Devil Dennis speaks up. "John, you best listen to that big-belly woman of yours." Because I was carrying our first child. Soon turned out to be our only child, too.

John shook his head. "I done listened to both of you all, sir. And I done said my say. Which one of you all don't know that no means no?"

I ain't never seen quiet like the quiet that came over Mr. Dennis, at that. He looked like a man struck by a revelation.

I'm whispering, "John, say 'sorry, sir.' Say you didn't mean it, John. *Please*, John," but John ain't letting on that he hears me.

Mr. Dennis heard me though. And he's twice as mad when my John doesn't say another word.

Next time Mr. Dennis opens his mouth, I hear fire roar and smell brimstone on his breath. "John, you are going to teach my field hands to mind me one way or another. It looks like you have chosen the hard way. But like I said, it makes me no never mind, as long as the job gets done."

And with that, Mr. Devil Dennis turns his back on my John and sticks two fingers in his mouth to whistle up some mens to come and get my John.

They don't like it. But they drag my John out and strap him to the whipping post.

Mr. Dennis comes toting a gun, long and pointed.

He lays it on the ground. He uncoils that whip off his hip. He hefts it, like he's measuring the distance between him and my John, where John's all tied up.

And then Mr. Dennis rears back and snaps his arm forwards and lays into my John's back.

One stroke. And the skin puckers like it's rising to kiss the whip. Blood runs behind the whip trail like juice from a woman in love.

Two strokes. The skin grabs hold and caresses that whip like it ain't never letting go. And now the blood runs like tears down my face.

Four strokes. Skin gets ripped across cuts already made. Nobody should be this close to my John, all up in his flesh and blood, but me and our baby. This is wrong.

Eight strokes. Bone shows, but my John won't let one sound come out from between his lips. So I scream for him.

Sixteen strokes. My John's blood runs like fire and the flood over the growing grass, both green and red where he sags on the sides of his feets because he can't stand no more.

Thirty-two strokes, and I'm shrieking like a madwoman, tugging and yanking at the arms that hold me back.

Sixty-four strokes. And I have fallen to the ground and broke their hold on me and crawled and scrambled to throw myself between my John the Conquer and that devil slaver Mr. Dennis.

I'm in the grass and the gore, piecing back together bloody strips of my John's back and pleading, "No, Mr. Dennis, sir. I'll do anything. Take and tote that whip my own self. Just don't whip my John no more. Sir, can't you see you killing my man?"

The whip falls again, and I'm face down in the blood and mud now, blinded.

When I come to, I find that folks have carried me and my John back inside our shack and laid us out like maybe we're dead, together.

We wake up alone.

I'm on my back. I can barely see the slabs of ceiling over my head for that whip cut I took across my face. I roll over and go to cry on John's shoulder. He's facedown, so still I think he's dead. But his skin burns under my cheek like cooking stones.

After a while, he turns his head so I can see where he's been crying like a baby.

I say, "John, I love you. And I'm still go'n love you when you live and take that whip in your hand and be the new whip man."

He fell asleep. Or passed out.

And next morning in the field, here comes the second sign. That devil's daughter, Heaven.

My poor man is bending over in the field. He can't rightly stand, but Mr. Dennis and his mens done dragged him here to make a point.

John is swaying on his feets, groping for cotton bolls like a blind man. And a chill wind blows like it's coming to hold him up.

Next thing I know, John ain't just standing and swaying but sets in to moaning and rolling his eyes all up in his head, like when we was young and had run off in the trees and the swamp together. Some of that moaning might be pain, but some of it? I'm ashamed to say what it sounded like to me.

"John," I called, and ran and caught him by his arm before he fell in another faint.

But them Quarters mens? They never looked up.

When my poor man woke the next day, he stumbled up to Mr. Dennis in the field and took that whip right out of his hand. Not another word of complaint.

Maybe I'd done wrong to set my man to take that whip and live. But now that he'd done it, there wasn't no turning back.

Maybe I got what I deserved. Because in a couple more days, the third evil sign ripped my life in two: the first half was happiness, which was gone for good, and now misery came to stay forever.

The devil's daughter came on home.

She came out of the woods with her brother and his bride, laughing and crying, clean out of her mind. But she wasn't so out of her mind that she couldn't keep her beady little eye on my John.

Two or three weeks, and my John and that devil's brat are hightailing off to the woods together. And fool me, I'm off after them, steady telling myself, "Has my John gone crazy, or has he lost his mind?"

Because a blind man can see that if Mr. Devil Dennis catches hold of my John one more time, my John is going to have hell to pay.

And Heaven, too. That devil's brat.

So I'm off after them.

And I fell and twisted my leg in the burying ditch.

I told you that burying pit got full up when Mr. Peter was around here, cursing people with his evil eye. But that was some time ago. Folks in the pit have been gnawed down to bones by time and the seasons and the wild beasts.

Now, I have never been one to say a mean word about the dead. I say prayers for them and to them, when the mood strikes me right. You can get you some good results that way. Only, most of the dead, once they have turned to bone and ash, you have got to be careful dealing with them.

They have changed on you.

If you go out there and rustle their skulls and disturb their rest, that's a different matter. I wouldn't recommend it. Not unless you're hardheaded and just don't care what happens.

But me, I wasn't like that. I had John's baby bigging in my belly, and I wanted to live. So when I fell in that pit and couldn't get out, I set in to screaming and clawing my way through them dusty bones.

And they started in to rattling like they was telling me off. Bones said, "Woman! What you doing in here?"

And I said, "John! Come find me!"

And bones said, "Let me catch on that warm slim ankle, there. I ain't felt nothing that good in a long time."

And bones said, "She don't want that wet warm body of hers, I know somebody can use it."

And bones said, "Baby, too. Feel on that big hard belly." And their teeth was just clacking and grinning in the dark.

And me, I was screaming for help.

Me and them bones was at it all night. I don't know to this very day where my John and that devil's wench had got off to, that they didn't hear me.

If John heard me, he didn't care. I was out of my mind with fear when folks found me in the morning.

Why them folks come looking for me in the burying pit, I'll never know. Maybe they figured that devil's brat did away with me, once and for all.

And my John was in the fields that day, toting the devil's whip.

Me all limp in the people's hands, I opened my eyes in the sunlight and dust and seen the evil growing out of my poor John like horns on his head when folks carried my body on home past the field. My John turned and watched, giving me his new evil eye.

John ain't come to see about me for two or three days. I lay up in our shack just wishing I was dead, aching with the pain in my heart. If I could have moved, I would have crawled on back to that pit and flung my fool self in it. Lucky for me, I guess, that John had become the Whip Man, because I couldn't have crawled out to go pick that cotton, even if Mr. Dennis had whipped me to death.

I couldn't move. But my baby sure could.

It made my belly climb up like it was going to push through the roof and greet the day. It made my belly roll to one side like it was going to fall clean off and crawl across the smooth dirt floor. Then it made my belly roll to the other side like it changed its mind and was going to split and go two separate ways, like me and my John.

Then one night, something like strong hands came and started pressing that baby right out of me.

Pain whipped up my spine and shot out between my teeth in screams.

The pain was sharp and deep. And, I'm telling you, I'm a woman who knows pain. That lash I caught for John wasn't my first. My poor back is a sight that can shock your eyes.

But that little baby getting rocked out of my body by hands I couldn't see was pain such as I ain't never dreamed it could be.

Awake, I called for help.

Fainted to sleep, I'd see claws rake my belly from the inside.

But the baby ain't came. Just rocked back and forth and up and down, like he traveled alongside me on a sea of despair.

For days, my John ain't showed.

The womens came and tried to help me with my busted leg and my baby. They said, "Push, Rhea!" and, "Don't push!" and "Lay still," and "Roll over on your side." Because, truth be told, nobody had no idea what was wrong and how to fix it.

Till I woke up in the darkest part of one night and seen sitting here beside me my John. Only, when I opened my eyes all the way and said, "John, it's you," he said back to me, "Don't you never call me that fool name John the Conquer no more. My name is Whip Man now." And he set his hands on me, and that pain shot through me like fire.

I tried to pass out but the pain slapped me awake. All I could do was close my eyes. And when I did, I seen claws sprout right out of my John's hands to match the horns shooting out of his head. He turned and looked at my closed eyes with his own glowing red just like that blood he spilled at the devil's feet, getting whipped into the Whip Man.

And I said, "John, the Whip Man ain't you."

And he said, "I told you, woman. My name is Whip Man now." And he dug in and gouged out my belly like a wild beast.

I knew I was a goner. I'm lolling and rolling my head to one side to see what might be left of my John catching my blood in a cooking pot to drink it down. I beg him, "John, baby, where is the womens who was helping me?"

And this new man who ain't my John says, 'If womens come through that door, I swear I'll eat them alive." And he licked his tongue out between his lips.

And just in the gray light of morning when I see the bones crawl out of the burying pit to come get me and my poor baby, I hear that baby cry.

I opened my eyes.

And it was John. My old sweet John the Conquer. And he's holding my little wiggle-butt brown baby to his chest like any woman couldn't do more gentle.

Singing to the baby, too.

John looked at me. And his eyes was brown as the good earth. And his smile lit that shack like the sun.

I said, "John, it's you."

And he said, "Rhea, woman, I love you." And he put the baby to my breast and hugged us all three together.

But no time, and the devil's daughter ups and drops her a baby, too.

Wasn't we all scared, out in the Quarters? "What will that crazy Mr. Devil Dennis do to us hardworking folks, now?"

But my John ain't quivered, and he ain't quaked. He stood straight and tall and said, "Wasn't me did no wrong."

Even when that whip-happy Mr. Dennis came for him, my John said, "Rhea, you got to believe me, baby. I ain't touched that woman. Her baby ain't mines."

I shook my head. It hurt me to do it. But I said, "John, you ain't never studded when Mr. Dennis told you to. You ain't studded for good times nor for money. But you was always one for love, John. I believe you done loved that devil's daughter, and the devil's come to make you pay the price."

That devil said, "I ain't meant my gal to love no fool ain't even free. I ain't got no family left but her and my boy. And I had it in mind that she'd be a wight woman for me, never mind her ma'am was one of you all. Now look, you worthless no-account field hand, what you have done. You gave her your baby and ruined her for good."

And Mr. Devil Dennis whipped my John without mercy and said, "Whip Man, you ain't bigged the bellies I told you to, and you turn around and big the only belly you know I didn't want you to touch. You don't even know what to do with this here. I'd better take it and keep it out of trouble for you."

And he cut my John till he wasn't a man no more.

Tears stood in my eyes till I couldn't see. There comes a time when you daren't cry.

I stood still and close by my John while his good blood ran and my baby slept. When he hushed to screaming, I said, "I don't care what you done, John, and I don't believe no lie, neither. I'll stand by you till you die, and it looks like that might be any minute now, baby."

I wanted to take him on home.

But wouldn't none of the mens touch him to drag him back to our shack. They turned away and said, "Let the womens lay hands on a woman." Because what happened to my John was a curse and a shame.

So it was me with my baby strapped to my back who had to drag my man, my own self.

The womens came and saw me and said, "Rhea, we'll help you, child. You're a good woman who never gave up on your man."

I said, "We made us a promise long ago. To stand together till the day we die."

Only, he ain't died. Not yet.

I pulled shut our rag door, and I lay myself and my baby down next to my John. I ain't tried to staunch no blood. Figured that wasn't no use, with him already dead in the sun, like that.

Day turned to night. I couldn't figure why John's body ain't set in to stinking, in this heat.

Then I woke to find him nuzzling after my breast milk. So I turned on my side and fed him.

The next day, a woman named Sister came to me in our shack. She said, "Rhea, evil days done fell on us around here. What can I do for you, to help?"

And I said, "Fix my baby boy a sugar teat. I need my milk to nurse his pap. John ain't died, but he can't live on air."

So Sister held our baby boy. And John the Conquer died under the whip and the knife, and we watched him get born anew, taking suck like a child.

Now everybody called him Whip Man. Not because he toted that whip no more. He didn't. But because when you looked at him, all you could see was what the whip had left behind.

The whip ate deep and drank plenty of blood. You couldn't rightly tell what you was looking at, when you looked at my Whip Man.

Watching Whip Man suck, Sister said, "Rhea, look out. That devil's daughter done up and died. Could be you two is going to have more hell to pay."

I said, "Sister, we done paid hell and Heaven, too."

And Sister laughed a little because that crazy Devil Dennis done named his evil little wench "Heaven."

And then the dead bones of Heaven's conjure woman grandmother, laid up alone till she shriveled and died in her shack, rose up and started to dance.

It was night. The sky was bright with stars. Somebody lit a fire near our shack, so folks could gather and recount all the strange goings-on at the farm.

And that dead body, wrapped in a little skin and a winding cloth around her hips, came wiggling and stomping in the dirt.

When this woman was alive, she was a powerful conjurer. She could tell the future. She could make babies in your belly, or bring Mr. Dennis and whatever overseer crawling on hands and knees to beg her please make things go right around here.

But when the spirits seized her, told her, "Come on back to the land of the dead and the ain't-happened-yet," that conjure woman would lie right down and sleep so she took neither food nor water.

But when the devil's brat came straggling home, her old conjure grandmother had up and died.

Folks said, "She must have looked down from the starry sky and said, 'I best get while the getting is still good.'"

And she got. Didn't leave anything but her body behind.

And ain't that just what that grabby devil's brat seized upon? The conjure woman's dead body.

Heaven put it on like a dress and set it to dancing.

It danced around the fire and made the flames flicker in its empty eye sockets. It stared around at the people like it was fixing to drag you down to hell, crying mercy.

Folks shied away. They went quietly home in the night. They pulled shut their little rag doors and hoped that death would dance on by.

At dawn, the death dancer's rotted meat bones shuffled on back to the conjure woman's shack.

Folks heaved a sigh.

Some went to help her devil pap bury Heaven's body, and they whispered to it, "Rest in peace, now." Only, we all knew she wasn't about to rest.

And the next night, sure enough, Heaven rose in the conjure woman's clicking bones, searching out some more fire to dance by, and staring them empty eyeholes around like she dared anybody to tell her to get back to the grave where she belonged.

Next night, the womens get slick. They build that fire near the conjure woman's shack so her bones ain't got so far to go to dance.

The mens stand around, jeering. "You can't do no better than that? We can take that rotted corpse and pitch it in the burying ditch for you, if you scared."

Womens said, "If you that stupid, go ahead."

So the mens sneak in by the light of the next day and lay hold of the sleeping bones.

It sits up. Fixes its eye sockets on one of the mens.

And he drops dead. Blam on the floor.

The mens skedaddle.

Then one or two of them get up some nerve and sneak back in the shack. They haul the dead man out and dump him in the burying pit in the conjure woman's place. His widow's screaming.

Folks run around and say, "Now who's go'n try to get rid of this dancing dead thing? I know! Go ask that John the Conquer. He was always brave, and we hear he ain't even dead yet."

So they come to my shack.

I slap aside that rag and say, "You all must is crazy. My man ain't lived but for the milk out of my breast, and I

27

swear if it will be the last thing I do, I'm going to make sure he dies easy."

They all look shamefaced at each other's feets and say, "Come on now, Rhea. That death dancer is haunting everybody. Send the Conquer to help us out."

I say, "You should have thought of that when I was hauling the Conquer home with my baby on my back. Shoo! Get on out of here."

Now what did I mention babies for? The womens pipe up. "Now, Rhea. You know we helped you, and we all got babies. What do you want to sit back and see them go all zombie-eyed for? How will that keep your man from dying?"

And they was right, come to think of it.

So I said, "What you all womens want from me now?"

They said, "From you, nothing. From your husband, go see that dead woman and tell her scram. Tell her these Quarters has got enough trouble without her kind moving in."

They had me there. But I said, "No. I didn't ask what you want from my man. I asked what you want from me, my own self."

They gone away, but they must done talked.

Because at nightfall, they straggled in off the fields and crowded around outside my shack, peeking and turning their backs till I shouted, "Now what?"

They said, "Rhea, we helped you drag your husband home to die. Do us this one thing. Go ask that man who is alive from the sweat of our hands to go see that death dancer and tell her to hit the road."

So I dropped shut my rag door and went to my man where he lay on our mat.

I said, "Whip Man. You know I love you. If these here womens ain't helped me drag you home, you and me both would be done lain down in the bloody grass and died on top of the baby. So I am bound to ask you this one favor. Are you going to do what they say and go talk to that walking dead woman?"

Whip Man broke my heart again. He opened his eyes and said, "If I can, I sure enough will."

I said, "No. You ain't understood me right. If you say you can't, I'll go tell them womens to get lost. Tell me you can't even move, Whip Man."

He said, "But, Rhea, I can. Look here." And he reached off that mat, grabbed a handful of dirt and pulled his self on out of my door.

It was slow going. My heart and my mind scraped every inch of ground my man's body covered. I said, "Whip Man, look at you. You're crawling dead, your own self. Please don't do this, baby."

And he reached his nails and dug in that dirt and pulled his bloody body along. I couldn't do nothing but follow.

He got all the way to the conjure woman's shack. Womens fall back before him, like in the old days.

The possessed conjure woman's body ain't up yet. Still some sunlight left. So Whip Man props his self against where she's got to come out the door. He says, "I'll sit here and wait."

I say, "In this sun? You go'n be dead for sure by the time she rise."

And he says, "Rhea. I used to be John the Conquer. Don't you all never call me that fool name no more. But I'm dogged if I don't sit here and see if I can't do me one last brave deed before I lie down and die."

Folks whispered, "Just look at him."

The sun went flat. And the rag door parted.

The death dancer came on out.

She set her little foot dainty on the soft dirt outside her door, stirred up from all this dancing. She leaned her body out of the shack and raised her can't-see-nothing eyesockets to the sky, as if to gaze on the moon and the stars, or maybe just to feel the fresh air blow through her skull. Then she turned her face like she could feel that fire the womens had lit near Whip Man, warming her dead bones.

Then she came on out and started to dance.

All of us stood around the fire and stared. But my Whip Man looked like he had died in his sleep and wasn't thinking about that death dancer.

The flesh was falling off her arms when she raised them and dropping off her thighs under her rag skirt. Strings of meat hung off her bones a starving dog wouldn't sniff.

And she just danced.

Head thrown back, skinny skull bouncing. The sun set and the moon rose, and the fire's flames licked at the black night sky.

And she danced on.

Mens started creeping around Whip Man. "John the Conquer? You ain't rested up yet? Death be dancing now. What you go'n do about it?"

Whip Man raised his tired head. "Me, I'll do anything you all want. But John the Conquer is dead and can't do nothing. I told you all don't call me that fool name no more."

Mens said, "We right behind you."

And Whip Man said, "Ain't nobody behind me but my wife. Now get on out my way. You all makes me tired when I needs my strength." And he hiked his self up, hanging off the conjure woman's shack.

He started in toward the death dancer. Looked like she didn't see him.

He got closer.

She danced on.

He got right up on her.

And she turned them empty eyeholes in her skull on him and stared.

Womens bit their fingers and shrieked. Mens fainted away. I went down on my knees and prayed.

But Whip Man? He didn't move a muscle. He stood still and stared at the death dancer. "You want me? Take me. But first you go'n tell me why you here." And he stared where she didn't have no eyes.

She slowed her dance to a little shuffle. She came forward towards my John.

Me and all the womens screamed and raised our hands to the sky. They asked him to do this, but all of a sudden they don't want to watch.

They fell in the dirt on every side, crying out and talking about, "Tell him shut his eyes, Sister Rhea! Tell him don't look! Don't even speak to her. She's the devil's daughter, for sure."

And that's when I knew it was Heaven.

Not her conjure grandmother, Mammy Water. Nobody but that sneaking, man-stealing little troublemaker, Heaven.

It hurt me. But I crawled as close to her as I could stand the stink and the sight and said, "Heaven. You already took my man from me once. You made me fall in the burying pit. You took him again, and sent me the devil in his place to come birth my baby. You took him a third time, and now he ain't even a man no more. Heaven, when are you going to do right by me and quit to taking my man? What did I do to you but ask my man to be careful or you'd get him killed? And ain't you done just like I said? How did I ever wrong you, to make you do me this way? Leave him be, I'm begging you. Just leave us alone."

You could hear that fire snap.

You could hear them crickets hum.

You could hear your own heart beating. I know I heard mine.

But you couldn't have heard nothing else. Not a fall. Not a scream. Not even one child whining. Folks sat where they fell in the dirt and watched that dancer with my man.

She dragged her foot and the skin rolled off so the creamy bone showed. The death dancer dragged her body dropping pieces everywhere till she got right up on my Whip Man. And Whip Man just swayed and dipped and stood still.

She raised her bony arms ain't got much flesh left.

My man leaned on in toward her.

She laid her stringy dead arms on both his shoulders and looked him in his bleary eye.

I heard him say, "Heaven, I see you."

And she leaned in so her yellow bone teeth scraped his lips and left a line of blood trickling down his mouth.

My Whip Man didn't move.

Now I knew he must have loved that devil gal something terrible.

He shivered. His eyes bugged out and his teeth knocked. His body shook till I was scared his good new scabs would rip on open and bleed him to death. Blood flew off his wounds. He opened his mouth and tried to cry out.

The mens bellowed, "John! Move, you fool!"

The womens prayed, "Save us!"

And I crawled closer to the death dancer, to her bones and her stench, and pulled on her skirt wrapped tight with a scent likely to drop you in your tracks, and I said, "Heaven! You're a woman. I'm a woman. Hear me. Let go of my man and send him back to life!"

I raised my hands. I reached for my husband, to pull him back from the edge of where Heaven wanted to take him. But Whip Man shook so he threw my fingers off.

And that was it.

I rose up, baby strapped on my back and all. I stood solid on my two feets. And I hauled me back my solid right hand and smacked that death dancing wench till her teeths rattled in her head.

And I said, "Now you little spoiled rotten hussy brat. I told you to get your hands off my man. Them big eyeholes and you can't see? If you don't get your death grip off my silly husband, he won't be around to dance with you much longer. You go'n drag your bones around here dancing long after you done laid him in the burying ditch. And then you go'n have to deal with me. And I ain't go'n be dancing when I get my hands on you."

She turned them eyeholes on me like she was shocked.

I stood firm.

And sure enough, she made up whatever was left of her silly little mind and let him be. She crept on back toward her grandma'ammy's house, a shuffle and a step and a slide.

And here is me once again. I hauled Whip Man home by one arm, scolding all the way. What can you do with a man who won't ever learn?

I get him home and lay into him. "Whip Man, you done laid up and died two or three times now for this knock-kneed skinny wench who ain't never meant you no good."

Whip Man mumbled, all in a daze, "Rhea, you right."

I said, "Shut up and drink your milk. You're getting on nerves I ain't got left."

Whip Man nursed till he slept. Morning came, and he opened his eyes and said, "Rhea, I swear. I feel healed. Look. My cuts ain't bleeding no more."

And it was true. His scars had all healed up and covered over with tough shiny skin.

But did that Heaven do him a dirty trick. Whip Man healed like he'd been dead for decades.

My poor man makes you cringe and hide your eyes. Even me, every now and again, and I have learned to stand almost anything.

But me and our son are getting used to him. And Mother Magdalen. She has seen so much death around here, she don't turn from nothing.

But I'll tell you what I turn from: the devil's granddaughter.

That Mr. Devil Dennis come and seen his daughter dancing in the conjure woman's bones, and he grabbed his daughter's baby brat and hightailed it off the plantation for good.

And the devil's boy took his bride and all the field hands too, talking about, "We'll take off and make a plantation of our own, share the crops and split the profits amongst ourselves. Rhea, you ain't coming with me and my wife and everybody? We're emptying out these Quarters lickety-split. If you want to come, you best step lively."

And I said, "Sir, you telling me my man can come, too?"

The devil's boy said, "Rhea, your man has dishonored my sister."

And I said, "Sir, I am going to stay right here and tend my man. You all better make tracks while the sun is high. Nightfall, don't forget them patter-rollers will be out looking for you."

But truth be told, after Whip Man danced with death, he didn't need my milk no more. Didn't need much of anything else, neither.

He is dead now, his own self. Though he tries to take a bite from time to time, just to be sociable.

My Boy grew up, just us three and Mother Magdalen.

And now here comes the devil's granddaughter.

Back from wherever that Devil Dennis took her and raised her. Solace, Heaven's brat, so white-skinned she's likely to blind you if you don't shade your eyes, looking at her.

I almost wished my poor Boy was blind. Because didn't he get one look at this baby gal of Heaven's and fall right in love with her?

Like father like son. Got the devil's curse on him, my poor Boy. But we don't talk about that.

And me a praying woman, too. I can't win for trying.

# CHAPTER TWO

## THE WARMTH BETWEEN: ELLA, BORN 1800

Mr. Dennis's Widow disappeared one night from the town house, just like that.

The maids said, "Did she run off to the plantation?"

They answered, "And didn't take us with her, to wait on her hand and foot? Not likely."

"Did she run off with that no-account gallivant who had his eye on Mr. Dennis's property?"

"And left all of Mr. Dennis's money and jewels behind with us in the townhouse? Doesn't ring true."

So then the maids all slid their eyes at each other and said, "Was it haunts that got the Widow?" Because nothing was left behind to mark that she was gone but a bright light streaming through the night sky. "That's a sure sign," the maids said, "of spirits at work."

But "Which haunts?" they asked.

"Why, Mr. Dennis's own haunt," some thought. "The Widow paid good gold to get him denounced dead in court. The judge banging that gavel likely killed Mr. Dennis in his tracks."

"Or Mr. Dennis's grandbaby's haunt. The carriage driver says the Widow tried to get him to kill Miss Solace so she wouldn't inherit the plantation."

"But he didn't kill her. He said so."

"The Widow wishing and thinking might have killed her. You don't know. If Miss Solace is safe and sound at the plantation, how come nobody's heard a peep out of her? Who's taking care of her? I heard that plantation's been abandoned and shut down as long as she's been alive."

"Maybe Miss Solace got to the plantation but the bats flew down out of the ceiling and sucked her blood and killed her dead. It happened to a horse just down the street a ways."

"Bats can kill you?"

"Fool. Nobody lives to tell about it."

"But I've seen-"

"Hush. You've been locked up all your life as nursemaid to a Widow who's mad at the world and as mean as sin. You haven't seen anything. None of you all know what you're talking about."

The maids hung their heads and wondered, all the same.

Except I didn't hang my head for anything or anybody. If the Widow dies, I say good riddance and a quick trip to wherever she's going, no skin off my back. She's never had a kind word for me. So I didn't do a thing for her that I didn't have to.

Like that night she disappeared. I picked up my little bit of candle and followed the others down the steep attic stairs to make sure the Widow wasn't hiding out in the house with us.

It was a strange night when the Widow disappeared.

The black sky was ripped with a light like stars bursting and shrieking to be free. The cook woke up and screamed.

Cook and her husband, the carriage driver, and their boy Zion lived way out over the stables, clear across the courtyard. And yet her screaming tore over the cobblestones up the backside of the townhouse and rattled our attic windows.

The maids were asleep when the screaming started. It raked our dreams to shreds. We all sat up like one body. "What was that?" one of the maids said.

"Screaming," another maid whispered in the dark.

"Well, sshh," some other maid said. "Listen."

They all crawled close in across the splintery floor and hugged each another. Except for me. None of them got too close to me, if they could help it.

Off in my little corner, I hugged my knees in tight and watched the maids. We all listened.

And then stomp. Stomp. Stomp.

Heavy boots coming up the shaky attic stairs.

"Oh, thirteenth woman in the circle," one of the maids commenced to pray. That's a spirit dance they do. The thirteenth woman is the life and death figure. You call on her when you want the one, but you're getting the other.

Not that the maids ever let me in on the dance. But I used to spy on them late at night when the soles of their feet brushed the wood floor. So I knew.

"Is somebody breaking in this house?" one of the maids said, catching the shiver of those stomping steps on the stairs.

A couple of maids couldn't take it anymore. They hollered out.

In the dark, the flash of other people's hands slapped down on their mouths. "Hush, you!" other maids hissed like snakes. "You want to lead him to us in here, trapped like sitting ducks?"

"Him who?"

"The break-in man."

"How do you know what we hear is a break-in man?"

"How do you know it isn't? What else could it be?"

38

"Don't answer that."

"Something sneaking and creeping up the stairs."

"Who just screamed? Slap her."

"I'm about to scream my own self."

"And I'm about to give you two good reasons to hush. My fists and my feet."

"You shouldn't talk like that to your dance partners."

"We're not dancing now."

"You all keep talking and you'll lead the murder man right to us!"

"So now it's a murder man! And the silly wench hasn't seen hide nor hair of anybody yet."

"Well, why don't you get out and go take a look and see, if you're so bold?"

"You sass me one more time, and I'm going to show you some get out."

"Would you all raunchy heifers hush?"

The maids were always fussing. But they lived in each other's apron pockets. I swear you couldn't catch them apart. It seemed like they loved each other so much that they hated how much they were stuck together, like there was nobody else in the world.

Not that I knew that feeling. They kept me on the outside. Sometimes I was probably jealous.

Like when that stomping stopped right outside our attic door.

They all were tangled arms wrapped like twine on a package left at the door. They all were one mouth hung open. They all were one bright staring bug eye.

Whoever was at the door had started working on the latch, trying to get the door to open. I buried my face in my knees, went cold inside, and waited to die.

The door creaked, and I raised my head to peek and see my death coming. The door swung on its hinges till it stood gape-mouthed, waiting to swallow us down the stairs. A light floated and flickered in the stairway's throat.

Was it a candle? We couldn't see anybody behind it.

And then that light like fire streaked through the black outside and made a white rainbow across all the attic windows at once. It lit the attic like day. And it was gone.

But by that light, we saw a tall man had come into the room.

He had one hand raised with something in it, and one hand down with a long heavy weapon like a black stick.

Windows were open somewhere and a breeze gusted in, following the death of the rainbow. The breeze ruffled the hem edge on everybody's nightgowns and blew out what the man had in his raised hand, a candle.

Some of the maids let loose and shrieked.

That man shrieked too.

Then he said, "What you all screaming for? What is it about that light scares you womens so?" It was the voice of the carriage driver, Mr. Tim.

I heard some of the maids sigh like, "Huh."

I fell over on my pallet and lay there breathing.

One of the maids, the lead dancer, said, "You old fool, Mr. Tim! What are you doing sneaking and peeking at midnight around the women's Quarters? If you don't hightail your long scrawny carcass out of here, I'm going to have to tell your wife what you've been up to."

The carriage driver said, "Sneaking and peeking? What're you talking about? Ain't a one of you dried up old maids got a thing I want to see. You flatter yourselves."

His shape kneeled down in the dark and set his weapon and candleholder on the wood planks of the floor. On one knee, fishing around in his pockets for some flints, he steadily grumbled, "Trying not to wake a passel of fool womens, and I like to scared myself to death."

The lead dancer, Myra, said right back, "If you didn't want to wake anybody, why did you shove a candle in everybody's face?"

I'm telling you about the dancing maids. If you get them riled, they get smart at the mouth. Myself, I was always kind of quiet. Maybe the dancing keeps folks' blood boiling.

The carriage driver fumbled with the flints and got mad his own self. "Why my wife got me on these stairs, about to trip and break my neck for a bunch of silly womens, I still don't know."

Somebody said, "Why don't we let the man have his say? Mr. Tim, what was that screaming we heard? It woke us up. And then it came again. And that light that went through the sky! What's going on around here?"

Mr. Tim finally struck a flint so it lit. His hands shook while he guided the flame to his candle. He mumbled like folks do to work up their nerve. "Long as I live, I don't see why womens start bawling soon as the sun goes down and good people want their sleep. It raises a man's hair on his head, to listen to scared womens bawling."

Myra said, "Or in your case, his hair falls out. I'm going to tell you: the womens start bawling because the mens take out after them."

"Myra!" A whole bunch of maids said that.

Mr. Tim stood all shaky and raised his newly lit candle high. Silver and flame shone on his dark skin. You

41

could see the puckers and lines around his eyes that didn't show in daylight. Mr. Tim said, "That's the second time tonight that light streaked through here. First time, it was like a giant fire boomed and got lit and burnt. My woman woke up and made that first scream."

"Where are your wife Miss Vivian and your boy Zion now?" Some of the maids started to creep up from the floor to crowd around Mr. Tim.

"Hugged up and hiding under his cot back at the carriage house. Vivian sent me to check on you all. See if the house burnt down or what."

"What did you see coming through the house, Mr. Tim?" They leaned in close to him and stared around at the dark beyond his candle.

Mr. Tim said, "Nothing. There's no light in this house but in the Widow's room. The door's a little open. I didn't go in there, though. I called inside, and the Widow didn't answer."

A hush ran like water through the attic. Nobody enslaved wants to be the one who finds a dead slave-owner. When some of those people get too broke, they just make sure you're the fool who stumbles up on their murdered relatives. You hang, and they inherit.

I ought to know.

And a handful of maids now piped up and said, "Let's send Ashy Ella in to check whether or not the Widow's in her room."

They looked at me. I stared back and didn't say a thing.

They looked away, and one of the maids said to Mr. Tim, "Maybe the Widow's somewhere else in the house." Then they had that long talk about where the Widow might have gotten off to.

Till Mr. Tim said, "All right. I say we all get a candle or some kind of light and go search through this house. See what we can find. Stick together, and call out if something doesn't seem right. I'll come running and see if I can help you, me and my iron stick here." He shook his weapon in the candlelight.

Maids started choosing partners to go hunting around the house. Some of them called out what rooms they wanted to search. They all pulled little pieces of candle out of their tote bags and stood and reached up to light them off Mr. Tim's.

They didn't look at me one time.

And neither did Mr. Tim. Not even when he started out of the door behind the maids, calling over his shoulder, "Ashy Ella, you search the Widow's room."

Then he was gone behind the maids. Left me alone in the dark with one little piece of candle standing in its own wax and burning on the floor at my feet.

I knew they'd do that to me. Just because I don't say anything, they think I don't care.

But there were tears running down my cheeks while I felt my way down the attic stairs in the dark. Because I do care. I'm sick of catching the blame for every somebody who gets killed by somebody else.

And I was getting to like being a scullery maid. I didn't even care much that they called me "Ashy Ella" around the townhouse. Ash on my skin showed I did honest work for a living.

The maids and Mr. Tim didn't know or care about the life I used to lead: lying up with some man my owner lost to in cards or billiards, waiting in the dark for his breath to slow and my owner to slide in the room and slip a knife between his ribs.

My owner, Mr. Dennis, loved to gamble and didn't like to pay up when he lost. Along the big river, there were plenty strangers passing through that nobody would miss.

It was safe to gamble with strangers. They come and go and kill each other. Dressed every kind a way, not just the scruffy ones. Men of all kinds dressed like gentlemen and vagabonds, too. *A man's race and his clothes don't tell you what he's got hidden in his pocket,* Mr. Dennis used to say.

I don't know why Mr. Dennis gambled with that last riverboat man. You could see he was trouble. It was in his eyes.

Either Mr. Dennis figured nobody would check up on a renegade Comanche running loose. Or else he just got himself a big head, like he did now and then, and figured he couldn't lose.

But he lost big. So big that at last he pulled me from standing around behind his chair and told the man, "Take her."

The man said, "I'll take her for starters." He was already pulling out his pistols. Cards were on the table and everybody could see the man had won fair and square, no contest.

This was probably one of those men who escaped the massacres and lived by his wits all alone, dealing out death. A trapper, maybe, with no business hanging around the riverboats. You know that much fur money makes some men go crazy.

This man wasn't too far from crazy his own self, to judge by his eyes. But his pistols were steady in his hands.

His gaze was straight like he might have shot a dust speck off Mr. Dennis's eyelash, if he had to. He didn't look at me but nodded his head for me to come around and stand beside his chair now. His long shiny hair grabbed up the firelight and swished like a black river running down his back. I came over beside him and reached out to touch that river of hair.

He jabbed his elbow back at me so I dropped my hand from his head. The whole time, he didn't take his eyes off Mr. Dennis. "Time for that later," he said through his teeth, to me or my owner, I couldn't say. "Now ain't time for nothing but paying up."

Mr. Dennis, you could see, was thinking hard whether or not to try his good buddy smile on this one. Then he must have figured this particular Comanche renegade must have seen too many bloody times and didn't buddy with the likes of rich planters who cheat at cards.

Mr. Dennis's smile faded.

Everybody around the gaming tables stared. Mr. Dennis said, "Now, you know nobody carries that kind of cash. You just give me till morning, and I'll bring you every penny I owe. Redeem the girl, too. But you can have her for the night as my pledge and with my compliments. I don't know how much you know about men of honor. But you can trust my word. I'll bring you what I owe." Mr. Dennis's voice dropped on the last words so I knew what he meant to do. Send me to put this man to sleep and then wait and watch to feel Mr. Dennis kill him.

The other man nodded. "Morning," he said. And he pushed his chair so it fell behind him to the floor between his straddled legs. He backed up and out of there with his pistols and his eyes fixed straight on my owner, a loner.

I followed after him, looking back at my owner, too.

I don't know what got into Mr. Dennis. The sun was striding the sky, making gray, by the time he showed up at the Comanche's room. By then, I knew his name and wasn't sure how I'd bear to see him die. Jim Feather.

We had talked about living in a log hut in the woods where he liked to trap and hunt. I was even talking too, trying to tell him how I missed scullery work, scrubbing and sweeping like I used to do for that loud baker woman, and Jim Feather just looked at me in the dark like my jabber made sense, till his eyes shut just like that, and he fell asleep on me.

I held him. The weight of his long strong body pressed my heartbeat so I felt it, and felt where we ran together like one. Closer than one.

He had nuzzled me with his nose and even kissed me.

I held him and figured Mr. Dennis couldn't find Jim Feather's room to kill him. Or maybe Mr. Dennis figured he'd get off cheap, swapping me for his gambling debt and a chance to get out of town alive. Everybody knew Comanches would rather kill you than deal with you.

Was I glad. Hadn't occurred to me I might get away from my owner and the life he made me lead.

When he first bought me, I thought I was coming into heaven. Long as I could remember, all I ever did was scrub and clean and keep that stove lit at the boarding house kitchen run by the baker woman. She would knead and cook and rail at me all day, her arms all pale in the bread dough, pounding and slamming. She'd go on about damnation and jumping devils till I swear I saw little evil things leap among the flames in the open red mouth of the kitchen oven.

When I had to clean it, I'd close my eyes and reach in the back, and every cinder burned me, I knew it was hellfire punishment. Every morning, early, I went to hell in the back of her oven and burned.

So when Mr. Dennis spied me carrying that bucket up the boarding house back steps, and he smiled so sweetly, it went right to my heart. Nobody ever smiled at me before Mr. Dennis. Nobody. He touched my chin and tears fell right out of my eyes.

He leaned down and kissed my nose and looked really close at me. I stared back.

And when he walked away on down the hall, I slid down on the floor between my bucket and brushes and rags and sat with my mouth open.

The mistress came and kicked my behind to make me stand and said, "Get up and get out of here, slut. I know what you did to get this man to buy you. Good riddance to your evil. I'll never take your kind in to work in my house again, after you repay my charity with whoring."

I walked out of her house into heaven.

Mr. Dennis just covered my skinny little body with sweet-smelling grease to make my skin shine like he liked it and with flouncy bright dresses for me to swing down the street like the rich ladies. I didn't do anything day in and day out for the longest but bathe and grease my skin and dress and eat meats and treats, following Mr. Dennis around the gambling tables and the rooming houses.

I don't know how long this lasted.

And then Mr. Dennis lost a gamble.

The first time he sent me away to some man's room, I cried all night. What was wrong with me? I had come to think of myself like married women and kept women flouncing up and down the riverboat ramps that men would kill to keep to themselves. I thought for sure Mr. Dennis was through with me, and this man he had handed me to didn't look like the type who'd give you good things to wear and eat.

I cried for shame that this stranger had me and for shame I that I didn't know better than to think this wouldn't ever happen to me, so vain and stupid I thought I was special to Mr. Dennis, a man who had everything.

I was so worn out from weeping and sobbing up under that stranger, what with his rattle breath snores, I didn't even hear when Mr. Dennis jimmied open the lock and sneaked in the man's room.

I didn't know he was there till I saw him lean over the man's back, looking in my face with his finger to his lips.

I hushed my fussing.

And I watched and heard that grate and slick sound when the dagger slipped into the man's side, clean and easy. Felt like that knife went through both our bodies. Mr. Dennis had his lip between his teeth, and a tiny spray of blood got on his chin.

The man groaned and went straight, like when he'd been taking his pleasure. Then his weight crushed me. He didn't thrash. Just his hot blood seeped down my side. I just knew Mr. Dennis had killed me, too.

Till Mr. Dennis rolled the stranger off me and tugged me to my feet. I looked down and in the gray dawn saw the blood drip and pool at my feet on the wood floor and get sucked in among the splinters.

Mr. Dennis rifled through the dead man's pockets and hauled out the man's pocket knife. He opened it and stuck it in the man's bleeding side. Wet slippery crunching sounds.

I was weaving and fixing to pass out.

Mr. Dennis wiped his bloody hand on the blanket on the bed and reached over, and quick pinched my nose. "Open your mouth and breathe, Ella," he whispered. "Deep breaths, now," he said.

I breathed with my eyes shut while Mr. Dennis dried the blood off me with the blanket he snatched from the bed. I opened my eyes to see him drop the blanket on the dead man. He fished my clothes up from off the floor and pulled them on me, fast and sloppy, everything hanging open, unfastened.

He dropped me out of the window. Then he slid out and fell down after me.

We ran through bushes till we got to a tethered horse he said he bought last night. It acted like it knew him. It waited till I was slung up and Mr. Dennis was almost in the saddle. Then it bolted out of there.

We never showed up at that particular river town again. There are a lot of river towns.

So Mr. Dennis never had to stop his murdering ways. Only, he says it isn't murder cause the men he kills aren't gentlemen. They're no-account.

They still feel dead to me. But I said nothing.

Till I met Jim Feather, I hadn't talked in a right long time. I tried. But I would open my mouth, and crazy stuff would come out. Not what I meant to say at all. After a while, Mr. Dennis would see me fixing to speak and he would up and say, "Never mind, Ella. Conversation's not what I like most about you, anyway."

We had a few signs he understood. We got used to each other, how we lived along the big river, what we did to people when Mr. Dennis didn't win or didn't win as big as he wanted to. I thought we'd be doing that game till I got too old for anybody to take me off Mr. Dennis's hands for a debt.

Till I slept with Jim Feather.

I slept and dreamed about that cabin in the woods Jim Feather talked about till I could see it with my eyes closed. Dreamed I was still talking to Jim Feather, and he was listening and smiling and nuzzling my nose and kissing my lips, like before he dozed.

I told myself Mr. Dennis either lost his way to Jim Feather's room or had grown tired of me. I slept and dreamed and woke and lay there looking at Jim Feather and thinking I ought to wake him so we could get out and head to the woods before day. But he slept like he trusted me.

So I just held him closer and closed my eyes to feel how good it felt to want to be with someone.

I'm going to die someday regretting that feeling of love.

Because the next thing I knew, I was waking up to people gathered around our bed shouting and grabbing at my bare body.

They hauled me out from under Jim Feather, and it was odd that he didn't protest or say anything, or try to get all these people out of his room.

Knives clattered to the floor as they dragged me to my feet across Jim Feather. Two knives, both with streaks of blood on them.

I got to my feet and fell. There was a gash in my thigh, deep and painful. But that isn't what sapped me.

What got to me and just about dropped me to the floor was, off the bed and on the floor this way, I could see why Jim Feather wasn't saying or doing anything. He was stretched out, bloody head to foot, with his head thrown back and his arms outflung. There were knife wounds in him.

There was a pain in my head where somebody must have bashed me. But through the shock and pain that made me squint till I was nearly blind, I could still hear the people say, "Knife fight between a red man and a black woman: savages, both of them. Haul her on down to the sheriff, and see what he wants to do with her."

That was the first time I ever got dragged through the streets naked, a rope around my wrists, hauling on me.

But not the last time.

The sheriff said, "No use hanging her. The government's paying folks to pick off red renegades, running loose. But no need to get carried away and pay her, either," he said.

He kept me in his little jail and collected money from whoever wanted me for a little while in a dirt cell on a dirt floor, till the next coffle came by.

It's a chain gang. They shuffle along like they're doing some kind of chain dance. Folks can buy you off the chain gang if they want to take a chance on your cheap labor.

I got hooked on the chain and walked out of town covered with dirt and old blood, mine and Jim Feather's together.

I guess we didn't pass any towns where anybody wanted to take a chance on me. Till we got to this town here.

I had walked in those chains so long I couldn't remember how it was to walk without them. My hair grew in tangles like ropes and my eyes were infected from staring into the burning sun. I walked ducking my head against my arms, but that did nothing but rub the dry crusts deeper into my eyes.

That pain in my head I got when I woke up and found Jim Feather stabbed grew so it weighed my mind down, and I couldn't stand straight to save my life. Scars striped my back where the gang driver beat me, saying, "Ella! Stop that dipping and swinging and stand straight so decent folks can think to buy you off my hands! Folks are going to think you're hoodoo, crazy, or dying, with all that weaving and wobbling you do!"

True, my mind was fried and my legs were sore tired. And that knife gash in my thigh hadn't healed right, in the jail and walking on the road.

I gave up hope anybody would ever buy me off this chain. I wasn't hoping for anything but to die.

So imagine when some shape that looked like a gentleman on a horse drew up one day between me and the sun.

I couldn't close my sick eyes and rest them for fear of bad dreams, nor could I open them for the glare and burn, and sickness had near on glued them tight with strings waving and blocking my sight between the lashes. The man and his horse were a shadow out there beyond the eye-sickness strings.

But I could hear his voice, deep and quiet like. "I know your name, Ella, and I know your crimes. Whoring and murder. Now, if you want to get off this chain gang, answer these three questions. Answer carefully. You and I will both be disappointed if I have to leave you here."

Oh no. Answer? I hadn't talked right in years, except for that one night, to a man now as dead as I wished I was, in his stead. No way was I going to be able to answer questions.

Could I?

I worked at cracking my dry lips apart. *Best to get started trying.*

The gentleman said, "Ella, to whom do you owe your greatest loyalty? To your former master, should you ever see him again, or to the master who buys you now?"

My lips broke apart but shaping them to words was making them burn. I gave up and nodded my head toward the shape of the man on the horse in the sun. Ropes of hair fell forward and covered one of my eyes.

"To me, Ella?" he said. "You owe your devotion to me, if I take you off this chain, don't you?"

I nodded my head.

"Good," he said. "Now. What if I wanted you to do something that went against your heart or your conscience, if creatures such as you have such sensibilities. Something, say, that frightened you or made you sad. What would you do, then?"

My burning lips shaped the words, "Do it." I would have said more, something for sure about no conscience, just to please him, but my lips gave out. And besides, he seemed satisfied.

"Twice well spoken," he said, "even if you don't make a sound. Now. Think carefully. Did you, Ella, love your former master?"

It hit me like a rock and made that pain I carried in my head blaze up till I thought I would faint away.

Next thing, I couldn't see him anymore. Couldn't see a thing. I felt the sun on my face and the pebbles strike my cheek as I went down.

I came to with sharp slaps and cold water stinging my face, together. When I realized what it was, I licked my tongue out to catch the water drops.

"She all right," I heard the gang driver's voice say. "You teach her who's boss, and she'll be just fine from here on out, sir. Pleasure doing business with you. Pleasure."

I felt chains fall away from my wrists and ankles and ropes get lashed on to cut me where the chains had rubbed my wrists raw. I heard the gentleman's horse clop away, and I got pulled to my feet behind it, tied to the gentleman's horse.

He had bought me. I was off the chain.

If the sun hadn't beaten what was left of my brain, I would have been happy walking to my new home behind my new owner. Did I say walking?

Walking, sometimes. Falling and getting dragged, most often. The gentleman had to stop so my weight wouldn't tire his horse.

But my heart was light.

Did I love the man who used to own me? Wasn't that who slashed me and Jim Feather and left me to take the blame for killing a man I could have loved? *Why did Mr. Dennis do that to me?*

Last time I fainted and got dragged, I came to slung across the horse's back with little rocks all up under my skin, grating against the horse's hide. The gentleman held me down with one hand.

I twisted my head around to see him. He looked down at me like I was filth. *But at least,* I thought to myself, *I can see a little bit. I'm getting better already.*

The gentleman pulled his horse up round the back of a big, tall skinny house. Women all shades, brown, black, gold, and cream, came around me saying things I couldn't make out.

The gentleman swung his leg off his horse and got down. The women hauled me off. Gabbing and chatting, they carried me to a big, slatted wash tub in the courtyard and leaned me on a clothes pole while they poured kettles of steaming water and whipped up suds in the tub.

I slid down the pole and sat on the cobbles. Cool damp linen flapped and brushed my face. Somebody put a scoop of water to my stinging lips. I must have dozed in the shade.

I woke when the women hauled me into that boiling hot tub of suds piled so high the soap got in my eyes and burned at the sickness. It smelled like something you use to scrub the floor.

But I don't care how it burns my skin and my eyes. I love me a good bath.

The women scrubbed and gossiped, telling each other who I was, and they said I was bought to bait Mr. Dennis back home.

"What would he want with her, no more? Look at her. Scarred up, ashy, and nasty. Been on the road too long."

"Don't talk stupid. What do your hands feel up under this water? When that ash gets scrubbed off this gal, and they get some food and water into her, she'll be a sight to knock Mr. Dennis's eyeballs out of his head."

"Only, Mr. Dennis isn't here to see."

"I'm sure the Widow and her gallivant will figure out a way to get Mr. Dennis home for this."

Listening to the gossip, I learned that this was just after the court gavel killed Mr. Dennis and his wife got declared "the Widow." Only, she seemed none too sure the court had killed Mr. Dennis dead enough to suit her.

Someone laughed. "What are you fretting on Mr. Dennis for, anyway? You'd best think about that young man of your own, delivering his eggs here every morning."

More laughs.

"Instead of studying on Mr. Dennis, plan on keeping this wench far from that back door when your young man hands over his dairy goods."

Guffaws.

"Some very good dairy goods."

Shrieks of laughter.

"If I do say so myself."

Screams.

"That's it! What do you think you know about my young man's dairy goods?"

Cackles that hushed suddenly to tsk-ing and soothing sounds.

"Come on, you all. No need to fight over one silly young man. There's plenty more where he came from."

"And where was that?"

"My cot last night."

Howls. One of the maids flounced off in a huff, her bare feet slapping the wooden steps up to the back door of the townhouse.

"Come on, you all!" someone bossy commanded. "The Widow is in such a hurry to see this gal with her knots cut off her head and that sweet grease she bought spread over her cuts and sores, you'd think it was the Widow and the gallivant that want to get in bed with her."

Easy laughter as I was pulled to my feet.

The long tangled locks fell softly past my shoulders and handfuls of water rinsed my bare head. The weight and the pain I had carried in there inside my mind fell away with the cut hair. A light breeze blew through my head, as if it went in one ear and out the other, cleaning my thoughts. I felt myself smile.

I heard a little sound go up from the women as I stepped out of the tub.

"How can dead skin and dirt hide a woman like that?"

"Look at her color. What do you call it when somebody's color shifts and dips all over her body like that?"

"Look at her eyes. A woman doesn't need hair when she's got a face like that on her."

"Face. Men don't study on a woman's face. Where have you been locked away? Look at-"

"Enough. Get to rubbing with this sweet grease here. The Widow will be down here in no time and whip you for spoiling Mr. Dennis's goods, if you let her skin dry out again."

Strong hands flowed from my head to my tender feet, and wherever they touched, they left a trail of scent like flowers and perfume all running together.

"Why doesn't she speak?" someone said. "Is she stupid or what?"

"You'd best be glad she doesn't speak. With what she's been through, to hear it from the Widow and the gallivant, if she told you it would turn your hair to gray. Leave her as dumb as she wants to be."

The women stepped back, holding damp towels and scissors and looking at me, nodding and staring and smiling.

Sweet smells rose all around me and felt to me like they filled the courtyard. I was the wind and the earth and the sweet seasons. I was whole and healed and someday, someday soon, I might just be happy, too. Maybe even today.

One of the women said, "I don't trust somebody who doesn't speak her mind."

Someone else said, "I won't dance if she joins the circle."

I heard a loud slap and a cry. "Hush on that! Don't you ever talk about that, in broad daylight!"

And silence as the back door to the tall house creaked open. The mistress came through it.

She walked tall and stiffly, like most of those women do. Only, she kept her eyes on me like the sun that used to burn me. I stood still as I could and looked at the Widow coming in the sunset.

She came right up on me and stopped inches away.

I could see in the fading daylight where something that looked like pain pulled her brows together. Like she would never stop eating me up and spitting me out with her eyes.

There were tears starting up in her eyes that she had closed to just about slits, staring at me almost from the side now. Like she didn't trust me, or maybe like I was going to do something to her. I tried to smile at her.

She let her eyes drop to study my body. She touched the scar on my thigh, all purple and pulsing from the bath. It was tender now where it used to be numb, so I jumped from her touch.

"Whoring and murder," she said. She backed away, still staring into my eyes. "Ella, I've saved your life," she said. "Don't ever forget that."

She turned away and got all the way up the steps and halfway through the door before she turned back one more time and said, "Follow me, Ella."

She led me, still naked and a little too cool now, up a back stairway. It was steep and twisted. You could hear how the steps wanted to crack and split if you rested your weight on them. I held onto the walls, still dizzy and lightheaded. I was scared I might fall and bust my happy head on that bottom step.

The Widow went into a big hallway, clean and carpeted and painted in bright colors cool to the eyes. *If I could be in a house like this,* I thought, *you would never catch me outside.*

I would have loved to linger in that hall just staring at the flowers and vines and colors all woven into the carpet, painted and framed, and twisted to hold candles out from the walls. But the Widow was at a door, working with a key, and she called me when she got it open. "Ella. In here."

I came into a big room full of dark wood and hung with blue at the tall windows and draped down over the wide deep bed and sewed and tucked on the carved wood chairs. Blue like the river wasn't but the sky in the soft part of night before the bad dreams rise in your mind.

I made some kind of little sound in my throat. I think it bothered the Widow because she shuddered and went a little away from me.

"Get in that bed," she said.

And I went and leaned and fell into it, slid between the covers. I didn't even know if I picked the right covers and sheets to be between. You know they've got rules about that kind of thing.

59

I didn't care. The bed rose up all around me and was soft and touched me all over and was the whole world.

The Widow came and sat on the far edge and said, "Ella. Ella, listen to me. I've been looking out to buy you for a long time. This is a dream come true for me. And if you want to survive, to be all right, maybe even to be given your freedom, this is what you must do. Can you understand me, Ella?"

I nodded yes.

The Widow leaned to a little table beside the bed and opened a drawer with one hand. She reached in and pulled out something that caught the last light coming through the blue at the windows. Silver and some kind of shell handle.

A knife. *Not another knife.* Something in my stomach turned and knotted up.

"When Mr. Dennis comes for you, whenever that is, you must wait no longer than the first evening that he sleeps in here with you. Then use this on him. Do you understand? Make no mistake. He is not to live one solid day and night in this house, with you here. He is not to leave this room, once he's come in-" Her voice went tight and then broke. She was hurting badly. I suspect she loved the man she was getting me to use that knife on. What was wrong with this crazy woman?

But I nodded yes. I didn't need to be yoked to another chain gang.

I took the knife from her shaking hand and made a quick jab just at the pillow next to me where a man's heart might have been.

Then I stopped because someone shimmered there and was gone. *Someone looking at me, who trusted me.*

*Jim Feather? Could I have hurt my own Jim Feather?*
Was I the one who stabbed him, after all?

No. Mr. Dennis sneaked in and did that. Why am I thinking crazy like this? It was Mr. Dennis who killed Jim Feather. Not me.

Killed Jim Feather.

I could kill Mr. Dennis. I should kill Mr. Dennis.

I would kill Mr. Dennis. With pleasure.

The Widow was working the knife out my hand.

I buried myself in the spreads and sheets, in the blue of the room and the black that spread in through the windows. I heard the Widow shut and lock the door. And then nothing for I don't know how long.

One time I woke in sunlight soft through the blue hanging drapes and found food and tea on a silver tray near the bed. I ate that. At other times I woke and ate like on the riverboats, food too sweet and salty and wine that makes you drowse.

Sometimes a maid would come lugging a little wash tub of water and haul another jar of sweet grease out of her apron pocket, for after my bath. Sometimes they would come take my chamber pot away, so pretty a pot I took to leaving it out in the middle of the carpet just to look at it. Nobody brought me clothes or monthly rags, though.

So I took to tying on Mr. Dennis's hankies out of his knife drawer next to the bed. And when they were all used and taken away and didn't come back, I started using his shirts.

And then one night I dreamed of Jim Feather. All that blood when he got rolled off me, like that first man Mr. Dennis killed.

61

I woke up in the bed and just knew Jim Feather was there next to me. And after all this time wishing for him and wanting to kill Mr. Dennis for killing him, I was scared to turn and look at my Jim Feather.

I reached toward him, just to touch him and be sure. I felt a strong warm body roll towards my hand. Crush it. Keep rolling on my arm towards me. Pinning me.

Any minute, I would have to turn towards my arm to pull it free and see this face rolling close and closer.

And all of sudden I knew what was wrong.

This wasn't Jim Feather, rolling on my hand and pinning down my arm.

This was Mr. Dennis. Barreling down on me. Trapping me. Going to kill me like he did those poor men, all those years.

The Widow is out of her mind to think that I could ever kill a killer like Mr. Dennis.

As soon as I knew who he was, Mr. Dennis reached over me and yanked open the knife drawer. I tried to get out of bed, out from where he pinned my arm under his weight, and he got his other arm around me to get to the drawer, and now my leg was split open from that old scar and spilling blood at the thigh, and the sheets were stuck to it. They wound around both of my legs so that I got tangled and trapped, and Mr. Dennis roared behind me, "Kill me, will you, Ella? Kill me, will you?"

I felt him scramble to get at my hands and pin them both and drag me back into the bed where for sure now he had that knife and I was done for.

Just when I thought it, that knife come arcing up from the drawer and then down to stop me from dragging my legs out of that bed, that knife so shiny I saw the blue bed curtains in it, under Mr. Dennis's pale fingers. "Kill me,

Ella?" he bellowed so my ears ached. "KILL ME, WILL YOU?"

Sharp pain ripped my legs again, back and front. They were slit now. Fresh cut. Useless. I couldn't go anywhere. I was helpless and stuck. Mr. Dennis was going to kill me now for sure.

I screamed my throat raw.

The screaming stopped him. Or stopped me feeling the damage he was doing. But I had to stop screaming to draw breath.

When I stopped, I heard knocking. Pounding. The Widow and her gallivant both banged on the bedroom door.

Now nobody pinned my arms and no sheets wound round my legs. I crawled to the door and pulled myself up on the handle and worked it open.

Just when I was rising to my feet, the door flew open and banged into me. The Widow and the man who bought me off the chain gang stumbled into the room, and we went down on the floor together.

The man had a candelabrum. He held it up even while we fell, and its light spread to the bed. We all turned back and looked.

It was empty. Tumbled and mussed from my kicking at the sheets. But nobody was there now.

I pointed anyway. Tried to tell the Widow. *Mr. Dennis was there.* Crazy sounds flew out of my mouth like when you fling waste water in the street.

The Widow sat right there and took her free hand and smacked my head this way and that. "Crazy, wretched, whoring wench!" she yelled. "No wonder your master won't come back for you. I was a fool, a fool to buy you off that chain gang." She pushed herself up on her knees and made her hand into a fist and used it to pound some sense into me. I tried to turn my back to take the blows. "Worthless," she hollered. "Worthless, crazy, murdering wretch!"

She must have worn herself out, pounding on me. I was face to the floor, curled in a ball to take as many blows as I could on my back, with my heartbeat rushing in my ears and my face still stinging from the slaps, when all of a sudden she just stopped.

I heard her crying like her mouth was stuffed with something. I looked up. She was in the gallivant's arms and he was trying to comfort her, still holding his candelabrum. "There, dear," he said. "Come now. A girl as smart and brave as you've been, to carry on so? Let's give it another try, shall we? So maybe old Dennis has lost interest in his favorite whore. I'm sure we'll soon discover his new whereabouts and his new weakness. You're a clever dear. I've seen you. Come on, now, love. You'll break my heart if you break down now, like this."

He went on till she lifted her head out of his nightshirt and smiled at him. His shirt was wet where she cried, but he didn't seem to mind.

The Widow said, "Of course, we'll find a way, darling. But enough of this wicked, evil thing lying up in state while-"

"Never mind," the gallivant said. "I'll put her away with the other maids for now, shall I? We can figure what to do with her in the morning. Or some other time."

"Some other time. Please?"

He kissed her on the nose, like Mr. Dennis did me when I met him in the boarding house hallway where the devils jumped in the oven downstairs.

No more thinking of Mr. Dennis. I might have more bad dreams.

I followed the gallivant and his candelabrum, feeling his way up the steep rickety steps. Then the gallivant stopped and banged on a shut wall in the dark.

It was a door, and it opened to him after a bit.

He took me with his free hand and shoved me through the door and turned and was gone.

Now that I know them better, I wonder if they were dancing when me and the gallivant showed up. But when the door opened, the maids were still and sitting up on their pallets in the dark, staring, as I stood in the doorway.

I went across the attic with the moonlight on my greased skin and trailed flower and sweet scents behind me. I stood in the middle of the floor till someone said, "Ella, you can have my pallet. Or share it with me, if you don't mind. I'm a little big, but I can keep you warm."

I went toward that voice and slept in those arms that night.

Next day, Myra woke me with a scratchy dark dress like all the maids wore, only mine was stretched too tight cross my chest and too loose at my waist. "Perfect," Myra said. "The Widow wants you to do scullery. She says I don't have to teach you anything. She's heard you know all about it."

I followed Myra down to the kitchen where the stove didn't look like the one I remembered, scaring me, but the buckets and brushes and rags were waiting, and I was glad to see them.

No time, and my skin had dried and flaked to ash again. Dry peeling skin gray and dusty and plain. The Widow took one look at me in a few days and took to calling me Ashy Ella. The maids giggled behind their hands at first but soon picked it up.

Well, didn't I want honest work? Just like I told Jim Feather.

At night I'd lie on the pallet I shared with the big maid till Myra gave me scraps and ticking to sew my own. I'd sit and sew and then lie down on what I had finished and pretend to sleep, slitting my eyes and steadying my breath so the maids might dance. I loved to watch them dance quietly in the attic just before night trembled and broke in a crack of thin morning like lightning.

I'd watch their soft feet shuffle, step, press the floor and leap, land quietly on the foot below the toes, catch and brace and hold themselves, spin and reach and clasp hands, circle and circle, spinning dreams.

I'd dream of the dancing maids, my best dreams.

What would I pray for, if I could pray to the thirteenth woman for anything, like they did?

I'd pray for somebody to take me in his arms and hold me gently and never hurt me or frighten me, and I would eat plenty and well and wear pretty things and smell sweet and sleep deeply, and never have scary dreams about anybody.

But Jim Feather. Because now, it seemed, he was dead. Was I going to find the Widow dead, too, tonight?

Serve her right. But I didn't want to be the one to catch the blame for it.

Yet, I took my little bit of candle, the night the Widow disappeared, and went slowly down the steps, feeling my way to the door that let into the Widow's hallway and pushed it in.

I thought I heard windy sounds like a storm starting. But when I stopped and held my breath, I heard nothing.

I got through the thick dark to the Widow's door and found it a little open, like Mr. Tim, the carriage driver, said. But none of that light he saw.

Speaking of Mr. Tim. Where was he and all the maids? Just because they didn't want to be in the Widow's room didn't mean they needn't be on the whole floor. *Maybe they gave me the Widow's whole floor to myself.* How scary.

The Widow's door creaked open under my hand.

I lifted the candle into her room and looked around. All the shiny stuff the Widow owned, jewels and silky things draped and dropped on the vanity, the chair, the bed, and her mirrors, all gilded and silver, sparkled through the dark in my bit of candlelight. I never saw a woman with a room and dresses as fine as the Widow's, even her black ones. Her fake mourning didn't fool anybody.

I came on into the room behind my candle. *Hey. Feels like somebody is in here.* I stopped and listened but didn't hear anybody. So I crept to the middle of the room and turned all around, taking in all that glittered in the dark, losing my fear that the Widow might come on me and punish me for idling.

I edged up on something shining, draped over the back of her chair in front of her big mirror. Lifted one edge of it. It was somehow light like it should float but so heavy it was limp with real silver sewed all through it. I held it up. It was a dress like a necklace. I'd never seen such a thing.

There were tears burning my eyes. They flowed before I could stop them.

How come I never had anything so fine all to myself, too? Me, off making my owner rich in one gambling den after another. Laying up under strange men bleeding to death. Whore, she called me. Murderer. Like I wanted to.

Jim Feather.

I picked up the shiny limp thing shot through with silver and smashed it against my face, to take it all in and catch the tears and smell it, make it mine.

*What did the Widow ever do to make Mr. Dennis as rich as I know I made him? What did she do to get all this?* I wiped my tears on her dress, or whatever I was holding. And then, I stopped crying.

Somebody had called me.

I went to the Widow's dressing table and lit her candelabrum there with my little candle. Then I picked up the candelabrum and held it to the dark heavy mirror right over her vanity table, its tarnished old silver frame worked with vines and flowers.

I looked in it at myself.

"Ella," I heard, really faint. Barely there. But, "Ella," it seemed so clear.

Almost like the Widow's. But far away and odd. Sad and shut off, like a door had gotten closed between us.

I turned to her wardrobe and again to her mirror. "Ella!" Sobbing now and fading. *Maybe I'm just so crazy, I made it up.*

I studied my face in the glass, the soft look of a child, really, still on me even after all I'd been through. The curled lashes Mr. Dennis used to love. Little smile puckers he used to kiss around my lips.

But look at my little, short hair, sticking up now in spikes, growing back. *Ugh.* I reached up to touch the spikes of new hair.

68

"Ella!" I heard it again. Clear this time. The Widow's voice, moaning.

I picked up the candelabrum and went hunting around her room. Under her wide bed, dripping wax on her thick bright carpet. In her wardrobe, pushing aside all the heavy gowns, rustling like they were scolding me. *Nothing*.

But that voice never stopped sobbing and calling after me. "Ella!"

But after a while I stopped listening, went back to the dressing table and just stared long and hard at the pretty girl-woman I still was, at all the places where the candlelight dipped and curved around my face, my cheekbones, my neck, and my throat. At the light in my eyes, how the whites glowed. At my brown lips, warmed by a pouty smile and framed by little dimples.

I reached down and picked up a pink crystal bottle that looked like it held scent, pulled out the stopper and dabbed it on my neck. I lifted up my nightshift and ran the stopper up my legs, first one and then the other, and a smell wafted up to me like purple flowers and soft face powder and rain when there's new grass to fall and get caught on.

I clinked the stopper back into place in the scent bottle, found where the bottle had been among the combs and cremes and knickknacks on the vanity, and arranged it carefully to look undisturbed. Then I picked up the Widow's candelabrum and went out of her bedroom, shutting her door firmly behind me.

I climbed to the attic and let the candles burn while I sat alone on my half-sewn pallet and smelled the scent floating up all around me. When I couldn't fight it any more, I lay down and drifted to sleep, watching so many candles burn and feeling beautiful. I have no idea when the maids came back in, or where they were all that time. I slept too deeply to think about them. But I know this: even in my sleep, I could still feel myself smiling.

Every day after that, me and the maids just kept on cleaning like always. The Widow's gallivant and her lawyers showed up so often we had to stake young Zion at the door, just to let these meddlesome menfolk in and out. It seemed they couldn't get enough of searching the Widow's room and asking to hear what happened, one more time, the night she disappeared.

The gallivant sat around in the parlor on the sofa where they used to make love and cried, acting like he hadn't been living right here most of the time and should have known more than he was saying. Like all he ever did was come calling. We all rolled our eyes at him when he got wound up and started in to moaning, "Oh, my sweet darling," and such like.

Maybe they caught us at it because, next thing you know, the lawyers started in to hinting out loud that maybe the gallivant might have been up to something. "Lonely woman all alone and scared, looking for a man to lean on?" They would shake their heads at each other. "Too easy to get rid of such a trusting soul, for a man who knows his weapon and his way around the swamps. Rich, too? Be worth hanging around taking chances, waiting to settle on some money like that."

The gallivant dried up and started listening.

The lawyers sat at the parlor table and clicked their little china cups down into their saucers and looked his way, over there staring red-eyed on that sofa where he should have been ashamed to sit in broad daylight, if what folks were saying about him using the Widow was true.

Pretty soon the gallivant took to not stopping by so frequently. And then he disappeared altogether.

And now the maids started sneaking out of the attic in the middle of the night to do their dance. I listened in on them during the day, but I didn't learn where they went.

I would wake in the night and find them gone. They must have sneaked back up while I was asleep because they would be in their beds when I woke again in the dawn. But they'd be tuckered out and kind of agitated and quarrelsome all day, like they had secrets wearing them down. And they'd nap in the afternoons wherever they dropped. Got to be a real chaos around the townhouse.

Till Miss Solace, Mr. Dennis's granddaughter and last heir, came and took everybody away.

What am I saying? Of course, that is, everybody but me.

But this time, I wanted to be left out and left behind. I wanted to stay.

Lawyers had us all lined up to meet Miss Solace at the front door. She rode up on the front seat of a cheap old cart, like real ladies never should go to town. There was a young man, brown muscles bunching out his loose white shirt, who came riding up on one of the horses hitched to the cart and guiding the other with his free hand.

The young man hopped off his horse before it stopped trotting and ran back to grab Miss Solace's hands and help her down off the cart. She stepped down right into his hands, lifted up to catch her, and she looked deep in his eyes and smiled.

The lawyers and all the maids watched him still holding her hands and her smiling into his face while they moved on up the stairs. *They sure enough look like they*

71

*are in love, to me. Isn't she supposed to be a wight woman?*

Little sounds went up amongst the maids. "That there is Mr. Boy, you know. Miss Solace's husband. I kid you not at all."

"Mm, mm, mm," somebody else said.

"How is she supposed to make like she's a wight woman when she's running around town making eyes at a man the law wouldn't let any wight woman touch?"

"She can't take me to no plantation till she learns to keep her eyes and her hands to herself. She'll get us all killed, the way she acts."

"'*And* her hands?' *First* of all, her hands. She can look all she wants to! Wight women do!"

The lawyers cleared their throats, like they wanted to shut the maids up before they had to take notice of what the maids were saying and do something about this.

Mr. Tim and his wife, Miss Vivian, moved forward to take Miss Solace's hands from Mr. Boy. Miss Vivian said, "Miss Solace, ma'am. You done come into your own, ma'am," and she swept Miss Solace a curtsy, like the Widow hadn't raised Miss Solace in the attic wearing rags the maids wouldn't have dusted furniture with.

At least, that's what I heard the maids whisper at night, since I had never laid eyes on Miss Solace before she came and took the others away.

Miss Vivian straightened up and stared Miss Solace straight in her eye. "Miss Solace, I wish your grandpap Mr. Dennis could just see how you done went out to the country and become every inch the lady he always wanted you to be."

Miss Solace was working a black lace glove off her hand. When she got it off, she laid a little golden hand on

Miss Vivian's arm. "Thank you, dear Miss Vivian," she said.

Miss Vivian said, "Now, ma'am, Miss Solace. You too kind. But now that you grown, you can't go around 'Missing' and 'Ma'amming' the help. People will wonder about your upbringing, if you take my meaning." And she gave Miss Solace an arch of her eyebrow before she looked down at the tell-tale dark hand and said, "Well, ma'am, you done finally went and got you some color, too, now, ain't you? Maybe a little too much color for a lady of your station?"

Miss Solace said, "I've been working the cotton with everyone else. We're shorthanded, Miss Vivian, I'm sure you've heard, and we need all the help we can get if we're going to get back on our feet." A little quiet groan drifted up around all the maids. *Oh no. Field work. If the mistress is doing it, you know what's going to happen to the housemaids.*

But like every maid was thinking the same thing at the same time, *Maybe there are a few more out in those fields like that Mr. Boy,* eyes slid back over his way.

Mr. Boy stopped a little ways down the front steps. But he had his head up, and he smiled, looking around at everybody. You could tell he made the lawyers uncomfortable. You could hear them under their breath, "Wight woman alone can't keep these people in line. Look at that young buck just grinning like the cat that lapped the cream."

Miss Solace stopped in front of Mr. Tim. "Dear Mr. Tim. I owe you everything. My happiness and my very life. I hope you and your family can make yourselves comfortable at the plantation. I've heard that, for some, country living is much harder than city."

Mr. Tim said, "Evident to me it ain't been hard on you, Miss Solace," and he winked before he bowed over her hand. You could hear Miss Solace chuckle behind that little ladylike smile.

And then she went down the line of maids till she stopped at me. Looked at me close and long and took her time, still smiling.

Then she said, "Miss Ella, I hear you don't talk much. I also hear you knew my grandfather, Mr. Dennis. I'm so glad you've come to live with us here. Mr. Tim tells me that you've raised your hand to stay behind here at the townhouse, in case my grandfather or stepgrandmother should return. You're ideal, since we won't have to worry that the wrong people may come along and pry information out of you." That smile again.

She drew in closer. "But if you should ever wish to share memories of Grandfather with me, I would love to help you talk. When I was a little girl, I always wondered where Grandfather went and what he did, when he was away from home. You see, he was my happiness, and I missed him so. Meeting you, at least I know he must have sought out beauty and peace."

I curtsied like I seen Miss Vivian do and wished Miss Solace would go on by. After a while, she did, and the lawyers followed her into the house.

I stood at the door, helping the maids and the cook tote their bags down to that cart Mr. Boy was driving. Soon as I locked the door and was alone, I pocketed the keys in my work apron and hung it right on the coat rack in the entranceway. I started unbuttoning my plain dark dress and had it off by the time I stepped into the Widow's bedroom. My room now.

"Ella?" Oh no. That voice again.

"Ella!" No doubt about it. The Widow's voice. Sobbing, "Ella, child! Can't you hear me?"

Did I hear her? Yes, but what difference did it make? Didn't I see Mr. Dennis in the bed trying to stab me, and the Widow had to make it clear I was just crazy? Crazy then and still crazy now. Seeing things. Hearing things.

I heard her, but no matter. I lit every candle I could reach in that room, till they blazed, and started pulling open chests and drawers, wondering which clothes I was going to try on first.

And near about wore myself out to sickness that first night, trying on all those clothes, underthings and all, tying all the little ties and hooking all the tiny buttons. I was overworked, dressing myself, and overjoyed. *How do ladies walk, carrying all this weight?* I set myself to practice, prancing around that room and then up and down the hallway till I could do it without tripping even once. *How do they see to their needs if you can't even find your body under all this stuff?* I went down the hall to Mr. Dennis's room to find my favorite chamber pot, brought it to my new room, and waited for a chance to straddle it and practice on it.

*There is so much to get used to!* How could people living in the same world with you be living in such a different world from you? How was I ever going learn to enjoy what Mr. Dennis had given to his Widow?

The thought made me sit down on the edge of her bed and have a good cry.

But when sunlight brought a new day through her heavy damask bedroom drapes and little lace curtains peeping from between like a lady whose underslip is showing, I woke from a nap and dressed in a tea party gown, making a new plan.

*So simple.* I could do it. I could learn to wear all these clothes and own this house. I could live like I had been given what I deserved, for making Mr. Dennis so rich.

All I had to do was take my time. *Wear one new outfit every day. Underthings, too.* Perfume on my body and something fresh to sleep in every night. I figured, one year or maybe two, and I would wear everything the Widow had at least once.

Miss Solace wouldn't be in a rush to sell off this townhouse, just in case her grandpappy or that cursed Widow should show their faces around here. She might give them two or three years, if I got really lucky.

Poor Miss Solace is near on as loyal and stupid as I used to be.

But I had a good plan. Now I could get some sleep and start fresh.

I woke up again around noon, just like in the old days on the big river with Mr. Dennis. I got up off the Widow's bed and heated some water in the bedroom fireplace to wash and start over again dressing.

"Ella." That voice still. But tired and sad now.

I stopped pouring a kettle of boiling water into a china wash basin to look into that twisty silver mirror over the dressing table. *I could have sworn that voice came from*-but no. *Why, I surely have never seen myself so lovely in all my life.* I looked so soft.

I thought of Miss Solace. Calm looking. *She takes her time before she speaks.* If I tried to calm myself like her, could I maybe learn to speak again? Not long speeches like she said. *That would wear me plumb out.* Just a little something here and there that might be important to me. Someday I might even say, "Miss Solace, let loose of your memories of your grandpappy.

You got a much finer man right there beside you."
Meaning Mr. Boy.

"Ella."

Still that voice!

*Go on and fade!* I thought at it. Wherever she was at, I was glad she was gone. *And I hope she loses her way coming back, too.* I took a soft cloth and ran the wash water right down my body to the roses on the carpet, still hot.

After I was washed, I took a bottle of perfume and sprayed till shivers made me stop. I almost laughed out loud. And it was a good sound I made, whatever it was.

After that first day alone, I made myself a routine. I got up and dressed every day in my maid clothes, gathered the money the lawyers dropped on Monday, and went to run errands and buy the little food I was to keep fresh stocked. Took the shop owners no time at all to figure they had to let me point at what I wanted and nod when they guessed right how much of it. They couldn't cheat me on money because I knew from Mr. Dennis how to count it and how to be cheap and stingy. I did well for myself, if I say so myself.

Spent a little time in the afternoon cleaning that big empty house, fast gathering dust.

And then I spent the evening washing myself and trying on pretty things, prancing up and down the hallways and dancing in the front parlor.

I changed again for nighttime into something sweet and lacey and maybe a little bit bare to wear to sleep, like I'd seen ladies do along the river.

I'd stand in front of the wrought silver mirror and stare at my narrow hips all curved out in a round high bottom, and glossy skin shining with lotions and cremes and that sweet grease I would never run out of again in my life, and stockings easing up over high calves and stopping short on my long tight thighs.

*Now, where did I put those little button-up shoes I promised myself I was going try on with this flowered silk thing?* I bent over from the stool where I sat to look around on the floor for where the little cloth shoes might have gotten off to.

And the knocker pounded on the front door.

I sat up.

The strings of jade and pearl around my neck clattered. *Is somebody here? This time of night?* I ran through in my mind who it could possibly be. Couldn't think of anybody. No lawyer. Certainly not Miss Solace.

Got to be that gallivant, back looking for trouble. Maybe I shouldn't go see who it is.

The pounding started up again. Knock.

Knock. Knock. The brass knocker shook the door so you could hear it even upstairs where I was.

I put my stocking feet down and stood straight up from the stool. Never mind the little button-up shoes. I reached around and pulled on the silk flowered dressing gown over my lacy underthings. *Maybe I'd best creep up to the attic and lock myself in and hope he'll go away.*

But that gown wasn't half on one shoulder before I heard that front door opening.

I could hear it plainly, the heavy front door swinging right open with a creak of its hinges. Wind swooshed up the stairs. I could feel it as well as hear it, and it chilled me. Then the door creaked closed.

Somebody had just walked right into this townhouse with me. The cold the intruder brought made a dive for my stomach and dug in its claws.

Where am I going to hide? In the attic? Get going, Ella! Move!

I couldn't move.

*Yes, you can. Get out of here.* I backed up against the dressing table so the perfume bottles on it rattled. Then I couldn't move anymore and just stood and listened.

Steps. Heavy. Like a man does. Step. *Oh no.* Step. Step.

If this is the gallivant, what does he want? How did he get a key? He isn't even going to call out? Announce himself? Ask for somebody? How does he know I'm alone and it's safe to let himself in here like this?

What if he really killed the Widow for Mr. Dennis's money? *He had to come back and find the money. Or her body.*

Either way, *He's got to look in her room.*

I have to get out of here.

Already I could hear the slow steps outside in the hall, and the opening and closing of doors. *Checking. Making sure nobody's here but him.*

Why hadn't I thought to lock this blasted door when I heard that wind rush up the stairs?

Lock it now, Ella. Just two or three steps. Get to it, and lock it.

I felt my body start forward on tippy-toe. I had my hand on the latch to turn the lock when that shoulder of the dressing gown I hadn't got all the way on slipped and the sleeve slid and got in my way. I fumbled for the knob.

And the door was yanked out of my hand and scraped me, coming open. I stumbled back.

Sounds caught in my throat. Nothing came out.

Oh, if I could have talked. Asked. Accused. Demanded to know, "Why have you done this to me?

79

Why? Killed a kind man and left me to suffer for it?" Said anything. *Anything.*

Because here was Mr. Dennis, standing and holding open the door on me. Alive and well.

His hair was gleaming gray where it used to be dark, in waves like moonlight on the big, long deep river that takes your thoughts and goes on and on. But other than the gray of his hair, Mr. Dennis didn't seem to have changed.

He stared at me. His light eyes went wide. "Ella?" he said. "So my wife didn't lie. You really are here."

He was frowning now. He reached out one hand, like he was going to touch the little spikes where my hair was growing back from being cut off. But he didn't touch them. He left his hand in the air. Left the frown between his brows. Frowned deeper.

"Your hair's been cut," he said.

I was staring at how his eyes moved all over my head and face and down my body, jerking and checking. *He must think fast, to keep up with eyes that move like that,* I thought. *What is he going do to me now? He'll have his mind made up before I can figure it out.*

Mr. Dennis said, "I looked-" and then his pale face flushed with color. His eyes stopped jerking all over my body and looked into my eyes.

I made no more moves and no more sounds. *He's going to kill me. He tried to get me killed by those people. He's going to kill me now.*

Mr. Dennis pressed his lips tighter together until they went white.

And then he opened wide his arms.

I threw myself into the warmth between them.

# CHAPTER THREE

## SOMETHING LIKE GOD: MYRA, BORN 1790

It isn't easy to be lead dancer. I've always been lead dancer, and that means I lead everything. That's what lead dancer means.

I've been lead dancer as long as we've danced the magic circle at the town house. Before, really. Because I was dancing by myself long before I came to Mr. Dennis and the Widow's place. She's always been the Widow, before and after she married Mr. Dennis. She was born to be the Widow. And I was born to be lead dancer.

If I couldn't have been lead dancer to Mr. Dennis and the Widow's silly maids, I would've kept on dancing alone.

But there's power in a circle. That's why I lead. Twelve women in a circle, leaving room for that magical thirteenth woman, each one of the twelve gives her power into the circle and gets back the power of all creation. The power to make. The power to be. That's what thirteen is all about.

Thirteen moon months in a year. Thirteen times a woman's body plays god and weeps for evil like war and slavery and starts new. A woman's body is everything that ever happened in all creation ever since that first breath god ever blew over the stars. Twelve women plus that magical thirteenth woman is creation made perfect right there in our circle.

I know a lot of things. I have to, to teach the magic circle to plain ordinary silly wenches like the kind Mr. Dennis and them like to buy.

The lead dancer works to keep her circle strong. Mr. Dennis and the Widow's maids never knew a thing about what I went through for each and every one of them.

And rowdy? Those maids were one raucous bunch of hussies.

Like when Miss Solace and them came to get us out of that townhouse and carry us off to her plantation. Most of the maids giggled and stared at Mr. Boy, sitting up there driving that cart, and I couldn't fault women who've been cooped up in the attic and couldn't get out and meet anybody.

And that Mr. Boy was one good-looking hunk of something. I can't lie. Got his back all strong and long muscles pushing out that fine linen shirt his wife stole out of Mr. Dennis's wardrobe and making hearts jump every time he cracked the whip over the horses. Cotton chopping can't be all bad when it renders a man's body fit to bring eyesight to a blind woman.

But, it's like this: look all you like, but Mr. Boy is poison to think about. Much less flirt and sneak in a little touch on.

If the maids thought they had problems demoted from housemaids to field hands, and from the townhouse to the plantation, they hadn't seen a problem till they try to wrap their legs around the mistress's man. A mistress who used to starve and shiver in her rags in the attic right alongside maids trying to steal her husband? Trouble.

And don't let the thirteenth woman find out her dancers are messing up and doing wrong and stealing husbands and carrying on. She'd give that circle so much power for Miss Solace's revenge, we'd all be lucky to crawl out alive. That thirteenth woman take her perfect creation to heart.

So I sat in that cart looking the other way. Enjoying the country air, trying to catch Miss Solace's eye and give her a little smile and a little nod and let her know she has no call to keep her eye on me and my maids.

Then that sassy, loudmouth, empty-headed maid Layla, whose got the last place in the chain before it makes a circle and better learn to stay there, asked me, "Miss Myra, why you so bitter and down at the mouth?"

I don't have it in me to like this gal, Layla. She's trying to cut into my place as lead dancer, and a child in the street would have sense enough to know last place doesn't lead to first place. And besides all that, I think Layla undercuts whatever I tell the maids to do. I told them to leave that Ashy Ella woman alone, she's got danger all over her, and what's the first thing Layla did? Shared her sleeping pallet with the woman. She's probably in love with her. That's why Layla's got the virgin's place in the circle, anyway. I don't think she likes men.

So I told her in the cart, "Leave me be. I'm thinking."

Layla said, "About what, Miss Myra? How it's going to feel to be outside plowing fields?"

I turned to her slowly to give her time to dread what I'd say. I thought I'd see that cat-ate-the-cream grin on her face that I hate, but it wasn't there. She looked as down in the mouth and bitter as she'd just asked me if I felt.

But I went on, anyway, and warned her, "Layla, child. If you don't leave me be, you're going to get to Miss Solace's fields and start plowing them with your coffin."

That put the fear of the thirteenth woman in her. She shut up.

But some other dimwit woman scooted close to me, away from Mr. Boy's back, and said, "Field hands get a coffin? I heard, when field hands die, they get thrown in some big pit out in the woods where the wild animals get to eat their bones."

Somebody else came close to me from Mr. Boy. "That's right. And I heard they rise out of the pits at night and walk the woods looking for runaways, to eat their flesh and drink their blood. That's why slavers throw dead field hands in the pit. After they spent their whole life plowing his fields, they don't want to see you come along and run away."

Somebody said, "The spirits of the dead field hands kill the runaways in the woods? I thought they had patrol come along and do that."

Somebody else snorted out a laugh. "Patrol? Runaways would be chasing patrol trying to catch them and get a ride on their horse, patrol would've lit out of there so fast, trying to get away from the dead field hands rising out of the burying pit. Don't tell me about patrol. Nothing but a bunch of poor farmers. They're only tough in the daytime."

"And in big groups."

"With guns."

"Guns can't kill spirits."

"That's why patrol would be running from the woods. Knocking on your shack talking about let me in please, ma'am. I won't hurt you."

"Hurt me? They better hope I don't get in my circle and call some spirits to come hurt them."

I got in the middle of this. "I don't care how lonely you maids get. Don't let me hear about any of you all shacking up with some patrol. Spirits or no spirits."

They all gathered closer around me and started laughing together. Would there be more men like Mr. Boy over at Miss Solace's plantation? Was she going to sell the townhouse to get money for more men? Maybe if we let on we couldn't work the field, Miss Solace would have to go out and buy us some men. One man for every woman. Make the men plow the fields while the maids take care of the house. What did I think of that plan?

"Don't get me started," I said, "talking about men plowing the maids' fields."

And then they really screamed.

Everything was going along fine, and then that Layla had to un-shut her mouth one more time. "That Miss Myra," she grumbled out loud. "Always letting on like she know everything. She don't know what Miss Solace go'n do."

I doubled up my fist like I was going to haul off and bap Layla one. Oh, but I was tired of her.

But somebody put a gentling hand on mine. "Ignore her, Miss Myra. She's sad and lonely and missing that Ashy Ella."

Somebody else said, "Won't be any men plowing Layla's fields, will there be, Layla?"

And she put her face on her knees and started to cry.

*Good*, I thought. *Let her cry. And let her leave me alone, too.*

Somebody put a hand on Layla's back, like I should stop picking on her, which I wasn't doing. So I said, "Look, you all. You're sitting up here beating your gums and flapping your chops about men and plows and nonsense, and I have other worries."

And I looked off at the passing trees, big and clumped together like you don't get in the city, and let all that green just take my mind, so I could think.

85

It was true. I had to figure out what we would do at the plantation about our magic circle.

When somebody owns you, you have to stay one step ahead of them. We needed to get to Miss Solace's place already knowing if we wanted to stay in the shacks or play scared and ask to live in the big house, like we did in town. I heard from Miss Vivian that Miss Solace's plantation had both shacks and an empty attic. *Choices.*

Shacks puts you outside the big house in the dark and in the night, where you can slip off whenever you want to and form your magic circle, if your owners don't have dogs, drivers, and overseers.

But, on the other hand, I've seen shacks in the country so bad that if rats broke in they'd be scared to piss in the chamber pot, if they could tell it from the cooking pot, which I doubt, with everything so filthy.

I heard that the old plantation house was falling down around Miss Solace's ears. So if we got put up in that attic and danced in the middle of the night, we might just bust through the ceiling and find ourselves in bed with Mr. Boy and Miss Solace, after all. And that wouldn't work.

So maybe we'd best take the rat shacks so we can dance in the open air, and then take so long fixing them up, Miss Solace would run out and buy some men. I've seen women miss the dance and lose everything the thirteenth woman ever gave them and have to crawl back to the magic circle and start all over again. And I can't have that thirteenth woman mad at me. She hasn't granted my wish yet.

I wish just once, before I die, I could gaze on that thirteenth woman face to face. Just to see her and know her by sight as well as by power. Power is my circle. I've got everything else I ever wanted.

It wasn't always this way. Before I learned the magic circle, I was a cane-cutter like my pa, before he got killed. Dancing alone got me out of the cane fields.

Dancing in a magic circle got me everything else. When something doesn't suit me, I dance on it. I danced the Widow and her gallivant out of the townhouse. It was either dance on them or put poison in their afternoon tea because the Widow and her gallivant were planning to sell off my maids.

And before that I danced on Mr. Dennis. For years, that rapscallion destroyed every virgin I got for the magic circle. Every time I saw that blood running down the legs of my newest virgin, I'd scoot her out at night to meet up with some young man of her own. Next morning, she'd come sneaking back good and compromised. And then I'd go to the Widow and say, "Ma'am, it looks like your property just keeps growing." And she'd start looking at the new maid slant-eyed and seeing little cream-colored babies all over the townhouse, any minute now. And that maid would soon be gone.

Except for one particular maid. I was so mad when Mr. Dennis started sending her chocolates and little sweet treats and she'd giggle and blush instead of run that I got her outside at night to a randy young man that got her with child before Mr. Dennis ever laid a hand on her. She was still putting him off, talking about how she couldn't creep down to his bed at night with the Widow in the hallway, watching. Silly maid took the chocolates anyway, telling me they were good for her cravings. So I was there when he sneaked up on her with her apron off in the townhouse foyer, stretching her aching back.

I walked in just as Mr. Dennis dropped the tin of chocolates at the sight of her round belly. I said my line:

"Sir, looks like your property is just growing apace, isn't it, sir?"

Mr. Dennis smacked his crop in his hand, eyeing me, figuring it all out. Then he kicked the tin so it skidded on the foyer tiles past the maid, fumbling and trying to tie back on her apron, already weeping because she knew she'd be back on the chain soon, marching to find a buyer.

At least, if the circle couldn't have that virgin, Mr. Dennis couldn't either. Not as a virgin.

But then he took to sneaking around, cutting evil eyes at me, and I knew I was fixing to end up dancing in chains, myself. I'm happy to dance alone, but not that chain dance all alone. That's when they're fixing to kill you.

So I danced on Mr. Dennis. And he hasn't been back since.

And that last virgin I talked the Widow into buying, Layla, is going to be a virgin for life, unless she gets loaned out to some breeding farm.

Like me. I'm a virgin, and I can dance the virgin. And I have, when I had to. But it puts you at the back of the chain, just before it forms a circle, and I was born to lead. *Someday, I will lead my dancers up to heaven to look on that thirteenth woman and understand pure power.*

And just when I thought that last thought, the cart bumped to a stop and something like a strong wind whooshed around me and yanked me over the back of the cart and off onto the shell and pebble drive.

We had pulled off the road and rolled up Miss Solace's front drive, but I was so caught up that I didn't know anything until I landed face first in the pebbles with that soft wind whispering around me, *You, woman. Myra. I've been waiting for you. Come here.*

I tried to rise up on all fours, but I wasn't even standing when that wind shoved me stumbling around the side of the house.

I heard the maids' voices call after me. But I couldn't fight that wind nor quite make out what they said.

Round the side a the house, I rushed upon two little grassy hills rising between some willows and vines. Topping the rise on one hill, I slammed upside something hard like a stone growing out of the ground. Fell. Reached up and grabbed to pull myself back to my feet.

I stood, wobbly, and looked at what I was holding onto. Two things, scratchy, rough and pale. Oh, thirteenth woman, protect me. *Two white gravestones.*

Growing right next to the house. *Does Miss Solace know about this?*

The back of my neck started itching at the collar on my dress. I felt like somebody up in the windows of the house was watching me. I looked up to see.

Way up high, the top window slit open. A light was in it, like candles. And birds? Something looked like feathers.

The lace curtains dropped, and the light was gone. But the lace still waved, like feathers fanned it.

I don't scare easily. But I felt fear of *That* in the window and *This* wind tugging at me.

The wind kicked up and shoved me on my face to the bottom of the hill. I lifted my head to see around the backside of the house where the grass gave way to dusty dirt spreading to the Quarters, like piles of kindling stacked and leaning, so as not to fall, just splinters and filth. Like I feared.

I pushed myself to my hands and knees again and felt my lip peaking in disgust. Who would make people live this way? Pigs wouldn't feel at home in a place like this.

And while I looked, from among the splintered shacks, that wind swirled up gray and twisting underneath the darkening sky.

It was gray like a tumbling cloud or a hand that flicked in on itself and stuck out a finger that motioned, *Myra. Told you I was waiting. Come here.*

I don't know what got hold of me. But I got pulled through the dust, pushing back with my hands and screaming, "No! No!" toward that gray moving cloud. I squeezed my eyes shut and put my hands up to keep from getting my face shoved clean through the splinters till I got slammed upside the worst of those piles of filth.

When I stopped, I leaned a little away and brushed slivers off my cheeks and away from my lashes. I was breathing hard and kind of shaking, telling myself, *Myra, just get to your feet. Don't let on you're scared or those silly maids will lose their heads.*

But whatever was pulling on me changed its direction and tugged me a bit to the side. I had my hands still up and felt something wispy, in strings like spider webs or rags, swaying a little in the breeze, caressing my face.

And some kind of sound, hushed, saying, *Got something for you, girl. Come on in this shack and see this. You just dawdling.*

If I listened, I was going to get drawn in. *I'd better not listen.* I leaned in through the wispy rags and couldn't see a thing. But I heard breathing.

And I felt power.

And then a smell hit me full in the face that stank of old rot, ruin and decay.

And another sound, like when a star bursts in the sky and falls in sprinkles like bright rain, but dry, like when the marrow sizzles to powder in a dead woman's bones.

That was it. Dead bones moving and stepping, slowly, with a click and a drag.

And a drag.

I felt the hair on my scalp prickle upright. The smell drove me back till I sat in the dust. But I stared, wanting this.

Wind called, stronger now, *You, Myra. You prayed, you wanted to meet me so. Here I am. Meet me.*

Through the dark, something white came at me, moving closer to the dark gathering all around me, this click and drag bringing *It* saying, *Look on me, Myra. Find my eyes and look inside.*

I blinked through the dark and strings, trying to see into the failing light where the gray twisting cloud blocked the sun as it fell. Something pale and sharp came through the spider webby strings and played on my face, stroking my splinter-stuck cheeks.

And then all of a sudden this thing was on me and sank little knives into my cheeks and pulled.

I screamed and pulled back.

And my pulling brought that thing full forward till I could see that *It* had dug bone fingers in my face, and that's what was holding me so *It* could look into my eyes, like *It* said. I grabbed at what was holding my face till the blood ran, and now, for sure, I screamed.

The power and the stench choked me, but I kept grappling to free my face, and my throat burst out something that might have been blood because it tasted of salt, but it might have been snot, I was crying and fighting so.

91

I fell back, and then I was up and scrambling on all fours and falling and scampering and crying, swimming over the ground like I couldn't take time to touch it, listening to my old dark dress rip and tear against all the sharp little stones between the weedy Quarters and the back of the big house.

I was close to the big back door, set to fling myself on it and pound to be let in, when I felt fingers sink again but, this time, in my hair. Fingers yanked and snapped my head on my neck till I knew that hair was flying. I grabbed at that hand jerking on my head, meaning to fight this time, but I felt flesh. Warm and plenty of it. No bones.

I heard a country woman's voice. "You siddity no-count from the city, what you doing, back here howling and tearing up the place? Ain't nobody round here wanted none of you all. We told Miss Solace sell the lot of you and get some money up in here to fix this place up, but Miss Solace and them fetched and carried you here, and this how you thank her, rutting in the dirt and banging on the doors?"

"Quit!" I shouted.

And she hauled off with her free hand and slapped me in my face, whoever she was.

Nobody can slap me who doesn't own me. I yelled and told her so.

And she yanked me round forehead first till I thought she was going to slam my head into something. But she let me loose, and I stood up, surprised.

I cast my eyes back at the shacks, wondering if that bone thing that grabbed my face also sent this country woman with the rag around her head to work some kind of devilment and humiliation on me, when all of a sudden she said, "Don't nobody slap you, Miss High and Mighty? Well, remember this. Miss Rhea done slapped you good. And if you get wild and foolish round here some more, I be right back to slap you again."

And she got hold of that door and shoved it open. I was just about to ask her about those shacks and what was in them, or if I was losing my mind, when she planted both hands on me and shoved me inside the house.

I lost my footing and stumbled and fell. Oh. More splinters. This place was falling apart everywhere. The floor felt like somebody had scrubbed the boards day in and day out but forgot the wax.

Miss Rhea banged that door shut behind me. I looked around in the dark.

There was a man bent low near me. At least, I thought it might be a man. I could hear his breath rumble, neither going in nor out. Just trapped in his body.

And there was that awful smell again, like a body that might have been dead in those pits in the woods but wouldn't stay put and had come walking.

I raised my head, looking up the worn trousers and the loose, frayed blouse that kept falling away from the strange bulky shape of this man, up to some kind of croaker sack that cloaked his head.

He tried to wrap that burlap sack tighter around him as I stared. But the sack kept twitching and falling away because the man's body was twisted all wrong.

While I watched, trying to take in the sight of this man, something slid out of the front of his cloak toward me. His hand.

I backed away.

His hand moved closer. He followed it. He tried to make the fingers reach toward me, like the fingers back at

93

the shack, only his weren't bone. They were rotten but alive. They moved.

All that reaching and moving made his burlap sack slide up his arm, where coils of ripped, swollen, and dried flesh shone.

I kicked at the dead hand and the walking dead man in front of me. "Get away," I told him.

But he was bending close, so my foot got caught in the tail end of his sack and carried it up and away from his face. He reached up to latch tighter onto his croaker cloak.

But I had seen what he was trying to hide.

Where there should have been a jaw there was just a torn space that he was working and shaping to speak to me. His face had scars like purple folds pressing his eyes almost closed, but dark pleading lights glinted out at me in their distress.

I jammed one hand in my mouth to stop the screams. Too much screaming in one day can make you dim-witted.

That only left me one hand to push myself up off the floor. So I was backing up and getting up and slammed upside something that felt like a bench. It toppled, and I fell over it face up to the ceiling.

I lay there looking up at dead things, shriveled plants and splay-legged animal skins, hanging to dry off the ceiling beams like they dried still struggling to get away from whatever had hunted them. A fire somewhere burned and threw light and shadow, making the dead things change shape while I watched.

What kind of place had Miss Solace carried us to?

My back felt like it was broken. The dead man slid his face between the things hung on the ceiling and me, and from behind him somewhere I heard the maids' voices call my name.

The dead man opened his rope-string mouth, and I looked into the pit it made and gagged on something caught in my throat.

Then I heard a voice like honey pearling in the wintertime on biscuits just out of the oven and broken open with steam, melting and sweet, saying, "Little miss, I ain't go'n hurt nobody. I come to show you your new room, is all. Everybody looking for you. Come on. I help you up."

His strong hand closed on mine, warm and tight. Then I was on my feet, and I wasn't a hand's-breadth away from the man's eyes.

There was somebody in there, calling to me. I swear it was as if the man he used to be was calling out to me from inside his walking grave.

The dead man said, "You want something, little miss, you just call on me and I take care of it. Call my name: Whip Man." It was enough to make the spirits sing and the demons weep, to hear that voice like flowers and warm earth under the winter snow come floating out from his dark burlap cloak.

This kind man, this gentle soul still had my fingers. I didn't want him to let go. My tired heart flew out to kiss that poor ropy gap he worked as a mouth. But all I did was say, "Mr. Whip Man, my name is Myra."

He gave my fingers a little squeeze. "Myra. Is that on account of how the mens make 'miration over you?"

I couldn't believe it. Myra. 'Miration. Admiration. He was flirting. *This dead man is standing here under a ceiling full of dead things, flirting with me.*

I put my free hand to my face. It was sticky where the blood those bony fingers drew was starting to dry. But under the blood and the splinters and the soreness, my cheeks were burning.

Either I was feverish, or I was blushing.

I don't blush for men. But men don't come along and touch my heart like this one.

I guess you start to take to the sight of those who please you. I was wondering how bad I looked my own self, with blood and cuts on my face and my hair coming undone from that Miss Rhea snatching at it, and twigs and dust all over my dress.

Whip Man was steadily feeding my too-hungry heart with his sorry, sorrow-filled, and wretched eyes. Something about him, all torn up and yet alive like this, and that voice, and those gentle big whipped-up hands, cool and warm both at once like where you plant flower seeds outside when the rain has stopped.

Whip Man said softly, "Miss Myra, why you want to look at me like this? Why you ain't turn away?" His eyes said, *Don't be disgusted by what you see.*

"I'm looking, I think, at how you used to be, Mr. Whip Man," I said and moved my free hand from my own cheek to touch inside his cloak.

The sticky blood on the tip of my fingers got in the way, at first. But then, under that, I felt something move under his skin like what runs through dark earth, humming and waiting to make planted seeds grow. Like when a woman comes to you to lose her baby or to save her child, dying of fever, and you can feel life wanting to break through.

I said, "Whip Man, be still. Now I'm the one who won't hurt you." I moved my hand up to his croaker sack

96

cloak and touched it. It was rough. Wearing it must have scratched his ripped skin dreadfully. I eased the cloak from around his head and let it drop down behind him.

"There," I said. I didn't want to scream or even look away. Once I saw him all, and all at once, I only wanted to eat his wounds with my own mouth and spit him back out as the man who I could see flicking like a gutting candle inside that long-dead body.

I gazed at the wheals that rose and fell all over his head and ran my hand though patches where his hair couldn't for the scars. "There's life in here," I said. "Your head rises and falls like the houses and the streets in the city. Touching you is just like looking out from my attic window over the city at night. You don't scare me." I let my fingers dip and rise on the curves of flesh that roped his skull.

Shy, he lowered the lids over his eyes.

I said, "Who did this to you, Mr. Whip Man? It was a whipping to death, wasn't it?"

He squinted up at me. "Yes. Mr. Dennis done it. Years and years ago. A whipping to death. But only my body dead. I'm still live in it, as you can see."

I said, "Too bad I only danced for Mr. Dennis to disappear. Had I known he did this to someone as kind as you, I would have danced him to a slow death."

Whip Man closed his eyes under the slow stroke of my fingers on his head.

I was looking for something. I let my fingers roam, soothing and caressing, till they found a place full of hurt and heat. I rested them there.

"You don't have another name I can call you by, Mr. Whip Man?" I said. "I can't bear to call you after the thing that did this to you."

97

The heat was gathering in my hands. My palms started to ache and arch high like mad cats.

But he didn't pull away, if he felt it happening. That was good. You can't heal a body that won't give in to your hands. And this was a healing that would take all I had. Or more.

But I couldn't stop to think about that. Because I might not go through with it, if I thought.

And this was a healing that was mine to try. His wounds cut in me as if I had suffered them myself. Worse. As if someone I owed my life to had suffered these very wounds.

I would die to heal these wounds, if I had to.

"John," the dead living man said. "My name use to be John. But don't you never call me Conquer."

The power gathered. "John," I whispered. "Pretty name, that one. No need to tack a silly title on it. I've got no use for men who brag and swagger. I don't have anything for them to conquer, either."

He chuckled.

I closed my eyes to feel the power come together. When the time is right, be ready.

It crept up my hands till I had to cup them on the heating spot on his head. Between my palms, the power worked up to break out.

It circled round and round, drawing itself tighter and then back into me, starting to burn because it was flowing as if in my blood to heal old wounds of a death long ago, raising the dead that never laid down and rested, not just to walking, but to life.

How long had I been storing up power to draw that thirteenth woman to me? Maybe that's why this was circling and never breaking loose. It might explode. It was too much.

My arms shook. I said, "Power," and my voice was low, trembling, "you are mine. You do as I say. Heal this good man! Never mind if I meet that thirteenth woman before I die. Leave me, and heal this man!"

Tears seeped out of my shut eyelids. I felt them get caught in the sticky blood on my cheeks. I pressed my clacking teeth together to still them.

I was shaking too hard. My own blood was burning too hot for me. As it raced, the sweat popped and ran, trickling down from my armpits, tickling between my breasts and down my stomach. My legs shook. I felt like I was falling, fainting, trying to hold on.

Then I heard John's voice say, "Myra," soft and far away, calling. And that did it.

At that sound, all my burning, racing power gushed like rivers scorching my hands and drenching the dead man in waves that rocked us both. John grabbed hold of my hands on his head and pressed them down harder. The healing poured. I could feel John trembling, too. But he was brave and held on and didn't pull away.

And then I felt him melt. The healing was going to change him.

I started to work on him, trying not to gouge or dig too deeply. I thought of his face as he used to be, flickering in and out of sight in my mind, and slipped my hands out of his grasp and ran my fingers over his head and spread the hair tenderly all around. I slid my fingers down to shape his face and felt where he had started to cry. So I wet my fingers and spread them around too on his skull, to keep it soft till I was done, scooping those rich tears into the new shape.

I pursed my lips and set in to blowing all over John's face and head, following my fingers.

Now I was shaping his missing ears and smoothing the coils of his neck, and now forcing shape to slide behind his head and down his back, leaning in close to reach around and press along the spine, smoothing and chasing away the memories of pain where death flowed in and life flowed out.

He turned under my hands so I could reach his back.

Down his butt and legs to his feet so that now muscles rose and bunched as they ought to, and up again to his arches, his shins, his knees. I was working quickly up his thighs, shaping and blowing to cool, and the cool air was bouncing back to me, when he grabbed at my hands and pulled me to stand.

I had to keep working. So I ran my fingers down his face with my eyes still shut tight and felt the power dip down his throat to his chest and blew on the trail to cool it in place.

I was blowing the life out myself. His tears had dried and gone, so I spit on his chest and swirled my hands around to spread and shape it.

The chest was broad and curved with a generous beating heart, and I worked it out into long muscle-bound arms that I followed out with my fingers. I was gasping now.

But I worked my way back up the inside of his arms to his chest again and now down to the flat of his belly, and here he did it again. Grabbed at my hands.

I was so startled I opened my eyes.

He pressed my hands to his chest, to the warm little new nipples there, and pulled me in closer where his heart was beating. *Beating.* He was alive.

He threw my hands out of the way and pressed his heartbeat to mine.

The curves of his new chest and mine kept us too far apart for him. He grabbed my head and shoved his new lips on my face, down my bloody cheeks. *Good,* I thought. *Drink my blood down. It will keep the healing going.*

I could feel the power slipping away, my hands dangling at my sides, spilling the last of the power down on the floor, slipping and going to waste. But he was strong and healed, sucking on my lips.

I had never been kissed. Never wanted to be kissed. I had taken many beatings to keep from having hands and lips on me, as his hands and lips were on me now.

And then I heard women's voices: the maids, Miss Solace, and maybe even that wild-fisted Miss Rhea, calling out from behind John.

I sagged and fell and felt strong arms catch me back up.

But it was too late for me. When I opened my eyes again, Miss Rhea's face was the first thing I saw.

Then torches on stone walls flickering red flames and golden light and shadows that showed me I was lying on a stone floor, cold and bumpy under my back. Somebody had unrolled my pallet and stretched it out under me, but it couldn't protect me from the rocks that were the floor.

I hate stone walls.

I was aching and so tired. That Miss Rhea was sobbing, all scrunched up on her knees at my side and gibbering into her hands, like she was praying.

I closed my eyes. I was trying to remember something so sweet it hurt. Strong arms catching me up as I fell.

Now I remembered.

Strong arms that made me, like the thirteenth woman made a perfect creation. Brown and long muscular arms that swooped through the empty universe to catch me back up and hold me to a beating heart so I could listen and hear something like god that whispered in my ear that this world, my world, was a good safe place for me to rest in.

I opened my eyes after a long, long time.

This time, a man knelt by my side with my hand in both of his, touching his cool, smooth lips to my fingers, one at a time. Dry and soft, like breath on skin.

His breath was sweet, warm and alive. Why was he crying?

I looked past his bent head through the torchlight and beyond him. Lots of women, staring, shedding tears, scattered around this strange stone room, talking low.

"Not our Miss Myra. To lose her head like that, and risk her life for a man!"

"Hush! She might hear you and dance on you!"

"Dance? She be lucky to get up and walk, if you ask me."

"You better hope that thirteenth woman ask you before she curse you."

"Hush! You all want everybody to know?"

I closed my eyes again. Someone was waiting for me.

Behind my closed eyes, my mind opened like drapes over a window and dropped me into another room, stone and rock and dirt, like this one, cut out of the ground to lock someone in.

The rocky walls pushed in at me, and I couldn't back away from them. A shape pulled away from the rock walls.

A big man moved and stood between me and a little high window left in the stones in the wall, stuck with iron bars. When he moved, a sound like music, soft and with the rhythm of his steps, rushed to me.

Oh no. I don't want to see this. I don't want to be here.

I looked around. *How can I get out?* Stone walls and the barred window and a door locked fast.

Moonlight through the barred window fell on the man in the middle of the stone room where he raised his strong, long muscular arms, jerked them up high over his head and waved them like the sun dipped and rose. He threw back his perfect head against the soft moonlight.

His lips fell apart, and he moaned long and low and started to turn in circles with his chains still held up over his head, swinging and bouncing off his head as he waved his arms, slapping him in the face. He threw back his head and howled like music for his chain dance.

I said, "No, pap. Quit, pap. You scaring me."

I had never seen my father's strong arms flailing when he wasn't cutting cane, and I had never heard him moan like a dying animal, howl like a mad dog.

But I was most scared of something else.

The rising sun.

I screamed.

Arms circled around me, and a voice said, "No, Myra. Don't, baby gal. I'm here. It's John. I got you. Wake up."

I opened my eyes and grabbed hold of him. That dream, that other room, faded. "John, where am I? Where are my maids? Where is everybody?"

I could see his shape clearer now, right up on me. He said, "They in the fields."

103

"In the fields?"

"They got to haul in that cotton, Myra. But you ain't no country gal. I guess you don't know a thing about cotton."

"Cotton? What cotton? We grow cane round here."

John got quiet.

I felt strange. Something wasn't right. I said, "You, John. How come you're not in the fields with everybody? Are you in trouble? Have you done something wrong?" I sat up, pushing at John. "Where's that window?" I yelled. "Is the sun coming up? John, hide! You're not in chains? You're free? Then, get out of here! Run, John! The sun is coming up!"

But John was trying to grab hold of me again.

I fought him off and kicked at him, and once I was up, I dug my fingers in his arm to get him to come with me. "John, go see if the sun has come up, yet!" I hurried along the stone walls I hated so, feeling with my hands for that window. It had to be there. I just couldn't see it.

John came behind me, following and still grabbing at me, trying to stop me. I shook him off my arm. "Let me go, John!" I said. "I've got to get you out of here!"

No use. No windows in here. Something was wrong.

I had felt my way all along one wall till it gave way to a door. The door creaked open under my hands. I shoved it harder. "Look, John! The door's not locked! Let's get you out of here!"

Now I had power. Maybe it wasn't going be too late this time to save him.

Save who?

I had gotten to another door. This let outside. I shoved at it. Shoved harder. John was coming right up behind me. I had to get it open. *Don't stop me, John.*

The door gave and sunlight spilled all over me like fire.

Fire. That fire, burning my pap, making his running blood sizzle and go dry. Somebody was laughing and saying to me, "Your pap ain't go'n bleed to death, Myra. Fire dry that running blood right up." And it was drying it. All his pieces lay there dry and smoking and covered with soot in the grass from the fire. Grass with bleeding pieces on it, pale fingers getting dark with blood and soot, picking up smoking, dark body parts out of the blood on the grass.

The sun was high.

And the grass was covered with my pap's blood and his burned pieces. And I wouldn't ever be in time to save him, no matter how strong I got. No matter what dance I did. He was dead. Always already dead, by the time I knew who he was.

Strong hands grabbed me from behind. I went down, screaming. Somewhere, I heard someone say, "Too much power will make you crazy. Just look at Miss Myra."

The next time I came to, I was lying on stones again, with strong arms holding me. Far away, I could hear a man crying.

I closed my eyes to rest. My pap's cries made me tired. And wasn't nothing I could do.

And then I was out dancing under the moon and feeling its light melt my chains away. And then I woke up with John kissing my face, my cheeks, my mouth. "Come back to me, Myra," he said.

I took it as long as I could. Then I had to turn my face away. I sucked in air and must have swallowed some of the tears John left running down my face.

He let me loose. When I could breathe, I turned back to him. I tried to lift my arms to hold him, but they wouldn't lift. Chains tugged and clanked at my wrists.

I tried to sit up.

Something around my neck snatched me back. I heard more chains clanking before I hit the stones hard and went cold in my stomach. "John? What's happening here to me? Am I in chains?"

"Myra." It was John's voice, all right, near me in the dark. "We had to hold you. You was go'n hurt yourself or somebody. Listen. Mother Magdalen been putting something in your ear, calm you right down, she say. She told me, when you come to yourself, I was to have you drink this tea. It go'n bring you right around. Drink it, and maybe we get them chains off, baby." His voice snapped like broken twigs. "Myra," John said, "if you get hurt, after all you done for me, it go'n kill me. You got to hurt somebody, hurt me. I owe you that. You done gave me back my life. You can take it back. But please don't run round here, snatching at knives and threatening yourself."

"Snatching at knives? Never!"

"Yes, baby. Snatching at knives and talking about put that down or you go'n kill somebody, and how everybody better don't touch your pap."

"My pap has been dead, John. Nobody can touch my pap."

"Myra, you got to listen."

"John, I can't listen to you. You're talking too crazy."

"Ain't me been talking crazy. Myra, it's something in you. Trying to come out, I guess. But this ain't the place. Miss Solace talking about she ain't never thought to put no chains on nobody, and she can't take it. She ready to send you and all them townhouse maids back to the townhouse. What you think, Myra? That help you, going back there? Cause all you got to do is calm down enough to make that ride. I be right there with you. Go back with you, and stay. Only, one more thing."

"One more thing? John, you've told me too much already. I can't keep up."

John talked slower now, like that would solve it. "Listen, Myra. I want to take you back to town, stay with you there, heal you if I can, like you done healed me. Take care of you. But it's only right to tell you. If you hoping for a man, I can't be that to you."

I turned my head to try one more time to get a look at John in this dark. Again, I heard that clank of chains. If what he said was true, I wasn't making the chains up. I was chained, after I had gotten so much power.

I could just make out John's shape, standing now, working at something on the wall and grunting. When light flew in around him, I realized John had pushed open a shutter. I heard it bang on the wall.

John wasn't through, though. He stood where he was, in the light and worked at his shirt, till it fell around his feet, and then at his trousers. He looked down to watch them fall, too.

The light from outside shot around his body and seemed to cut off parts that should have been there.

John turned slowly in the light. For the longest, I couldn't tell what I was looking at. And then I understood why John had said he couldn't be my man.

"I see," I said to John.

He bent and got his shirt and trousers and put them back on. "Light bother you, Myra, if I leave the shutter open?" he said, dressing.

107

""Yes," I said. So he banged it shut, and I heard and felt him come slip his arm between my head and the stones. I said, "You shouldn't have stopped me, when I had the healing going. I could have healed that, too."

John said, "It was something in me. Shame, I guess. I just had to stop you."

After a while, I said, "John, I'll drink that stuff for you and get better. But you've got to promise to let me out of these chains by the time the moon gets new. I've found the thirteenth woman. She lives in a shack right on this plantation. I won't lie. She scared me when I first found her. But by the next new moon, she and I are going to dance to heal you."

"Myra, you can't dance. We got to come at this another way. Take me like I is. Don't ask for what I ain't got. And I ain't blame you if you seek what you need elsewheres."

I blew out my breath. "How you talk," I said. "You wear me out. I always heard that men don't make sense. Now I know it's true. Let's talk another time. My head feels like it's been split in two with an axe. Go ahead and give me that tea you told me about."

He had started up kissing on my face again.

I said, "And can't you get me out of these chains? Look at me. I'm too weak to hurt anybody. You say my chains hurt Miss Solace? They can't hurt her nearly as much as they hurt me. Why didn't she leave me a little more slack in them?"

John had propped himself up and brought something round and made of clay to my lips. I smelled something green inside. The first sip glided over my tongue, and I gulped the rest down. I had a terrible thirst.

I heard John working a key at the locks on the chains, scraping. First my neck lost that awful pull. I wanted to stay awake and feel the rest of the chains fall away, but Mother Magdalen's juice was knocking me out. The last thing I said with my thick tongue was, "John, leave me the shutters open after all. I've got to keep an eye out for that new moon. I'll dance for you, and you'll see."

I waked plenty of times to find John near, washing me or pouring something from a bowl into my mouth. "Me and my son Boy been hunting in the woods for you today," he would say. "Found you something got strong good blood in it, bring you back. I cooked this up myself. Try to drink it all." Or, "Mother Magdalen say this here make your heart strong. Pump. Drink it."

"John, all I need is sleep. Let me alone."

"Come on, baby. You can sleep when we get you back to that townhouse. Right now, you need to get strong enough to ride in that cart."

I groaned. "Don't even talk about it. Just thinking about that cart makes my bones ache."

"Your bones ache? Don't you feel this feather mattress I got under you? I took it right off me and Rhea's bed."

What had I heard?

Till then, everything John said run into one long ramble: everybody wanted me better; that cart was just waiting; any day now, I'd be bumping along the road to my attic room at the townhouse; we'd be together forever. He said the same things all the time.

But now, time stopped. He had said something that broke away and stood apart. I said, "You and Miss Rhea's bed?"

Quiet.

"John. You and Miss Rhea go to bed together?"

Still quiet. Bad, bad time for the man to sit there quiet.

I said, "Miss Rhea is your wife, John? Is that true? Am I right?"

Nothing. Nothing but a place where his tongue cut my heart out of my chest, still pumping, and swallowed it down.

I stared in the darkness till maybe I slept some more. I don't know. But when I came to myself, I hollered, "John, get this mattress out from under me! Talking about what you can't do. You can do something! You've got you a wife, haven't you? I said get this mattress out from under me! Now I know why I can't get better. You've got me laid up on Miss Rhea's mattress, and she's killing me! Get me my pallet back, John! Do you hear me? Get me my own pallet!"

John's fist hit the mattress somewhere down by one of my legs.

And I lay still. I guess I went back to dreaming.

Because in this dream, the moon was high and round against my pap's perfect head, and he turned toward me as I said, "Where that new moon, pap? Why it stay full and ain't never new? I got to dance for you. Set you free like everybody out in the fields be free."

He didn't answer. But while he looked at me, I heard that other voice say, "That moon won't be new for you again, Myra, unless you come cover it, yourself."

So I rose up to cover the full moon and make it new. That's all I meant to do. But it was far and high above me. So I kept rising. It felt good to rise.

Shutters banged open and shut behind me as I passed, and somehow I was out of the stone-walled room and looking up at the moon past the trees, reaching with my hand to shut out the moon's light with my spread fingers.

But I heard sobbing through the rumble of a gathering storm. I looked back through the banging shutters into that room where I had left John, just as a storm cloud burst and spilled. I reached for the falling rain, to catch it up to my heart and cool and heal myself.

Rain slipped through my fingers and slanted past me into that empty room where John was lying on my pallet. Around him were piled the chains he had unlocked off me, and it was strange. I could see him in there through where the shutters banged open and shut, and in the dark he was holding me, propping my head when it flopped back, and he was crying.

I felt for him.

But just now, I was so glad to be out of there. There was nothing back there for me. Not John, and not that thirteenth woman.

I could go without getting back into that weak stiff body to try to dance.

# CHAPTER FOUR

WHO: LAYLA, BORN 1788

The maids heard the storm that took Miss Myra even from where we was locked in a stone room with no windows.

We held on to one another while the house shook so that torches rattled in the wall sconces, and we closed our eyes even though we couldn't see the lightning. You could feel it in the air. Some raised their heads and started praying to that thirteenth woman. Some bowed their faces to their knees and cried.

When the house stopped shaking, I said, "I'll have a look-see. Something big is going on around here."

Nobody tried to stop me. They all wanted to know. The torch-fire jumped across the tears on their faces and lit them all red, lips trembling. They was weak and frightened, without Miss Myra.

I hated them.

Always making me prove myself. Here I was again, about to do something nobody in her right mind should have to do, always trying to get out of the back of that dance chain.

I told myself, *Don't think on it*, pushing open the door to the hall. *Don't think, and you won't be scared, Layla.*

But when you came out into the hallway, dark and bent between the stone rooms hanging off the side of that flung-together house, you couldn't help but think of it, whatever "it" was. And feel "it."

"It" was present, something like terror in the flesh, but grown old and getting up out of a squat, thinking about me, too. Maybe trapped right here in the hallway with me.

"Shut that door, Layla!" some of the maids screamed behind me. I pulled it to.

It clicked, and I leaned back against it to get my bearings. You want to feel out a place so you know what's coming at you and from where.

I could hear the storm crack and rock the stones in the walls. The torches that was stuck in the hallway sconces got caught in a big jolt and shuddered and dripped bits of flame on the floor around the hem of my skirt. I grabbed handfuls of black cotton and snapped it and flapped it to keep the whole dress from catching alight.

Then I pressed my back up against the shut door. I could feel somebody on the other side slide the bolt against me. Locking me out. So I hung on to the stones at the edge of the threshold and waited for my trembling to stop. Mine and the storm's.

I would have prayed if I believed in a god or in that thirteenth woman. But I didn't. So I closed my eyes and thought of the lightning and tried just to push it away from me and from this house I was in.

The third door at the far end of the hallway slammed open. I could hear the storm screech inside that room and water splattered on the stone floor in there, like windows was open.

Then Whip Man backed out of the door into the hallway, all bent over, like when we first saw him. I thought, *He must be deformed again. Maybe Miss Myra died, and her healing died away with her.*

But then Whip Man turned, and I saw he was bent over something in his arms. He was holding it up, and it was heavy.

He was soaked from the rain. Water streamed down off him onto the dry thing he tried to hold up. It sagged to the floor between his arms, dark and still.

I heard the storm in that other room pick up, like it was shrieking to get at what Whip Man was carrying away. I came away from my doorway and scraped my back against the stone wall, moving close to see what Whip Man carried.

He struggled to hoist it up. Its head flopped away from him. Its eyes was half open. It was Miss Myra.

I watched while Whip Man got Miss Myra up so as he could stand straight. Then he looked over at me. His eyes blazed red in the torch-fire, wet all around the sides.

He left the door wide and started coming with Miss Myra at me. He swung Miss Myra from side to side, moving fast. I tried to back up against the bolted door to the maids' room, out of the way. But he knocked one of Miss Myra's shoulders right into my chest, pushing hard.

He glared into my eyes, like he knew I had always hated his woman and wished her dead. I lowered my eyes. I couldn't help how I felt about Miss Myra. Whip Man spat out, "She ain't dead! Don't say nothing to me." I cut my eyes up at him. He pushed past, looking over her head at me. I still said nothing.

Almost past, Miss Myra's cold fingers touched me through my skirt like little trickles of ice. She was too dead, all right. Whip Man had been lying up in that room with a dead woman in this storm for who could say how long. Maybe he was as crazy as she was.

I came off the wall and followed him through the dark and the torchlight.

I caught up to him in Mother Magdalen's big back room, with the fireplace roaring and the dried things hanging off the ceiling and walls. Whip Man rammed up against that bolt at the back door with his side, trying to slide the bolt without letting loose of Miss Myra. She was getting stiff at the limbs from being dead too long. Only her head was heavy enough to keep on flopping.

I got around Miss Myra's body and slid between Whip Man and the door. Then I got both hands on that bolt and shoved hard. And here comes Whip Man ramming into my back, and that sent the bolt sliding.

The storm shoved the door wide open for us. Rain and flying rubble slapped me full in the face till I fell back.

I sat in the mud and turned away to keep the storm from cutting at my cheeks and at my eyes. When I looked again, Whip Man had already set out. With my arm crooked over my head, I followed him and left the door gaping. I couldn't have closed it, anyhow.

The whole world around me was gray up-heaving in the green. Trees tossed and broke up against the sky. Flying pieces of things struck at my face. Blood broke through and burned, and the falling rain washed it thin.

The wind ripped at my clothes. My skirt flew in my eyes so I had to stop to yank it down. I looked around and couldn't see Whip Man after that.

So I bent low, crawling over the ground. This way, I got around Mother Magdalen's garden and looked up just in time to see her rose vines reach out and snatch at my face with their little mean thorns.

I fell back and sat and pressed my hands to my cheeks. My salt tears stung the fresh cuts, and the wind whipped the tears around to plug up my ears. *Who wants to hear a storm howl, anyway?* I thought, but I looked around, good and scared now.

The sky glowed dark. Lightning like a knife slit the sky's belly, and it bled bright pink along the crooked cut. Thunder shook me on the ground where I sat, the mounds under Mother Magdalen's rose vines split along their grassy tops.

I had heard tell it was Mother Magdalen's own ma'am and papa buried there, in graves slit open while I watched. *I better get out of here.* No need to linger and see things I couldn't bear.

I got up to crouch against the flying pebbles. I couldn't get anywhere sitting down. I cupped my hands around my eyes and searched out that grieving mad Whip Man.

There he was, under the trees tipped low like they was reaching down to the burden in his arms amongst the shacks. He shouted up at the sky that was barreling down. And Miss Myra, in his arms, jerked in the wind.

*Follow on, or give up?* I got up on my hands and knees and followed. It felt like the woods beyond had crept close to face me down. I had to keep my eyes on Whip Man.

His legs was spread, so the wind shoved but couldn't bring him down. I crawled up close till I could grab Myra's cold body and ease her down from his arms. It scared me, to see him flinging her and bellowing so.

Whip Man looked down at me wild-eyed where I was under him, pulling on her, but he let me take her.

I sat and held Miss Myra. She froze me in my arms, stretched stiff with her head back over my shoulder, staring glassy-eyed at the dying storm. I turned away from her, holding her but trying not to think of her.

Whip Man, freed from Miss Myra, went scrambling close to the ground, running in circles, rolling flat stones together in front of one of the shacks. He dragged his fingers through the dirt, raking up kindling and held his little pile of kindling inside that ring of stones while he fished in his pockets, maybe for a flint to light him a fire.

I guess he found nothing. He stomped down to hold the pile of kindling against the wind and looked deep inside the shack where he stood. He shouted something, but what was left of the wind ate his words.

Still, something came to the open mouth of that shack.

White like china dinner dishes. Fine and fragile, but lined up tall like smoke from a dying campfire on a windless night.

It looked at him, like it was waiting. Just leaning a little and looking, like a woman who says, *I knew you'd come back.*

*A woman,* I thought, *alone in that shack through this storm? Who? So thin.*

At the top, her head turned this way and that, like to watch Whip Man still fumbling in his pockets and the storm blowing itself out, both at the same time. *But something about her is wrong.*

That's when I saw the shreds of rag draped off the wide white hip that snaked up into her ribs and twisted down again around her thighs, licking tight and letting go, as the wind blew them. Spiders floated to the bits of bone that made up her feet. They hid under the arch and

117

scuttled away back into the dark where the bone woman had come from.

*Bones!* I jumped and tried to make as if to move. But now Miss Myra, stiff, pressed me down.

The bone woman raised her fingers to touch at little shreds of headrag laced over the top of her skull. Her black holes for eyes settled, pointed straight at Whip Man.

The holes looked empty but even from where I sat, I could tell it was something in there, like a fire lit but burning dark.

The bone woman stepped out on the ground. Mud squished up between her toes. She walked like a candle flame blows out.

Wind tossed a few straggling leaves away in circles. The bone woman lifted a hand, like to feel and make sure she was seeing Whip Man out ahead of her. She tilted her skull on all the little neck bones. Her mouth opened, and she said his name. Or maybe it was the last of the wind, sighing.

I had sat still, cold and shaking and holding on to Miss Myra, thinking, *None of this is happening.* But the bone woman's voice trembled through me so I felt it in my insides.

She spread her thin arms wide. The last flicks of lightning washed over the bony white and turned it silver and then blushed it a color like apricots in early summer.

Whip Man turned from her to where I sat holding Miss Myra.

The bone woman stopped and stood still. Dropped her thin white arms and stared, first at Whip Man, walking away with his back to her. Then she turned the deep black pits that should have been her eyes at me.

She was still far away. But I looked in those holes like she was right up on me.

The black was pure like folks hope to find heaven and deep like folks fear to find hell. The longer I looked, the more I thought I heard screaming come from inside, and I felt pulled like there wasn't a world to live in but those pits in her eyes, and I had to go there.

*Stay here. Stay put. Don't look at her anymore.*

But in the quiet after the storm, I could hear the scraping and had to look at the bone woman, because she had started moving towards me again.

She had an odd style of walking. She had to kind of slide that wide hip bone, snaking her long thin back behind and above, dipping and twisting her whole body from feet to skull, gliding.

The last of the storm whistled through her bones and away. I kept my eyes on the space between the bone woman and where Whip Man was sneaking up behind her.

I didn't see when she reached me. I didn't know a thing till her sharp finger bones like spikes dug in my cheeks and forced my head up.

And then I was just lost, falling into those pits of the bone woman's eyes, like coming to the end of the stars in the sky and looking over the edge where there's nothing but black. *Fall into forever. Let the black soothe you and drain your mind free while you fall out of life and time.* A spider ran out of one eye socket and down the cheek like a prickly black tear, and the screams in her eyes died away, like drops of rain.

The rain had started up again, plopping between me and the bone woman's face, wet and cool. I pulled back and realized I wasn't holding Miss Myra's body. It was gone.

Miss Myra lay stiff on her side in the mud. Four trickles of blood made their way down the side of her head. I had the idea that the bone woman had clawed Miss Myra out of my hands, but I just couldn't remember.

Whip Man snatched the bone woman around to face him, and I got to my feet. Miss Myra was truly dead, and the maids was in the stone room waiting for my news, and this storm had paused for just a little bit.

I took off, making my way around the side of the big house, away from Whip Man and whatever he was doing with Miss Myra's dead body, and that bone woman. I hung on the willow branches, the wild vines, and the tombstones as I passed them, looked to the gray sky dropping rain, and wondered why that rim of nothing in the bone woman's eyes felt more real than this solid world.

I made it to the front of the house where the maids called to me. They gabbled, "Layla! Come on, girl. Where you been? Mr. Tim is fixing to get all of us out of here."

Surely enough, there was the carriage, and Miss Vivian and their lanky son Zion lurched around on the driver's bench with blankets on their laps and bundles at their feet, all set to go. They glared down at me, mouthing against the drip-drip of after-rain, "Come on, Layla."

Mr. Tim leaped down and grabbed my elbow, shoved me and shouted in my ear, "Miss Solace done ordered us all back to town. We was going to have to leave you, messing around in this storm, gal."

I got heaved to the carriage door. Miss Vivian, perched up there, turned away from me, and the rain dripped off the tip of her short nose. Her boy Zion stared at me and blinked his eyes.

Maids was piled inside the carriage one on top of the other like baggage. I stopped on the carriage steps with Mr. Tim's hand still shoving in the small of my back and looked around one last time at this strange place we was leaving at last.

Lights like little tongues of fire flickered up above the big house's front door. The light came from a woman up there, above the verandah, sitting right on the porch roof. She was curled up like she was just sitting and thinking and flicking her bright wings, where the light glowed.

Her gown glowed too, dry despite the rain but twinkling like stars hid under the cloth as fine as spider webs. Only the light in her wings sputtered when raindrops hit the feathers. She moved a hand up under her chin and looked straight at me, like she had just noticed me staring. Her big bright wings lifted up and down with a lazy whoosh, and she blinked at me like Zion and settled down to stare back.

I stumbled off the step and tried to point up at her because I couldn't choke out a word. But Mr. Tim lifted my feet back up on the carriage step and pushed my body through the narrow door.

I fell over on the maids all crouched and crowded on the seats and with their tote bags jumbled in wherever Mr. Tim tossed them, rocking and shaking, squeezed so close they couldn't settle back and get comfortable.

"Get off me, Layla." I felt a foot jab into my behind and heard the thin carriage door slam.

"Did any of y'all see-?" I said weakly, but we all got thrown upside one another as the carriage jolted and started to roll, and I sank my face into the black wet cotton between my knees and let the bone woman and the woman with the wings flit in and out of my befuddled mind.

I was burdened and weary now with something I could probably never tell. I wanted to lead these women, and I didn't need them thinking I was as crazy as Myra. *I've lost my mind. Seeing strange women. Why?*

And while the horses clopped and rocked the carriage, and the sweat mixed with rain and ran down my body, I thought, *What if some day I work up my nerve to go back and fall over that edge the bone woman offered me? Heck with the end of the dance chain. I could walk to the front of creation and claim it.* The thought soothed me to sleep.

Next thing I knew, somebody was shaking me awake and talking about, "Come on, Layla. Mr. Tim done pulled the carriage round back of the townhouse and is waiting for us all to get out. Climb down. We're tired."

Maids was kicking me, getting past. I crawled to the door, lightheaded, and tumbled down the rain-slick carriage steps. I landed hard right on my hands and splashed in the puddles on the courtyard cobblestones.

"Get on out the rain, you all," Miss Vivian called. Her husband snapped his whip through the night air to make the horses walk on into the stables.

Maids huddled under the service porch eaves and watched lights glow bright in the windows over the stables where Mr. Tim and them lived. After a while, Mr. Tim loped out of the stable door, shielding a candle in one hand. We moved off the porch to give him room and backed out into the rain, so he could protect his candle and work at the lock on the door with his latchkeys. He must have forgotten which one opened this back door.

The other maids was chitchatting about what they would do first, as soon as they got inside. How they would dry off, burning charcoals that don't spit sap. Rub their hair with towels still white and with no holes in them. What they would eat that was in a tin and cost the Widow lots of money and was salted down so it couldn't go bad.

Pretty soon, they got to laughing in the rain for no reason. It just felt good to almost be back home.

I looked around at them. I was shivering. Nobody remembered to pack my tote bag for me. I looked up at the dark where you couldn't see stars for the storm clouds, and I thought again about the bone woman's eyes and that other woman with wings. Was I just crazy like Miss Myra?

I shuddered and thought of Whip Man doing what-all to her out back of that plantation house.

"Come on, Layla," somebody hissed. "You done gone witless on us?"

The maids was all filing inside, slinging their bundles down and shaking out their clothes. I tagged a bit behind, wringing my skirt on the porch. Mr. Tim was patient for a change and held the door with one hand and the candle with the other.

"Mr. Tim, bring on that light here," someone called from inside.

"He's waiting on Layla."

"What's got into her?"

"Seen something out back at that plantation, I reckon."

"What?"

"Don't ask. I don't want to know."

"Poking around where she ain't got no business."

"Hush, you all. I'm looking for flints somewhere on this mantel. Help me find them." You could hear pat-patting around above the kitchen fireplace.

Somebody grumbled, "That Ashy Ella ain't been stacking the wood."

"Leave it for tonight."

"Yes, ma'am. Let's just get some food out of the pantry that don't need heating and head on up to bed."

"Me, I'm tired enough to drop and sick enough to die."

"What was that?" And we all stopped what we was doing, wringing and patting and knocking things on the pantry shelf, and looked up.

Looked around.

There had been a sound. I came through from the service porch into the kitchen, staring. I thought, *Mr. Tim didn't close that door behind me*. I felt a swift sharp breeze, and Mr. Tim's candle gusted out.

The maids panted, short of breath. One of them said, "Mr. Tim. What was that?"

But he didn't say anything. I think he was staring at the shape, tall and pale against the dark, in the doorway that led from the dining room to the kitchen. It carried its own light in its hand. *That bone woman!*

The light threw shadows up along the face full of sharp edges, flat planes. The face was still, just looking at us. You couldn't see anything but that one hand, and the face, and the white hair that lifted and drifted in a breeze made by the candle's flame.

Somebody screamed. Maybe it was me, at last.

Mr. Tim's voice came out weak in the darkness. "That you, Mr. Dennis? Sir?"

The shape moved a little in the doorway before it opened its mouth and said in a man's deep voice, "You are never to call her Ashy Ella again. None of you. You are to call her Miss Ella and serve her as mistress of this place, for she is indeed mistress enough for the likes of all of you, until I give you further notice. Do I make myself understood?"

Maids let out held breath in a gush of, "Mr. Dennis, welcome home, sir," and started dropping deep curtsies all around the kitchen with their heads bowed. I had never met Mr. Dennis. I stared.

This sharp, floating shape in front of me wasn't anything like the strong, angry, dark-haired man the maids made him out to be. But you could tell perhaps something wasn't quite right about this Mr. Dennis by the way all the maids and even Mr. Tim kept studying him sideways out of the corner of their eyes in the dark, peering into his candlelight, seeing it was him, but not quite. All faded and wrong.

Like maybe Mr. Dennis wasn't just back. He was back from the grave.

This was a sign.

Mr. Dennis's coming back like this from nowhere meant all Miss Myra's magic was gone with her. The rest of us maids was on our own, to start all over again working the world the way we needed it to be.

The maids gathered their bundles and pallets to tote them up the back stairs. We filed through the door and up, saying as we passed, "Good night, Mr. Dennis, sir. So glad you're back home, sir."

And all the while, he said nothing more.

It wasn't till we was all stretched out to sleep, me with nothing to put on once I took off my wet dress, but curled on half the dry side of somebody else's pallet and wrapped in half of her little rag quilt, that the maids took to talking again.

Voices echoed around the attic under the windows streaked black with rain. "Is that Mr. Dennis? Or is it his ghost?"

They talked a long time. But nobody let me get away with saying much of anything, since I had never met Mr. Dennis before and couldn't help them compare, and they was all afraid I might get started talking and end up telling them what I saw around back behind Miss Solace's big house at the plantation.

All us maids woke up late and starved the next day, with nobody calling and shouting and banging pots to wake us. But we figured we best go on down to the kitchen, get whipped for oversleeping and get it out of the way, so we could wash and hunt up some fixings to cook city food. Some for us and Ashy-Miss Ella, and some for that thing calling itself Mr. Dennis upstairs.

We was sidling down the steep back stairs, talking about, "You ain't never go'n get me back out to the country. Folks like to up and die with they feet in the air, eating wild like that," when we got stopped at the door. The maids at the bottom stood at the foot of the stairs, stock still, blocking our way to look at something in the kitchen.

It was that Mr. Dennis thing, standing before the big iron stove, watching the cold pots hang from the ceiling. The kettle was on the stove, but it was just sitting.

He turned to look at us crowding in the doorway to look at him.

In the daylight, you could see all of him, the dark holes in his face for eyes and the blackness in his nose to breathe. But other than that, he didn't look even real, he was so pale and dry. Something about him rustled when he moved, and his hands rose up and floated, like they wasn't used to the weight of being. And all the time those strings of his white hair wouldn't lie down or even stay still but drifted around him like he was always falling down from the sky.

Without Miss Myra, who was dead, and Miss Vivian, who wasn't around to be accounted for, there was no one to speak for us. So we all started dropping our knees and tugging our hems in curtsies at the same time and promising all together to make him and "Miss Ella some breakfast right away, sir." Still, he didn't say a word. Just listened and then floated on away.

I followed to the hallway. I shouldn't have. But so close to Ella, up there all alone where Mr. Dennis was going, I couldn't stay back. I stood under the wide stairs that curved away up to the second and third floors and watched him drifting up, staring right back down at me.

The maids gave me the tray, when it was ready, to take up to Mr. Dennis and Miss Ella. "Was you befriended her when everybody told you not to. You the only one not go'n slip and call her Ashy because you never did. Go on up there and no gawking and dawdling. Come back and tell us what you see."

"And don't miss nothing," somebody said as I started up the back stairs. "We all waiting to hear."

It wasn't anything on the tray but a silver pot of coffee, two tea cups turned into their saucers, and a plate of buttered buttermilk biscuits tucked around with yellowed linen napkins. Ella hadn't kept the place up while we was gone and the food stores was full of weevils and roaches.

And speaking of kept up. I looked down at my dress. It was near on dry by now but muddy and frayed worse than ever from where the storm had whipped me around last night.

How would I look to Ella?

I stopped on the second floor landing. It was too many rooms in this house. Which one was they in? And was they in the same one together? I started walking, my breath shaky. "Miss Ella, ma'am?" I called out to both sides of the hallway as I went.

A door far down the hallway nudged open. Used to be the Widow's room. I went to it.

Through the crack that had opened in the door, I could see Ella seated on a carved wooden chair before a fancy mirror. She was in a flowery silk dressing gown I used to see the Widow wear in the morning before she took callers, and Ella had draped strings of glowing stones around her neck.

She was looking in the mirror, but she turned her gaze to me. I said across the room to her, "Miss Ella, ma'am. Your tray. Good morning."

And Mr. Dennis's voice piped up beside me at the door and said, "Put the tray down on the table and go, girl."

Ella watched me with her dark, quiet eyes. She had finished draping on necklaces, I guess, because she reached for a silver-handled brush and started running it over her spiky coils of hair. I came further into the room with the tray. Did she remember it was me who gave her a place to sleep when she was naked and alone? Every move she made sent me smells from her body that was

128

like holding her those long ago nights and listening to her sigh in her sleep.

My hands was shaking when I set down the tray on the first table I came to. I looked up and saw Mr. Dennis in the corner behind the door, glaring at me.

I curtsied to him and then to her, saying, "Good morning, sir. Morning, Miss Ella." And then I looked at the bright flowers sewn into the carpet on the floor, hurried out and down the hall, and didn't stop till I got to the back stairs just outside the kitchen.

It was horrible in there. The beautiful and the dead, together. I was sick at my heart. But I wanted to get back in there and remind her she still had me.

When I wasn't shaking anymore, I walked into the kitchen and said, "You all, I think they want their room cleaned and their things washed. And it's no fire in the grate."

Just like I knew they would, the maids still hanging around in the kitchen said, "Then you go do all that, Layla. Like we said, you won't slip and call her out of her name."

Miss Vivian hauled more hot biscuits out of the oven. I snatched one off her tray, and she looked me in my eye and said, "Don't you go get in no trouble on account of that gal. She still ain't nothing but the trouble the Widow bought her for."

I shoved half the hot biscuit in my mouth before I remembered to say, "Yes, ma'am." I was in a hurry.

When I got back to Ella's room with my brooms and bucket, I knocked but didn't hear anything, so I let myself in.

Ella was still at the mirror, staring. Only, the ghost of Mr. Dennis wasn't anywhere to be seen.

The breakfast tray was still where I left it, untouched. "Ma'am," I said, "you're not hungry?"

Ella had her sad eyes on me. We stared at one another in her mirror. Then she opened her mouth and said the first words I ever heard out of her. "I don't know who I am." Took a long time and a lot of breath to come out.

I let my brooms and bucket fall and went over to her. When I got close, I reached my hand out for that silver brush she didn't know how to use. "Let me do your hair, please, ma'am," I said and started looking around her vanity table for oils and lotions that might smell sweet.

It took a long time to get all that thick short hair into neat rows of braids. A bunch of times I finished a row just to start it over. I sang little bits of songs I liked and hummed the parts I couldn't recall, which seemed to soothe her, and every now and again, I broke off to explain that Miss Myra was dead, and there was strange sights to be seen over at the plantation. All the while, Ella stared at herself in the mirror and didn't say anything more.

Maids came and went, though, peeking in and hurrying away. One of them asked leave to remove the tray. I shook my head into the mirror and motioned her with a jerk of my head to scram.

I had just finished Ella's braids when Mr. Dennis came back. I was patting her braids in place, trying to get her to look at how pretty her hair was and smile.

Mr. Dennis walked heavy and solid-no ghost now-over to where Ella sat staring at herself. "So you have chosen a maid, my darling? I'm glad someone here pleases you." It was an edge to his voice that sent prickles up my spine.

He bent and pressed his lips to her forehead. Dressed in a gentleman's suit like he was, you could almost feel that Mr. Dennis was real. He held on to Ella and watched her eyes in the mirror. She looked at him and shimmered in the glass.

Mr. Dennis stood up straight and turned to me. "Your name?" he said.

"Layla, sir."

"Layla. Get these filthy things out of this room," kicking at my brooms. "Tell the other women that someone else is to do this kind of dirty work. I need you to tend the mistress."

"Yes, sir." I dropped my deepest curtsy and picked up the scullery things as I backed from the room. I even closed the door behind me. Swinging my bucket and brushes, I skipped down the stairs. I could have broken my neck and wouldn't have cared.

The days rolled by like good dreams.

Ella liked to bathe and dress up, so that was all we did day in and day out. My hands lost those cotton-picking calluses, soaking and lathering her in all that hot water. And they even got soft for the first time in my life, oiling Ella's skin and hair after her baths.

I looked forward every day to how the Widow's wardrobe was going to blossom again and more than it ever had before, on Ella's beautiful body. But she couldn't be satisfied. It broke my heart to see her, the softest, loveliest woman in the world, staring, hungry and eager and hopeful, in that heavy mirror, searching for something I could see but not make her see.

Odd how that glass just shivered and lay flat before Ella's dark, searching eyes. I hated to look in the thing, myself. So I kept my eyes on Ella, when I groomed her.

131

We had every day to ourselves. Mr. Dennis went out in the mornings. Mr. Tim had to take him in the carriage and explained to all the maids that there was legal men to see about Mr. Dennis's property and what was going to happen to it now that the Widow had disappeared. And plus, every few days, Mr. Dennis wanted to ride out to the plantation and pester poor Miss Solace.

In the attic one night, I asked the maids, "What's Mr. Dennis going to do to Miss Solace and Mr. Boy, when he hears about that baby folks say they keep hidden upstairs?"

The maids was parting and braiding each other's hair in the moonlight coming through the attic windows, laughing soft and gossiping like it's good to do when the sun's gone down. But they broke off sharp with little frowns and tongue-clicking, like I asked something that just wasn't called for. I knew they was nervous because I had broken out and mentioned the plantation. They didn't know how far I might go with it, and they wanted me to hush.

One of them said, "Layla, you honestly don't think Miss Solace and them is stupid enough to get all hugged up right in front of Mr. Dennis's face, do you?"

I really didn't know. I said so. "She ain't got no call not to hug up on Mr. Boy," I reasoned. "She ain't wight."

Huge sighs all around me. "We all know she ain't wight."

"And Mr. Dennis knows she ain't wight."

"But he wants everybody else in town to keep on thinking he's got him a wight relative and heir."

"Otherwise, the Widow will come back and finish killing him off, to inherit his property."

"And that devilish good-looking Mr. Boy and that baby he done went and got off Miss Solace surely ain't helping Mr. Dennis's charade none."

All the maids but me burst out laughing. I'm just not one for acting silly. I asked, "Why she got to be wight to inherit?"

Laughter died like it had been run over under carriage wheels.

Sighs. Then, "Layla, you really shouldn't show off your ignorance this way."

"Some people don't know when to shut up."

"Don't shut her up. Tell her."

"Well, Layla, if Miss Solace ain't wight, and the Widow is gone, what's going to happen to all Mr. Dennis's property when he dies?"

"What?" I asked.

"Strangers will lay claim to it. So it seems Mr. Dennis would rather have it all go to a gal who has got his own blood than to strangers."

"That's Miss Solace. At least she's his blood."

"And I think he really loves her."

"He loves that she's the only relative he's got who doesn't want to kill him."

"Strangers might come and kill him off, Layla, to get their hands on his property faster."

So I answered, "How can you kill off somebody who is already dead?"

Fed up sounds, now. "Layla, they don't know he's dead."

"Well, they can look at him and figure it out."

"Layla, these wight people just don't believe in nothing like that."

"Don't believe in nothing like what? Killing dead people?"

But now the maids was tired of me and took the conversation where they wanted it to go, without leaving me room for questions.

"Talk about don't believe in nothing: I don't even believe Mr. Tim's stories about how that ghost of Mr. Dennis is going to see the legal men and the plantation. Mr. Dennis isn't doing anything but fading out and waiting for the sun to set. Ghosts can't stand daylight."

And they was off again on ghost stories and getting-over stories.

But I thought it was funny how, ghost or not, Mr. Dennis had worries just like everybody else.

And powers too. Evil powers, like whipping. Turns out he came back from the dead with a mean whip hand.

He let into Miss Vivian's boy Zion one morning till Miss Vivian lay down in the courtyard and cried, holding the bleeding and knocked-out body of her son.

And Mr. Dennis whipped the dress right off one of the maids' back, while she stood over the washtub. Blood ran in the suds and ruined the laundry. The maid fainted in the water, and he wouldn't stop the whip so somebody could get through and fish her out.

"He ain't but getting back to his old ways," the maids whispered in the attic at night, trying to nurse her.

"These is his new ways. Blood sacrifice so he can go on living."

That maid never finished coughing up water. She staggered around in the daytime and moaned at night till we feared Mr. Dennis might climb the attic steps to finish the job he started. But then she died in a few days, anyway.

"Now we can never make the circle and free ourselves of this Mr. Dennis ghost thing," the maids grumbled, wrapping the dead body for burial.

"We done lost two women out of the circle now," they said, fearing to name the recent dead.

I had been thinking on just this problem. Being with Ella every day made me happy, but it hadn't made me clean forget what else I wanted for myself. "I can get us two more women," I said. "Right here, right now. You name the night you want to make the circle and dance."

They hushed.

For one, they was all mad at me for getting the lady's maid job. Working for a woman as helpless and needy as Ella instead of a real lady was just too easy. And plus, she gave me a new dress and apron, too, a dress the color of lilac flowers because Ella liked them best, and the apron was trimmed with lace so flouncy and fine I was scared to take it off and wash it, thinking I might ruin it.

Didn't do any good to remind the maids that none of them had wanted to tend Miss Ella. And I didn't blame them in my heart for being jealous. But this new problem might just give me my chance to form that circle one more time and get to that edge of creation, like I saw it in the bone woman's eyes.

Late at night, I thought it was odd how both the bone woman and Ella had eyes that brought you to that same place: the end of everything and the peace when you can leap for the last time. Better than lead dancer, I would dance for the place in their eyes, for peace and beyond.

"If you can get us two women, go ahead," the maids said, tucking the knots in the dead woman's winding sheet.

135

Soon after that, I asked Ella to let me take some salve off her vanity table to ease the welts on Zion's back. Ella looked confused.

"He's been whipped, Miss Ella," I explained. She stared at me like she was working on recalling just who I was. "Mr. Dennis did it," I went on. "The boy is suffering bad. Miss Vivian done gone so distracted she nigh on is going to get her own self whipped, burning food and leaving stores open to the rats. Maybe this salve you got here can make the boy's sores heal less tight. Can I take it to Miss Vivian for Zion, Miss Ella?"

She looked back into her own eyes, in that mirror. The mirror rippled and lay still. I thought how she had eyes like brown earth melting in running water. I went to touch her.

But the mirror moved.

Miss Ella's reflection hadn't moved in the mirror. Something in the mirror itself moved.

I backed up a step, slipping the jar of salve in my apron pocket. I watched her in the glass. Nothing moved again.

I had felt this before. Something was wrong in here. Something besides Mr. Dennis. Ella was in danger, here in this room.

I knelt at her feet and reached for her hands. "Miss Ella," I said. "Listen to me. I know it's something you want. Something you need. I can help you get it. Come dance with me and the maids. In the dance, you wish for whatever you want, and you get it. This dance will destroy the world as you know it and put it back together the way you want it to be."

Ella frowned. But she looked from the mirror down at me.

I said, "You wear white, join hands where I tell you to, and move like everybody else moves. You ever done any kind of dancing? I mean, you know how to make your body move like you want it to?"

Ella rose to her feet. The necklaces that had pooled in her lap clattered and hung long and swaying. The scent that drifted around her came to me. She pulled at my hands till I stood with her. Then she started pulling and turning with me all around the room.

I couldn't take my eyes off her. She dipped and leaned back, her head to one side, her eyes closed like she was dreaming. She swung me and made me hold her up while she gave herself to whatever music was in her mind. Under her closed eyelids, her eyes moved, and she hummed something almost like a song. The smell of that sweet grease all up and down her skin wrapped us in a turning cloud.

"Ladies, may I cut in?"

We froze so fast we stumbled. I let go of Ella's hands, and she fell back away from me. It was Mr. Dennis, appearing all of a sudden and out of the blue, like I guess a ghost loves so much to do.

He had on a cape over his gentleman's suit today. He floated in it over to Ella and covered her away from me.

I felt sick like I hadn't in a while. I said, "Excuse me, sir. Ma'am. I'll go run that little errand for you, Miss Ella." I was trying to get out of there fast. But I stopped myself as I was shutting the door and looked back in.

In the room, you could see Mr. Dennis was dancing like it cost him no effort to hold Ella up, and she was sagging in his arms with her head lolling. She was all wrong, and he noticed nothing.

But in the mirror, Ella wasn't dancing with the ghost of Mr. Dennis, at all. She was sitting in her wood chair, carved all over with animals growling and rising on two legs. The mirror showed Ella just sitting in this chair, watching Mr. Dennis as he danced alone.

I closed the door on them quick. I leaned on it, but that wasn't enough. I was lightheaded. I slid down the door until I sat on the carpet in the hallway. "Most like," I told myself out loud, "if I was to open that door again, I would see that I just misperceived something, that's all. I'm going to open that door again."

But every time I started to rise, some kind of dizziness struck me. Finally, I just crawled away and sat at the top of the wide stairs that the maids wasn't supposed to use. And when I could pull myself up and hold on to the banister, I made my way down. I wasn't sure when I was going to be up to going back to Miss Ella's room.

I was still lightheaded when I made my way through the kitchen and across the courtyard to Miss Vivian and them's rooms over the stables. All the time I was crossing the kitchen and cobblestones, maids who never had a kind word for me in ages stopped kneading and scrubbing and hanging laundry to say, "You look peaked, Layla. You poorly? Want to go lay down? I can cover for you."

I kept smiling and nodding to show I was grateful. At the last, I even lifted the salve out of my pocket and said, "Got something for Miss Vivian's boy. Got to get over there and take that risk, myself."

The maids turned back to their work, shaking their heads.

I got to the dark in the stables. My knees went out from under me, and I went wobbly in the hay where I was walking. I fell into it, and lay down and just trembled.

After a while came a hand on my shoulder and Mr. Tim's voice, soft but sharp through the stable stink. "Layla? This ain't no place for shirking your work. Mr. Dennis come in here, you and me both get the whip."

I raised my face and felt the sticky straw fall from it. I dug into my apron pocket and offered up the salve jar with one hand, propping myself with the other. I said, "Miss Ella sent this so Zion's scars can heal."

Mr. Tim backed away in the cool dark, nearing a glossy horse with its muscles rippling while it stood and waited to be brushed. Mr. Tim answered while he took to brushing the horse strong and long down the flank and leg, "Layla, take that jar on up them stairs to Miss Vivian. You a good girl. She be glad to see you."

I hadn't ever been up to Miss Vivian and them's rooms. I looked around for the stairs Mr. Tim was talking about. Right behind me, rickety and thin. I made it up though, hanging on the splintered rail and steady calling out ahead. I came into a dark small box of a room that smelled like cooking grease and horse droppings.

Maids over at the townhouse attic had always envied Miss Vivian and them having their own rooms. Miss Vivian being the cook for the Widow, she would always fix up nice fine meals in the house and sneak us some good portions, too. But we all knew Miss Vivian and them never ate from that food their own selves. Miss Vivian cooked for her family up in their own rooms.

We was all jealous, the way everybody said "rooms" when they talked about Miss Vivian and them. Not one room for a dozen or so women, freezing in the winter and roasting live in the summer, like us in the attic, but rooms meaning more than one. Like Miss Vivian and them was near on rich as the Widow and Mr. Dennis.

Miss Vivian was ripping a white cloth to rags when I reached the top of the stairs. She looked shocked to see me, so I quick held out that jar of salve. "Miss Vivian, Miss Ella sent this for your boy's back."

"Zion," Miss Vivian called out, "pull your cover up, baby. I'm bringing a gal to see you who got something to make you feel better."

Miss Vivian grabbed my wrist and tugged me along into a smaller, darker room. She was steady explaining, "The grease I'm using on him don't make him feel so good. Ain't but cooking grease. Can't get my hands on no other. Get rancid, get hot, and get to burning. And it don't stop the bleeding. Sight of blood coming through my boy's shirt would send that Mr. Dennis back into a tizzy, like the beast he is."

Walking through the rooms over the stables made me ashamed of all the mean jealous things me and the other maids ever said about Mr. Tim and Miss Vivian. I looked at the little windows streaked with burnt grease fumes where no light could get in because it was blocked by the townhouse. I breathed deep of that stink they had to live with day in and day out and thought how the sound and smell of horses was just everywhere, in here. *Being in these rooms, you might as well be an animal, your own self,* I thought. *No wonder Miss Vivian and them stay so thin. Me, I couldn't eat a bite in these rooms.*

We had come up on the boy Zion's little cot. Most I can say for it is at least he was up off the floor.

The cot was up on sticks crossed and trembling till I thought any move he made must send him crashing down

140

onto that damp straw that covered the floor. He was still, facedown. He must not have heard his ma'am calling him because his worn little itchy bit of blanket was still down about to his thighs. His ma'am reached quick and pulled it up.

My eyes was getting used to the terrible gloom in this place. I could see how the jaggy whipscars crossing the boy's back one way and another had little worm-colored edges where the dry scabs was starting to pull at the smooth dark skin. This boy was going to be a long time healing.

Miss Vivian said, "Zion, wake up, honey. I got to get back to that kitchen. And your papa's going to need you down to that carriage."

She was all the time scooping two fingers full of sweet-smelling salve out of the jar and waving it under her own nose. "What in the world is Mr. Dennis go'n say when Zion opens his carriage door a-whiffing like this?" she said more to herself than to me.

I thought that was a good question, but all I said about it was, "I got to go, too, Miss Vivian." And then I added, "Only, can I tell you something?"

Miss Vivian got all stiff. She didn't look toward me no more. She got right to salving her boy's back.

I went on. "I know you never held with us maids dancing, Miss Vivian. You let on you don't know anything, and we have always been grateful and never meant to drag you into it, neither. But Miss Myra done died, and her magic died with her. You can see things is falling apart around here. What's Mr. Dennis going to get up to next? We just buried one woman for telling him it wasn't fitting he asked her about the stains on the underclothes Miss Ella got from the Widow."

141

"Hush," Miss Vivian said, her voice all stern. "If it wasn't fitting that Mr. Dennis heard about it from the maid, then it sure ain't fitting if I hear about it from you."

I got closer and dropped my voice so her son, if he was awake, wouldn't hear. "Then I won't talk about that, Miss Vivian, because it doesn't matter no more. What matters is look how Miss Myra's protection is coming undone all around us. First Mr. Dennis is hopping out the grave and heading home like death can't hold him. And what next? The Widow and her gallivant will be back, too, splitting up property and taking off folks one from another. You know how their kind of people do. You've got a family."

Miss Vivian's eyes had been shooting back and forth in her head like she could just see it all in front her, happening any minute now. But when I mentioned her family, her eyes jerked to my face and stopped there, staring. "Get your mouth off my family. You ain't got to carry on so. Ain't nobody studying about my family but me." She was still smoothing salve, but her hand slowed down almost to a stop.

"You right, Miss Vivian," I said. "No mother needs me, a virgin, to bring up the worry about families getting sold off. I won't talk but about one thing. I say, let's get to dancing while the dancing is still good. Before any more of Miss Myra's magic comes undone."

"Magic," Miss Vivian spat. "Mojo and hogwash. You all ought to be shamed, ain't got no better sense than leaping and shouting about some thirteenth woman. You think I don't know? I done heard you. Whole world done heard that ruckus you all kick up, up there in that attic, all this African *gris-gris* mumbo jumbo."

I got chills. I mean, you don't have to believe in something for it to take revenge when you disrespect its name. I had never heard anybody talk about the thirteenth woman worse than I did, myself. I had to stand up for her against Miss Vivian.

"We don't know anything about Africa, Miss Vivian. This is no *gris-gris*, either. This is just us women looking around and figuring things for ourselves and putting some spirit into it. You don't have to dance for the thirteenth woman. Dance for something you believe in. Dance for your boy, here. Me, I'm going to dance that I don't get sold where I've got to give my body to some man I don't want to. Nor am I hankering for Mr. Dennis to hang around here much longer."

"Coming between you and that Ashy Ella," Miss Vivian muttered. Then she caught herself. "Look at me, talking down on a woman who just tried to help my boy. Both of you. Listen, Layla. I'm going to give you something for what you done gave me. If you ask me, somebody should have done whipped some religion into all your hides a long time ago. But it's too late now. You all done went wild. But you tell me when you go'n stomp in the attic or get out-out there in the courtyard under the moon, am I right? Where the law and the lord can all see you-and I'll be sure to turn my back and not tell on you."

I said, "Next new moon, ma'am. Miss Myra taught us to believe in the new moon, when you got something you need to grow. But I'll tell you what, Miss Vivian. If you don't approve, ma'am, we won't do it. I'll just go right back and tell those maids to stay in the attic and act like they've got good sense."

Miss Vivian hadn't looked at me this whole time. She was studying on her son's back and smoothing the last bit of salve off her fingers onto his scalp.

She snapped all of a sudden, "Zion! Boy! Ain't you heard nothing I said? You want Mr. Dennis come looking for you up here? He be done cut these whipscars back open again, eavesdropping at the door on this nappy-head gal. She go'n get us all killed. Where them fresh bandages I ripped for my boy?" Miss Vivian bent and started searching under Zion's cot. "Let me wrap some of these rags around this wild gal's mouth. Pestering decent folks."

She had dragged a pile of brown bloody rags from under the cot. Now she started worrying to herself about whether she should wash them or burn them or just stuff them down my throat.

I said, "You should dance with us, ma'am. For your boy. For your family. Come dance. It can't do you all any harm. Good day, ma'am," and ran back through her little dark rooms to the stairs.

That night, I didn't think about the bone woman's eyes at all. I only thought about Ella sitting and staring in that one silver framed mirror and telling me she didn't know who she was anymore.

I wanted to blame that ghost of Mr. Dennis. But after what I saw today, I wondered if it wasn't the mirror itself doing something to her. "But how can a mirror do anything?" I said out loud.

"Sshh," one of the maids said, drowsy like in her sleep.

Mr. Dennis took Mr. Tim and Zion and the carriage off to Miss Solace's plantation, and they didn't come back for going on a dozen days. In that time, Miss Ella only wanted to sit and stare into her silver-framed mirror over

144

the vanity. But there wasn't no dreamy look on her face no more.

She had gotten a fierce look, still and quiet round the eyes.

I would come in first thing in the morning, and she would already be up and sitting. Did she want her coffee, her bath, or to try on some of the Widow's black mourning she hadn't touched yet? Miss Ella would flick a look at me, but not straight at me. In the mirror, like she would never again look at anything except through that glass.

And she was fading, too. Getting little around the ribs. Getting lighter than a feather when I went to help her up. She felt like almost nothing.

I would have my arms around her, leading her out of that chair with the wild animals carved on it, and she and me both would turn back, like we had been called, and look again in the mirror.

And sure enough. That mirror wouldn't show Miss Ella in my arms, walking away from it. It showed her still sitting in that chair and staring into the glass. Maybe her reflection flicked its eyes and looked over at me.

First time I saw this, I checked to see was Miss Ella in my arms, after all, the Ella in the mirror looked so much more real. Then I went straight for a shawl tossed on the bed and covered that evil glass with it.

Miss Ella grabbed my arm and went to shaking her head no, like I had done the wrong thing. I grabbed her back by both arms, like I could keep her here, solid in the room with me, and shouted, "Ma'am, it ain't right! You got to get away from that thing!"

She kept shaking her head no, and all of a sudden I wondered why I thought she was really in the room with me, at all. It was like I wasn't doing anything but thinking about her, trying to recall her features, but she was somewhere far away.

I had a crazy notion that Ella was really in that glass. I snatched off the shawl to see, and Ella in the room grabbed it out of my hands and wrapped it around herself. I could see her in the mirror, doing the same thing.

She turned away from me and waved me out of the room. When I came back later to bring her a tea tray, her door was locked. I knocked and called low, but she wouldn't open it, and I had no key.

I ended up leaving the tray outside her door. I went down to the kitchen to see could I find somebody who might know where keys was kept.

Wasn't anybody left in the kitchen by the time I got there but Miss Vivian, crying into her cooking pots. She had been in a tizzy over her son since the second day he was gone with the men off to Miss Solace's plantation. I went up to her at the cooking stove and put my hand on her knobby back, where the bones jutted through her dress.

She lifted her apron and covered her face with it and sobbed. "You know my Tim and my Zion, Layla," she said. "They won't tell nobody about Zion's back and how he needs it salved till the boy falls on his face from infection and fever. They probably got him out in them shacks on the dirt floor with the wild rats picking at his scabs all night. Beasts in the woods be sniffing them wounds and old grease going bad and coming to hunt him while he's asleep."

I said, "Everybody says that Mother Magdalen woman out there has got a gift for healing that works like magic. She won't let harm come to your Zion, Miss Vivian."

Miss Vivian cried out into her apron, "I don't trust that Mother Magdalen woman. It's some kind of evil hanging around her. Secrets and such! Stuff from Mr. Dennis's old family. Who knows what she did for them people?"

I had to put my arms all the way around her. It had never occurred to me that sharp-tongued Miss Vivian might really hate somebody. I held her close and said like to myself, "And I used to think I hated Miss Myra." Seemed like a long time ago that dancing at the end of the chain could have been on my mind. I almost laughed at myself.

I got Miss Vivian to leave her pots and go lie down over the stables on her boy's cot. That would make her feel closer to him, I said. She thought so, too. But then I had to find somebody to tend the food while I kept on looking for keys.

In the end, I got one of the maids to come with me with some keys she took out of Miss Myra's tote bundle that fit different doors around the place. She didn't want to part with the keys. Probably figured she'd never get them back. And I figured I'd be glad to have someone else come along and look at Ella in that mirror and tell me what she saw. So we went to Ella's room together.

The tray was still as I left it at the door. But when I reached for the knob, the door came right open.

Ella sat in the usual chair, looking weary but still staring. In the dark, she looked strong and clear in the mirror, but you couldn't really see her where she sat.

I said to the other maid, "Wait while I light a fire. I want you to take a look at Miss Ella for me."

147

She said, "I ain't got no leave to wait on Miss Ella. Mr. Dennis will come back and flay me alive for being in this room unasked. I'm getting back downstairs to my sewing." And she fled with me still behind her screaming, "But tell me what you saw!"

It was almost like a cold draft kept me from crossing that room alone to get to Miss Ella. I could do it, but only once I set my eyes on the empty fireplace and promised myself I wouldn't look at her or her mirror till the fire was blazing.

But I didn't look even then. I left the fire roaring and the door open and went to haul water for her bath. I had to fill her tin tub and set it in the fireplace to heat. When it was steaming, I dragged the tub off the fire and onto the hearth to cool a little while I undressed Miss Ella.

When I reached for her, for the longest I couldn't find her. I could see where she was shimmering, sitting still in the dark, even though the room was lit with firelight. But my hands kept sweeping through her. I fought down panic. I kept moving closer to her, closer in front of that hated mirror, calling out her name and feeling around with my hands in the air.

Straight in front of the mirror, my hands closed on something that didn't slip away. I held onto it and led it toward the tub. I felt like a little girl with her eyes closed, pretending she had a doll and undressing it.

When I had pretended to put Ella in the tub, she sat there shivering and rubbing her arms and legs and shimmering in and out of sight. She wept real tears into the bath water. I remember when they fell clear from her face toward the water, all of a sudden the tears looked more solid than Ella did.

I hated to leave her. But I had to get out of there. It wasn't like she ever looked at me anymore, anyway. For all I knew, she didn't know or care that I was in the room with her.

I got to the door and looked back at the mirror as I closed Ella in the room. The mirror showed Ella sitting naked in the carved animal chair, kind of turned, so as to watch herself bathe. She looked so intent. So solid. So evil.

I thought again I ought to throw something over that mirror, to cover that evil reflection. And as soon as I thought it, the woman in the mirror slid her eyes at me with a frown cut deep between her brows.

She had Ella's body, but everything about her looked more like the Widow, to me. That's who the other somebody in this room was.

I looked back at the Ella who was bathing. I was suddenly scared for her. I couldn't leave her. I came back in the room. Since I hadn't brought towels, I picked up that shawl I had used once to cover the mirror.

Ella in the tub looked concerned when she saw me pick up the shawl and spread it open. But when I brought it over to her, she stood from the water and stepped into the open shawl in my arms and leaned into me. I closed the shawl around her. The water off her body felt heavier than she did.

It was that very night I was lying on my pallet outside Ella's door, where Mr. Dennis told me to sleep while he was away, trying to shut the strange sights I'd seen since Miss Myra died out of my mind. I didn't think I was asleep.

But the next thing I knew, one of the maids shook my shoulder and said, "Layla. Layla. Get up and come on. It's

149

time to dance." And she was gone. I heard her feet pad away on the carpet and heard her weight on the back stairs.

I got to my knees and started knocking on Ella's door. "Miss Ella?" I called. "Miss Ella! Come outside with me and dance, ma'am. It's going be a new moon. It will be pretty. You can wish for anything. Come see."

I was still kneeling there, knocking, and wondering how long to wait till I tried the door, when I heard a sound down the hall the other way from the stairs, toward Mr. Dennis's old room.

Was he back already?

My throat went tight. I jumped to my feet and turned to face him, coming down the hall toward me.

It was something gliding close to me, all right. But it didn't look like Mr. Dennis.

It shimmered, now here, now gone, carrying something that glinted with a silvery light.

Whatever had come down the hall toward me went past me into Ella's room and disappeared. I felt it pass, but I couldn't see it, the closer it got.

Ella's bedroom door was now open, next to me. I had thought for sure this door was shut.

But it shut as I watched it. I thought I heard a lock click. I backed away from the door and ran out to the courtyard, calling for help.

As soon as I came down the service porch steps, some maids grabbed me and clamped a hand over my mouth. They dragged me across the cobbles toward the stables, and I saw Miss Vivian come from the dark in there.

I pried their hands off my face. I joined the maids coming out of the courtyard shadows, taking each other's hands. None of us said anything.

I had made up my mind to dance for Ella tonight. It was the only way left I thought for sure I could help her.

I was at the end of the chain. My old place, no longer hated. My always place. We all looked up to where the moon was a slice of bleeding light.

Our chain started snaking around the courtyard.

You had to work into the feeling of the chain dance before it made a circle. So we went slowly, stepping and crossing past the clothesline where the wash reached out damp and ghostly to caress your face. Past the cobbles where we first put Ella in the tub to wash the grime from the chain gang off her perfect body. Past that little patch of grass and flowers where we laid to rest the maid Mr. Dennis whipped to drowning in her tub of suds. And past the stables, where Miss Vivian's boy wasn't there to lie still while his back sewed itself shut on scabs. And past the kitchen, where Miss Vivian cooked food her family wouldn't eat.

Everywhere the chain snaked, I couldn't feel Miss Myra's magic anymore. Surely she took all her spells with her when she went away.

The moon rose high and hooked the sky to climb. The moon was sharp light in soothing black, a curved needle sewing. It was the sliver you look through when you close your eyes on what you still need to see.

And as it sewed its way up and up the sky, it walked through the secret places in our minds and bodies. Spinning and snaking under the hook, we could see why it was good to dance when the moon was new, just the size and shape of hope born fresh, when it still has a chance to grow.

I closed my eyes and let loose of Miss Vivian's hand and started to turn under the moon, still following at the end of the chain.

It is not a good sign when the virgin gets taken by the chain dance first. But it is a powerful sign.

I couldn't help myself.

I raised my arms. I dropped them in a flap like a big bird, snapping and humping my back, twisting to the side. I raised them and flapped them to the other side. From side to side, flapping and gaining power as I twisted and felt my long arms like wings raising me a little above the courtyard and the townhouse and the life I had lived here.

I turned and turned and turned, and the power of the beat of my arms like wings fanned through the other women, and I saw their arms start to flap like mine.

I felt the heat of all the women in the chain ahead of me fan back to me as we all twisted and beat our arms. Our feet stomped the beat of our arms, pushing us on and up. And I kept following the other women.

They wasn't closing the circle. But we was one, bound in the chain dance.

I felt like my back would break from the flap of my arms and the snap of my spine. But someone reached up and caught hold of my hand and pulled it down to hold.

It was my hand on the other side, away from Miss Vivian, the side where there hadn't been anybody because I was at the end of the chain. But somebody was there now, and she'd got my hand in a grip that was strong with a pull that was heavy.

Had the new lead dancer closed the circle? Who was going to lead?

I opened my eyes to see.

The woman who had my hand was Ella. She had closed the circle and taken the lead. And even on this moonless night, I could see her clear and bright.

She was in a white gown flowing with blood from waist to hem. She smiled at me over her bloody gown and squeezed my hand. She snaked after me, dipping and swaying like I had seen her do that one time before, when we danced together in her room. And she said in puffs of too much breath, "I had to kill her."

"Who?" I said.

The other women snaked in close to me on that word. That would be the word for our chain dance tonight.

A power shot through my throat, and I hollered, "Bone woman! Take me to the edge!" And I heard somebody shout, "Who?"

Then Ella cried out and spun so we had to grab at her hands to hold her, and she screamed so everybody heard that she could after all talk, "Jim Feather!" And somebody answered her, "Who?"

And Miss Vivian's face, running tears in the night that shone like stars on the black skin, sobbed out, "I have seen that winged woman, you all! Why won't she fly my boy back home to me?" And I answered, "Who?"

Somebody said, "I see Miss Myra!" And we all thundered, "Who?"

Somebody said, "I see all my dead babies!" And we all asked her, "Who?"

Something grabbed hold hard on Ella so she snapped back and forth from the waist, wrenching my arm, and she pleaded, "Get her out of my mirror!" And we witnessed, "Who?"

And though it isn't a good sign when the virgin gets taken, but I couldn't help it and we all saw this coming, now the power snaked through the chain and sent the women screaming and flapping and snatching at hands, and the circle went round and round the courtyard, whipping.

"Send me back my man!"

"Who?"

"Take this demon ghost to the grave!"

"Who?"

"Heal me!"

"Who?"

"I see my dead mother!"

"Who?"

"Set me free!"

"Who?"

"Where is my sister?"

"Who?"

"Who killed my brother?"

"Who?"

The word for those who had faith.

And that moon that had finished snaking its way through my brain and my body now burst out of me, and the pain was blinding and drove me to my knees.

The dancing women dragged me along in the circle.

My arms was up, and I set in to writhing, dipping at the waist, crawling and twisting and pleading. And that little hook of the moon stabbed through my raised arms just under the pit. It flashed in and out now, and I felt myself bleeding light. And every long drop of light from my raised arms grew hard like melted wax and flipped at the tip like a feather.

The curved needle of the new moon jabbed in and out, circling through my skin, shedding light in drops that all flashed and feathered out, and when my body was covered with feathers of pain and faith and moonlight, I broke from the circle and rose among the stars in the black sky above the women.

From there, I looked down to them, softly hooting, "Who?"

They all reached up their hands toward me, in their white underdresses, and Ella in her bloody white gown, and I watched that sharp little hook that was the moon now sew feathers of light and flight in and out, in and out of arms so fast it blinded me to see.

Women had let loose their hands from the circle and was on their knees on the cobbles in pain from the new moon needle, bursting drops that grew to feathers and screaming, begging to see loved ones and rising to meet me in the black moonless sky, all softly cooing, "Who?"

And as I flew under her power, I asked myself why I had never before believed in that magical, mystical, blessed thirteenth woman.

# CHAPTER FIVE

## TO FEEL EVERYTHING: ROSE RED, BORN 1787

I woke up one evening as a storm passed and took Heaven and her restless spirit from me.

I opened my eyes slow, my habit ever since my husband Boyfriend died, and looked around the room Mother Magdalen and Solace gave me when I was brought back to the plantation to recover from the lynching.

It was Angel Girl, running wild with her wolf, who cut me down from the lynching tree. She told me it was too late to save Boyfriend, or even just keepsakes of him out the fire. Patrol and scavengers must have took all the pieces small enough to tote.

The room Mother Magdalen and Solace put me in used to be my sister Rose White's room, with her husband, young Sami Wolf Water. That was when she came from the fields and our ma'am's shack to marry our owner's son and live in the big house. Blood-hungry Sami Wolf Water loved to shoot folks down, and he led my sister and my ma'ammy and all the field hands off to some farm he had far away, as a gift from Mr. Dennis.

I never did like that man.

And how I missed my twin, Rose White, the way she dimpled up when she laughed, showing off them white teeth that flashed between her pouty lips. Rose White understood me and was patient with me, till she left chasing after that Mr. Sami and some strange freedom.

Then I thought to myself, *I'm remembering Rose White so young. Barely a woman, just got those round breasts. She must be my age, as old now as our ma'am*

*was when she birthed us. Time pass, and everything you
thought would last forever is gone before you even miss it.*

My sister and my ma'am, gone, and now my husband
and my babies, all dead.

And yet, here I still was. Waking up in the big house
and wishing I could get back out to my woods. Or at least
back out to my ma'am's shack. *Old folks say the more
things change, the more they stay the same.*

That was when I sat up and looked around with my
mouth open. Because in my head, wasn't nobody talking
but me, about nothing but my own thoughts. None of
Heaven's wild dreams and her grandma'ammy's burning
river nightmares.

And that was how I knew, *I'm not possessed
anymore.* The storm had freed me.

I flipped back the moth-eaten covers Mother
Magdalen had tucked around me, trying to keep me tied
down against the tug of Heaven's spirit, and I stood up. I
was solid on the floor, no floating and no stumbling, all
light-headed.

I threw back my head and laughed out loud for joy.
Then I took off running out of my sister's room to find
Mother Magdalen and them and tell them the good news.

All along the hallway and stairs, somebody had lit the
candle sconces stuck in the walls. The hallway looked
swept and bright like I hadn't seen it since I was a young
girl.

I turned and looked at the stained glass window set in
the outer wall, just past Solace and Boy's bedroom door.
As the storm passed and clouds unwrapped the moon and
stars, sparks of light shot through the stained glass to me.
I braced myself to see something scary take shape.

157

But nothing rose out the glass but pretty colors, no special shape at all. Lights danced on my face. I smiled and started down the stairs.

The wood rails that curved down and out was polished, and the carpeted wood steps under my bare feet was swept. Everything glowed but them old paintings of Solace's ancestors, turning dark in the shadows along the walls. No more pale ancestors watching you pass.

That thought made me laugh some more. It was just like me to be laughing so, like a crazy woman. I sat on the carpet on the steps where it was worn thin, wrapped my arms around my sides, held myself, and rocked and laughed.

I wanted to go find everybody, but I was enjoying myself so much, I wasn't going to make it. I covered my face with my hands and gave my laughing over to sobs.

Through my noise, I heard folks come close, whispering about what could be wrong with Rose Red now. Their bare feet and shaved wood clogs and thick old leather shoes made hushed steps on the carpet until a hand rested on one of my shoulders.

I looked up from between my hands at all the family I had left any more. Angel Girl, with her tangled weeping willow hair like a waterfall down almost to her knees and mine too, the way she was leaning over me, with her good hand on my shoulder.

I brushed away a lock of her hair from my face. "Angel Girl, you ain't no loblolly pine with the moss hanging down. When are you going to cut that wild head of hair?" I broke out laughing again.

She looked surprised. But she smiled back and sat down careful right next to me.

Her silver wolf came leaping up the stairs to sit between us. I said, "You getting stiff, old man," and scooted over to make him some more room. Petting that woolly wild animal of Angel Girl's never felt so good.

Solace sat down on my other side. "Aunt Rose Red, are you all right?"

I looked at her, but I could only shake my head and laugh some more with the tears standing on my face.

Her husband Boy came up on the other side of her with their baby on his hip. All of a sudden it struck me that here I'd been missing my own dead babies and hadn't once thought to take and hold theirs, to see if she could soothe the ache in me.

The baby squirmed in Boy's arms because he was all tense, waiting to see was he going to have to quick hand the baby over to Solace and pin me down. "Take a load off your feet, Boy," I managed to say. "And stop squeezing that poor baby. Here. Give her to me." I held out my arms. My laughing quieted down, and my breathing slowed. I waited.

Solace's hand went to her mouth. Her great big blue eyes got bigger, but she said through her fingers, "Go ahead, Boy. Let Aunt Rose Red hold Baby Joy, if she wants to."

"What's going on, Rose Red?" Angel Girl said on my other side.

I snapped, "I ain't going to eat your great-grandbaby, if that's what you mean. Let up on me, old woman." My arms closed in on that warm sweet bundle of breast milk.

The baby looked up at me in the dark candlelight that barely reached the stairs and pulled a toe into her mouth to suck on it, thinking. Probably wondering did she know

159

me, and why was I holding her. Tough stuff calls for toe-sucking.

I smiled at her. She spit out that toe when she smiled back with her big wide toothless pink gums. "No wonder they call you Joy," I told her. Even Boy eased up and laughed. "You big-head proud papa," I told him. And he just chuckled and sat down near me to hear some more about his cute baby. Goofy thing.

I was just trying to think how to tell Solace and Boy that their baby was the single most wonderful one out of all these wonderful folks living at this plantation, when Mother Magdalen started up the steps.

She carried a silver candle tree all lit with little licking flames, staring up at me. The circle of light her candles threw back and forwards lit her long purple-lidded eyes and all of us, sitting up there on the steps.

I looked at her and said, "Mother Magdalen, it's gone." She would understand.

Solace said, "How do you know, Aunt Rose Red?"

Now, we had to be careful with Solace, since she learned the hard way it was her own ma'ammy, Heaven, haunting me.

So I said, "I'm free," looking at Mother Magdalen.

Mother Magdalen reached me and put her candle tree in my face and looked in my eyes a while. Then she said, "Welcome home, Rose Red. We've missed you."

And finally everybody hugged me all around.

We had just started down the stairs to the dining room, ready for some good hot stew that I was really going to taste for the first time in a long while, and they was telling me how the pesky city maids had just got sent back to the townhouse, when we heard Rhea scream.

Her scream died away to moans. And we snapped out of our happiness.

Boy said, "What the devil?" and took off running down the stairs toward the back door.

My hand under the baby's bottom got warm. I moved it and looked at the fingers, shining wet, but everybody was rushing past me after Boy. A light spilled through the doorway from Mother Magdalen's back room, as Boy went out. It was the Angel, Mother Magdalen's child.

Boy brushed her wings, getting past her, and she turned to watch him go. But she stayed in the doorway, lifting and dipping her wings in that way that made feathers spread like fingers and brush the wood of the floor and the doorframe. The women crowded around her, waiting to hear what she saw outside.

The Angel looked up at me on the stairs with Baby Joy, her face a carved moon. She said, "You're free, Rose Red. Heaven has found another woman's body."

Then the Angel turned in that way where you couldn't be sure you wasn't seeing all sides of her at once, like a candle spinning, and faced Mother Magdalen. "Heaven's taken Myra, Mother. Where should we lay Mammy Water's bones to rest?"

Solace made a little cry and bolted back up the stairs. She snatched the baby out of my hands on the way. Angel Girl and her silver wolf trailed Magdalen and the Angel back outside.

I couldn't bear just now to see more of what Heaven did to people. So I turned and went up the stairs to see if I could comfort Solace.

When I tapped on Solace's bedroom door, she called, "It's not locked. Come in," and I pushed the door. She was over by the chest of drawers. She had poured water from

161

her china pitcher into the wash basin and was just settling her chubby earth-colored baby in the bath.

"She wet on herself," Solace said without looking at me.

"So that's what that was." I came close and held out my wet hand, and then stuck it in the wash water to rinse it. The baby thought I was playing with her and broke out splashing and giggling. Her little fat foot kicked at me and sprayed water on my gown.

Solace reached to dry up the water with a piece of torn linen sheet she had as a towel. "I can't go out there," she said.

"Neither can I, Solace," I said. "Let me hide up in here with you and the baby. What was you all saying about sending the silly city maids back to the townhouse? Was that just today? Wish I could have been at the front door to wave them on their way."

"Just tonight," Solace said, wrapping her baby in the torn sheet to dry. I went to the table over by the window and sat down to watch Solace dress Baby Joy. "I can't say I was sorry to see them go," she went on, "even though they were a big help getting the field ready for this year's crop."

"What happened to Myra?" I asked. Without Heaven in my head, I didn't know anything.

Solace carried the baby to the bed now and set her down, rubbing at her tummy and her toes with a corner of the linen. She slid her eyes at me sideways and looked away. "Myra must have died tonight, Aunt Rose Red," she said. Rub, rub, rub.

"Died in your house and you don't know nothing about it?"

She blushed and kept on rubbing.

"Solace, you're going to rub that baby's skin right off till she's pale as you, and Boy will think he ain't her papa, after all. Now, what are you trying to hide from me?"

Solace sank on the bed and put her arms around her head and started crying.

"Oh, no," I said.

She said between sobs, "It never stops. Oh, Aunt Rose Red, Myra lay crazy and dying in that room ever since she got here. She would come to and try to get away and kill people. I had to let Boy and Whip Man chain her. I don't even believe in chaining people. What's happening to all of us? I thought our plantation would be different."

Baby Joy lay on her back and watched her ma'am carrying on. There went that toe again. She stuck it over in the side of her jaw like chewing tobacco and started talking to herself, like spring water bubbling aboveground into a brook.

I came to the bed and picked up Baby Joy. "Come on, now, Solace. You didn't make the world the way it is. Pull yourself together and show me how to dress this baby."

Solace lifted her face, tearstained and turning red around the biggest blue eyes you ever saw. I said, "Myself, I think this baby most resembles me."

Solace smiled like she was supposed to, since we are not blood kin. "What kind of world did I bring my baby into?"

"A world where everybody she knows loves her," I said. "Look at you. Got the man you love and the baby you two made, and your own home together where neither one of you has to answer to anybody you don't want to. What you got to weep for?"

Solace said, "I've turned out to be no better than any other slaveholder. I meant to make a place where people

163

would be free and would live and work together because they wanted to. You're all my family and my only friends, and look how I've treated you."

I sighed. "You fed me and put me in a bed way too big and soft." I started bouncing Baby Joy on my lap. "Call me selfish, Solace, but I just got free of your mother-beg your pardon-and I don't feel nothing but sorry for Myra and Rhea, and good and ready to get on with my own life. You feel bad, and you want to do something for somebody? Show me how to dress this baby. I can't wait. You know none of mine ever lived."

That got her. Solace had a good heart. She couldn't weep and carry on in front of a woman who had less than she did.

We was rolling on the bed and passing the baby between us with nothing but a fresh diaper tied on her, dodging her drool and giggling like little girls, when Boy came in. He stopped and leaned on the doorjamb to watch us.

The smile died on Solace's face as soon as she looked over and saw him. "What's happened?" Solace asked her husband.

Boy kind of shrugged and shook his head. Then he turned and left. You could hear him start down the stairs. Solace got up and went after him.

I stood up and raised Baby Joy over my head. She grinned and sent a cool line of slobber sliding right between my eyes. I wiped it with her diaper and hugged her. "Let's you and me find you some clothes," I told her. "Dressing babies can't be all that hard."

Solace had her top left drawer filled with little yellowed tight-stitched clothes with lace, ruffles, and ties crumbling off of them. "Mr. Dennis's baby clothes," I explained to Joy, propping her on my hip to show her one gown after another. "Never mind. There's nothing in the world can make you not look cute."

Solace didn't have oils or creams or anything to rub on the baby's skin. "Let's go down and see can we at least get some of Mother Magdalen's cooking fat." Baby Joy cooed.

I slipped a crumbly lace gown down over her head. "There," I said, plucking her sausage arms through the sleeves. "Now I have dressed a baby. I can die happy."

Wasn't nothing on my mind but begging some fat off Mother Magdalen when me and Baby Joy came through the doorway into the kitchen and saw everybody in the blazing firelight, covered with dirt.

Whip Man had his head in his hands. He looked up at me with his shoulders all strong and his face all good-looking like in the old days, but his eyes was bloodshot and weary. Boy was on one side of his father, staring at the air in front of his face. Solace was next to Boy, with her hand on his shoulder. Mother Magdalen and Angel Girl was sitting across from them, reaching out to touch Boy and Whip Man, now and then.

"What is it?" I said. *Get it over with,* I thought.

Mother Magdalen said, "We should have buried Mammy Water's bones in the same grave with my parents, where her husband used to help tend the roses and herbs."

I said, "Whip Man, you ain't still weeping over Heaven? Because you know in your heart she been dead since Solace was born-" and I could have bitten my tongue off. I had almost said "since Solace was born to you two."

165

And hadn't we all agreed to believe that Solace was not Whip Man and Heaven's baby, once we knew Solace and Boy was having a baby of their own?

Some miseries are only in your mind. Best to let them go.

"Where's Rhea?" I said suddenly.

And Whip Man just threw his handsome face in his smooth strong arms and shouted, "No! No!"

The fire in the fireplace leaped, I don't know why, and the baby on my hip squealed. I braced myself for the Angel to come and take away Baby Joy. The Angel never let anything distress Baby Joy, if she could help it. It was a sight, to see the baby disappear with the turning Angel, folded in her long and shining wings.

But the air stayed dark and the Angel didn't show.

"You all," I demanded, "where's Rhea, and the Angel, too?"

I was beginning to sweat in the heat from that leaping fire. It dawned on me in my happy freedom that Heaven could have brought something dreadful on the rest of these people.

The fire that had roared up now quieted down, and so did Baby Joy. In the quiet, Mother Magdalen said, "Myra's killed Rhea, Rose Red."

Some kind of sound got bellowed out somewhere between Whip Man and Boy.

Angel Girl looked away from them and said, "We buried Mammy Water's bones and Rhea near the tombstones and willows and vines."

I said to myself, *With Dennis parents? What on earth for?* But I ain't dared ask that out loud.

Mother Magdalen had got up and went to a big iron pot she had boiling in the fireplace. She was saying,

"Myra's disappeared. Angel's gone after her, to try to persuade Heaven to let her go."

I hugged Joy closer. "Oh, Whip Man and Boy. I'm so sorry for you," the one who'd lost his wife of all his grown-up years and the other who'd lost his mother.

Angel Girl went past me to gather clay bowls off Mother Magdalen's shelves and muttered under her breath, "Strangest killing I've ever seen, Rose Red. Next to lynching, that is. Be careful about going out. I know how you love those woods."

I nodded so she could see it in the firelight.

People ate supper that night in Mother Magdalen's back room, like in the old days before Solace tried to make us proper gentlefolk who ate at the dining room table. Mother Magdalen dragged her steaming iron pot a little off the fire and ladled out stew into clay and wooden bowls Angel Girl handed her. They didn't ask if anybody was hungry, so nobody could say no and fast from mourning.

Still, Whip Man picked at his stew. His tears kept ran into it, making little watery clear pools that sat on the dark thick broth.

Boy and Mother Magdalen both tried holding him to get him to eat. Finally, Boy grabbed his father by the shoulders to raise him up from the table. "Come on upstairs and try to sleep," Boy told him. "You can't do ma'am no good weeping yourself out of your mind."

Whip Man sputter, "It ain't just your ma'am, Boy," but Solace drowned him out calling to Boy, "Stay with him, honey," as he guided Whip Man through the doorway. So I thought nobody but me heard what Whip Man tried to say.

Solace went on, "The baby and I'll be all right on our own tonight." But they wasn't on their own.

All the women and little Baby Joy too sat up and drowsed through the night at the big wooden table in the back room, listening for Myra's dead body to come scratching and knocking at the back door to get in. Angel Girl's silver wolf lay by the door, got up, circled and growled, and lay down again.

In the morning, when sunlight finally sneaked thin streaky fingers under the bolted door, Mother Magdalen stood up and stretched and looked at us and said, "Tell me something. Why did my Angel have to go after Myra? Heaven never listened to Angel."

Angel Girl raised her head up from where she lay curled on the floor with her wolf. "The Angel will be safe, Mother Magdalen. She can't be killed."

Mother Magdalen said, "We hope."

And Solace got up to get a bucket and go out to the pump for water, to boil up some coffee. But she hesitated in front of the opened door.

I watched her and held her baby closer to my chest and belly, thinking, *I should offer to go out for her.* But it was too new to me to be free of Heaven, and I couldn't bear to take a chance on her repossessing my body. For the first time since Boyfriend got lynched and burned and cut to pieces, I wanted to live my own life. *Besides, Heaven wouldn't possess her own daughter. Would she? Solace is the safest one of us. Isn't she?*

But Angel Girl got up and called to her wolf, and they went out with Solace. Me and Mother Magdalen stood in the doorway and looked out to where Mammy Water's splintered old shack stood quiet and dark at last.

I asked, "Where are the stones that lined Mammy Water's fire pit?"

Magdalen said, "First we scattered them. Then we took them to line Rhea and Mammy Water's graves."

Baby Joy had her hand in her mouth and her face snuggled up under my neck. She was fighting waking up all the way. I started rocking her and said low, "Why did you bury them right there with Dennis and Jared's parents? Rhea and Mammy Water don't want to look on those people who owned them and held them prisoner, for the rest of forever. Them two short-tempered women will rise up out of that grave and come right back in this house to haunt us all, for burying them over there."

Mother Magdalen smiled. "Rose Red, they're strong enough to keep the evil of those two slaveholders down. If any more spirits besides my own Angel are going to rise around here, I want to make sure they're the ones that are on our side."

I looked at Mother Magdalen, but she wasn't looking at me. It was impossible to tell what was likely and what was just crazy thinking around here, anymore.

I shook my head and left the doorway. *Best not to think on it too much.* "We out of corn meal?" I asked, conversational. "You want I should help you get some breakfast together, Mother Magdalen?"

Solace and Angel Girl squeezed through the doorway together, struggling with a bucket between them. The silver wolf slipped in behind them.

Mother Magdalen blew out her breath and closed and bolted the door. From what I always heard from my own ma'am, it seemed Mother Magdalen spent her whole life grieving over and worrying after Angel. But it wasn't like the girl could die twice.

Solace took her baby from my arms. "I'll go up and check on Whip Man and Boy," she said and headed for the stairs.

Angel Girl slid the bolt back to open the door again. "Where you think you going?" I demanded.

Angel Girl started on her way out, snapping her fingers at her wolf, and called back over her shoulder, "Wolf and I might as well hunt up our breakfast in the woods. We can look for Myra while we're there." And they took off across the field, streaks of silver and gold legs trampling the stiff new green stalks of cotton.

"Watch out for patrol!" I shouted after them. How the sight of that growing cotton saddened me. I used to be out there, year in and year out, my hands and feet getting cut to shreds and rubbed to calluses right alongside Rose White. "I wish I would never see another cotton field as long as I live," I said and pushed the door shut.

"Someone needs to go to town," Mother Magdalen mumbled among her shelves of pots and bowls and supplies. "Those maids ate us out of house and home."

That was it. I would take a horse and go to town to shop. Solace and Boy needed to be with each other today, and I needed to get out of here alone.

It took forever to get me up on that old horse's back and ambling off to town.

First, everybody had to give their thoughts about whether or not and how I could get to town and back safe on my own. Next, they had to figure the best note that Solace could kind of write a little bit, to look like a pass written by my owner, in case some patrol tried to stop me. After that, they had to figure how long I'd be gone and how much food I might need and whether or not we had it, seeing as how the townhouse maids was such a pig and all. And wasn't it a trial when they had to teach me how to figure the money?

I just wouldn't reckon that folks with two new deaths on their hands could find room in their minds to get so worked up over a trip to the grocer. I thought for a minute there I was going to have to take all of them with me, even Whip Man, hunched over in a croaker sack cloak and wringing his hands, looking like before Myra healed him, up in the back of the cart. Patrol would see me and escort us all to the auction block instead of to the grocery store.

But here I was, finally, floating above the ground on a big powerful horse, with saddlebags flopped over his back and coins clinking in my satchel purse.

I hadn't ever carried money before. But I could hardly think about that right now, I was so caught up enjoying the feel of looking around and having nobody's thoughts in my head but my own.

How long had it been since I lived with the sight of Mammy Water's burning mother, a nightmare Heaven had inherited, always in my mind? And Mammy Water's village going up in rolling smoke, way back then and way over there? And what could I do about it but suffer for a dead woman who was long past suffering?

I was ready to live.

The trees was a high roof over my head, and the birdsong and clop of the horse's hooves was music for my ride. I drowsed on the horse's back and woke to more sunshine and good feelings. I swayed and hummed in the saddle and real eyes I was near on drunk with bliss.

Just like when me and Boyfriend used to make love in each other's arms in beds of moss and pine, the sharp scent of the crushed needles under our bare bodies sweet

171

and rising to mingle with the hot human smell of fresh sweat, running. Boyfriend's mouth made a hot dark world inside me come alive. Even now, my cheeks flushed thinking how many farmers and hunters and patrol must have watched us, lost in the woods in the morning, making love.

Why did it have to end?

And the dead babies.

But no. Not today. Today I wanted to be happy, going to town.

It wasn't really a town. Just a general goods store. Not like the real town where Solace and Boy went to fetch the maids.

But it was town to me, on account of you had to use or take money to bargain with the old man in the store. He never took goods for goods, only goods for money or services.

When Boyfriend was alive and we ran the woods together, I used to hide out in the trees at the edge of town. Boyfriend would kiss me long and gentle till I was ready to let him go on the chance that this might be the day everything would go wrong and he didn't come back, only then Boyfriend would leave me hiding to watch him stride into that store. He would put on like he trusted everybody and had no cares but carrying the bowls, cooking spoons, and clothesline pins he had carved and the animal skins he had cured, to sell.

He would come back to where I was hiding, and only when we was far from town and the road that led to it, Boyfriend would un-sling his sack off his shoulder and start unpacking it while I worked up a fire, pulling out things he had bought one at a time to ask me, "Well, what you think, Rose?"

Such things. Food cooked and wrapped by somebody else's hands, and all you had to do was bite into it. Sweet like you wouldn't believe. Or tough and chewy and last while we ran further into the woods for the winter, where the woods sloped up into the mountains far away and no patrol would come looking because they figured if you got up there, you was going to die when it snowed, anyway.

*Boyfriend.* No, not today. I would go home and bleed my heart out over Boyfriend one more time tonight. *But let me be happy, even with the sad memories he left me, today.*

I was still caught with shining eyes blurring my vision when I pulled up and tethered the horse to the hitching post and grabbed up the saddlebags to walk inside. If I had another thought, it was that everybody around here by now should know I'm a woman growing too old for shenanigans, minding my business and grieving over my man that got lynched not too long ago. *I shouldn't be too much fun for nobody to bother. Just get my purchases and get out of here.*

I ain't noticed nothing and nobody till I was right up on the two men, facing each other at the back of the shop.

It was dark inside, after that long ride in afternoon sunlight. Hot too, from the woodstove sending out heat so you had to walk around it in the middle of the store. The store owner must really be getting old, burning good wood on a day with so much sunshine.

I came around the stove and near on bumped into the two men. "Beg pardon, gentlemen. Good afternoon, sirs," I said, trying to remember how everybody back at the house had told me you talk to strangers predisposed against you. Then I dropped my eyes.

173

But it was too late. I had already seen what I had seen. And I couldn't wait to see it again.

One man wasn't nothing but the shopkeeper, washed out and dried up and plain as a dust rag hanging on the laundry line.

But the other was a man like I had never seen. His face was the woods in all seasons. His cheeks was the cliffs where you step out and see the treetops like the eagles do, spreading their wings to fly. His eyebrows was bird wings lifted for flight, and his skin was moist earth that smelled wet, and his hair a running stream thick from falling rain and black with the feelings that rise with the blind sky of night.

And when he turned and looked at me, I felt like I was falling. I could only look away and beg everybody's pardon.

Then I raised my eyes with something like pain and looked at this man again. He put me in mind of a doll Boyfriend had carved for me when my babies kept being born dead.

The doll was from a willow branch Boyfriend broke off a tree and carved, and it had black rabbit fur stuck on its head with pine sap. For the longest, I carried that doll in my dress between my breasts or in my apron pocket and loved it like a baby. I even gave it a name, so I could call it. *Willow*. It was a baby to me.

And more. It was my piece of the woods before the patrol lynched me and Boyfriend and drove me to live inside again. It was every night I fell asleep in Boyfriend's arms and every day I woke before the sun to stare at the shape of his face as it gathered dawn light.

I had hid Willow away when I came to from the lynching and found that Angel Girl had brought me to

174

Heaven, so I would have to live. I didn't want Mother Magdalen to know I talked to a wood doll and think I was crazy in the head. But worse, Heaven wanted me to go to Whip Man for her. I was afraid she would destroy anything that kept me in love with the memory of Boyfriend. So I hid the doll from Heaven, too. Could I find it now?

Mr. Wash-Out whined, "Gal, ain't nobody learned you no manners? I said what you want, now. Don't try my patience. This here is a place of business."

And on and on.

By now, the man I thought of as Mr. Woods was looking in my eyes. I couldn't have found the presence of mind to speak to save my life.

I was probably headed to lose all of Solace's money and get horsewhipped and thrown in the local jail for acting uppity. If I got off easy.

But Mr. Woods fixed it.

He snapped out of whatever had happened between his eyes and mine, and he put what he had been holding on a long wood counter that ran in front of Mr. Wash-Out.

It was a high thick pile of cured skins. Not skins like me and Boyfriend used to bring in, little and pale, to sew together to line some lady's cape or make a muff for some child's hands.

These skins Mr. Woods dumped down was as long as a man and rich and black and brown, some of them with stripes and spots running and leaping through the fur.

Mr. Wash-Out stopped talking but left his mouth open. And Mr. Woods took my saddlebags out of my hands and started moving around the shop, looking at things on the shelves and in the barrels, his head on one side and then on the other, making all that black river of

175

hair tumble and flow while he took and hefted and dumped stuff in my bags.

He moved easy, like Boyfriend used to do. I felt like I knew this man. Not to speak. To hold.

Mr. Wash-Out started in to protest. "Now see here, you! I ain't said I can rightly trade you for these skins. It's goods for money, and then only money to buy my goods. I ain't got this kind of money nowhere in my store. I ain't even sure I got the buyers to pay me and you for a haul like this. You could be buying me out of my store, taking and dumping things that way."

And on and on.

My presence of mind came back to me and I started to wonder how this was going to be paid for, after all. I went after the man with my saddlebags.

He had his back to me. I had to reach up to touch his shoulder. It felt just about like a steel knife. Hard. Sharp. Ready.

But when he turned to look at me, his eyes was warm. Asking and smiling.

"Sir," I said. "Thank you. I best start counting out my money now." And I went to take the bags from the man and give them to Mr. Wash-Out to calm him down.

But the stranger with a face like the woods did another strange thing. He said something to me, but I couldn't understand more than that I was inches from his face and breathing the very air he was speaking.

Then he hefted my bags across his shoulder and went on out the door with them. I followed at a run. In time to see him sling the bags over Solace's horse.

The horse shied and the man ran a hand down his flank and spoke to him, and the horse calmed. Then he took my waist in both hands and lifted me up into the air.

I landed on the horse's back, sitting sideways. And he held me there and looked up at me a minute.

I had just thought to untie and hand him my satchel purse, to pay for the purchases, when he smiled and pushed away from the horse, slapping its flank.

"But the money!" I called out as the horse walked on.

He raised his hand and waved aside the very idea of money. Then he turned his back and made his way into the store while I watched, drawing further away.

Would I never see him again?

All the way home, I thought my heart would break and run blood from the burden of hope and shame in it. But I loved the guilt of that burden. Now that I was free of feeling Heaven, I just wanted to feel everything.

The woods was washed clean from the storm the day before and sparkling with sunlight caught in all the little leaves, and the air was thick with the scents of ripe earth and evergreen. Birds and squirrels chattered overhead, and the horse's hooves beat a rhythm dancing down the dirt road under me. Every step my horse put between us was a step into yearning that ached.

I wanted that man like I never wanted anything or anybody ever before in my life. And here I was, a widow in mourning, living in a house circled around by fear and bloody death. I ought to be ashamed.

I came around the town road to the plantation drive and saw the house rising up, bulging white above the dirt and the green. *How can I go in there and look like I was sad over how Myra took on my curse and gave me back my life?*

All of a sudden, though I never wanted to, I understood Heaven. Love-if this that I felt for the stranger was love-was worth doing anything for. *Anything.*

177

Whip Man came out the back door to help me with the saddlebags, eyes red-rimmed and downcast, but he moved steady and with his head up, like he was trying to make out he could handle it and not be a burden to Solace. "Girl," he said, "what you got here in these bags? You done stopped along the way to hold up a couple of farms?"

His voice broke on the end of his joke, but I was already laughing for him. Whip Man slung the bags over his shoulder and disappeared back inside.

Mother Magdalen was in there tending one of her big black pots in the fireplace. Whip Man dropped the bags on her table and went out toward the stairway.

I caught up and grabbed his arm. "Where is everybody?" I asked.

He turned in the dark of the hallway to look at me. I had to catch my breath. Even after everything had he been through, you could see Whip Man used to be a powerful good-looking man.

Use to be? Still was, standing here today. Poor Myra, I thought. Poor Rhea, too. Today I could even say poor Heaven.

Whip Man said, "Miss Solace upstairs tending to Boy. He done nursed my feelings till he fell apart just now his own self. You excuse me, Rose Red?"

He went on up the stairs and turned toward Solace and Boy's room. When their door opened, I could hear Baby Joy crying and a man and woman's voices arguing like this was life and death.

*Angel and Angel Girl and the wolf must not be back from hunting Myra,* I thought. And just like that, I wasn't going to hang around to take part in all this sadness.

I knew I should go to Mother Magdalen and help her get supper on the table. But instead I went up the stairs to my own room, where my sister Rose White used to sleep with a husband that scared her. I shut the door and slid the bolt and searched under my limp pillows and lumpy soft mattress for that doll my Boyfriend had carved for me, calling, "Willow? Willow, baby girl! Don't play games, now! Come to your ma'am!"

I stopped when I heard a turtledove outside my window.

I stood up and listened and thought, *How strange. I ain't heard turtledoves call but in the early morning. And here it is, going on sundown. Oh, that is the sweetest sound!*

And suddenly I only wanted to get out of this house and go outside, anywhere. I would not, could not, wait.

I was on my way down the stairs when Solace came up from behind and called to me. "Aunt Rose Red," she said, "Boy and Whip Man would like to have us gather this evening around Miss Rhea and Mammy Water's graves to bless their deaths and help them rest in peace. Please don't go far. And don't forget the danger." Then she disappeared into the dark hallway.

It was like she had read my mind.

*Never mind*, I told myself. *I can wait at the grave good as I can wait anywhere. I don't have nowhere to go. I just want to listen to that turtledove.*

But I knew this was a lie as soon as I got to the bottom of the stairs and didn't go through Mother Magdalen back room. Instead, I turned the other way and went out through the front door, something I never did if I could help it, afraid of patrol spying on us from the main road.

*Never mind*, I told myself again. *I ain't acting peculiar. I just want to be by myself.*

I got around the side of the house and dropped on my knees by the fresh grave. You could tell where the grave was dug fresh because the grass was all turned under and nothing but dirt and tiny dying roots showed. I ran my hand over the dark soil and thought back on how Mammy Water used to look, when I was a child, all skinny and shrunk up, stretched out on her pallet, near on dead. And when I was young and afraid of falling in love, all the couples in the quarter wanted to be just like John the Conquer and Rhea, devoted, and refuse to be broke up for studding, no matter what the cost or the punishment.

And now two other women together had killed off poor Rhea, vying to get their hands on her Whip Man. *What, exactly, happened? How was Rhea killed? I ain't even asked nobody.* It was, truly, a shame.

My hand rested on the soil, and I finally found some tears for these two women. And that turtledove called soft again, almost like somebody whispering to me.

I looked up with wet all around my eyes just in time to see Whip Man bend close to me and say, "Rose Red."

He was just kneeling down beside me. When he saw I was crying, he put his arms around me and his head on my shoulder and cried, too. The turtledove went quiet, and all I could hear was Whip Man.

He was such a big man that it was hard to get my arms around him. His wide back kept heaving and shoving my hands so they slid across him and couldn't get a grip and stay put. While I was trying to hold him, I kept thinking about that knife-hard, knife-sharp back of the man in the goods store and wondering what it would be like to have him here in my arms.

Kneeling there in the presence of the dead, I started thinking I should call out to Boyfriend and ask him to forgive me for the way I felt about the stranger. But it felt like Boyfriend was far away and would wonder why I was calling him back here.

The others came around from the back, all together, Solace with her baby, Mother Magdalen, and Boy, who came and gathered his father into his arms, away from me.

Whip Man kept saying to him, "Your poor ma'am," and Boy kept saying, "It wasn't your fault, papa."

Solace and Mother Magdalen knelt across the grave from me. I said, "The Angel and Angel Girl ain't back yet?"

Solace said, "No, Aunt Rose Red."

Mother Magdalen said, "I should tend these rose and grape vines. This used to be a lovely place to sit and think about the dead."

Boy started to say what we all hoped was a blessing, still holding his father. "May all the good that be in the world of the living and the dead come around these two women and keep them in peace. We love them, and we go'n miss them. But we know they right here and still with us, just in a different way. Ain't that right, everybody?"

Solace said, "That's right, Boy."

But Mother Magdalen and me was quiet, holding on to our thoughts and feelings like we didn't want them to get out, in case they upset people.

Whip Man said, "Rhea, please forgive me, baby."

And when they all rose to go inside, I said, "You all, I got to go visit my ma'am's old shack."

181

Boy said something about was it safe on account of wild animals could have got in there to nest. But Solace said since it had a door kept shut and no windows, it was probably safe.

I said, "I'll stop by the tool shed and pick up a hoe to defend myself, just in case." And I set out.

It was a long walk across that field with the sky spilling shades of faded red all around me. I kept thinking time passed, and I couldn't say for sure why, but even with all the sadness and loss, things was better than I had thought they could be when I was a young girl not wanting to grow up.

When I got to the edge of the woods and turned my back on the trees to face my ma'am's front door, I stopped and stared.

The rose vines Mammy Water's husband had planted for my ma'am, the roses she named me and my sister for, had gone wild and was growing tangled in and out of the logs of our shack. They swept up to the roof and spread out. Even this early after the winter, they had little buds starting.

And that sharp sweet smell.

I took my hoe in one hand and pushed in the door with the other.

And that man with a face like the forest rose up from squatting on the floor of my ma'am's shack and said, "I shouldn't a called you. The wild cat is near. But I mean to trap it."

I was in his arms and feeling if he was really warm and hard and sharp and solid as he seemed, just like I had thought he would be, before I wondered why he was there.

If he was surprised, he ain't showed it. His arms went around me light at first and then firm, and his hair brushed my face when he turned to watch out through the open door.

It was me who pushed myself away from him. He let me go and went and shoved the door shut and bolted it.

"When did you call me? The turtledove was you?" I said, wiping my cheeks. *Just crying for Whip Man and them,* I told myself. *And maybe for surprise.*

"Yes. Bird was me. You ain't knew that?" he said, coming back. But he didn't open his arms, where I wanted to be.

*This ain't Boyfriend,* I told myself. *I got to act right.* "How would I know it was you?" I said. "I don't know you."

He kind of laughed. Then he said, "Jim Feather. Now you know me." He squatted again and made a motion with his hand for me to join him on the ground. Only, he wasn't nothing but a shadow in the dark, and I started feeling afraid.

But I sat on the bare earth floor not too near him to keep my head, and I listened to him rubbing up a fire in my ma'am's old fireplace. Soon he was blowing little whiffs of smoke up the chimney.

"Someone will see," I said.

"And think it just you," he answered. "Enough light to see. Here." He handed me something that felt like a strip of soft wood. "Eat with me," he said.

I raised the strip to my mouth. It smelled like meat smoking on a slow fire. I was sure I had smelled it before, sometime when Boyfriend showed me his loot from that goods store. I bit and pulled. It was meat, dry and chewy. Kind of wild in your mouth.

183

"Deer," Jim Feather said.

And I sighed. Because for just a little minute, my heart thumped on account of it sounded like he was saying "dear," like Boyfriend used to.

There was distance between Jim Feather and me. Not just the one I made between us on my ma'am's floor. The one he was making, like he was pushing me away at the same time he pushed his way into my life.

When the fire was going, Jim Feather cut himself a slice of the wide, thin, dark meat and sat chewing, watching me in the firelight. He drank from a skin of water and handed it to me to drink from, too. The water inside tasted like a running stream that sat and got a little rank.

Finally I said, "Jim Feather, why you here?" My voice quivered a bit. I ain't really wanted to hear what he would say. His answer would probably have to hurt because he didn't know me till today, and I wasn't nothing to him, yet. So he wasn't here for me. But I thought I should know, someday, that I had asked.

Jim Feather took another drink of water and washed it around in his mouth before he swallowed it. Then he licked at his lips like to clean them and looked at me a long time before he said, "For two people. And a wild cat."

"Two people?" I said, not sure if I should be disappointed just yet. "Who?"

He kept watching me. Then he put his knife and the meat and waterskin into a fur pack and slid the pack away from us across the dirt floor.

When he looked at me again, he opened his arms.

So I went to him.

It was different than with Boyfriend. Not just because of the hair that kept brushing my face and belly and because Jim Feather didn't use his mouth like Boyfriend. I was sure he wanted to hurt me, hurt my body and my feelings, and I was afraid.

Not just of being in love. But of the man I was coming to love. I hadn't ever been afraid of Boyfriend.

And all of a sudden, when the shoving and wrestling and pinning down was over, I lay there in the dark and missed how Boyfriend was tender and gentle and wondered why I gave myself to another man, this way. It was like I wouldn't ever be Boyfriend's widow again.

I started to cry.

Jim Feather got up on one elbow at my side and put a hand on one breast, where he had bit me. "I hurt you?" he said. "No blood." He ran his hand down my belly.

I don't care how many babies I had. My belly was flat and tight as any young girl who had been tramping across the fields and through the woods. To look at my body, you wouldn't think I was nothing but a growing girl, myself. Not like my ma'am when she was my age, wrinkled and scarred.

"Yes, Jim Feather," I said. "You hurt me."

He said, "No need to cry. I don't hurt you no more." He rolled over onto his back and pulled my head onto his shoulder.

I put my hand on his chest so I could feel his breath and his heart beat. At least Jim Feather was alive. Sometimes I wondered if I was mad at Boyfriend for dying and going away and leaving me behind, like he was one of my babies and not my man. *Am I just mad at Boyfriend? Is that why I'm here with Jim Feather?*

185

A wild cat coughed and then screamed outside in the woods.

Just when I was falling asleep, Jim Feather said, "Them two people. A man and a woman. I wait here to kill them."

I woke up. "Who, Jim Feather?"

He stroked my head like you do a child. He made that grunt that was his laugh again. He said, "You stay safe. Stay out of my way."

"Stay out of your way?" I moved his hand from my belly.

He put his hand back. "Till they die."

I know I was asleep when I heard Jim Feather say, "When they dead, you come away with me. What you say?"

In the morning, I wasn't sure I hadn't dreamed that.

Before the sun was up, we went out into the woods to find a stream and wash up together. It was good to be back out in the woods with somebody special to me, to get up in the daytime and not have to stay up all night, wearing out my body so Heaven's spirit couldn't take it over. It was going to be good to be in love.

Was I in love with Jim Feather? Or was this just wanting to have a life of my own again?

I watched him while we stripped off our clothes and waded into a stream to splash, only here because so much snow was melting from the hills.

We cupped our hands to feed each other running water. When Jim Feather smiled, his face got soft and old with lines that curved around his mouth and shot out from his tipped up eyes. His wet hair slapped against his back and stung wherever it hit me.

I started to shiver and got out the stream to get dressed first. He watched me dress before he followed me out.

Walking back to the shack with the sun fully up, he took my hand. "Go in that house so they not miss you," he said. "So they not come here looking."

"You sending me away," I said.

He nodded. "I told you why."

When we got to where the woods met the clearing for the plantation fields, he stopped and dropped my hand. So this was all?

I started to walk away but turned back to him. "Ain't you even wanted to know my name?" I asked.

He stood straight with his legs a little spread. His wild leather trousers blended into his skin, I thought, and made him seem to fade into the trees already, just watching me start out across the cotton field. He lifted his head a little. "What your name?" he said soft, but it carried.

"Rose Red."

"Rose," he said. And smiled a little and lifted his head again, like he was using it to point me to the big house where he wanted me to go.

When I got to Mother Magdalen's back door, I turned to look for him one more time. But he wasn't there no more.

I spent the day working in the field and washing laundry. Rhea's old jobs would be mine, now. I watched the sun rise and crest the sky and sink and couldn't wait to get back to my ma'am's shack and my new man, Jim Feather.

The pain he gave me didn't seem to matter anymore. It wasn't like I forgot it. It just didn't make me feel like he didn't love me. He was just different from Boyfriend, was all.

But Boyfriend was gone, and I was alive, and I was tired of being with people who all loved somebody else.

By the time I strung the last kettle of wash on the line, I had a thought that made me stop and drop my hands. *If Boyfriend was still alive, would I have wanted Jim Feather?*

*Of course not*, I thought at first.

And then I wasn't sure.

I tried to remember Boyfriend, but it felt like I had tried so hard to shut out that last memory, of Boyfriend hanging and burning in the tree, shouting at me to run and save myself, and that shout all caught up in his hollering from the pain of dying, cut and on fire, that I couldn't make my mind bring him back.

We was children together. I should be able to remember Boyfriend over his whole life.

I wandered away from the wash line. Mother Magdalen called after me, and I turned and called, "I'll be right back," and went in the house and up the stairs to the room I'd been in, fighting off Heaven, ever since the lynching.

I heard Solace down the hall, singing Baby Joy to sleep. I ran my hands more careful under all my pillows and far up under the mattress. Finally, just when I was ready to sit and cry, I got down on my knees and felt on the floor under the bed.

Far up under the middle, stretched till I was flat on my belly with my face in the dust of the carpet, I felt a sharp little splinter of wood prick into my fingertip. I grabbed the wood and tugged. Even before I hauled it out, I knew it was Willow.

How she got way up under that bed, I'll never know. I sat and held her to my chest and rocked her while Solace sang. Maybe this was all of Boyfriend that I could keep, if I wanted to live and not be crazy and sad and possessed.

I went down the stairs and found Mother Magdalen sorting through the supplies I had brought her yesterday. I said, "Mother Magdalen, I wonder why I ain't died when Mammy Water did?"

She shrugged and poured some corn meal in a bowl. "Who understands these things?" she said. "But I would guess that it was Heaven prolonging your life, Rose Red, using Mammy Water's powers. It wasn't Mammy Water. She was dead long before Heaven moved into her bones. Maybe you're alive because Heaven is still alive and well in Myra, now. Please, let's not talk about it anymore."

We went back, that night, to eating in Mother Magdalen's back room without discussing it. I guess we was just trying to stay near the back door, where we could have heard if the Angel or Angel Girl came back from searching for Myra. Or anything else that might come knocking at the door. All we heard was the calls of that wild cat out in the woods.

Whip Man dipped some cornbread in his stew bowl and said, "You a grown woman, Rose Red. Don't none of us want to tell you what to do. But maybe it ain't so good, you staying out there alone in your ma'am shack, by yourself." Then he studied his sopping bread and ain't looked at me.

I tried not to let on. But it rankled me something terrible to have Whip Man all of a sudden take an interest in my comings and goings. Wasn't three women killing each other enough worry for him?

I said nothing.

189

Boy and Solace shared a look and ain't tried to hide it. Solace cleared her throat and tried to get Baby Joy to take a bite of that soft fresh cornbread. Boy said, "Miss Rose Red, us all go'n feel like it was our fault if something happen to you out there in that shack alone."

I looked around at them all. Even Mother Magdalen was watching me. I said, "It ain't no good, me being in this house with you all right now. Too hard for me, sharing this sadness. You don't want me creeping around in the shadows in this house, afraid to show my face because I feel I'm disrespecting everybody's mourning. Including my own mourning. I need to get away. I promise you all I keep the bolt slid on my ma'am's door. Ain't like them other shacks, got a rag door can't even keep a breeze out." It was quite a speech, and it was all I was going to say.

Whip Man said, "I told you all. Hard-headed."

Mother Magdalen said, "Be fair. Rose Red always hated being in this house."

The meal got quiet, and we listened to the wild cat cough.

I was in a hurry to help Mother Magdalen wash up after we ate. She waited at the open back door to watch me run to my ma'am's shack, facing the woods. Wasn't no smoke curling out the chimney against the graying sky. Maybe Jim Feather wasn't going to be there.

By the time I pushed open the shack door, I was sure I was just a crazy widow in mourning who went and made that man up because I was lonely. Used to hear about that kind of thing around the Quarters, when people who loved each other got sold apart or one of them got killed or just died.

190

But in the dark, there Jim Feather was, squatting by the cold cooking stones and skinning something. "These little ones bring lot of money," he said, pointing at his pile with a knife.

I left the door open just a crack so I could still see his shape. I went to sit near him. The heat from his body near me was like a touch. My heart reached out to him, and I said, "I'm glad you still here, Jim Feather."

He said, still skinning, "Thought I be gone?"

"No," I said. "Scared you'd be gone."

He only said, "I be sure and tell you before I go." I waited for more, another promise maybe that I could go with him when he left here someday. Like I thought I heard him say in my sleep.

Nothing.

I wanted to feel like we was close. I reached in my apron pocket and held out Willow to him. "Look," I said.

He stopped scraping at the little shiny black animal he had stretched on the floor. I felt him take Willow from my hand and heard him get up to carry her to the slit of light that was still coming in at the open door. He stood in the doorway with his head bowed over her so his hair waterfalled around them and left me nothing to see but the line down the middle of his back.

I thought I must seem like a crazy old coot to this wild, free man who lived killing and skinning animals and moving on through the woods. I went to him at the door and reached around him for Willow.

He closed his hand around her and turned to me, holding Willow in his fist behind him.

I looked up at him. What was this all about? Was he teasing me? *Why?*

I said, "I just wanted you to see all I got left in the world. You can give her back to me now, Jim Feather."

He shook his head so his hair flowed into the shadows. "No, Rose. I got this now."

I went cold. *What have I done? Just gave my whole life with Boyfriend, the man who loved me since we was little kids together, to a stranger.* I said careful-like, "But I ain't meant you to keep it, Jim Feather. It ain't got no meaning for nobody but me. It was a toy for all my babies that was born dead."

He pulled himself up, like putting a little distance between us. "Not lie to me." He moved me aside with his free hand. "I know what this is." He went by me to the other end of the shack at the fireplace.

I stood at the door and felt like a fool. This couldn't be happening. What had possessed me to put Willow in anybody's hand but my own? Even Boyfriend ain't touched her after he gave her to me.

This was wrong.

I heard the scraping sound of a fire being laid and lit.

It lit with a roar so the puff of dark smoke swept out and then up the chimney. The fire died to sparking coals. Jim Feather put the skinned animal carcass across my ma'am's old cooking stone where she used to fry corn pone. Then he went to scraping the inside of the black fur with his knife on the floor.

I stood there shaking. Now I was really alone in the world. "Jim Feather," I said. "Give it back."

I must have said this two three times. I don't know what-all I was going to do if he didn't respond.

He put his knife in his pack and laid some smooth stones around the edges of the skin. Then he stood up and came back to me.

He came so fast I had no time to back up and get out of there or even put up a fight. But who could bear lovemaking with a hateful stranger who just made a fool of you?

And me just a harmless lonely woman.

He pulled me to him with one hand and pushed the door shut with the other. I remember hearing the bolt slide, but I couldn't think about being trapped because he was using his mouth this time, and it felt like he loved me.

By the time I thought to push him away, I didn't want to. Alongside all my anger and shame at having handed myself to a man who stole my wood child was all the wanting to be held, in just this way, by just this man right here.

He leaned me against the door after the bolt was slid, so we could find out how far this kiss could go.

And not till we was lying still with my head on his shoulder, and I was thinking , *Can love so deep be between bodies, or is it between people? How does somebody who just met you and could leave any day make you feel like he brought you a new somebody you could be who you never was before?* when the cat coughed outside.

Jim Feather said, "Out of season to catch a cat." The cat coughed again and screamed. He lifted a hand and started stroking my braids.

They was getting long and bent, like they do when you lay on them and don't use no head-rag. I had always had way too much hair for one head, anyway. Couldn't do nothing with it.

But Boyfriend used to like me to unplait it so he could bury his hands up to the wrists in it. I reached up and started unplaiting.

193

I was thinking how Jim Feather was good as his word and didn't hurt me this time. And I wondered what happened to all my pain that he took Willow away from me. *Where is she? In his pack? Maybe I can wake before him in the morning and look in there for her.*

We had no appetite for that animal he had smoking on the cooking stone. After I got my hair undone, I guided his one hand into it, and he fell asleep like that. Then his heartbeat put me to sleep like a lullaby.

I woke to hard knocking at the bolted door.

Jim Feather slid out from under my head and went for his pack. He slipped out a knife and went and crouched in a corner just as Boy shouted, "Miss Rose Red!"

Jim Feather pointed his knife at the door and nodded his head to it.

I called, "Boy, what is it?" and started pulling on my dress.

"Got to tell you something, Miss Rose Red."

"Well, Boy, I'm listening." Buttons down the front of this blouse. At least you can see them, but they still take forever. Now how to untangle my apron in this dark?

"Solace said for me to talk to you face to face," Boy bellowed.

I was losing patience. What could Boy-or Solace, too, for that matter-have to say to me that couldn't be said through a shut door?

"Well, go on back to the house, Boy, and I'll be up there soon as I fetch me some water and wash up. You banging on my door like this ain't even decent. And you go tell Solace I said so."

I could hear from the stillness outside that he ain't moved. I was tying my apron by the time Boy said, "I really think I should wait and walk with you to the house, Miss Rose Red."

So I looked one more time at Jim Feather crouching in the corner, and he looked at me and nodded, *Go on*. I pulled open the door just enough to slide through and shut it on the smell of roasting animal and sweat inside the shack. "Well, come on then, Boy."

It was a misty morning and gray. I took deep breaths of damp air while we walked without speaking. Boy toted a shotgun. He ain't tried to explain it, and I ain't wanted to think it might be important.

I wondered to myself if, this time for sure, Jim Feather would be gone for good when I got back to my ma'am's shack. *Why you have to outlive the people you love? It's too hard to live without them and just as hard to love somebody new.*

And why did I ever think I was coming to love this stranger, this Jim Feather, with no promises but that one, once whispered in my sleep? *I should hate him.*

We came into Mother Magdalen's fire-lit back room, dark compared to the gray outside. My eyes drew to a glow on the far side of the table, on the floor. When Boy closed the door behind me, the glow inside got brighter in the black, and I could see that it was the Angel.

She was on the floor at her mother's feet, brushing her wings over the floorboards with soft swishing sounds. Mother Magdalen's hand was lost in the light around her head, but she must have been stroking the Angel's hair.

"Welcome home, Angel," I said. "Did you or Angel Girl find that Myra?"

She nodded. Seeing her face move in all that light, you couldn't be sure what you was looking at, one face or

195

a thousand faces lined up in the blazing light, but you felt like you just had to watch her, even if she blinded you.

I said with my eyes still on the Angel, "Mother Magdalen?"

The Angel rose and then she wasn't there no more, by her mother. She was by Solace, sitting on a bench holding the baby. The Angel bent and spread her wings around them. The baby and the Angel flared like grease on a fire and disappeared in a scent like roses.

Solace sat there in the dull glow of firelight, after the Angel was gone, looking a little shook up.

Mother Magdalen said, "Solace has news for us, Rose Red."

Solace looked up at me and said, "I just got a note from my grandfather's lawyers. This morning, by pony. Aunt Rose Red, you won't like this." People rose up from the benches around the table, and now I could see Whip Man and Boy edging close to me.

Solace said, "Aunt Rose Red, Mr. Dennis is back."

I sagged, but Whip Man caught me and eased me onto a bench. Maybe I fainted. Next thing I knew, I had my head on the table, and Boy and Whip Man each had one of my arms.

I sat up and shook their hands off. "Let loose of me," I said. "Of all the dead to come back to life, who went and resurrected that buzzard?" I managed to get to my feet. "I best get back to my ma'am's shack. I can't bear to hang around here and have to see Mr. Dennis again. After all these years."

Mother Magdalen said, "Sit down, Rose Red. We know how you feel. But we have to stick together right now and make some decisions. Angel Girl hasn't come back, and what my Angel found in the woods isn't good news."

Boy stood and went to the back door, yanked it open, and went out.

Whip Man said, "How we planning on protecting my son from Mr. Dennis?"

Mother Magdalen answered, "Boy will be all right if he'll just move into that outdoor kitchen. He can bar it at night against-" *why she hesitate like that? We all knew what she was going to say* "-against that wild cat that's been prowling around. You should move out there with him, Whip Man."

Solace said, "And Baby Joy? How will I explain her to Grandfather?"

Mother Magdalen said, "That's why I asked you to send for Rose Red. Rose Red, you can take Baby Joy to live in your mother's shack with you. Should Dennis find out she's there, you simply claim her as your own baby."

I sat, after all. When I could speak, I said, "But Baby Joy is brown. Look at me. I'm quite black. And so was Boyfriend. Mr. Dennis ain't never going to believe that the two of us made Baby Joy."

Mother Magdalen said, "Maybe not. But maybe Dennis will think you've had, possibly, one other man since Boyfriend died. Maybe a man light enough in color so that Baby Joy would be brown?" She made it sound like a question.

But that sound was for everybody else.

I could tell Mother Magdalen knew. She was hinting to my face about Jim Feather. *That witch. How does that purple-eyed hag already know a secret that still makes me feel so ashamed?*

I fumed. Mother Magdalen tactfully looked away.

Whip Man said, "Woman enslaved could a had a baby with anybody, for all Mr. Dennis know. Patrol man on the road-"

"That's enough, Whip Man," Mother Magdalen said.

"Oh. Excuse me. Why don't I help carry the baby things, Rose Red?" He got up looking troubled and went out to the stairs.

I carried Baby Joy with me back to the shack that very morning. No telling when Mr. Dennis might show up to be reunited with his granddaughter, Solace.

Whip Man carried the cradle he had carved when Heaven was carrying Solace. Solace herself brought so many diapers and washtubs and little ugly tight lace clothes till I said we wouldn't have no room for me and Baby Joy in that shack.

Boy couldn't be found.

But we tried to make light and talk merry. I made sure we made plenty of noise coming up on the shack, in case Jim Feather was still there.

The door was left a little ajar. I shoved it open with my foot. Solace and Whip Man came in, crowding up the room, putting things where they might look homey.

"She will get used to me?" I asked, nervous, watching Solace give the baby her breast.

Whip Man came and put one of his big arms around my shoulders. "We go'n go buy you a milk goat for feeding Baby Joy. Solace can't come down here all hours of the day and night. And if we can keep Mr. Dennis from catching sight of you and looking for more trouble, be that much better."

I slipped out from under his arm, pretending I was in a hurry to go through the tore-up sheets Solace brought. Whip Man bothered me these days.

And where was Jim Feather? I had to get to him and tell him what was going on. Wasn't no trace of him in here. Was this the day I was to finally find out I made him up?

I took the longest strip of sheet and got Solace to help me tie the baby to my back. I said, "That cat don't come around here this early in the day. I got to get out of here, off Mr. Dennis's land. I'm taking a walk with Baby Joy, you all."

Whip Man said, "I come with you. Keep you safe."

I said, "You go with Solace and get a milk goat, like you said you was go'n do. I been walking these woods all my life."

Whip Man grabbed and held my arm. "Why you hate me all of a sudden, Rose Red?" he said, hurt and angry.

I twisted my wrist and snatched my arm out of his grasp. Out the corner of my eye, I saw Solace come close. "I don't hate you, Whip Man," I said. "I hate what happened to the women who loved you. Just like you should hate it."

I was out of the door before they could say another thing.

I went crashing between the trees. If that cat was prowling close by, after all, I ain't wanted to sneak up and surprise it.

Wasn't no way I could work up at the big house today. Might as well gather kindling, like a child, while I walked and looked for signs of Jim Feather.

Walking made the baby doze. So I just kept on. The mist had burned off and the sunlight that sprinkled through the tall trees was easy on my eyes and on my mind. I started remembering how Boyfriend had run with me through these woods as a child. Now there was a good memory.

But it led to lovemaking in hidden little burrows and beds of leaves, after Boyfriend beat them to drive out snakes.

I forgot why I was walking. I blinked, and Jim Feather stood on the path ahead of me. "What you thinking?" he said.

I stopped with my hand to my heart. "How you do that? Show up so quiet you don't press a twig or snap a pine needle? You been following me?"

"Since you left the shack. You couldn't tell I was with you?"

I spotted a log nearby and went and sat on it. I had walked far and fast and just real eyes I was tired.

Jim Feather came up on me with that quiet walk of his. "Whose baby you got?"

"You know that man came to call me this morning? And that woman you must have seen go with me to the shack, just now? Their baby."

"Why they give it to you?"

He sat near me. As he sat, I watched his eyes. It seemed like there was a rush of feeling in there, pulling at me, and I wondered what it was. Looking at him close and in the light like this, my own feelings rushed toward him and the woods and the freedom stretching out behind him.

I said, "When you go away, Jim Feather, will you take me with you?"

He came down off the log and squatted in front of me. He took my hands and put one of my hands over his heartbeat. "When I kill these people I came to kill, I take

200

you with me when I go." He nodded, like he wanted me to believe him.

I went a little cold, like when he took Willow. *But I will get Willow back.* "Who did you come here to kill, Jim Feather?"

He turned and looked back over his shoulder in the direction of my ma'am's shack and the big house beyond it. He said, like to himself, "One of them coming today." He looked at me. "You stay away from that big house. More danger there than these woods."

I stayed around my ma'am's shack after that.

And Mr. Dennis finally came there looking for me.

I kept Baby Joy tied to my back most of the time she wasn't in her cradle. Solace and Boy came along that first evening, trailing the baby's new milk goat. I kept it tethered to a post between the shack and the woods. Jim Feather warned me that it would draw the big cat. So I kept Baby Joy tied to my back most of the time when she wasn't asleep in her cradle, in case I had to run.

Sometimes at night, I thought I could hear the wild cat coughing and whining close, just beyond the wild grass. The goat would bleat and Jim Feather would creep to the door and unbolt it, squatting just inside with a bow in his left and arrows in his right hand.

I had asked him not to shoot with his pistols from inside my ma'am's shack. Everybody in the big house would come running if they heard shots, knowing I sure ain't had no gun. And I didn't wanted to find out what would happen if they all met with Jim Feather.

I wasn't none too sure who he had showed up here to kill. And that Whip Man struck me these days as none too stable. So Jim Feather would wait quiet just inside the door, his bare skin gleaming with a layer of sweat that grabbed at locks of his moving hair, watching the woods and notching an arrow in his bow.

*What is so special about that cat?* I wondered. *And why does it hang around here so?* For sure not on account of one skinny little tethered milk goat. Besides, it came before the goat got bought. Almost like it came with the man who hunted it: Jim Feather.

Sometimes I stared at his pack while he watched for the cat and wondered what would happen if I sneaked a hand into his pack while he was so intent on the shadows at the edge of the woods. Would I find Willow?

I asked him once, while he was watching for the cat beyond the wild grass and the milk goat, "Jim Feather, why you take my wood child from me?"

The goat had stopped bleating. Baby Joy had stopped making little gurgle baby sounds in her cradle and slept. In the quiet, Jim Feather ain't even turned to look at me.

So I asked again.

He put his bow to his lips, like for me to be quiet. He shook his hair further back from his face. He was always so still, watching for that cat. Like he was made of wood his own self.

After a while, I sagged into the pallet of skins he was piling up for me, day after day hunting and letting me choose before he took the skins to sell. I started falling to sleep.

Maybe in my sleep I felt Jim Feather lie down next to me, put his hand on my belly, and heard him say, "I took her away cause you got her with some other man. That's why."

I tried to wake up several times that night and ask him. I dreamed over and over again about what he said

202

and how I was trying to wake him and ask him what he meant.

In the morning, when I woke up all the way, he was gone.

The day Jim Feather was gone when I woke was the day Mr. Dennis came down to my ma'am's shack to find me.

I was just back from bathing me and Baby Joy in that little stream nearby, steady drying up in the warming spring days. I was kneeling by her cradle, rocking Joy and wrapped in just a strip of sheet myself, some of what Solace carried down here, wondering should I get dressed and why didn't I give Solace back that money from the day she sent me to get supplies, when a shadow fell on me from the doorway.

I looked over, thinking the shadow was too tall for the goat, and how did it break loose, anyway?

Too quiet for Whip Man or Boy, unless they took to peeping on the sly at women who wasn't dressed for company, and I was going to point this out to them, make no mistake.

Just when I had made up my mind it was Solace come down to my ma'am's shack for the baby, my eyes wandered across the floor and got to the figure in the door.

Mr. Dennis.

Couldn't be wrong about that.

My insides went to ice. Then to sickness. Then knotted up.

His face hadn't changed much, but for his eyes, cutting and cruel, more than ever. Not like there wasn't feeling in them. More like his brother, long dead and

203

gone, he had plenty of feeling. Too much feeling. And all of it vicious.

Mr. Dennis said, "You haven't come up to the big house to welcome me back, Rose Red. Why haven't you?"

His hair had gone from that burnt red brown to silver white, almost like Angel Girl's wolf. It lifted around his shoulders off his black suit while he just stood there, like the Angel's wings lift. He had a cape on over his suit, and his hands trembled. I wondered if he was cold.

He looked so old.

"Sir," I said and tried to wind the sheet a little tighter and tuck it a little more snug without him seeing it, if I could. I felt young again and scared.

Can I say anything to make him just go away?

Mr. Dennis said, "All these years, and that's all you can say? 'Sir.' Did you, too, think I was dead?"

I licked my lips. Funny they got dried out so fast. Like he said, it wasn't like I was doing much talking. "Yes, sir."

More quiet still, Mr. Dennis said, "You didn't just think I was dead. You hoped I was dead, Rose Red. Admit it. I know you." He laughed short and hard. "You never change," he went on. "Well, I guess I don't need to wait for you to invite me into my own property. Seeing as how you don't plan to invite me in."

He came forward.

I was thinking, *I ain't the only one who ain't changed.*

He didn't stop till he was right on me and the cradle, so close his trouser leg touched my knee, where I was crouching. I wondered would he notice if I backed a little away.

Mr. Dennis looked down on Baby Joy. "So this is the baby," he said. He looked at me. "Who is the father?"

I said, "Boy." Quick bit my lip and kicked myself in my mind while I added, "friend."

"Boyfriend?" Mr. Dennis said and laughed. He threw back his head and the silver hair lifted. He straightened and looked at me with venom. I looked away again.

His voice cut at me. "Rose Red. Remember all the lies you told me, to throw me off that man's trail? Well, don't bother lying now. Did Boyfriend believe you when you told him he was the father of this baby? If he did, he was a bigger fool than I ever was. Well, I hear he's dead now. And you're all alone. Except maybe for whoever gave you that brat."

From the corner of my eye, I saw the black-trousered knees bend and felt the cape brush me. Mr. Dennis crouched down next to me.

His hot dry fingers came under my chin, and my face got pulled around to look at his.

Eye to eye with me, his pale lean face peering through the silver, Mr. Dennis said, "Just goes to show that nobody can be a bigger fool than I was and still survive it. I think I hate you, Rose Red. So many of my dreams invested in you and lost to me. And you still don't even care." His eyes on mine was frost on the pond in wintertime: cold, cracked, and covering away the warm life inside. Or was it already rank and dead in there?

This man still wanted me. After all these years. And he still owned me and could do anything. It didn't bear thinking about.

My mind went blank as he leaned in toward me. *Not this. Not again. Not like when I was young and in love and hunted. Not more of that fear and confusion.*

There was a sound, like a snake slithered quick across the floor.

Mr. Dennis's eyebrows, still dark on his white face, went up, almost like he thought of something very important that couldn't wait. His mouth fell open like he wanted to ask me something. But instead he reached around like to scratch his back with both hands.

And then he slid slow over on his side, stretching out on my ma'am's dirt floor, like to sleep.

But instead of closing his eyes, he lay there and looked up at me, breathing loud with his mouth open. He left off scratching at his back and reached his pale fingers up at me.

They was smeared with blood.

I leaped to my feet and backed away from him. Then I grabbed hold of the cradle and pulled Baby Joy to the wall with me. I slid to the floor and shoved my fingers in my mouth and ended up covering my mouth with both my cupped hands, trying not to cry out. All the while, Mr. Dennis lay looking at the blood on his hands and then looking at a spot somewhere in the air closer to his eyes.

Jim Feather's shape came through the door behind Mr. Dennis. He crossed the floor and knelt and tugged at Mr. Dennis's back. It was a quick scraping sound.

Mr. Dennis jerked and arched his back and cried out and finally closed his eyes.

Jim Feather held up a bloody arrow to his lip, motioning with it for me to stay quiet.

I sat on the floor with my back to the wall of logs and sank my face against Baby Joy's neck. She woke and began to fret.

I shivered, and warm arms went around me. That black river of hair brushed my cheek and tumbled down my shoulder.

"You not got to cry," Jim Feather said. "You ain't loved him? No one find out. We feed him to that big cat tonight." Jim Feather let me go.

I looked up at him with my tears all over my face. "Where you been, all the time he was in here? Why you didn't just tell me you would do something like this?"

Jim Feather was lifting Mr. Dennis by his armpits. "Like what?" he grunted.

I screamed, "Like killing this man here in my ma'am's shack! Why you do this?" I clapped one hand over my mouth to stop myself.

Jim Feather dragged the body just to the inside of the door, barely ajar. He dropped the body and looked up. "Sure, I told you. This the first one I come to kill."

He sighed and came back across the room to me, sat and lifted my chin with his fingers like Mr. Dennis had just done minutes ago. "I kill two. Then we go away, you and me," Jim Feather said. He leaned in close and touched the tip of his nose to mine. Rubbed them soft together round and round, and breathed in the air that I was breathing out. Touched his lips to mine, light, like his name. A feather.

Only a touch. And then he backed away a little and let go of my face. He reached for Baby Joy and returned her to her cradle for me, and she settled down and returned to her deep sleep.

I had let my hands down. But when he came back to me, I reached to hold some part of Jim Feather, where all the strength was right now, so unafraid of what he had just done.

Jim Feather squatted and looked into my eyes. "You ain't want him?" he asked and jerked his head toward where Mr. Dennis's body had opened its eyes now and lay

207

staring straight at me. Jim Feather's black river of hair flew and fell with the motion of his head.

"No," I said. "But don't leave him in here. Drag him out, please."

"Tonight." He smiled. "Call the big cat with him."

He pulled his pack off his back and took a long drink from his waterskin. Then he sat next to the cradle, quietly checking over his old scraped skins. After a long while of not looking at that doorway, I shifted to the fireplace and cooked up a wild meat stew and sizzled corn pone on my ma'am's old cooking stones. The only thing different was Jim Feather had to take the bucket to go fetch stew water. No way was I stepping over Mr. Dennis.

The sun took forever to sink.

I couldn't tell was I happy or horror-struck, with that particular dead body lying by the door, watching me. What did Mr. Dennis say right before he died? Something about me and his dreams. I ought to know about lost and wasted dreams.

We was eating, scooping the sizzling pone like ladles into the pot of wild stew, when the cat made its coughing and whining sounds.

"Sun down?" Jim Feather said and smiled over his shoulder at the door. He turned the full glow of his broad smile back to me, dropping his bitten piece of pone into the pot. He leaped to the door, squatting and easing it a little more open so he could look out.

The cat must have smelled the big dead body in here. The sky was still bleeding the day away, and it sounded like the cat wasn't no further away than the edge of the wild grass.

I was holding Joy. I pulled her in tight to my chest and crept to the door behind Jim Feather, to look out.

Right at the open edge of the woods was a shape, dark, slender, hunched over, hulking low and lifting its head like to sniff the air.

"There it is," Jim Feather whispered and frowned in the blood-like sunset. "Something ain't right," he said to himself.

"Maybe just too hungry to wait," I offered.

Jim Feather did that little grunt he sometimes liked to do. Then he squat-walked quick like running the little space across the shack floor and grabbed up his bow and some arrows and came back to take hold of Mr. Dennis's feet, to drag him.

I tugged open the door with one hand and hunkered down in front of it over Baby Joy, to brace it open. Joy nuzzled around on my breasts, looking to nurse like on her ma'am. She started in to whimper and whine. "She cry when she don't find no milk on me," I warned Jim Feather. "Maybe you shouldn't dump the body out there till we done brought in the milk goat for her, first."

"Then do something," Jim Feather said. "I got to get this body out quick." So I smiled down at her and started to croon out some little song in a whisper. My heart was slamming in my chest.

I looked at Jim Feather easing Mr. Dennis's body by me. "Don't back out," I whispered. "I don't want to lose you."

He stopped there in the doorway and said, "Keep your eyes on that big cat. It move toward me, you tell me what it doing. Got that? You say walking, jumping, running. You tell me."

I nodded.

It was best not to say nothing just now. If I opened my mouth again to sing to Baby Joy or answer Jim

Feather, I was going to let loose and scream at him to get back in this shack and bolt that door.

I was asking myself what was I going to do watching one more man who maybe loved me get killed right in front of my face. Mr. Dennis shouldn't have counted, right in there with Boyfriend and Jim Feather, but in a way, he did.

Mr. Dennis had always been a sore trial. But while he was around, for all I know, he kept worse trials from getting their hands on me. Maybe sending his body out with these thoughts was almost like the memory service at the graveside for Rhea and Mammy Water.

Jim Feather made it through the doorway. I could hear the pebbles up the walkway grating under Mr. Dennis's black clothes, getting frayed.

I could feel Jim Feather's eyes on my face. But now I kept my own eyes fixed on the dark, prowling shape of the big cat.

It was inching forward. Sniffing at the air. Lifting. Ducking. Steady coming slow, one soundless step at a time.

Like Jim Feather could do. Steps that made no sound at all through the tall wild grass between the woods and the shack.

All of a sudden it leaped and disappeared forward in the grass.

"Run!" I screamed. "It jumped, Jim Feather!"

He cleared Mr. Dennis's body in one stride, bent and staying low, notching up an arrow as he ran back toward me. Before he was at the door, he swung around and took aim behind him for the cat.

You could see the top of its head bounding closer in the grass. But it didn't come past the still body of Mr.

Dennis. It slunk low over the body and started to circle it, rustling grass and making black shadows stretch.

Jim Feather stayed his ground outside the door and kept steady aim with his bow and arrow.

And then he started creeping out there towards the cat. He stayed so low it was like he was walking with his knees bent. He slid along just above the ground like he was walking in a ditch, his head never bobbing.

You could hear the cat growling and starting to yowl, slurping and crunching on Mr. Dennis's flesh and bones.

And you could hear the goat out there bleating and begging to be got out of the grass and brought away from the cat. I ignored it and kept my eyes on Jim Feather and now my hand on Baby Joy's mouth, so she wouldn't distract me nor him nor draw the cat to us.

So noisy out there for a night when people and creatures was hunting each other and trying to be quiet.

Jim Feather rose from the grass to get a good sight on the cat and shoot it. For the first time, I saw where some old scar zigged like lightning across his back and down. I wondered, out of the blue, if that old raised scar had anything to do with Jim Feather coming to this plantation to kill Mr. Dennis and some one other body.

Jim Feather froze. He lowered his bow.

He stared. The cat caught sight of him so close and stopped its guzzling on Mr. Dennis. It stood.

High on two legs. Like a woman.

It was a woman. Better dressed than me, in a black gown spattered with dark running blood. Mud, old blood and fresh.

She was dark and slim and long and tall, standing, so you could see how, prowling through the grass, she could have looked just like a big black slinking cat. She stared

211

at Jim Feather for a minute, the blood and gore dripping down off her jaw. Her mouth hung a little open, her eyes round and staring.

Then her lips peeled back and her fang teeth, white and pointy, hung down on the sides. She curled her lips back in a wide stretch and screeched, still staring at Jim Feather, warning him back off her kill.

He held her eyes and started back.

He crept and crept back, still standing straight so she could see him, till he was upside the goat. He kept his eyes on the cat woman while he reached for the goat tether and unwound it off the post. Still holding his bow and arrow and the cat woman's eyes, he backed on into the shack, pulling the goat behind him.

I crawled to the wall, out of their way, till they was inside. Then I kicked the door shut on the nightmare in the grass.

"What was that?" I demanded of Jim Feather.

I ain't never seen him so rattled. He stood in the middle of the floor with the goat, breathing hard and with his eyes wide.

He shifted his eyes to me. "You ain't seen it?" he asked.

"I did see. I just don't believe it."

"Believe it," he said. He threw down his bow and arrow and the goat's tether and went to slide the bolt.

And now at last Baby Joy bust loose and started to cry.

I held her to the goat's teat. I ain't never seen a sight so silly like we must have been, trying to fit the goat and all of us in that tiny cabin space with Jim Feather's pelts and pack.

Jim Feather held the goat standing still, and I slid my legs up under its belly and laid Baby Joy face up, propped up on my thighs, so she could just reach the teat with her mouth and suck on it. I had no patience for milking nor steady fingers for feeding a baby from a bowl or a rag teat tonight. So this was just going to have to do.

She did all right. Then I rocked her in the cradle till she quit her fussing, but she wouldn't sleep till she wet through two diapers, and by then I was crying, my own self. But when I got the third diaper tied on her, I found she was finally sleep.

I covered her with a little bit of one of Jim Feather's furs, just in case it was as cold to her as it felt to me, cause I had the shivers.

Jim Feather surprised me and sang her a lullaby while I rocked the cradle. My throat was too tight and dry. I couldn't have comforted no baby who had to listen to me.

When Baby Joy was good and sleep, I crawled into Jim Feather's arms. My shaking died down under how tight and warm and close he held me.

He leaned back against the log wall and kept up his song. It kind of had a lift and drop to it, like a heartbeat that you sing. After a while, I drowsed.

We spent most of the night waking off and on and making love, like we hadn't just killed the man that owned me my whole life, and then watched one of his slave women eat him. It seemed like we should be doing something. Dancing or praying or something. Maybe lovemaking was just as good. It would surely have to do.

We three woke up to the sound of pounding on the door. Whip Man was out there yelling and so was Mr. Tim, that carriage driver from the townhouse. "Rose Red! Open up! You and the baby okay in there?"

I sat up and looked at Jim Feather in the dark.

"Tell them yes," he said. "They must found the dead man."

"We fine!" I shouted. "What you all doing out here?"

Whip Man yelled, "Come to bring you safe to the house, now. Unbolt the door and come on."

"But why?" I didn't want to go. I held on to Jim Feather.

"Don't ask none of your fool woman questions." That was Mr. Tim. He had a reputation. "You snatch up that baby and just come on, like the man told you, woman!"

Jim Feather was easing my fingers off his arm. I shouted back, "Give me a minute." I turned towards Jim Feather in the dark and said, "But I don't want to leave you."

"You ain't leave me," he whispered back. "And I ain't leave you. We leave here together, real soon."

I got up and wrapped myself back in my piece of sheet and lifted Baby Joy from her cradle, waking her as I hugged her to my chest. I didn't look at the watching shape of Jim Feather no more. I was mad at him and hurting for him, I wanted to stay here with him so bad.

He had my secrets. He had my doll. He had murdered Mr. Dennis for me-or was it just for himself?-and was sending me away, alone, with the burden of what I knew.

I made a show of dragging that goat out of the shack behind me and pulling the door shut, holding Baby Joy with only one hand and the goat tether with the other.

Whip Man and Mr. Tim just waited, staring around at the sky and the grass, the longer I took. They ain't dared come close, on account I ain't had nothing on but a sheet.

But I must have been too long at the goat and door business because Whip Man came up and snatched at

214

Baby Joy, and then Mr. Tim took my elbow, and they hustled me across the field between them, whipping my bare legs against the growing stalks of cotton.

Mother Magdalen and them was all gathered in the back room and turned like one body to stare at me, wrapped in a sheet.

"Angel Girl!" I said. "You came back. Where you been?"

"Tracking Myra," she said quiet-like and looked away from me.

Boy leaped up off a bench to take his baby daughter from Whip Man and hold her. Solace made a sound like a little sob and ran to hug the two of them together in her arms.

"You all act like you thought I wasn't going to take care of the baby," I pointed out.

Mr. Tim slid the bolt on the door.

Whip Man said, "Rose Red, listen. Mr. Dennis come see you yesterday or today?"

I dropped my eyes. Here I stood in a sheet and with my hair all wild and undone, when I had left this house with proper clothes on. I knew full well what they must be thinking. And it bothered me something terrible to know they would think that about me and Mr. Dennis.

Angel Girl said, "Rose Red, I think that, between you and me, we can explain what's happened."

Solace had her breast out for Baby Joy, who was making loud sucking sounds. Other than that, it wasn't no sounds but the snapping of a fire in the fireplace.

I gave up and sat down near Angel Girl. "Tell whatever you feel these people have a right to know," I said. "I got guilt, not shame."

"Let me start at the beginning," Angel Girl said. "Wolf and I caught up with Myra pretty soon after she ran away from the plantation."

Mr. Tim snapped, "Then why ain't you brought her back here?"

Whip Man said, "Shut up and listen and you go'n find out why."

Angel Girl said with great patience, "Because it seemed like something strange had happened to her. So we followed her, to find out what it was, if we could. Why just bring her back if what she's become endangers everyone here?"

Mr. Tim said, "Become? What you mean, 'become'?"

Whip Man sat and buried his head in his hands.

Angel Girl said, "She's become something like a wild cat. Remember that she killed Rhea, and then ran away? Well, last night she killed and ate some of Mr. Dennis."

Whip Man raised his head. "What I found of Mr. Dennis, nothing but a wild animal could a did."

Angel Girl said, "Myra is a wild animal, now."

Mr. Tim said, "Ain't possible. She ain't nothing but more crazy in the head than she used to be."

Whip Man said, "I thought sure I told you shut up."

Mother Magdalen said, "Let's keep our heads. Rose Red, Mr. Dennis's body was found near your mother's shack this morning. Whip Man was drawn to it by vultures and raccoons. Can you tell us why Mr. Dennis might have been near your shack? Or can you tell us anything about Myra?"

I said, "You all know darn right well why Mr. Dennis might have been hanging around my shack. And every one of you knows just as well wasn't nothing I could ever do about him. He owned me, not the other way around.

And whatever got him, I ain't going to lie. I'm glad. But I never met Myra. Remember? Those was the days I spent asleep or locked up in my room upstairs. So I can't tell you not one blessed thing about her."

I made as if to rise and go up to that room I just reminded everybody I had. I think that was what I meant to do.

Instead, I passed out and dropped to the floor.

I was already coming to as Whip Man gathered me up off the wood plank floor and lifted me in his arms to carry me upstairs. I could hear Mr. Tim mumbling, "Single womens is more trouble than they worth," and for a minute I wasn't sure was I young again, and was it that field hand name of Bully trying to stop Boyfriend from helping me escape a beating in the field?

But by the time Whip Man had got me up the stairs and Mother Magdalen was spreading the covers on Rose White's bed over me, I knew everything.

Where I was. How I felt. Why I felt this way. I had carried-and lost-enough babies to know what was happening to me now. I was carrying another baby.

From Jim Feather. Along with Jim Feather. Now Jim Feather for sure would leave without me, laying up here in bed sick and not able to run through the woods.

I couldn't bear to run through the woods again, dropping another tiny dead body in a river of blood, like when Boyfriend was alive.

Mother Magdalen and Whip Man couldn't get nothing out of me. So they left me to my staring at the wall, thinking.

Pretty soon, Angel Girl and her silver wolf came quiet into the room. She sat on the edge of the bed and took my hand in her good one. Her wounded arm hung, limp and curled in, at her waist. She said, "Rose Red, my dear. Would you like to talk to me?"

I turned my head on the pillows to look at her and said, "Just this. Why some women won't never be alone? And other women won't never be nothing but on their way to being alone again?"

Angel Girl said, "Are you on your way to being alone again?"

I said, "You and Mother Magdalen know who been in that shack with me all this time. I'm sick with his baby. He came here to kill two people. Mr. Dennis was one. It's one more he ain't got to, yet. And then he will leave here. And I can't run through the woods no more and watch one more baby die out of my body."

Angel Girl said, "Let me tell you what I saw out there." And she told me how her and the wolf was out there watching for Myra and keeping an eye on me and Baby Joy, and then she saw what a good hunter Jim Feather was, and how he was always keeping an eye on me and Joy at the shack in-between the kills he went and made in the woods. And then she knew she ain't had to worry over us no more.

"Rose Red," she said. "He's a good man. Only, now that he's killed Mr. Dennis, he'd better get away from here. Let me go tell him about the baby and ask him to come back for the two of you next spring. Solace will have her hands full convincing Mr. Dennis's lawyers that he went for a stroll in the woods and got killed by a wild cat. Strangers hanging around won't help her story."

I thought this was a rotten idea. But I said yes to it because I ain't seen no other way out. Then I lay in Rose White's bed with my hands on my belly where I ain't wanted to lose my last chance to have a child, listening like I could hear Angel Girl and Jim Feather talking way out there near the woods.

Solace and Mother Magdalen came to see me and try to get me to eat. They talked about burying Mr. Dennis on the side of the house with his parents and Rhea and Mammy Water.

"Those two women will have their hands full, holding down slaveholders, won't they?" they tried to joke. Hadn't neither one of them ever been good at making folks crack a smile.

Still wasn't no good.

I drank some of that strange green stuff Mother Magdalen is always pouring down people's throats. Then they left me alone. The green stuff knocked me out till morning.

Boy was back in the house, now that Mr. Dennis was dead. He brought my breakfast, and I asked him where was Angel Girl. I needed to know how her talk went with Jim Feather.

"Angel Girl and that wolf took off yesterday and ain't been back. They probably hiding out till all this about Mr. Dennis's death blow over." Solace was on her way into town, tearful and pale, to explain to her grandfather's lawyers about his tragic accident.

I passed the day in a stupor, drowsing. When I woke toward nightfall with a head that felt like it was cracked in two, I swore I wouldn't never touch those green hot teas from Mother Magdalen, again.

I could hear voices downstairs, all of them excited.

I pulled myself out of bed, still wrapped in my little bit of sheet, and made my way down to the back room.

Only Whip Man and Boy, holding Baby Joy, was in there. They said Solace and Mother Magdalen was up front in the parlor, treating some lawyer like company.

Boy's face looked like a storm-cloud.

Whip Man rubbed his back and shook his knee. "Don't worry, son," he kept saying. "Solace ain't but putting on company manners. Got to, if she want his help. She ain't never leaving you for no wight man, no matter what her grandpapa use to want. She love you, son."

After a while of this, Boy took the baby and banged his way out the back door.

Fire in the fireplace leaped from the gust of cool air. Whip Man rubbed his head and said, "Rhea knew how to talk to him." Then he heaved himself up from the table and followed his son.

This was my chance.

I sneaked out the door after them and ran towards my ma'am's shack.

The door was left swung open, and it wasn't no sign that Jim Feather had ever been there. It was just the baby's cradle, the piles of rag strips for diapers and swaddling, my dress and apron with the satchel purse still tied to it, and me and my ma'am's few cooking things.

No sign of no man at all.

I searched the purse. Full of money. At least, he never robbed me. Then I hunted everywhere for Willow. Gone.

No, he robbed me, all right.

I knelt in the middle of the mess I had a made in there and shouted, "No!" *Lost them both, Boyfriend and Jim Feather, my memories and my future, being greedy and reckless and wanting more than I can have. And trying to have a baby.*

220

A breeze picked up and blew in through the door, carrying a sound like a bleat from the milk goat.

I looked around. *Where has that stupid thing got to? Will Solace make her way down here, looking for it? I best find it and haul it back to the house, so she won't never stumble on Jim Feather. If he comes back for me.*

He still wanted to kill a second somebody around here, whoever that was. Maybe Angel Girl hadn't for real gotten him to go. I could hope.

If I made two or three trips tonight, I could haul back the cradle and the sheets and things to the big house, close myself up in my ma'am's shack and just wait for Jim Feather.

Or lie down and die here, if I'm lucky. What an old fool I turned out to be.

I was out in the wild grass, clutching my bit of dirty winding sheet and calling, "Nanny! Nanny goat. Nanny," when I heard the big cat cough and mew.

I froze and turned so my back was to the shack and my face to the woods and started backing toward the shack, like Jim Feather did.

The dark gathered from the trees and the fields on all sides of me. The world looked big and hateful, and I was alone out there in the middle of it, way too small.

My mind so set on grieving for the loss of Jim Feather and Willow, I had walked right out here to hand myself over to-whatever Myra was now. I should have stayed safe in the big house.

A form crept closer from the woods. The long shadows between the trees dipped and danced in the little breeze that had brought me the cat's cough. Soft shadows slid together, rose up, and walked like a woman on the prowl.

Myra lifted one leg like a woman sipping from a china tea cup with her finger in the air and pressed her foot to the ground so no noise was made. She eased her body forward and lifted the next foot. Her head never bobbed and her eyes never blinked.

She stared at me and kept coming.

Her lips was parted so you could see the fangs glint with the first drops of moonlight. She ran her pink tongue over her fangs.

Her hands walked in the air too, like her feet. One step at a time. She kept her shining dark eyes on mine as she kept coming.

The dark closed around her and behind her till I couldn't make out nothing clear but the black of her eyes fixed and burning out from the whites. I ain't snapped out of it till she sprang at me.

She sailed into the air, and her face folded in on her wrinkled nose, so her teeth was coming at me first.

Then a scraping yowl tore out of her throat so the spit flew from her mouth. That pointed tongue licked at the flying drool as she flew through the air to get me.

And I finally broke loose from her spell and ran, falling back and twisting round and pushing myself up off the grass to make it to the safety of my ma'am's shack.

Air whistled right behind me and I felt the burn of something sharp like a handful of shaving razors graze my back. I threw myself through the door and back up against it and felt something hit it and bump me forward.

I turned and pounded at the bolt and slid it into place, just in time to hear a roar like thunder come out of that animal throat and feel a shove like the door would splinter under my own hands.

She yowled in rage and raked the door to get at me.

I pressed on the door to steady the bolt because it was old and cracking with every thrust she made against it. I screamed and cried out with my terror every time the door and the bolt both bulged.

But I stayed and held the door with my body against whatever Myra was. My own screams rang inside my ears, and Myra's roars made them throb.

And then I heard two pistol shots.

They was loud like stones cracking and they was close. One and then another.

I heard Myra yelp and whine. She must have stopped her attack on the door. It stopped bulging in at me.

And then I heard grass rustling. I waited and listened, and the ringing and throbbing in my ears died down till I could hear voices, men's voices, shout from over by the big house.

I sank on the floor and pressed my ringing ear to the splintered door and listened to the men running closer through cotton stalks and then wild grass. I waited. I ain't opened the door until I heard Solace's own voice call, "Rose Red! It's us, Rose Red. You're safe now."

I pulled open the door and seen a man with a moon white face and screamed again. I thought it was Mr. Dennis, back from the grave yet another time.

But Solace pushed past the man and reached for me and said, "Rose Red, darling. This is Mr. Sacks. It's all right, Rose Red. We heard shots, and he's come to rescue you."

So this was the lawyer man Whip Man and Boy ain't trusted.

I started gibbering. "Miss Solace, it was the cat. I remembered the baby things and came to get them. And the goat was gone, and when I went towards the woods to find her, this big cat came screeching and leaping and I ran-" I broke off and hid my face, making sounds to cover what I couldn't tell in front of this lawyer.

Solace said quick, "That must be the same cat that got Grandfather. Mr. Sacks, you see how it is. Whip Man, Boy, Tim, please help me get Rose Red back up to the house. Now, I've told you, Rose Red. You and your baby must stay in the big house with me and the men until the cat has been found and shot. We're none of us safe this close to the woods. Boy, please carry that cradle."

Solace had let go of me to grab up my dress and apron and the strips of sheets and point at the cradle and look at Boy.

I was standing alone with my arms wrapped around my breasts, shivering again. You know them nipples starts to burn when you're carrying a baby.

And Mr. Sacks just stood off to one side holding his pistol and staring at my legs where the stripped sheet ain't covered them. He said, "I begin to understand, Miss Solace, why your grandfather was out here, walking so close to the woods that the wild cat got him."

Whip Man was carrying a hoe, I guess for a weapon. He swung it so it bit into the dirt floor and quivered there, stuck upright.

Solace dropped the clothes she was gathering, blushed bad and stared at Mr. Sacks. The lawyer man had his eyes on Whip Man and his jaw hung slack. Boy dropped the cradle and looked at his papa, waiting for somebody's next move.

Solace recovered first. She bent for her bundle of clothes again and said, "Whip Man," without looking at him, like nothing out of the usual was going on, "we're all upset by Grandfather's death." She straightened and looked at the lawyer man. "It's almost like losing him twice. We had just got him back, you know. We've been very lost, out here trying to run the farm without him."

"I understand, Miss Solace," the lawyer man said, nodding. "It especially grieves me that you've never enjoyed the peace of mind afforded by a man's protection on your premises. Why, just last year with those patrollers-"

"Please, Mr. Sacks. I'm so grateful for your concern. But if we could just get to the house before that cat returns?" Solace was brushing past the man to get out the door.

Whip Man snatched his hoe out the ground and guided me out the door with one arm round my shoulder. This time, I ain't pulled away. Mr. Tim and his son was waiting in the grass. They took the bundles from Solace and came on behind. All the men had come down there carrying some kind of weapon.

But seeing them there with their hoes and axes put me in mind we had to talk Solace into buying some firearms. As we walked, with Boy and the cradle trailing behind, I thought I heard Mr. Sacks say, "I only wonder who fired those pistol shots that brought us running?"

Solace said, "Oh, probably some patrol or other, invading my woods. Everyone who's heard of Grandfather's tragic death will rightly expect a handsome reward for catching that cat."

Mr. Sacks said, "Surely you don't mean 'catching,' Miss Solace. We mean to have that creature killed. Once they've a taste for human blood, you know, there's no alternative. And speaking of a taste for human blood." He chuckled. "I'm glad I don't see any dogs around here to chase patrols away any more. You've gotten yourself quite a reputation, after that incident last year." Mr. Sacks laughed. "But allow me to say, Miss Solace, that I do admire a feisty woman." He cut up his eyes up toward Solace, like to see how she was taking the news that he admired her.

I dropped back to walk with Boy. Since Whip Man was touchy about me pulling away these days, he waited till we caught him up, and then he put his arm back on my shoulder to walk together again.

After that night Mr. Sacks was a very regular visitor.

The Angel stayed away when he came, so as not to risk he would see her light. Solace or Mother Magdalen would come and bring me Baby Joy. I would tie her to my back and try to keep the knotted ends of the rag that held her from rubbing my sore nipples or pressing my tender belly. My belly gripped on me now if I so much as moved wrong, making me bend over and breathe deep to ease the cramp.

I spent all my time cleaning house, learning to care for the baby, or sleeping. Now that I wasn't possessed by Heaven wanting Whip Man, I dreamed a lot of Boyfriend.

He'd come and sit on the edge of my bed and listen to how I hadn't meant to fall in love with Jim Feather, but I had done it and there it was, and now I was going to be raising a baby me and Boyfriend should have had together. But it was strange, I didn't really mind because maybe the baby would give me back the two men I loved.

Only, I got so tired of holding somebody else's baby nowadays that I was carrying my own, meaning I was fed up with tying Solace's Baby Joy onto my sore body, though I loved them both dearly, but really, why couldn't Solace just up and tell that lawyer man Sacks to get out and stay out, now that Mr. Dennis wasn't around to try to get her to marry a wight man?

Boyfriend listened and smirked and told me I would know what to do when the time came to change things.

Sometimes Jim Feather would walk in on these dreams and tell me, like Boyfriend wasn't even there, "Come on. We got to go."

And I would look again at Boyfriend's face and go cold from the loss and the loneliness haunting him and wake up and throw up on the floor.

I took to keeping a bucket by my bed for these dreams.

One night, right while I was throwing up and listening to it splash in the bottom of the bucket and waiting to feel that dizzy relief, I heard shouting. Boy's voice, saying, "I'm go'n kill him! Let me go, pap. This it. I'm killing him dead."

I heard scuffling and something sounded like Solace's voice but strangled. I wiped my mouth on a rag I kept tied to the bucket handle and came out into the candlelit hallway, holding the doorjamb and the walls to stay on my feet.

There was Whip Man, tussling with Boy outside Solace's closed door. Every time Whip Man got Boy pinned a little bit, Mr. Tim and his son Zion would grab a couple of Boy's arms or legs and try to hold him a while. Mother Magdalen swept up the stairs carrying a candle tree and a basin with something in it that smelled right pungent.

The Angel floated through Solace's shut door, sparkling like the stained glass behind her and the candles in her mother's hand. She had Baby Joy in her arms, protected from the solid door by the Angel's wings that lifted out and closed again around her. The Angel smiled at me before her and Baby Joy disappeared.

Mother Magdalen said, "If you gentlemen can spare some shouting and swearing, will two of you go to the edge of the woods, where the soil stays shaded? Mud full of lichen might do Solace's face more good than another fist fight."

I said, "I'll go, Mother Magdalen."

Whip Man shoved at Boy's head one more time and said, "Cut it out, Rose Red! What good you do anybody dead? You all know Myra won't hurt me. I go." And he turned without looking at me and headed down the stairs at a run.

I said to his back, "Me, I don't know no such thing. Nor do I think you rightly know what Myra's going to do." I was light-headed from dreaming and throwing up and wanted to go back to bed and see could I bring Boyfriend back and reason with him some more. But I went toward Solace's door, following Mother Magdalen.

Boy was still on the floor under Mr. Tim and Zion. "Ain't I a man?" he demanded. He stared around at the men holding him. "Look what that sneaking thief done to my own wife! And you all telling me ain't a thing I can do about it? Ain't I a man?"

I went to him and put my cleanest hand on his mouth. "Sshh," I said. "You a man. Question is, you going to do Solace more good as a live man or a dead one? I take it Mr. Sacks done got tired of being turned down and beat her?"

Mother Magdalen tapped at Solace's door and said aside to me, "I think he meant to persuade her that she is badly in need of his particular protection. Our men managed to throw Mr. Sacks out without breaking the law and doing him any actual physical harm, but who knows what he'll do next."

Boy got a fist loose from Zion and slammed it backward into Solace's door. "Let me in!" he shouted. "How much of this you think I can take? First you flirting with him, Solace. Now he beating on you. And you still telling me watch and do nothing? What am I to you?" Bang, bang. "Tell me that! What am I?"

I sat on Boy's chest and covered his fists with my vomit-smelling hands. Mr. Tim and Zion got hold of his legs and arms again. Mother Magdalen got Solace to open the door at just this second, so she could slip in with her basin and rags.

Boy yelled through the closing door, "You don't let me in there, I'm going after him, Solace! I swear it. I swear it!"

Mr. Tim said to me, "Why we don't just knock him out? Fool go'n get us all killed."

I said, "Boy, listen. You ain't doing nothing but scaring her. You know Solace don't want you to see her and go off and get lynched, trying to avenge yourself on that wight man. She is trying to protect you. She don't want to see you like I last seen Boyfriend, hanging and roasting from a tree. You got to let on to her that you are calm and can handle this."

Boy didn't say anything, but he was lying still now, staring up at the ceiling with his jaw stuck out and tears coursing down into his hairline. I continued more softly, "She want you in there more than she want anything. You quiet down, you be in there in no time. Tomorrow or the next day, we all sit down and start figuring how can we get back at that Mr. Sacks."

I kept on till he went limp. A few tears was still sliding out the side of his eyes, but he was still.

I got off his chest and slid my lap under his head. Mr. Tim and Zion let him go but sat down near Solace's door, just in case. Boy buried his face on my sore breast, rubbing that aching nipple. Must have been something he got in the habit of doing with his mother. I chewed on my lip and held him.

I ain't made it back to Rose White's bed till dawn was spreading pink and gray across the sky. But by then Solace, face packed brown with mud, had wept herself to sleep in her husband's arms, and none of us needed to watch at no more doors.

"I ain't ready to go back to sleeping my days away," I told myself and ain't woke up till sunset.

I dreamed that Boyfriend had come back and sat on my bed to take my hands and say, "See, this the problem. Man loves a woman, and if he try to protect her, he go'n lose her." But Jim Feather burst in the room and looked at Boyfriend for the first time, admitting he seen him, and started shouting, "Ain't my fault you dead! I was dead, and I come back! You want her? Come back for her, and fight me fair! What stopping you, if you want her?"

I woke up retching dry in my bucket.

Mother Magdalen's voice was calling through the door, "Rose Red, aren't you joining us for supper?"

I rolled over on my back and said to myself, "I just got to tell Mother Magdalen I'm pregnant and see does she have anything I can take." My stomach gripped me at the thought. "For the sickness," I explained to myself. "Not to lose the baby. To help me keep it." Then I wondered who I thought was in the room, listening to me talk.

House madness. People wasn't meant to live in houses like this. *House like this one can eat your mind right out your head, and you never notice.*

What ever made me think staying in this place would help me give birth to a live baby?

I really should have known better.

But then things calmed down. Mother Magdalen brought me some soothing tea without my asking, and I lived on it even when I couldn't hold nothing else on my stomach.

And then Mr. Sacks stopped prowling the verandah every night banging on the door and pleading with Solace to let him in, didn't she know he could use the key her grandfather left him, but he was being a gentleman? Didn't she know everything he done was on account he was out of his mind with worry over her, inheriting this big plantation all by her little self? And on and on.

Boy locked himself with Solace in their room to get through these nights, and all of a sudden they ended.

And then one night the Angel came in my dream and met Jim Feather and told him, "It's almost time." And Boyfriend came from a long way away and kissed my forehead and said, "Listen now and look in my eyes. Rose Red, you know I will always love you. You know that, don't you, babygirl? I be here when you need me." And I said, "I will always love you, too, Boyfriend."

And after all, everything become peaceful.

Until the night Angel Girl came banging on the back door to be let in.

She rapped on the door with both fists and called out to Mother Magdalen and Solace. Whip Man and Boy let her in. She looked at them, tears all over her face, and said, "It's my wolf. Mr. Sacks' men have him."

"Why?"

"Mr. Sacks is going to tell Solace that it was my wolf that killed Mr. Dennis. I begged him to understand that he had it all wrong. But he said only Solace could convince him of that."

"Then I will," Solace said. We had all crowded in the kitchen to hear.

Boy said to her, "Don't go out to him. He just trying to force you to talk to him, Solace."

She said, "But I have to. I can't just let him kill Grandmother Angel Girl's wolf."

Outside, a howl split the air.

We looked through the open back door, across Mother Magdalen's garden and past the old kitchen and shacks to where men and dogs were crossing the fluffing cotton in the fields.

Among them, twisting and leaping in the blackened light from the new moon, was Angel Girl's silver wolf.

It lunged and got all tangled up in the ropes and chains Mr. Sacks' men had strung on it. Then it cringed and hunkered down among the scratchy cotton stalks as the men beat it down again. Sometimes it jumped to break the bonds and then fell with a thud and jangle of chains. It raised its head and howled as it struggled to its feet with the dogs snapping at it on all sides, staggering and running blood in the men's torchlight, by the time they got it out of the field and coming up the cobbled path to the back door.

Solace slipped her feet into clogs at the back door and ran outside.

When we caught up to her, Mr. Sacks had struck a pose with his rifle aimed square at the silver wolf's weaving head.

Foam dripped from the wolf's bloody jaws. It was shaking its head and looking for Angel Girl, but Angel Girl couldn't get near her wolf for the snapping of the dogs.

Mr. Sacks shouted, "Here's the beast that murdered your grandfather, Solace! My men and I caught it still lurking around the very shack where his body was found."

He cocked the trigger on his rifle.

"No!" Solace shouted, running up close to Mr. Sacks. "This is my dog. You're wrong."

The silver wolf pulled back against the ropes and chains, jerking so some of the men holding the ends stumbled and fell. Their dogs was frenzied and snapped at the men that went down, too. Dust and more shouts rose up all around them. Solace eased up closer to Mr. Sacks and put her hand out to grab his rifle.

But he had got aim, and his rifle went off. The thrust threw them both back. And the wolf leaped backwards in the air and lay still on the ground.

Angel Girl screamed and ran through the blood-mad dogs to throw herself on top of her wolf where the blood pumped.

And Boy ran and snatched up Solace off Mr. Sacks, who had tossed aside his rifle and went to slide his arms around her and grapple with her on the ground. Whip Man, Mr. Tim, and Zion all threw themselves between Mr. Sacks and Boy.

Mr. Sacks' men tried to get out from under their own dogs and let the dogs get close enough to the wolf to keep biting chunks out of it till they got their bloodlust sated. Mr. Sacks had just hauled off and hit Boy solid in the face and sent blood shooting out under his fist.

And two small sounds like thin snakes sliding one after another across a dirt floor slit the night.

Mr. Sacks grabbed at the side of his head, and then at his chest, and he dropped his head back and fell forward on his knees, and then to one side.

The men with the dogs started shouting and whirling to see where was the person who shot the arrows that killed Mr. Sacks.

And then there was the cough.

The whimper.

The roar. The sounds of the wild cat following the scent of all this fresh blood. Everyone stopped in their tracks.

And turned in time to see Myra bound high, crashing through the cotton stalks toward us.

You almost couldn't tell no more she used to be a woman, except she had on shreds of a black dress in rags hanging between her thighs, and she could stand on her hind legs to bare her fangs at the dogs.

She swiped one claw at a dog tangled in the wolf's chains nearest her. It yelped and blood leaped in a spurt, and Myra lapped at it right there in the air.

Mr. Tim and Zion crashed past me into the house.

Whip Man shoved Boy and Solace toward the door, too, shouting back over his shoulder, "Myra, this me! Can't you remember me, girl?"

A man whose dog wasn't nowhere near the wolf nor the cat took aim with his pistol, looked like at my head. But someone grabbed hold of my arm and pulled me to the ground just as the bullet went by.

I landed on top of Jim Feather and cried out at the sight and feel of him. He rolled me over to one side and snatched a pistol out from somewhere around his waist. He shot the man who had shot at him and me.

There was another shot.

A man had let his dog loose to meet whatever fate. He was on one knee taking aim at Jim Feather, to shoot again. Jim Feather grabbed his chest and grunted, and then he hauled out his other pistol with his other hand.

The man watched while Jim Feather shot him. He flipped backward and lay beneath a spreading red spot where his face used to be.

"In the house," Jim Feather said to me, grabbing up bow and pistols in one hand and still pressing the slick dark place on his chest.

We got through the back door just ahead of Whip Man hauling Angel Girl by one arm and saying, "You can't help him, Angel Girl! Your wolf gone."

The dogs that hadn't been brought down was leaping and growling over the place where the silver wolf fell. Somehow, they seemed not to pay no mind to the big cat till she came right up on each one of them, swiping them into the air with first one set of gleaming bloody claws and then the next.

She walked easy among them on her two thick hind legs, turning so you could see her long fangs dripping spit and blood. She had got strong. You could tell when she caught the dead men upside the head with a paw and sent their limp bodies flying.

The men who wasn't dead yet had let loose their dogs and took off running. Their torches bounced in the air, lighting a way to the woods through the cotton fields.

But the dead men had dropped they torches. Some of the dropped fire landed on the cobbles and snuffed out, sizzling in the dirt to nothing. But some of the flames leaped and licked at the puffs of white cotton and caught them and lapped them up and burst in bright sparks and spread.

Solace watched at the back door with the firelight full on her face. "We've got to put this fire out!" she wailed.

Whip Man was still holding Angel Girl back from the door with his eyes on Myra, where she prowled in the flames and yowled and bit into the bodies of dogs and men and then raised her head to slurp at her fangs, feasting.

I hung on Jim Feather, where he had caught himself up against the table. "Mother Magdalen," I begged, "help him. He been shot." She was already going for her kettle on the fire to pour water into a basin of rags. I eased Jim Feather down onto a bench. His pistols and bow clattered to the floor.

Boy went past Solace out the back door with buckets, heading for the well and the pump past Myra. Myra, squatting among the bodies and flames and licking her paws, turned her head to watch Boy run by.

Her ears pricked forward.

She rose light and graceful off her heavy haunches and started after him.

Whip Man shoved Angel Girl over to Solace and took off out the door. "Myra!" he shouted. "Take me! I'm the one you want. Take me!"

Myra stopped and turned to watch him come.

Solace and Mr. Tim and Zion had started out the door, too. But they all drew back open-mouthed at the full firelit sight of Myra's snarling,, curious, catlike face.

But Solace said, "Please! The fire." And they ran on after Boy with more buckets. Angel Girl crept out after them into the chaos to search out the body of her silver wolf before it burned.

I was holding Jim Feather's jaws shut as Mother Magdalen dug out his bullet and washed the wound. And then a sound like wings filled the sky. Heavy flapping.

Outside the door, I could see Myra swing her head on her long-muscled neck to look up toward the new moon. I left Jim Feather with Mother Magdalen to go out and look, too.

At first, I could only hear wings.

But then the black sky filled with long beating bunches of gathered feathers and women's bodies hung between them, flying. As the field took light and belched a ball of fire and noise at the sky, the winged women flew down closer.

As they drew closer, I could tell it was the maids from the townhouse. All had claws and a few had beaks.

A shout went up. Zion raised his arms to the sky and cried, "Mama!" One of the winged women circled low and landed and folded her wings around Zion.

Boy and Solace stopped hauling on the rope at the well to watch. But the flames didn't stop spreading.

The women hovered and beat their wings like to put out the flames in the field. I could smell the sharp smoke from their singeing feathers. It stung in my nose and made my eyes water.

Myra watched and twitched as the flames started to puff into smoke and die. Then she left off prowling after Boy and Solace and went for the winged women.

She had gotten in good among the wings and the smoking cotton stalks, batting at some of the flying bodies, when the women turned their claws and beaks against her.

The cat woman sat still, aiming one paw, as the first women swooped on her. Before she could stretch out an arm to paw at them, they had made quick jabs with their clawed feet at her eyes and nose, making her leap and mew. Then they lifted into the air, out of her reach.

Myra screeched and ducked down into the crumbling stalks. More women dipped into the stalks, after her. You could hear rustling and yowling. The women kept rising and dipping. Every now and then, Myra's black claws reached up and scratched blindly at somebody. The women screeched, diving straight at her now with claws stuck out before, gripping in spasms as if to gouge out her eyes. They would crash, wobble to their feet, stand, and flap up again into the air only to dive one more time for Myra's face.

Myra batted, flipping and twisting to get at the swarm. Her yowls turned to mewls. She was getting scared. She hunkered down low into the smoking stalks, and all of a sudden it was like the fire and the claws shook her. She leaped up out from between the stalks where the fire was edging closer and closer and took off bounding low toward the woods. The flying women kept dipping low and spreading their claws to swoop down at her till she got to the woods and blended into the blackness. We all stood in the smoking field among the fallen and burned bodies and watched the winged women dipping scorched white dresses in the smoking stalks of cotton, chasing the sleek giant cat.

It was powerful and so beautiful, but it was ugly and savage and couldn't no way be really happening.

Then I real eyes that my Jim Feather had come out of the house and stood beside me, leaning on Mother

238

Magdalen. I turned toward him. He spoke first. "Rose Red, go get me one of my pistols."

He had his eye on one of the flying women. She had turned and come back from the woods and was fluttering to the ground in front of us.

She was as small as a beautiful child. Her long white gown was splashed with blood drying down the belly. Tight little braids framed her face and her body dipped and curved, shaping the ruined gown.

She landed and started toward Jim Feather, smiling and holding out her hands to him. Her mouth moved like she was trying to say his name but couldn't.

He wanted his pistol? Was this the other person he had come here to kill?

I went toward the woman. I said, "Go away. He don't need you no more. If you don't go away, you'll get hurt." I shooed at her with my hands like she really was a wild bird. She stopped coming on and looked at us, her little head tilting quick this way and that.

A rustle of wings, and another woman swooped down in a loud flutter. This one was bigger and stronger and as soon as she got to her feet, she reached for the hand of the little, lightweight woman, tugging at her.

The little one, perplexed, pulled back a little. Jim Feather said to me, "Rose, you didn't do what I said?"

I said, "Look at her. She loves you."

She looked at me. The bird woman with her, the bigger one, rose into the air, her powerful wings beating against the still smoke. The little one was lifted by the pull.

She looked back at me and Jim Feather and seemed to spread the sight of us away from her face with the spread of her own wings.

Jim Feather said, "You cost me my kill." There was no anger in his voice.

I said to Jim Feather, "Don't tell me who she was. I don't ever want to know." And I watched her beautiful flight till Jim Feather pulled away from Mother Magdalen and buried my face in that safe space between his chest and his arms. The rag bandage pulled against his muscle and drank up the sweat and tears on my cheek. I rested in the darkness there until he let me go.

And then I turned to see that the whole flock of women, except Zion's mother, rose again into the sky, until you couldn't tell that they wasn't really birds. They didn't glow from inside like the Angel, but they ate light from the moon and stars around them into the feathers of their wings.

They floated on the night air until they disappeared in the dark above our heads, waving back a breeze that smelled of burned meat, charred green cotton stalks, and gunpowder.

Most of us spent the night dragging the torn and burned bodies of the dead wolf and dogs and men into the old burying ditch where the slaveholders used to pitch the field hands. Jim Feather watched as Mother Magdalen packed his wound with herbs.

When the ground was clear of bodies and splashed with buckets of well water, so the sparks couldn't relight, we sat together in the back room and decided on our story.

Mr. Sacks had been hunting the wild cat that killed Mr. Dennis, we would say, but he caught Solace's wolf dog by mistake. And the wild cat just followed the hunters to the farm and killed off as many of them and their dogs as it could.

And if anybody in town real eyes the townhouse maids had flown the coop, we'd just have to say we didn't have no idea they had turned to runaways. That's just what happens when folks is left alone and unsupervised for any amount of time.

Besides. What we all saw was that as soon as Miss Vivian touched the ground and held her boy, her wings was gone. So you could never be quite sure she ever had them. And what if the maids, without their wings, decided to go back to the townhouse? It wouldn't do to have them arrested for running away once they got back home, would it?

Jim Feather and me went back to my ma'am's shack and slept on the bare floor with the door bolted. At night, you could hear the big cat yowl off in the distance.

In a few days, Jim Feather's wound had stopped bleeding. So we left through the woods.

I didn't know how to say goodbye to Angel Girl and Whip Man in their grief, and to Solace and Boy and everybody in all that confusion.

So I didn't say goodbye. Just turned and looked at the plantation stretching gray and black and green up to the crumbling shacks and the dirty big white house. And I looked at my ma'am's shack with its roses, blooming now, white and red. And I wondered if we might ever find my ma'am and my sister.

Could Jim Feather ever stop and settle down, if we did find them? In the meantime, if we kept to the woods and avoided the towns, we just might stay safe.

So in the middle of some strange woods, in the middle of the next winter, my baby was born.

She was pale, almost creamy green she was so light in color, with a swatch of black spikes sticking up off her head just like that fur Boyfriend stuck on the doll he carved for me.

So I named her Willow. And she lived.

# CHAPTER SIX

NOW WHAT DO YOU BELIEVE: VIVIAN, BORN 1766

I didn't believe none of it.

My own boy and Miss Solace too tried to tell me that me and the runaway maids came flying through the sky like birds to the plantation. So I said, "How come you all ain't reached up in the sky and snatched them silly womens down and told them to get back to work?" And I said stuff like, "How come I don't remember flying?" Because sometimes you just have to make your point.

The truth was I did remember flying. The only thing was I knew it never happened because it couldn't happen.

You can't pull nothing over on me. I tend to be strong that way. But my poor Miss Solace, now.

That comes of not having a real ma'ammy to raise her up. She never had no ma'am but me. And I couldn't do nothing more than what the Widow let me do for her.

It broke my heart to come to this plantation, here where Miss Solace had come at last into her own, and find her weeping her eyes out and talking nonsense just like the rest of them ignorant maids. Flying women.

I said, "I don't know how they did it. But I know them *mojo* women drugged us all so they could make a getaway while the Widow was out chasing after her gallivant. And now we got to do the decent thing and bury these here patrollers as good as we can."

The air was thick with smoke and the sound of rushing wings. It felt like any minute vultures and wild chickens would fly down and peck the dead bodies out of your hands.

The dead bodies lay on the ground limp and warm, ripped where the dogs went crazy chomping and munching on a feast of meat and bones before the wild cat got to them, too.

My own boy, Zion, jabbered like a fool, trying to tell his ma'am that the wild cat was a woman. One of the maids, a nasty secretive wench name of Myra. Used to put on airs.

I let loose on my poor boy. Wiped my running eyes and said, "Zion, you ain't never seen no such foolishness as bird maids and cat womens. Let me set you straight here and now. Grab hold of this leg and help me haul this dead man to the burying ditch before he set in to stinking."

Sparks kept setting alight the cotton stalks, all dry and crackly.

I ain't never before set my bare foot on a cotton stalk, thick with blood and bright with a flame waiting to burn. And I was tired from whatever them maids had done to get me out of that townhouse and all the way to the plantation.

We must have run all the way.

I could almost remember running, seeing the maids' faces up close to mine, excited and scared, and something like trees all around us, passing fast.

That must be what the goofy juice done to me: made me so I couldn't remember nothing straight. It was strange to come to, hauling the violated dead to an old burying ditch for field hands that dropped among the cotton stalks. Every time we tossed another body in the pit in the dark, you could hear dry bones crunch and move. And the bodies falling made some kind of sound like, Ugh. And

244

the tree leaves all around just sighed like they was the mourners at a funeral.

No wonder these country goings-on drove my boy to superstition. But I set myself to fight against it.

Soon as we went in the back of the big house to Mother Magdalen's table to drink some hot chicory and get our story together. *What to tell them angry wight peoples when they send the sheriff and a full-blown posse to look for the murdered patrollers? And that stone dead lawyer man.*

I lifted up the wood mug Mother Magdalen set in front of me. "This is your trouble," I told all of them folks. "You don't put fork to mouth that you ain't eating and drinking some *gris-gris* this old conjure woman done goofied up for you. She got you sitting here thinking the maids got wings and Myra done up and killed all of them men and dogs with her bare hands. You just go ahead and tell a story like that to The Man when he come from the city with his guns and his chains. See don't he slap some of them chains on you all and whip some sense into your nappy head. It wouldn't surprise me none if I see you strung up right outside here on some of Miss Solace's willow trees, begging to get cut down and stretched out in the burying ditch with everybody else running around here dying on this property."

Mother Magdalen, that batty old voodoo woman, mumbled something that had nothing to do with it: "Nobody is dying around here while death is dancing."

I looked her straight in her eye. *Enough of signifying. Time to do some specifying.* "That's what I mean," I said. "Listen to her, ranting mojo and nonsense in your face every minute. This claptrap can drive you out of your mind."

I slammed down that mug and slid it back across the table to Mother Magdalen. "I done drunk enough *gris-gris* for one night. Zion, boy, get up and get your ma'am some fresh water."

Zion, all sheepish, looked around the table at this bunch of bedraggled backwoods field hands. I was fixing to remind him I was his ma'am when my Tim said, "Zion, boy, you heard your mother."

So I put my foot down and said, "I ain't seen nothing tonight but how them maids sweet-talked me into dancing and then drugged me to help with their getaway. And I ain't telling no different story and get myself sold away from my boy and my man when The Man come out here with a chip on his shoulder in the morning."

My Tim said, "Shouldn't we have kept out the lawyer man's body from the pit, then? Show the sheriff and the posse how we tried to treat him with special considerations, due to his rank and calling?"

That big bully Whip Man-what an ugly name-said, "Too late now. Unless you want us to drop you down in the pit to go fetch him."

Mother Magdalen cut in again. "Enough of that. Let's burn them all."

*What a hideous woman. What a terrible thing to do.* I sucked my teeth at her. But then it came to me, *On second thought, it might do some good if we could tell the sheriff that, after the fire in the field, we couldn't tell the bodies apart.*

Got to hand it to her. Magdalen may be mojo, but she got her uses.

We all got up from the table but that hag they call Angel Girl. (Lord, the names these people pass around in this house.) And we made our way back through the tree-whispering dark to the burying pit.

The sun just wouldn't rise. I could have sworn we hauled them bodies all night till dawn. But we went off and sat and argued and cussed and hollered, and the sun still wasn't out.

We stood around the pit and tossed in forest trash and dried hay, and then we followed that with kindling and torches, trying to get the bodies and bones to light. Maybe it was the dust of the long dead together with the wet blood of the fresh dead that wouldn't light. But the smoking leaves and hay sizzled out like wet grass.

We decided to cover them with dirt and mulch and tell The Man he can dig them up again, if he want to. None of our affair.

Miss Solace stood on the edge of the pit wiping her eyes and staring down in the trench. She shuddered now and again.

I went over and put one arm around her. I wouldn't want no one to know this, but I always pretended to myself Miss Solace was my own daughter. All my little gals born to me was sold away.

Tending soft scared little Miss Solace, who would pass out in the kitchen with my hot buttered biscuit clutched all soggy in her hand, was my way of getting by.

How I loved that girl child, staring at the charred bodies and breathing their stench and letting these ignorant darkies tell her what to think and how to do.

I would set this whole situation straight after I begged some herbs off that Mother Magdalen to heal my boy's tore up back.

They tried to put us in a room in the big house, talking about, "Everybody has to sleep inside since Myra turned into a cat woman."

I said, "My man and my boy ain't sleeping nowhere near where The Man can say they almost got their hands on a wight woman."

Tim said, "Vivian. It ain't no wight womens around here."

I said, "Did you tell the lawyer mens that?"

And Mother Magdalen dropped my jaw open. "Well, now. There is the outdoor kitchen. It has a large fireplace, so you can cook for your family, and a very solid door."

And when we walked into the kitchen house, with a door and fireplace and a big table with *two* benches pulled up to it, and a hardwood and stone floor swept clean, and a solid roof that never had a leak, I was so glad I remembered my manners enough to say, "Thank you kindly, Mother Magdalen, ma'am."

Copper pans gleamed in the light of our candle on the walls, much better than the savage black iron pots in Mother Magdalen's room. Stacks of china bowls and plates on the walls and metal cooking spoons hung below the mantel above the fireplace. And there was even a long brick oven where a body could lay down and sleep in the winter, if the snow made him sick like it do our Zion.

Me and my man and my son had at last found us a home. We took the bundles of burlap sacking in the corner and spread them out along the wall opposite the fireplace.

That night I dreamed I was flying with the runaway womens. Only this time, I stretched and felt my feet touch the solid ground, and I turned to Myra and said, "See? Your mind can fight the mojo."

248

And she turned and opened her mouth to speak but it was fangs in there that could rip a woman like me in two.

I woke up sweating.

Tim was up and about, heating well water in the fireplace. He has always been good about helping with women's work. He said, "Vivian. You look poorly, baby."

I tried to shrug it off. "Running away do that to you, old man. What you cooking? Coffee?"

Seemed too good to be true out here in the country. But that voodoo Mother Magdalen woke my Tim, knocking at the door to bring us coffee beans and molasses to sweeten it and fixings for cornbread.

I drank down two mugs full, thick and tasty.

Zion was still asleep. I peeled up his shirt where the scars healed good. Went back to the table and said, "Tim, what we going to do?"

Tim shrugged. "Ain't up to us, Vivian. Miss Solace own us now as much as the Widow and Mr. Dennis done before."

I said, "Wait till somebody discover that the maids is run off."

It's a devil skulking through the world and he be listening to every word you say. Because that very day, up to the plantation rode a man in a long black cloak on a gleaming black horse talking about, "Let me speak to Miss Solace, please."

I was in the back room of the big house trying to tell Mother Magdalen that I should cook for everybody and she should stick to her laundry, and it looked to me like the house could use some scrubbing and mending, if she ever got through with the washing.

That old hag Angel Girl was sitting and staring like a zombie. And Whip Man and Boy took Tim and Zion out to clear the burned cotton from the fields. I said, "Plow it under."

And Miss Solace went upstairs with her little dark baby that's going to get her secret husband Boy lynched someday.

That baby sleep uncommon good. Wouldn't surprise me none if we all find out Mother Magdalen done doped up Baby Joy, too.

And, *Wham bam bam.*

Somebody at the door.

I quick told Mother Magdalen, "Go upstairs and tell Solace to primp up her hair. I know how to handle these folks." And I went to the door smoothing my apron.

It was the lawyer man all dressed in black. I know him. But I gave him my little frown like I disremembered.

He said, "Vivian, auntie. You don't remember me?"

I said slow, "Well, sir, Miss Solace and them sure do get a lot of pleasant company out here in the countryside."

He chuckled. "I'm Mr. Shavers, one of the family's attorneys. I've come on some pretty urgent business. I hope my coming so unexpectedly doesn't inconvenience Miss Solace." He took off his hat like he had already been invited inside.

I opened the door wide enough for him-no use putting up a fight before you can win it-and said, "She's poorly, Mr. Shavers. But I'll call her, sir. She'll be that pleased to speak with you for a minute or two."

I showed him to the parlor and near on ran up them stairs. I pushed my way into Miss Solace's room as soon as she undid the bolt. Her and Mother Magdalen stood around gape-mouthed holding Baby Joy.

I said, "It done started. Mr. Shavers here looking for that wretched Mr. Sacks."

Mother Magdalen wanted to offer him some of her green tea.

I sighed. "You can poison him some other time. Today, we already in enough trouble over these folks breaking down the door to get they hands on Miss Solace. Mother Magdalen, you stay out of it."

Then I said, "Miss Solace, mind me like when you was a little bitty girl. Let me dust you up with something smell good-nobody can be so country they don't have no talcum powder-and you go down to him all faint and weak. Leaning on me. Wiping at your eyes like you mourning your beau on top of your grandpap, who lost his life last night defending you."

I said, "And you don't know nothing-*nothing*, hear me?-about them runaway maids till he open his mouth and tell you about them."

And ain't that greedy-eye Mr. Shavers done let his self out of the parlor like he got no home training. He waited and watched at the bottom of the stairs for Miss Solace.

She leaned on me and shed some very real tears in my apron. (It's a shame when the lady of the house can't even carry a hanky.) I guided her down calling out, "She done had a terrible scare, Mr. Shavers. You got any more bad news for her, I don't know what we going to do, sir." And I ain't let go of Miss Solace till I eased her into a parlor chair.

That crazy Mr. Shavers throwed his self on one knee at her feet and said, "Oh, mistress of my heart. Let me help you, my dear Miss Solace. Tell me what has become of Mr. Sacks."

The parlor was dark, but not enough to make you blind. I grabbed Miss Solace shock-looking face and buried it in my thin little bosom and said, "Oh, sir. Let me tell it."

So she hid her face and grinded on her teeth while I told Mr. Shavers how that brave Mr. Sacks had got up a posse to go after the demon cat. I spilled every foolish little thing, wolf, dogs, fire, and all of it but the flying maids.

Mr. Shavers just ate it up. Till it came time for us to hand over the body.

I said, "Sir, we are so sorry. But we can't."

You could feel the anger rise in him. Now he was going to doubt every word I said. These is a bunch of distrustful, suspicious, petty-minded people.

"Can't?" Mr. Shavers asked me.

Miss Solace freed her head out of my grasp and looked up. "Mr. Shavers, what the wild cat left of Mr. Sacks, the torch fires burning out of control further destroyed."

Then she screamed.

And dog my hide if she ain't for real up and fainted to the floor. Me and Mr. Shavers knocked heads, leaping to get to her.

Me, I'm steady shouting fit to bust a lung, "Mother Magdalen! Mother Magdalen, come help me get Miss Solace back in her bed."

Mother Magdalen appeared at the door looking down on Mr. Shavers like he was the lowest kind of trash. I swear that woman wouldn't last a day answering the door at the townhouse.

Between us, we dragged Miss Solace up to bed, with Mr. Shavers talking about how he wanted to help.

I just bet he wanted to help.

252

I said upstairs to Mother Magdalen, "We best get that fool out of this house before the baby wake up and scream and he set himself to searching the rooms."

Solace come around and opened her eyes, big with red veins shot all through to the circles of purest blue. She snatched my hand. "Yes, Miss Vivian. You've got to send that man away. We're in terrible danger, if he stays. I just know I'll betray how much I hated Mr. Sacks."

I worked my hand free. "You both just leave him to me. I'll send him packing to mind his own business."

I went down to him. "You see how it is, Mr. Shavers. The poor thing done lost her grandpappy, and her grandpappy's wife, and now her suitor, all at once and under such dreadful circumstances, sir." Then I looked all hang-dog and went for his hat.

He took it and stood there looking mighty unprepared for the door. He said at last, "Well, I had been taken into Mr. Sacks' confidence. He had his hopes, I daresay, but I'm afraid there were justifiable questions about"-he cleared his throat-"Miss Solace's more distant blood antecedents."

Stopped me in my tracks. "What about her blood, sir?" I said, right puzzled, but he must have thought I was throwing him a challenge because he looked at me like Mr. Dennis had come back from the grave and pulled a sword on him.

Then he drew his self up, above such slanderous gossip about Miss Solace. "Of course, I'll do all I can for her, as a gentleman," he said. "There will be the difficulty of notifying Mr. Sacks' next of kin. They'll want to inter him in their family mausoleum, I'm sure. He comes of old stock."

*Like every brood sow,* I thought. But I tried hard to look impressed.

Only that Mother Magdalen had followed me down and now said from the doorway, "He comes from old stock? As do we all, Mr. Shavers."

Mr. Shavers looked at her sharp-like.

I could have throttled her. I caught Mr. Shavers' eye and twirled my finger around the temple of my head, to show him he was to pay her no mind. "We thank you kindly for all you can do for our poor mistress," I was steady saying as I got him to the door.

And did he do all he could.

We hadn't hardly cleared the burned part of the field and learned to lock that skinny hag Angel Girl in at night, to keep her from hightailing it to the burying ditch and getting herself ate by the wild cat that liked to sit there yowling for blood and pawing at the buried corpses, when a letter came.

From a city far away, on the edge of the sea, with long, sloped handwriting that looked like spiders trailing webs all down the page. Poor Miss Solace tried but couldn't read it.

So me, my Tim, and Zion took her to see the lawyer mens. Tim drove the carriage with Zion along as footman. And I rode beside Miss Solace, so she could have a lady's maid.

Didn't she look miserable.

Zion leaped right smart from the driver's perch and swept that door open for Miss Solace with a bow. Took her fingers as she floated to the ground. She ain't thought to tell him he done good, her being so nerve-racked. So I told him what a gentleman he growed up to be, on my way behind her.

I don't reckon our clothes looked none too good, me and Miss Solace. But she carried her head up and her feet light on the carpet of that office, like her breeding was all on the inside. Folks rushed from all sides to seat her.

Miss Solace held her letter up to Mr. Shavers and a pair of old men who called their self Shavers and Sacks, attorneys at law. She looked sad as was in her heart and said, "Will you gentlemen please explain this to me?"

Just like I told her. "Ladies that can't read and ladies that can is all expected to say the same thing, anyway: 'Will you gentlemens please tell me what's going on?' So just you say what they expect to hear," I told her. "They will take it from there, and it will all work out just fine."

And it kind of did.

Old Mr. Shavers sat stiff in a chair pulled up near Miss Solace and said, "My dear, it's to be expected. Mr. Sacks' relations hope to rely on your near inclusion in their family to assure them of your hospitality, when they come to pay their respects to their lost kinsman. It's quite the proper thing for you to host them. There will be ladies in the party, I understand."

Young Mr. Shavers said, "It's as I forewarned you, Miss Solace. They accept that Mr. Sacks has been interred on your property. You cannot object to their calling."

Miss Solace said, "Of course, I'd never. It's only that the farm is drab and presently so sad. And I am so unused to entertaining."

Young Mr. Shavers said, "May I suggest you offer them the use of your grandfather's townhouse? Surely the Sackses intend no inconvenience to a single young gentlewoman obliged to comfort the aggrieved."

Old Mr. Sacks just sat there looking stern.

Miss Solace rose. "I have been meaning to open and air the townhouse," she said. "While I'm in town today, I suppose I shall have to undertake that sad obligation. So many memories. So many lost loved ones." And she fetched a sigh, deep and good. Near on brought tears to stand in my own eyes. She finished up with, "Would you gentlemen be so kind as to write and invite Mr. Sacks' relations on my behalf? I believe that would be best."

They was already up and bowing. Young Mr. Shavers beat his pap to hand Miss Solace to my Tim, saying, "Miss Solace, I've no wish to distress you further. But we have had odd complaints from neighbors. Other duties have delayed my investigating-"

Miss Solace had her lace-gloved fingers to her mouth. She looked good and shook up. "Complaints, Mr. Shavers?" she said, and her voice was all a-tremble. Right proper, too. Because he was much too close for manners or for comfort.

He said, "We must never forget the savage inclination, my dear Miss Solace. Unsupervised, there is no predicting their behavior."

She said, "You mean my maids."

Young Mr. Shavers was calling for his horse. He rode right alongside our carriage to the townhouse.

I said in her ear, "Miss Solace, why you out here drawing attention to how them maids done flew the coop?"

And she said, "They're going to find out anyway, certainly by the time Mr. Sacks' relations have descended upon us, Miss Vivian. At least let Mr. Shavers witness my surprise."

Mr. Shavers about knocked Zion out the way to hand Miss Solace out of her own carriage and up her front steps. He took her key out of her hand to open her townhouse door.

And a wave of stink that made us all retch and double over came sweeping down the main stairway and out the door to greet us.

Mr. Shavers gagged into his riding gloves. Miss Solace sat down slow on the top step, with her back to the open door. My Zion sat next to her and threw up on the step between them.

Me and Tim staggered all the way back down to lean on the horses.

I recovered myself first. I covered my face with both hands to go back up to the open doorway and shout, "Miss Ella? Myra? You all? Come on out here and explain this, now!"

Then I turned to Mr. Shavers and said through my hands, "Smell like they done been poisoning rats in there like I told them and was scared to pick up the bodies and get rid of them. Bet they all hiding in the carriage house."

He went green around his cheeks. Leaned away from me over the rail to the neighbors' flower bed and threw up in it.

Miss Solace said, "Please, Vivian. Close the door again."

Mr. Shavers took that as a sign we was all leaving. He said, "The farm should do quite adequately, my dear Miss Solace, since the Sackses may there visit their relative's gravesite as often as they wish. I shall write to them immediately to that effect. And you, my dear, must leave me your key so that I may return here with my own hands to search and rid the house of the source of that disreputable odor."

257

Miss Solace said, "You'd bring your own people to clean my house, Mr. Shavers? You are so kind." And she shivered.

He said, "For you, my dear, I'd do that and more. But this is not the time to speak of my intentions."

She said, "How can I ever thank you for your solicitous attentions?"

And he left, weaving, with her key in his vest pocket.

When he was gone, we got in the carriage. Miss Solace said, "Mr. Tim. Let's pull around back to get water to wash the porch and refresh the horses. You do still have your key, don't you? Good."

We stashed the horses in the back and let ourself in through the kitchen door.

The stink was less powerful this time, like it took a breather through the gust at the front door. We took candles and set out to search the room for the source of the stink in pairs, me with my Tim heading upstairs.

The stink cut a path to the Widow's bedroom. We went down her hallway with our candles shaking in our hands. When we pushed in her door, I dropped my candle and strangled on a scream while it was still in my throat.

Horrible, horrible sight, and in the glow from Tim's candle, I could still see it.

The Widow's body had slid out from the mirror and down over her dressing table till her feet stretched out towards us on the floor. But her one arm was caught up and behind her, still in the mirror, so you couldn't see it below the elbow, except like it was a reflection, all bent. The Widow hung from it, like she had died trying to pull it free.

She had been hanging there for a while.

Rats infested our townhouse, like all the houses all over the city. They had gotten to the Widow's cheeks, her eyes, her open mouth. The soft places.

But worst of all, they had gotten to where it looked like somebody stabbed the Widow when she slid out of the mirror, if such a thing could ever happen. The knife was still stuck in her gut, even though the rats ate clean around it.

What was it stuck in? You would have thought the knife would fall out. Maybe all that dried blood held it in there and held it up.

Somewhere downstairs I heard Zion call, "Ma'am? Ma'am, where you all at?" And feet on the stairs, like he was coming to find us and try to help.

Tim hauled me out of that room and pulled the door to behind us.

When Zion and then Miss Solace made their way to us, their candlelight fell on our faces, and I could feel mine was firm and in charge.

"Listen here," I said. "Both of you. Hitch them horses back to the carriage and bring it around close to the kitchen door as it can get. And don't come back in here. It's nosy neighbors got they maids out hanging wash and snooping round. If that Shavers man come back here spying, you all tell him me and Mr. Tim is in here trying to find the maids, cause they scared and hiding. Tell him if he tromp in here like the law and the lynch mob, we never go'n find them. Best he get going. Promise him anything, Miss Solace. You do just like I say, and do everything I say, if you don't want us all to get sold every which way apart."

Then I looked straight at Miss Solace and gave her a look that said, *You included, Miss Light Skin and Blue*

*Eyes. You don't look so wight that those wight lawyers won't be happy to make some money off of you, too.* And I said careful so she could catch my meaning, "Sold if we be lucky. Something else go'n happen if we ain't. Now get."

When I heard them let theirself out the back I turned and said, "Tim, honey. You still with me, now? I think I know what to do."

It was even harder to look on the Widow a second time, knowing what was coming. I said, to build up my nerve, "Poor fool of a woman. Letting that evil gallivant do this to her."

I dropped my eyes to the floor and came up on her. The sight of her stiff feet stuck out and twisted back got to me.

And that sticky pool of dried blood below, evidence of so much pain.

I said, "We will wrap her in this carpet and get her out of here, Tim. Can't save it. The blood done soaked in for weeks now. It's so stained till even I can't get it clean."

And Tim, being such a good man and all, started in to snatching the corners of the rug out from under chairs and bed legs and stools. The hard part was raising up the carpet in our hands to reach around behind the Widow and wrap her in it.

She was stiff as a board, and my eyes fell on her face at last, up close, where the pain had wrinkled up her brows, and the shock stretched down her mouth, and the rats ate the lips away. But I could swear there was still anger where the eyes was gone that led into darkness where she still stared out at us, demanding and disapproving.

Threatening us. Even here, caught and hanging dead on that one arm.

I reached up and tried to pull her arm out of the glass. It wouldn't come. The mirror lifted and thudded back on the wall when I pulled.

I sighed. "Tim, don't look at her. Just reach up behind her arm and lift that mirror off the wall. I'm too short. We going to have to wrap the mirror in the carpet with her."

He set his candle on the side of the dressing table, and the flame started licking up wisps of the Widow's hair where it had worked its way out from her hairpins.

"Hurry," I told my Tim.

And the candle flickered and danced up till you smelled little singes along with the cleansing scent of flame.

I urged him, "Both hands, baby. I got her so she won't fall."

But I was a lie. Because as soon as he brought that mirror down off its nail on the wall, the Widow slid, her head swept the candle to the floor, and she fell.

My stomach went in my mouth in the dark.

I didn't let loose altogether of the Widow. I clutched when she fell, reaching low on her body so as not to touch her face and feel where places was missing, and grabbed at that knife and felt it resist me, like it was coming alive now that she was dead. I could still feel her through the carpet wrapped part way around her, on my side.

I held on under her head with my other hand and said quiet, "Tim? You still got hold of that glass?"

"Yes, baby."

And then he went back to wheezing.

I said, "You a good man, honey. Now take and lay that mirror flat over her somewhere in the middle. Don't feel around on her"-like as if I needed to tell him that, poor man-"but try to recollect where the knife is at and set the mirror over it. Then we going to just flip the carpet over that and wrap it around from your side, too. That should keep her still and in one place till we can get her to that burying ditch back at the plantation."

Tim grumbled at me, "Hope that yowling cat get her and take her off our hands."

But he started in to lower the mirror down so I felt the tug go out of the Widow's body, and I scooped my other arm under her, to keep her from sagging to the floor too soon.

A whiff of rot came up and caught me with my mouth open. "Now, Tim," I said, weak and sick to my stomach, "toss me your side of the carpet."

It came arcing over the Widow's body with a flurry of dust and dead bugs and more deep stink. I threw up in my mouth and ain't had nowhere to spit it till we stumbled out the door, down the stairs, and out the back to the cobblestones.

There, I sprayed my mouthful on the stones and dropped my end of the Widow's carpet, doubling up and retching.

Zion leaped out the carriage, where he had been hiding with Miss Solace. He grabbed my end of the Widow's carpet and held her high so Tim could work his end in through the carriage door.

Me and Miss Solace sat with our feet on the dead body, feeling where the mirror rose up over the knife under the carpet, while the men pumped water in a bucket to slosh away the signs of sickness from the cobblestones and the front porch. They looked in to see could we really stand to ride so cramped with such an awful smell for so far.

I grabbed Tim's hand. "Let's get back to them lawyer mens before that young one come back around here. Tell them we found what was that stink. Say it was fresh meat went bad and rats ate poison and died and rotted, and we dumped it all in the latrine out back and covered it with lye. And tell them they right, can't no Sacks folks stay here till we done had a good long scrub and airing out. And we suspect the maids is run off, scared when they got word Mr. Dennis was dead. Even Ella."

Miss Solace said, "Miss Vivian, I owe you my life. It's the Widow in this carpet, isn't it?"

I said, "Begging your pardon, but what you don't know, you can't tell, Miss Solace. And another thing, Tim. Tell that Mr. Shavers Miss Solace don't want no notice put out against the runaways cause she is hoping they decide to come on home. Now drive on, Tim. We counting on you to pull this off."

I could see his lips mumbling, going over his story, while he shut and latched the door. Then I heard him let his self back in the kitchen and come out again. He went for the lye, to pour it down the latrine. You couldn't never tell if them money-grubbing lawyer mens might check up on our story.

Then me and Miss Solace took off rocking with our feet propped on the woman who used to run and ruin our lives, me thinking, *Strange how the world come around.*

We stopped and my Tim scared me by pulling open the carriage door. He said, "Miss Solace, it ain't no use. I'm sure you the one need to come in and talk to these lawyer men. I know what to say. But it's a safe bet I won't have my mouth halfway open before that young Shavers will be out here all over this carriage, trying to get to you."

I said, "Oh, Tim, please tell me you don't never mean it."

He said, "Yes, I surely do mean it. That young Shavers rapscallion has got that old gleam in his eye, now Mr. Sacks is out the way."

Miss Solace climbed on the seat opposite so she wouldn't have to sit on me nor walk flat-footed on the Widow to get out. I followed her, and Tim and Zion both held me up when I thought I would land on my face on the sidewalk.

I was sure we stunk like the dead.

Mr. Shavers rushed us out to the carriage to talk.

My Tim explained all about the stink and the runaways and don't post no notice on account of our Miss Solace here has got too soft a heart and too many recent shocks. All the while, Miss Solace kept her face in a hanky, turned from Shavers, wiping at her eyes.

She didn't speak till she was turning back to the carriage. Then she laid a hand on the man's arm. "You will be kind enough to return the key?"

And she closed it in her fingers and snatched her hand away just before Mr. Shavers' lips touched her.

Zion and my Tim crowded close to block Mr. Shavers' view inside the carriage while me and Miss Solace climbed back in. I glared at him like I had caught him trying to stare at my mistress's behind through her thin skirt with no stays and hoops to protect her modesty.

He turned on his heel and went back in his office.

Not till we was all the way out of town did I open my mouth and say, "Playing coy ain't go'n do nothing but make him want you more. Right now he's back there wondering what Sacks knowed about you that he don't. Let him wipe his mouth on your hand next time he sees you, if he want to, Miss Solace."

She sighed and looked out the window.

We clopped the carriage around the backside of the plantation house past the shacks, as close to the woods as we could get. Whip Man and Boy sighted us from the field and came running with chopping hoes.

Zion helped me and Miss Solace stumble on up to the house where Mother Magdalen was at the back, holding Angel Girl's hands.

That Angel Girl had aged till she looked gray from hair to dress. She was fading to dust right before our eyes.

Mother Magdalen said, "Solace, Rose Red is gone."

Miss Solace sat on the plank bench pulled up to the big rough table. "Did she come up to the house to say goodbye?"

Mother Magdalen looked up at Miss Solace a long minute. "No."

Miss Solace nodded. "Let's hope for her happiness."

All this eye contact wasn't doing nothing for me. So I said, "One less crazy to feed," because somebody has got to be practical.

Miss Solace went upstairs to wash off the stink and lie down. And I went to my family's kitchen house out back to do the same.

It wasn't till I had eased my back onto my burlap pallet on the floor that it struck me what was so strange, coming back into that house. Baby Joy's ma'ammy been gone all day, and that baby still wasn't crying. *Is it more people in this house caretaking and hiding away that I don't know nothing about?*

I woke when it was night out. You could hear the wild cat coughing over by the burying ditch. Tim and Zion was at the table, slurping stew that had to have come from Mother Magdalen.

I said, "If you all keel over poisoned, I'm going to kill you for touching that woman's grub."

Tim said, "We got the carpet in the ditch and covered it over with dirt."

I harrumphed at him. "Not so deep the cat ain't found it. Long as I'm living, don't you all never let me catch you eating after Mother Magdalen again."

And I turned over and gone on back to sleep.

Relations of the dead patrollers kept showing up for weeks after that, demanding money and pity. I had them stand outside the front door while I went for Miss Solace. She would go get her little set of coins and come down the stairs slow, stirring them around in the palm of her hand with one finger, like she could make it be more of them if she stared hard enough.

I told her, "Charge them for the cotton that patrol burned up for you. That patrol came here to help Sacks, not you."

But she only said she didn't want no more trouble.

The flow of poor wights had barely slowed to a trickle when Mr. Shavers was back at the door with his hat in his hand.

I led him back to the parlor telling him the relatives of all these deceased was wearing poor Miss Solace to a frazzle, like it was her who set the cat upon Mr. Sacks and them. I wanted Mr. Shavers to go after them lowlifes and make them give Miss Solace her money back.

But all he done was wait for Miss Solace to come in the room and leap to his feet saying, "My dear Miss

Solace. May I have the pleasure of reading you the Sacks' reply?"

*Here we go*, I told myself.

That letter was so full of lies about loving Miss Solace like a sister and a daughter already that I couldn't make head nor tail of it. When he finished, Miss Solace just stared.

Mr. Shavers said, "Members of the immediately bereaved Sacks family will be here any day now. This is quite an honor, Miss Solace. It erases any doubt as to your social standing."

Then he bowed and said, "Forgive me," and was gone.

"Lordy," I said. "Now what we go'n do with Baby Joy? You still could pack these peoples off to the townhouse, if you ask me."

Miss Solace shook her head. "And if the maids return, Miss Vivian? Or Ella? It's better not to risk it." Then she looked up at me sharp and sudden. "You could keep my child, Miss Vivian."

The good thing was that tending to Baby Joy over in the kitchen house kept me out of the big house, where Angel Girl sat crumbling to dust in the back room, and Mr. Sacks' sister stalked Miss Solace up and down the stairs. I would come in early in the morning with some breakfast cooked like city folks likes it, because that Mother Magdalen didn't cook nothing but cornbread and stew and witches' brew day in and day out. I would set the hot breakfast in its covered pots and trays on the dining room table and leave it for Mother Magdalen to sweep down cobwebs and set everybody's places. And then I would go on up the stairs to help Miss Solace get her hair looking like a lady should.

267

Not that I was good at it. But anybody was better than Miss Solace.

She'd be standing at the wash basin fretting over Boy, out with his pap nights in Rose Red's old shack. And I suspect she fretted about her baby, too, though she was too courteous to let on about it to me.

We would talk while she sat at the table by the window, looking down at the gravestones and beyond, where the woods led to the burying ditch.

Which was no longer all that covered up, mind you.

That cat ain't never stopped scratching to get at them ripe-smelling fresh roasted bodies. You could fall asleep listening to its yowling rage and hear it prowling closer amongst the open shacks in the Quarters, sniffing old rocky animal droppings and hissing at the moon. You could hear it bumping through the empty doorways and knocking around abandoned cooking stones.

Sometimes the cat come clawing and sniffing around Mother Magdalen's garden right upside our kitchen house. It would be the middle of the night, we all been asleep for hours, and Baby Joy would like as not wake up and whimper for me to get her out of her cradle. Scared of the cat.

I'd come get her and sing, "Hush, Baby Joy. Hush-a-bye."

You could see poor Zion's eyes bugging and shining in the dark. He ain't said nothing, though, but once he asked where was our chamber pot.

I said, "Zion, baby, you send that cat some fresh strong smells like that under our door, and it is like as not to pounce and come down our chimney, looking for you. Just wait till it's gone."

Every day the men went out to shovel and pack the dirt down on the burying ditch again. We listened to the shovels and hoes whacking while I did Miss Solace's hair and caught her up on Baby Joy's doings. "Shame that child ain't going to grow up knowing her ma'am, if these freeloaders don't soon hit the road," I took to saying.

Because time was passing, and them Sackses wasn't getting no closer to the door. It was only two of them. But they was about to send for more.

Daughter Sacks, young and single and with a sharp eye like a knife that cut you up and down every time she caught sight of you. And Father Sacks, leaning way back in his wicker chair.

The chair had big wheels at the bottom that would creak and grind when Father Sacks used his legs to make the wheels go: shuffle, shuffle, scuttle, scoot.

You'd be walking down the upstairs hall, minding your own business, and you'd see Father Sacks down below, scuttling from parlor to dining room like some big bug, trying to get to the table before Mr. Shavers and Miss Solace and Daughter Sacks. Sneaking food.

Oh, yes. Mr. Shavers turned up right often these days. Not that he needed the food. He claimed he was paying his respects to the close relations of the deceased, carrying Father Sacks and his chair up and down the stairs all day. He didn't fool me. He wasn't here doing nothing but edging up close and making sad eyes at Miss Solace.

Or maybe you'd be downstairs trying to get out the house, and Father Sacks and his chair would go scuttle-walking by in the hallway upstairs, heading to spy on Miss Solace alone in her room or go hole up with Daughter Sacks, whispering and snickering till late in the night. He would come out and pause from these midnight parleys with the light from the stained glass bursting on him like fire sparks while he glared down at you, staring up at him from below.

I always wondered why Father Sacks wouldn't just get up and walk.

I broke down and asked Mother Magdalen to give me some poison to cook in some food and leave it around, waiting for Father Sacks to sneak and steal it and eat it and die.

But Mother Magdalen let on like she ain't heard me.

I got up in her face. "They go'n live here for the rest of they life. That Daughter Sacks and Mr. Shavers has got a foot race on to see who can get Miss Solace to the altar first and lay claim to the most of her money. They got Boy setting up in my house day and night bawling his eyes out over Baby Joy, talking about his wife done left him, and she a prisoner in her own home."

Mother Magdalen was undressing and washing up Angel Girl and ain't said a single word.

It was strange about Angel Girl.

She was all humpbacked and withered up at the table, bent in like something hurt her so bad she couldn't straighten up. You hated to walk through Mother Magdalen's back room for fear of catching sight of this miserable old hag hunkered at the table, one arm all curled in like a dead leaf and the other hanging limp like it was going to fall off and hit the floor.

But let Mother Magdalen strip her to bathe her and change her clothes, and you wouldn't know it was the same woman. You'd swear she was her own grandchild, a woman fresh and lovely enough to turn my young Zion's head.

Of course, I ain't let him nowhere near the house when Mother Magdalen was bathing Angel Girl. I shut and drew the bolt on the back door, too, to keep the rest of them mens out.

But I couldn't keep out that creeping Father Sacks.

Wasn't a thing I could do about that bug, crawling up on people and letting on like he was crippled and not to blame for his actions. I looked up from Angel Girl's bath many a time and seen that sharp-faced Father Sacks rocking back in his wicker chair in the doorway, watching with a little bright line of spittle trailing down the side of his chin, till Mother Magdalen got Angel Girl dressed back in some clothes and hunched back in her corner at the table, old and bent and crumbling to dust again.

Maybe it was Angel Girl I should have got that poison for. But I ain't thought of that till it was too late.

I let myself into my little kitchen house one night just after sundown, back late from attending on Miss Solace in the parlor with that Daughter Sacks again, trying to talk Solace into marrying some Sacks cousin or other who wanted to come a-courting.

I wasn't thinking about nothing but how was I going to teach Miss Solace to say so little she wouldn't need to back up and take her foot out of her mouth the next day, cause them Sackses was going to have Miss Solace married to one of them in no time, at this rate. She just couldn't out-think them.

And the door to the kitchen house creaked inwards.

I could have sworn I seen and heard wings, bigger than a vulture and making black shadows all around me. I felt the feathers brush me and the wind from them wings fanning me.

And then it was gone. But it felt to me like something else was gone, too.

I went to the cradle, peered in and screamed.

What was gone was Baby Joy.

The men had finished in the field and was packing down the dirt on the burying ditch for the night. I heard them come running.

They broke in through the open door and my Tim grabbed me. "What is it?" he said, shaking my shoulders.

"Baby Joy!" I sobbed and pointed to the cradle.

Boy let out a holler and took off running to the big house. He slammed open that back door, and we heard shouts and loud calling that carried back and told us Boy was on his way up them stairs, no permission asked.

Whip Man and Zion got to the house ahead of me and Tim. Beyond their broad shoulders, I seen Mr. Shavers loading his pistol at the bottom of the stairs.

When did he get here? And what's he doing calling so late?

Mr. Shavers started up the stairs after Boy. Everybody followed him, shouting and pleading.

Everybody but Father Sacks.

And me.

Father Sacks waited till they all rushed up the stairs after Mr. Shavers on the hunt for a darky gone wild, like he figured they was all prone to do. I backed into Mother Magdalen's back room, out of Father Sacks' sight.

I couldn't have said why. But it looked to me like he was a greater danger to Miss Solace and all of us tonight even than Mr. Shavers' pistol.

Father Sacks turned that big wicker chair and started down the long stone hall, creaking and grinding and shuffling.

That was where the maids and Myra used to be locked up, losing their mind. Didn't nobody never go down that way no more but Mother Magdalen, leading Angel Girl to bed after the wild cat stopped coughing over the ditch every night.

I didn't like to go down there. But it surely looked to me like Father Sacks was up to no good.

So I followed after Father Sacks.

The torches wasn't never lit no more on the stone walls in that hallway. I had to follow with my hands on the smooth stones, listening to the scuttle and creak of Father Sacks' chair to guide me.

It was easy, all the way to where he turned his chair to go into one particular room lit by some strange light, like candles that don't flicker.

I crept in right behind him.

And stopped, bumping upside the back of his tall wicker chair.

In the far corner, you could see Angel Girl on a bed, sitting up a little more alert than usual. But in front of Angel Girl, shedding light everywhere, was a woman lit from the inside and fanning the most tremendous, glorious wings, swish on the floor, and swish in the air above our heads, sending a scent like flowers on a breeze, like a fresh wind.

She was holding Baby Joy who was not, in no way whatsoever, crying.

Angel Girl, and the winged woman all alight, and Baby Joy in her arms, they all turned to look at me and Father Sacks, standing in the door like we came in together.

And then the winged woman looked right in my eyes with something like the deepest sorrow I have ever seen. She tilted her head to study me, and her face was sweet.

And then she started to fade, right before my eyes.

Just before she was gone, and the baby was floating alone in the air, I rushed forwards. I had to shove that giant wicker bug chair out of my way. I heard Father Sacks cry out when the chair went over.

I caught the baby, but she wasn't floating. I felt warm arms, tingling like I was touching-I don't know-sparks from a fire. Warm arms still had Baby Joy, even if I couldn't see them.

I snatched Baby Joy and looked at Angel Girl, who stared back at me in the sparkling light left by the burning woman. She looked calm, like she was questioning me and waiting, saying, *Well, Vivian. Now what are you going to do? Now what do you believe?*

Father Sacks yelled bloody murder on the floor with his giant wicker chair tumbled on top of him, wheels spinning.

I pressed Baby Joy in close to my chest and took off running for the stairs.

I could still hear shouts and bellowing. *Good! That fool young Shavers ain't killed Boy yet.* I followed the noise to Miss Solace's room, panting and calling out, "You all! Stop! I got the baby. Look! I found Baby Joy."

But when I squeezed inside that room, I could see Baby Joy wasn't the point no more.

Boy and Miss Solace looked over at me, and relief and happiness was all over their faces, for the whole world to see.

And that Daughter Sacks sure did turn and see it.

But Mr. Shavers was struggling with Whip Man and even my Tim and my poor Zion, who plucked at his fingers to try to get his pistol.

But as soon as Zion got the pistol free from Mr. Shavers, Daughter Sacks came and took it from his hand. "I'll keep this for our guest," she said.

So the men got him wrestled out the room and down the stairs, Mother Magdalen following behind saying, "I'm certain Miss Solace has stocked some nice brandy, Mr. Shavers. That will calm you down, sir."

Us three stayed behind with the baby. I held her out for her ma'am to see and not touch in front of Daughter Sacks. "See," I said. "Angel Girl came and took her to hold. Crazy old woman like to scared me to death." And I chuckled to show it wasn't no big thing, after all. "Must have heard her crying while I was waiting on you all in the parlor, ma'am," I blathered on, trying to warn Miss Solace away with my eyes. "I'll just take my baby on back to my kitchen Quarters now," and I backed towards the door cause Miss Solace was fast chasing me down.

I tried to turn my back and keep her hands off her baby, but she got hold and pulled the baby from me. Soon as Baby Joy was in her mother's arms, she went to reaching for her mother's teats and smacking out her little sucking sounds. She wanted to nurse. I said, my voice all stern, "Miss Solace!"

But she had already pulled down enough of the front of her dress to give Baby Joy her breast. And Boy went to put his arm around her shoulders and started in to laugh and wipe the worried tears from his face and his wife's.

And only then did Daughter Sacks say from her corner, "Solace. Solace, dear. Would you like to be alone now? Should I send away Vivian?"

And they finally looked up and realized what they had done. And in front of who.

Daughter Sacks came forwards at last to rest her hand on poor Miss Solace's burning cheek. The baby gooed and cooed, so glad to have a real breast after all them treacle teats.

Daughter Sacks said, "Solace, dear, I've always suspected. My brother, God rest his precious soul, suspected, too. But he wanted to give you a chance. And respectability. And I am determined to honor his wishes. So, Solace, dear, is this the child you had with my brother?"

I made a sound like I was strangling. Boy's face went slack with shock. Only Miss Solace ain't seemed to understand what this woman was saying.

Daughter Sacks tried again. "So this is the child you and my brother had, in your love and loneliness. Your poor child betrays your unfortunate lineage, doesn't she? I understand why you are forced to keep her hidden. If your race were known, you'd lose everything, wouldn't you, Solace? But never fear, my dear. For I love you like a sister, as I've told you. And I will treasure all your secrets, shared with me because you trust me. The secrets of your sin and of your shame. The one which betrays the other. For your sake and my brother's, who loved you, Solace, I will shelter you in his family, as he would have done had he lived. Now do you understand me, my dear?"

Daughter Sacks let go of Miss Solace's cheek, where the blush had bleached whiter than Daughter Sacks' hand. She said, "It is time we got rid of your rather bothersome new suitor. I believe he came tonight in such a lather because he has worked himself up to propose. I admire your resolution to have nothing to do with him. If he discovered your race, as my brother did before his tragic passing, there is just no telling what Mr. Shavers would have done to you."

As she left, Daughter Sacks closed the door behind her. And Miss Solace and Boy sat there on the bed, still staring at Baby Joy between them.

I said, "Oh, Miss Solace. Leave it to me. I will think of something."

As I clicked the door shut behind me, I heard Boy say, "Solace. I was so scared it was the cat woman who got our baby. Can you forgive me for what I done tonight?"

When I got to the bottom of the stairs, my Tim and Zion was wheeling Father Sacks to Mother Magdalen's back room as he moaned and swayed in his wicker chair, his feet still scuttling underneath him.

Daughter Sacks stood at a distance, saying to Mother Magdalen, "As soon as you are free, I'd like that brandy for Mr. Shavers. He and I have some talking to do."

I went up close behind Daughter Sacks in the doorway, just to make her jump when I started talking. "Mother Magdalen, don't you think it's time you brewed up that special potion I have been asking you to make for Father Sacks? It's a stone shame how you let that man suffer, Mother Magdalen, with him and Daughter Sacks near on family to our Miss Solace, or so they tell me. Why you don't make up a nice warm mug of brandy for him, too?"

Daughter Sacks gave me a look like, if she missed my meaning, it couldn't have been too important, anyway.

In the darkness of the back room, Mother Magdalen stoked the fire till it flared. She said, "Yes, Vivian. I have

277

that potion all ready. I suppose it has never seemed urgent that I offer it. I've been short-sighted."

I clicked my tongue and said, "Oh, Mother Magdalen, when you get our age, you figure out that if you don't take care of what don't seem important, you go'n be taking care of it when it gets crucial. Like Father Sacks' condition tonight. It's crucial."

Daughter Sacks said, "I *have* asked you for a brandy for Mr. Shavers, Mother Magdalen."

Mother Magdalen's hand reached out of the darkness with a curved bowl of clear glass on a short, thick stem. Dark liquid sent up fumes from inside the crystal goblet.

Mother Magdalen's voice drifted out of the darkness. "This is for Mr. Shavers, and I'm preparing one for your father now, Miss Sacks."

But Daughter Sacks was already on her way.

I told myself, *Think fast*. And just in the nick of time, I said to Father Sacks, who was moaning already, "We best get that brandy in you and get you upstairs. You don't want to still be sitting here when Mother Magdalen gives that dimwit Angel Girl her bath."

He looked up at me with his watery eyes jumping. Now he was going to stay put for good. That line of drool was already running when I left him to go after his daughter in the parlor.

She already gave the brandy to Mr. Shavers and was watching him drink it down. Whip Man stood guard and looked up at me, wary. Daughter Sacks said, "Leave us, you two. Mr. Shavers and I would like to speak privately."

I said, "Why, Miss Sacks. Landsakes. I couldn't never leave a gentlelady such as yourself alone with a gentleman so distressed and not his self. Miss Solace would never forgive me if I let Mr. Shavers up and do something to you he's going to regret later. Gentlemens do these things sometimes. It be in they nature."

"Shut up, Vivian," said Daughter Sacks. "Listen in all you want to. You can't affect anything. Mr. Shavers?"

He looked up from his glass, woozy with high feelings and fumes, and said, "Yes, miss? Am I alone in my concerns for Miss Solace's safety in such a house? Where any buck can take a notion to violate her privacy and tear through the rooms, bellowing like a bull? Don't you understand that she's at the mercy of her own property?"

Daughter Sacks had a smile on her lips like a curled snake. "I fear it is you, Mr. Shavers, who do not understand. I have always heard that these women's charms surpass understanding in their power over men such as yourself and my brother, our society's cream. But I have never before witnessed how they captivate and reduce otherwise insightful and discriminating men to helpless emotionality."

Mr. Shavers, losing patience, said, "Meaning, Miss Sacks?"

Daughter Sacks sneered in the man's face now. "Meaning that the misplaced baby had our Solace so distracted because it is all she has left of my brother, Mr. Shavers. Had you really no idea why she had no interest in you?"

Mr. Shavers and Whip Man both leaped toward Daughter Sacks. It was me held back Whip Man, and that barely."

But Mr. Shavers ain't stopped till he was facing down the barrel of his own pistol.

He stopped, red-eyed and roaring like a castrated bull, "You dare! You *dare* imply! If you were a man, Miss Sacks! If you were *only* a man!"

Daughter Sacks waited till he backed away from the gun. She was shaking, but she went on talking in the face of his rage. "Dear Solace has commissioned me to undertake to free her of your oppressive suit, Mr. Shavers. You cheapen her devotion to my brother with your passionate attentions. Your presence in her bedchamber tonight has blasphemed the honor he intended to bestow upon her and compromised the protection with which he sought to shroud her unfortunate history. All his talk of marriage was a gentlemanly charade. Yours is a travesty. You have been fooled."

Mr. Shavers threw his brandy glass against a wall. "Lies!" he shrieked as it shattered, and his voice shook.

Daughter Sacks went on like a sledgehammer to the brain. "No, Mr. Shavers. Not lies but the brutal truth, made necessary only by your importunate indiscretions. I have taken it upon myself to safeguard our Miss Solace in my brother's memory and with my family's name, as indeed he wished to do himself. We have, I believe, a great-uncle in your office who may supervise Miss Solace's finances, in future? It would be indelicate to have you, her rejected suitor, continually interposing yourself in her affairs."

Shavers pointed a trembling finger at Daughter Sacks' face. "You are discovered!" he intoned. "You know that Miss Solace is the rare solvent planter, due to her grandfather's inheritance and her own frugality. You mean to defraud her, Miss Sacks."

Daughter Sacks smiled. "As did you. Come now, Mr. Shavers. No more feigned innocence. Miss Solace will not thank you for bringing her secrets to light in your efforts to protect her. Her race. Her baby. Poignant, is it not, that Miss Solace and my brother's passion should gain such dignity and-dare I suggest-morality, upon his death?"

Mr. Shavers turned and yelled at Whip Man, "My hat, boy! My cape!" And as he banged open the front door with his pistol still pointing at him from behind, he shouted back, "Lady Sacks, you and I are not done!"

His horse hooves ain't stopped clopping down the drive before you could hear another sound rumble up from the back room.

Daughter Sacks had been standing in the parlor, fingering the gun like she was trying to figure it out. I begged her to take a brandy toddy to bed to steady her nerves just as she sank to the sofa and said, "My land, but that man was bigger than I ever realized." She went to laugh off her nerves after the encounter with Mr. Shavers.

But then the gagging and thrashing and banging broke out.

I couldn't stop her from running to the back room. First we seen Angel Girl gleaming in the firelight with water running down her lean young body. Mother Magdalen washed her, stooping and rising all around Angel Girl, sloshing and sending down the water in little rivers and streams from her washing rag.

Next I seen my Zion and Tim upside a wall, staring someplace in the direction of Angel Girl's feet, standing in a basin.

I yelled, "What have I told you about standing round watching these country womens bathe in the kitchen?"

Tim looked at me and pointed.

Father Sacks done slid out his chair and lay wriggling around on the floorboards like he done finally lost the use of his legs. While we watched, he stopped breathing and sent a glob a something dark and thick out of both ends of him.

Mother Magdalen and Angel Girl kept washing. But Mother Magdalen said, "Oh, Whip Man. I did warn Father Sacks that if he drank his brandies so quickly he might choke. And now he has. So many deaths, such a shame. But we can't risk drawing the wild cat to our door with this smell, can we?"

Behind me, Daughter Sacks took off running, shouting out the front door for Mr. Shavers to wait for her. I told Zion and Tim to go after her.

Whip Man hefted the body off the floor like he ain't even minded all the filth that was touching him. And he went for the back door round Angel Girl, while she stepped from the basin for Mother Magdalen to dress her.

Mother Magdalen said, "Nobody touch the basin. I'll use the water to wash the death throes off the floor. I had no idea he'd drink it down so quickly. Did we disturb the conversation in the parlor?"

I started to explain but closed my mouth. Another sound.

Whip Man and Tim and Zion had left the front and back doors open. Wind gusted straight through the house. Just a little breeze, but steady.

Carrying the clear cough of the cat.

I turned and went after my men, out the front door yelling, "Tim! Zion! Get back in here. That cat is coughing!" I heard shouts and ran down the gravel to see could I catch sight of where they had got to.

That's why I seen the tall thick shape, all curves, like a cat but like a woman, too, with breasts, sleek and black upside the night that couldn't be as black and as huge as she was, walking on her hind legs up to the edge of the stand of trees along the side of the main road to watch and wait and tense and then leap forward on all fours.

The cat woman leaped and landed square on that thin line that was Daughter Sacks. Daughter Sacks' skirts had been flying out behind her while she ran. Now they fluttered to the ground under her.

I heard screeching and screaming. Ripping the throats that sent them. Tearing into the night.

And under the screams as they died rose up a sound like purring. Like a tongue drumming on the roof of the mouth.

And then a gunshot. Soft, like in a pillow. The purring stopped.

The cat grunted.

Zion and Tim caught me at both my arms and I let them carry and drag me back to the house, where the great front door still stood open to the light inside. I was sobbing when they got me into the back room.

Mother Magdalen had finished washing up after Father Sacks on the floor. She stood at the back door with the basin of filthy water and rags at her hip, looking out towards the burying ditch.

My Tim and Zion sat me next to Angel Girl, on her bench. I fumed, "You all can*not* go out there, you hear me? You *stay* in this house!"

Mother Magdalen fretted, "I do wish Whip Man would come back and dump this basin for me. What could be keeping him at the trench?"

Boy came down into the back room and looked around, fretful himself. "You all. What is it?"

Solace probably sent him. Tim said, "Mr. Boy, Father Sacks dead. Your pap went to drop him in the burying ditch."

Zion said low, as if to nobody in particular, "The cat is out there, eating on Daughter Sacks right now."

Boy took off past Mother Magdalen. Soon you heard arguing, loud, coming all the way from the ditch. Shouting and the whack of garden hoes biting into the packed earth. Even if Boy was helping Whip Man dig, they wasn't getting that ditch open too fast.

Mother Magdalen dropped her basin and took off after them.

Then you could hear her voice, too, raised. You could almost see the shape of Mother Magdalen, out there just into the trees in the dark, wave her arms and tug now at Boy, now at Whip Man. Where was that demon cat?

I went to the stairs and called to Miss Solace. She came to the head of the stairs with her baby. "Yes?"

I pleaded, "Miss Solace. Mr. Boy and them is out there at the burying ditch, trying to get rid of that Father Sacks. He died, you see. But the cat be prowling, and we afraid they're in danger. Mother Magdalen went to fetch them back in the house, but that ain't did nothing but make more ruckus to draw the cat."

Miss Solace flew down them stairs and handed me the baby in passing. Baby Joy clung and cooed while I held her in the doorway, watching Miss Solace disappear into the dark that had gathered like a friend for the cat.

You could hear more shouting break out. They was all calling to Miss Solace to go back.

My Tim yelled at me, "Get out that door, Vivian! You deaf and can't hear that cat coming?"

It was true.

You could hear her coughing and yowling and steady coming on round the side of the house where the gravestones leaned and, beyond, where the burying ditch stank.

She was already between the ditch and the back door. How was they going to make it back here?

As Tim yanked me out the way and went after the door, to shut it, I hollered out past him, "You all! Come back *now*. She's coming!"

A loud roar like thunder split the black air just when Tim slid the bolt, and we stood together, shivering. Only Angel Girl sat still and stared, not quite into the fire.

A crack on the door like somebody buried an ax in it and Boy's sharp voice said, "Let us in!"

Tim tried to snatch at Zion and keep him from the door, but my boy broke past his pap and said, "Pa, we got to open up. They could get killed."

All of them tumbled in through the open door together. They eyes was staring scared and big, and they was breathing hard from running and from fright.

But not Whip Man. He wouldn't let nobody bolt the door, nor even shut it. He stood in the doorway and stared off towards where the cat screeched in the dark though it had got so dark you couldn't see nothing past the Quarters.

Mother Magdalen went and put her hand on Whip Man's shoulder. "When death danced out back, no one died here," she said, and he tilted his head over toward her like that meant something to him.

285

I said, "Miss Solace, we can't go out now. Tell me where me and my poor Zion and Tim go'n sleep tonight."

We got one of them big stone rooms with hay on the floor, next to where Father Sacks had went after Angel Girl. I had to sleep light. It made me sad to admit to myself I was afraid what my Zion might do, so close in the night to that staring, dimwit, young-in-body old hag, Angel Girl.

I kept waking up to feel for Zion in the dark. When my fingers ain't reached him, I shot to my feet. "Zion!" I called. In the black, I couldn't see Tim neither. "Tim!" I screeched.

I felt around in the hay on the stones. Gone. For sure. Both of them.

I went to the doorway. You couldn't see nothing but the light where the stone hallway let out near Mother Magdalen's back room. The torch sconces on the walls was empty.

"Angel Girl!" I pleaded. "Tim? Zion? Where you all at?"

I found my way to the back room. I couldn't take no more how everything around here always went wrong.

The back door was open, but nobody was in sight.

Except way far off, over at the covered up burying ditch.

The gray light of early morning filtered through the trees at the edge of the woods, and I could see the clustered brown lumps of all the people from the house.

I went towards them. I was close up when I finally realized what they was doing: standing around and kneeling to be close to Whip Man.

He sat under the still cat on the burying ditch, where the earth was filled in and packed hard. You could see the

286

dents of the chopping hoes, where the men tried to dig up the earth in a hurry last night. All around the ditch area, moss and wild grass still grew undisturbed. And a little ways off, that silver mirror from the townhouse gleamed out from under shreds of the carpet we had wrapped around it. I fretted for just a moment, *How'd the cat get that mirror out the ditch? And where has the Widow's body got off to? Has she crawled out the mirror, dead and stabbed and whittled down to pieces of herself? Or did the cat eat her out?*

But now I had to think of Whip Man, who looked dead, pinned under the great wild cat. I said, my voice breaking, "Why don't you all pull him out from under her? Bury him decent over there where you say you put his wife." I pointed back towards the headstones under Miss Solace and Mr. Boy's bedroom window.

Whip Man raised his eyes and looked at me, and I could see now they hadn't really been shut. Just looking down steady at the head of the great cat resting on his lap.

The folks turned towards me as Whip Man explained. "This my fault, Miss Vivian. Help me tell them. I can't rest easy with my good wife. They got to leave me with Myra when I die."

Miss Solace came to me, still holding her baby, and took my arm with her free hand to lead me to the group. She muttered, "He's blaming himself. I made them leave Father Sacks' poisoned body on top of the ditch last night when the cat came. Myra ate Father Sacks and died."

Whip Man moaned, "Slow. She was still suffering when I found her out here this morning. You ought to understand, Boy. You know about love. I love this woman. She gave me back my life. Don't take me from here. Look what I done to her."

Mother Magdalen said, "You, Whip Man?"

Whip Man nodded. "Was me took Myra out to the death dancer to be brought back to life."

Mother Magdalen shook her head. "You took Myra out to the death dancer to be saved, Whip Man, but, instead, Heaven took Myra's body and all her powers. Just as she had taken Mammy Water's bones and powers. How were you to know what Heaven would do?"

Angel Girl squatted on the ground near Whip Man. She looked up now from her endless silent staring and said, "You couldn't do a thing about Heaven, Whip Man. Heaven did this to Myra. You didn't. Leave it."

Angel Girl stood up. She looked down at Whip Man and said in a voice all of a sudden strong, "Or die in peace, if you want to die. I'll make sure they bury you with Myra, when you're gone."

And then she sprinted toward the woods.

Her long clawed toes gouged up moss and pine needles and tossed them behind her in little tufts as she ran, and I blinked after her, shocked at how she'd talked.

Next thing, I was watching a silver wolf run after her trail. *She better be careful*, I thought. *We'll be burying her, next.*

Tim said, "This a shame, you all."

Zion said, "Ma'ammy, you talk to him."

Mr. Boy joined in. "Miss Vivian, won't you help me save my pap?" His voice choked.

I raised my hands, helpless. "Boy, I feel for you, with everybody thinking about they self and acting in such a way as to tear you up. Whip Man, look at your son. Your womens is gone, but your child still need you."

Whip Man did look up from under the weight of the great cat on his lap, and I seen for the first time where a line of dark slobber trailed out from between her fangs and down between Whip Man's legs to make bloody mud.

Whip Man was grim. "I done everything I can to help Boy have the woman he love and they baby, too. He need to let me go in peace now, like Angel Girl said. Some you all don't understand what it feel like to lose... " and he let his voice trail off while he stroked the cat's fur and looked at it like this was his first time seeing it up close.

Up close and still like this, it really did look not just like a woman, but like Myra. Darker, shiny black with that fur, and stronger, with them giant cat muscles rippling under the skin. But softer, with Myra's nose poking out between the whiskers, and the fangs looking so shiny and pointed and pearly, now she couldn't hurt no one. Her little bright pink tongue lolled because of the way Whip Man had moved her to talk to me, with her head tilted back so sunlight fell on it.

The first fly came and landed where her eye was part open.

Mother Magdalen reached down to brush away the fly and press the lid closed. She said, "Whip Man is trying to tell all of us that we don't know what it feels like to lose someone we're bound to."

I thought, *How could Whip Man think that about Mother Magdalen?* Because even I knew who was buried under the angel statue in the gravegarden by the house. *How could Whip Man think that about anybody here?* I thought of my lost babies and glared at Whip Man.

Mother Magdalen was still talking. "Heaven brought him back to life once, and he was bound to Heaven. Then Myra gave his body life, and he was even more bound to Myra. Now that Heaven and Myra are one, and dying, we can't imagine the pull they have together on Whip Man.

We can't tell him that he should bear and resist something that would kill anyone."

*Didn't kill you,* I thought. *Didn't kill me, no matter how much you and me wanted to die.*

But Mother Magdalen had had her say and now left, too, dragging that silver mirror through the dirt to the back door. I stared after her, wondering what crazy things she had just poured in all our heads, and we ain't even resisted it.

After a while of fanning Whip Man and the flies off that cat woman, me and my mens had to go inside, too. That kind of thing will get to you. You feel helpless and can't take it no more. And when the sun got high and Baby Joy started to crying, Miss Solace came in at last.

But the day dragged, and some folks went back and forth to the ditch, never resting nor really working, just trying to beg Whip Man to let loose of the cat and come back in the house and keep on living.

We never knew how he made it through that first night. He might not have made it, if Boy hadn't sat guarding him with a chopping hoe from the prowling beasts. Boy said he would keep an eye out for that crazy Angel Girl, too, who chose now to turn up missing.

Boy dragged in tired in the morning. "Angel Girl said don't neglect my family. Said she can keep watch at night from now on."

I said, "Angel Girl? When she say all that? I ain't heard her say all that to you, and I was there when she left. What good she ever do anybody anyway, unless she go'n throw herself to the wild beasts before they get to Whip Man?"

Tim said, "Vivian, you don't never catch on how you don't know everything."

I got quiet. Cause Tim don't tend to talk to me like that. What was wrong with me trying to make sense of things?

The second morning Whip Man woke up laid out on the burying ditch, I begged Mother Magdalen for some more of that stuff she gave Father Sacks. None of us didn't need to watch no more what this crazy man was up to.

Mother Magdalen put it in brandy and wouldn't give it to me. I followed her out to where Whip Man was stretched out.

His lips was crusted gray, and his head was lolled back against a little tree. It looked like a cramp in his leg had hooked his foot up ugly. But he wouldn't wiggle out from under that stiff cat.

Flies was burrowing in.

Mother Magdalen got on her knees by Whip Man. "I'd give you something milder, but wouldn't you rather go quickly? Or I can go get you fresh water, and you can live."

Whip Man said thick, "Tell Boy... " and then he shut his eyes.

Mother Magdalen said, "I'll tell him, John."

And she put her clay mug to Whip Man's crusted lips and poured, so most of the brown stuff went right inside and not down his chin. He gulped, thirsty.

And then Mother Magdalen sat on the ground and eased his head off the tree and onto her lap, sideways, and she stroked his brow, like he had done the cat. She said, "Take this mug back to the house, Miss Vivian, and wash it well. Wait till you've stopped crying. And only then, go call Boy and your husband and son from where they're burying the Sacks' remains and burning that wheel chair.

Tell them we need them to come here and open this grave for Myra and John."

Boy came from the field with his hoe and stared at his pap a while and swung into the ground near Mother Magdalen, chopping. For the first time since I'd seen him in pain, he didn't cry. Mother Magdalen said, "Asking your father not to go with Heaven and Myra would have been like asking him to go back to being a walking dead man, Boy. He was bound to them. He called it love, but why don't we call it magic or healing?"

I thought with some shock, *She's almost begging.* I said, "You talking about that hoo-doo, ain't you? Boy, don't listen to her."

Boy ain't answered. When the ditch was dug open, he took his hoe and bit it into that tree trunk nearby and left it jutting out while the rest of us tumbled the bodies in the grave.

Dead, Myra looked awful little. Even as a cat. Whip Man's big arm flopped over her, and you was almost glad he was going to be there to protect her.

Before we shoved the dirt in over them, I said to Mother Magdalen, "Where you done scared Boy off to now, filling his head with that crazy talk?"

Mother Magdalen's legs must hurt from sitting up under Whip Man and Myra's weight, both. She rolled over onto her knees to help shove dirt and said, "Leave him alone, Miss Vivian. None of us can judge what he's going through, any more than we could judge his father."

So me and Mother Magdalen and my Tim and Zion, and then Miss Solace and Baby Joy, we stayed to say words over the fresh grave. When we was leaving and the sun pinked the sky, I told my Tim, "After all I done for you, don't you never dare go to the grave with no other woman. I swear I'll haunt you."

He put his arm around me.

And now it was Zion taking turns with Miss Solace at the back door saying, "Where Angel Girl? Where Boy?"

And through the night you don't hear that great cat coughing no more.

But I still wasn't easy in my mind about going back to live in the outdoor kitchen. Because now at night you hear a howling, like that wolf I seen track Angel Girl.

Close, like it's waiting at the burying ditch.

# CHAPTER SEVEN

## ONLY ANGELS: BABY JOY, BORN 1821

Daddy was still there sometimes when I woke in the morning. I would open my eyes just above the thick white quilt on my bed and I could just *feel* that he was there that day and I could see him if I hurried.

Hurry meant slide out from between the feather mattress and the feather quilt like sleeping in the clouds or flying with birds or my angel and run barefoot through the dark in the hall.

Miss Vivian told me it was the Boo-Hag riding me in the clouds every night. But when I got afraid to fall asleep Mother Magdalen found me crying alone in my bed. And I told her what Miss Vivian said about the Boo-Hag and how I was afraid to sleep now.

Mother Magdalen said, "Joy, there are no witches to fly with you at night. There are only angels."

As soon as I heard it, I knew it was true. So I thought I shouldn't talk to Miss Vivian about it anymore.

And Mama taught me to see the angel in the stained glass in the hall.

The glass angel looked just like my angel. So then I really knew old Miss Vivian was just trying to scare me.

And every time I forgot that and started to believe her, I would only have to stop and study that angel in the stained glass a little before bedtime.

Sometimes me and Mama would sit there on the floor together in the hall to study our glass angel. If you're not careful, you're likely to miss everything.

How she's rising above the flames and her hands are spread to give the light from inside her to the sad people below. And her face is sweet and she's not scared by the flames leaping up from the field like they want to get at her.

And the people working hard and burning in the sun can look up at her and all the faces that see her are at peace.

I didn't see any monsters in the stained glass. I only knew that one was there because one time Mama said, "But, Joy, honey, why hasn't the angel blessed the beast and made him happy?"

She gets like that sometimes.

She forgets I'm little and she wants to protect me and she'll all of a sudden just say things that are so different from what she says most of the time that I can't answer before she snaps to and looks at me and puts on that smile that closes up her feelings again.

So by the time I figured she was asking about a monster in the glass it was too late. She had already jumped a little where she was sitting and looked over at me with her fingers on her lips and said, "Oh. Oh, Baby Joy." And then she said, "What foolishness your mama talks sometimes," and hugged me and put me to bed.

But after that I knew there was a monster at the end of the hallway trapped and hiding in the glass.

So I would hurry toward it like I'm brave because my angel said you can't show fear of evil. And then I would turn quick to the write hand and shove in at my mama's door so I'd be safe before the sunshine woke the monster from the glass and he could look at me.

I didn't know what would happen if he looked from out of his glass at me. But monsters have powers. Especially if you're the only one who really knows they're there. Then their secret is like a power they have over you because nobody else believes you so they can't save you from the monster.

I always ran right up to that monster and turned my head away.

And if I saw my daddy's head on the pillows just when I pushed through my parents' door I might say to that old monster, "See. I'm not scared of you. I'll get my daddy on you."

But I wouldn't.

Cause he wasn't always here. I hoped the monster didn't know.

But when my daddy was home, he was wonderful.

Mama never locked the door on me. So I just ran through and landed smack on the bed. And Daddy started smiling before he even got his eyes all the way open.

And by the time I crawled across the rose quilt right up to him, he'd got one eye peeping out of the covers at me. And by the time I crashed onto his chest and just lay there he'd got both arms free of the covers to hug me.

Daddy'd say something like, "How my Baby Joy been doing, now?"

And I wouldn't say much at first. Just to punish him for always being gone. And then after he woke up some more and sat up to curl around me I'd go ahead and say, "I'm fine, Daddy. Good morning and how are you?" like Mother Magdalen taught me.

But kind of more shy.

Cause every time I saw him again it felt like maybe I didn't know him any more. Not like I knew Mama and Mother Magdalen and Miss Vivian and Mr. Tim and Zion. And my angel.

But then Daddy would start to tickle me and ask me riddles and even if I knew the answers I wouldn't say them till he made me laugh cause he'd been gone and I didn't want to be too easy on him. Mama's thick hair was all over the pillows everywhere in the morning.

When Daddy was here and we were playing, she might wake up a little and move her hair like a big soft rug and look at us.

But like as not she'd just snuggle over so she could touch us more than just when we bumped her. And then she'd keep on sleeping.

Till Daddy said he had to go. That always woke Mama up like a shot.

And she couldn't wait to get up and get dressed over her white gown and try to get Daddy to stay just for coffee or maybe honey biscuits with me.

And he'd say, "Solace, baby, you know I can't. It just ain't in me right now. I'm sorry."

And she'd say something like, "Boy, you could try harder to come back and be with us again."

I always got out of there when they started talking like that. I didn't want to see Mama try not to cry.

She never cried in front of Daddy. She tried not to cry about Daddy in front of anybody. Not even me.

But I would come back in her room after Daddy was gone for my reading and writing lessons and see the red round her eyes plain as day.

She would do that smile and pretend she wasn't crying. Like she thought I couldn't tell.

I didn't know why Daddy did that to her.

It would just make me angry all of a sudden till I was sorry that I had let him tickle me and tell me riddles till I laughed.

And next time I was going to turn my back on Daddy just like Mama did that lawyer man from town when she wanted him to go. I'd even cross my arms and tap my foot like Mama and not look at Daddy till he was almost at the door, gone.

I wished I wouldn't break down and run after him to get that last hug. Cause if I didn't, then he would really know how I was angry with him and might not ever forgive him again.

Ever.

And then he'd have to be afraid to go.

I could figure out what I should do. I just couldn't stick to it and do it. I'd lie in bed at night and wait for my angel, and most nights, that was what I'd be thinking.

How to learn to be brave and not give that last hug, to scare Daddy and make him wait here to get it. And I would never, ever give it. So he could never go.

And Mama would stop crying.

Mr. Tim told Zion to stop cutting my mama's own flowers to bring her and hold her hand when she cried. And Mama told Mr. Tim, "He's just a boy."

And that really upset me too, because I wanted my daddy to be the only Boy.

At least Mama never called that lawyer man Boy when he brought her flowers. If she did, I would have flown away with my angel and maybe never come back to her, either.

Once I asked the angel to fly me away and find me my daddy because my mama wasn't ever going to stop her crying if he didn't come home soon.

Could people just cry to death?

And my angel flew me in her arms to where the trees in the woods blocked out all the moonlight till I was scared. And there on the ground where the trees grew thick was my daddy's wolf, stalking something.

I didn't like my daddy's wolf.

It was big and pretty, so shiny black, but all its muscles felt like they could hurt you, when I petted it, but even worse were its teeth.

Long and dark white and curvy and pointed at the tip. Sometimes when Daddy was already gone his wolf was still here, prowling.

And Mama would pet it and call it Boy, too. And talk to it till the lawyer man asked her to put it outside. And she wouldn't answer him, but keep petting.

I bet she was glad to have some part of Daddy left behind when he was gone.

I got like that with my angel. One time, I found one of her feathers in my hair after she flew me back home to get my sleep for the night. I pulled it from my braid and held it and didn't drop it the whole time I slept.

And then in the morning I showed it to Miss Vivian without saying anything so she could figure out for herself that she was wrong calling my angel a Boo-Hag.

But all Miss Vivian said was, "Baby Joy. What you doing ripping feathers out your mattress for? Don't you let me come in this room and catch you with that quilt and that mattress rip to pieces all over this floor. Too much crazy doings round here. I'm after you people from day-clean to day-lean and I'm tired of it."

None of it was true.

We weren't crazy. And nobody wanted Miss Vivian following around after them telling them what to do, either. Especially not me and Mama.

But that Miss Vivian would come and pester. Like when the lawyer man came for a visit. Mama wouldn't be halfway done with my lessons and Miss Vivian would burst in her bedroom or come stomping up under the willows by the graveyard and say, "Miss Solace, ain't I just told you so? If that Shavers ain't back again spitting a mouthful of questions about everything you done already told him plain as day."

And Mama was off to talk to Mr. Shavers and I just knew she'd be all pale and her face would be all pinched through dinner and supper, too. And worse, I'd have to hide in the back kitchen with Mother Magdalen so Mr. Shavers wouldn't see me and fret.

I didn't know why I should make him fret. It was my house with him always barging in not invited. If anybody ought to fret, it should be me and Mama.

Mother Magdalen said Mr. Shavers was just peculiar that way and I was to pay him no mind. Mama said she only let him come over, anyway, to help her figure her money and how to keep the plantation.

So I told Mama that if she would just hurry up and finish my lessons, I could get smart enough to help her figure all that.

She would do that smile and say, "I know you will someday, Baby Joy." But I could see she didn't believe me.

I didn't know why people figured I couldn't do anything. Someday I would show them all.

I would save the plantation and bring Daddy home and tell him to stay put and listen to me. Then Mama would stop her crying and she'd have all the money she wanted and Mr. Shavers could never come back.

And we'd all be happy.

And everybody would know that it was me that fixed it. And it would be even better than chopping vegetables for stew because even Miss Vivian who bossed everybody couldn't figure out how to fix everything like I would. I didn't care if she never let me use a knife.

Because I could fly. Even if Miss Vivian didn't believe me.

The way I knew I was flying with my angel was that the wind was in my face like sitting on the roof with my angel's arms around me to look out over the field of weeds to the shacks where I couldn't go for fear of snakes and to the woods.

Only the wind blew stronger when we were flying like it was pushing us back where we came from.

We could see more when we were flying than we could see from the roof. Like lots of trees all at once so thick you couldn't see the forest floor and you thought that if you got too sleepy and fell off the angel's back that the treetops would feel like your feather mattress.

Or we'd see a flock of birds that when you got really close you could see they were women in long white gowns with long white wings that beat the air so strong you couldn't catch your breath till you got so far away that they looked like beautiful birds again, just soaring.

Or we'd see that big river where there was a cave set in a hill and people lived far down and hid away from other people, and my mama didn't know where to find them, either. But my angel took me to them when I asked her how I could help my mama keep the plantation.

My angel lay on my bed one night before we flew holding me and the light shined out of her till I had to squint against it to still see her inside the glow, shifting.

And my angel said, "I know what to do, Baby Joy. If we bring your mother's uncle back home, he could protect her. And he could bring lots of people with him, and they

301

could all work the farm together. Should we go look for your mother's Uncle Sami?"

So we did.

Night after night we looked for him till I didn't even believe any more that there was an Uncle Sami and I went and asked my mama.

She said, "Oh, Baby Joy. Who ever told you about him? Yes, your daddy used to tell me that my mother before she died had a big bear of a brother named Sami Wolf Water. He even wore a bearskin, and he shot the last overseer that ever worked this plantation, and he freed the people, and then he led the people away to freedom." She shook her head and looked away from me. But I heard her say, "I wish I could be freed of this plantation."

And the next time Mr. Shavers came I didn't hide in Mother Magdalen's back room to peek at him and listen for when Mama told him go.

I made myself real quiet and tiptoed right up to the parlor door. And I listened to every single thing they said and I even leaned a little around the doorway and looked straight at them. So I could understand just why my mama needed Uncle Sami and what to tell him when we found him. And maybe Mr. Shavers even knew where Uncle Sami was?

But they didn't really talk about my mama's Uncle Sami.

They talked about selling a place called the townhouse, and Mr. Shavers said maybe he should buy it from my mama, but he wanted her to go there with him first and pick out things she should keep to remember the grandfather that gave it to her.

And Mama was quiet most of the time Mr. Shavers was talking. But when he touched her hand she slid it away under her shawl and said, "I simply can't bring myself to do any of those things, Mr. Shavers. Won't you just buy someone else's house?"

And Mr. Shavers said, "My dear. If I let you lose your grandfather's things to neglect or to the greed of strangers, won't you resent me someday for my negligence? I've promised to protect you, and I shall."

I didn't understand it and I was sorry I had come to listen. But I was stuck. If I tried to tiptoe away, I might make noise.

And then Mr. Shavers might see me and fret. And Miss Vivian would say it was all my fault. And I really didn't like to hear Miss Vivian fuss.

So I stayed and fell asleep where I was till Mama woke me up and when I jumped she said, "Don't worry. Mr. Shavers is gone. But what are you doing here, Joy, outside the door?" She tried to look stern.

I said, "Listening to see would you and the lawyer man talk about where was Uncle Sami and how could me and my angel find him for you."

She hugged me like I was still tiny. I loved it when grown ups hugged me like I was still tiny. She said, "Why do you want to know where Uncle Sami is, Baby Joy? Has your angel told you that he's in some kind of trouble?"

I said, "No one's in trouble but you, Mama." And I fell back asleep.

I didn't mind sleeping in the daytime. It meant I'd stay awake and not fall off my angel when we flew at night.

But Miss Vivian fussed and said I was too big to still be napping every afternoon. She said Mama was raising me to forget my place and put on airs like I thought I could ever grow up to be a lady whatever that was.

Mama told me, "Uncle Sami is somewhere where there's a big river and lots of small towns along it. I've written him many times. He doesn't answer. Maybe he doesn't get my letters. Even Mr. Shavers can't help me find him."

So that made me feel better when I fell asleep.

Cause you just can't do anything when all the grown ups are already doing it first and better. But when they give up and you do it on your own they have to be proud of you.

Even the mean ones like Miss Vivian. So I told my angel about the river.

We went out on the roof when I woke up from my nap and all the grown ups were in the field, weeding.

My angel squinted up her eyes to look far and the sunlight shot yellow all in the blue till I wondered how she could see me at all.

But after a while she said in her voice like singing, "Baby Joy, there are no big rivers close by. I've searched all around here. Maybe I have to keep going until I find one." She turned her head to me so it blocked the sun from my eyes and smiled like this idea would be all right in the end.

I loved my angel's smile.

It was soft like Mama's but close like Daddy's. Plus my angel never used a smile to shut me out from knowing something.

She said, "Joy, I'll be gone for a while, looking for this river with the towns. But never mind. That will give you a chance to sleep at night. And soon I'll come back to you."

I must have frowned at her.

Because she took her fingers that feel like when you run your hand quick over a candle flame and smoothed my forehead between my eyes.

"Don't worry," my angel said. "I'll be back as soon as I've found your Uncle Sami. And you'll have something good to tell your mother."

So I slept every night after that till it felt like when I woke up my angel was just something I made up when I was a baby and she wasn't real anymore.

And I told Miss Vivian to get her old broom out from under my bed because I was old enough to know there wasn't any Boo-Hag and I didn't need to trick a witch into counting bristles at night.

Miss Vivian said I could get the broom out from under the bed myself and use it to clean my bedroom, too.

And I did. And left it up against the wall in Miss Vivian's outside kitchen where she slept at night with her husband and her son. And then Miss Vivian caught me looking through her pans on the big table and her fireplace for maybe biscuits from breakfast and some honey and molasses to dunk them in. Miss Vivian spoils everything.

And she told my mama I was big enough to help in the field and stay out of trouble and it wasn't good to spoil me so and leave me to learn to sneak and steal hardworking people's food. My mama said I couldn't steal what was already rightly mine.

Miss Vivian and Mr. Tim too said they didn't know we had a system like that. And Zion said that wasn't what my mama meant and they weren't trying to hear her out.

And Miss Vivian said the point was people like us couldn't have anything if they didn't work hard for it every day and I might as well learn that now.

And Mama said there'd be plenty of time to learn to work when I was a little more grown and she wanted me to have some fun right now cause we all knew that it couldn't last.

We were all in the field where Miss Vivian had hauled me by my arm after she caught me with a biscuit looking for something wet and sweet or even milk from that old goat tied in the garden.

And Mama said that settled it and she would have to find a new law office because we were all turning against each other like enemies.

Mr. Tim said, "And risk that Shavers fellow turning against you? After all you done to keep him on your side?"

Mama said, "I've been thinking of selling the plantation land, too. All the woods and most of the cleared fields. We'll never keep up. None of us know farming, and without Boy I can't even buy a good plow or a cow that won't die or have her milk give out. I'm tired of trying. Maybe we can survive, at least, in the townhouse. I can take in sewing, maybe, and the men can hire out."

Miss Vivian went to put her arms around Mama. So me and Zion looked at each other like we knew the fight was over and we could stop being scared of what might happen next. Miss Vivian said, "Miss Solace, you don't never mean to go sit in that townhouse and think you go'n ever get Mr. Shavers off your front steps. It must be another way."

But Miss Vivian surely looked happy. So I knew me and Zion were wrong about not being scared anymore. Miss Vivian was up to something.

I ran to the house and told Mother Magdalen.

She had been roasting wild plants till they dried in her fireplace. She put them in a clay bowl and sat at the table and said, "I see what you mean. Miss Vivian loves that kitchen house, but she might think it would be nice living in the city with your mother for a mistress." Mother Magdalen looked toward the shut door and said, "Where are my angel girls? How can I leave this place?"

I said, "There are no witches and no angels, either. Only little children believe in that."

And then I looked down at that hideous biscuit that started all this fuss and bother. Why had it ever looked good to me? Sitting here with Mother Magdalen, I knew she would give me anything to dunk it in, anything she had, but I didn't want it anymore. I went outside and checked all the oldest, nastiest, weediest latrines I could find, risking snakes and everything, and I threw that biscuit down the stinking hole in the ground that made me feel the sickest. Flies burst out of the hole at me and I knew Miss Vivian would have been upset if she knew what I did with her good food.

I came out of the latrine wishing she would catch me. But she was far away in the field where everybody was leaning on their hoes talking. I wanted to run and hide but I didn't know where to go without that angel I made up when I was a baby. I wished I could fly through the woods.

That night I woke up and cried in my bed till the sun rose because I thought I could hear the monster coming out of the stained glass at the end of the dark hall to sneak to my room and get me.

Only when he got so close I could hear him outside my door trying to unlatch it I would cry just loud enough so my daddy or my angel could hear it if they had got back home, but not the monster.

He must have been afraid. Because he never did unlatch the door and come inside my room. Could my angel have come home, after all? Someone must have scared off the stained glass monster.

I spent the whole next day downstairs searching the stone rooms for my angel. Sometimes she liked to hide there so people who didn't believe in her couldn't find her.

I hated to go in the stone rooms.

They let off the main part of the house which was dirty white wood into a strange kind of dark that glowed but there was no light in it. Just something like arms jutting out from the walls like they wanted to hold candles but the candles were gone. And big wood squares like shutters that you couldn't open in some of the rooms.

And smells. Like when you found old clothes folded in the wardrobes with little pale bugs dead in them.

And sounds. Like if you listened real close you could hear a girl screaming far away. Or a long time ago. I couldn't tell which. But her screams were an echo that bounced off all the walls.

And other voices, whispering. And the stones moved closer.

I got scared and curled up in a corner and called out, "Angel!"

Someone hurried to get me. It was Mother Magdalen calling, "Joy!" I started sobbing and couldn't say a thing.

She stumbled right up on me in my corner and put her arms around me. She said, "Why are you hiding in here and crying, Baby Joy?"

And I said, "Cause I lost my angel and now the monster came to get me in my bed."

So she picked me up and I tried to feel like nothing to carry because Mama says Mother Magdalen is getting real old and weak. But she carried me all the way up the stairs and down the hall to the stained glass and said, "Show me where you see the angel."

I showed her with my finger.

And she said, "What have I told you? There are no witches. There are no monsters. There are, Baby Joy, only angels."

So I hid my face in her neck where the wrinkles are soft and said, "But Mother Magdalen. When will my angel come home?"

And she said, "I don't know. But it's good to know how to wait. Do you see how your mother waits for your father? Let's be like your mother and wait for our angel. And when she comes home again, she'll know we trusted her."

That night I lay and listened and wondered should I ask Miss Vivian for her broom back under my bed. And I fell asleep and slept so sound that I didn't wake till Daddy's wolf was licking me good-bye.

I sat up in my bed and called out, "Daddy!"

But his wolf was out the door and bounding down the stairs and Mama said, "Let me let Daddy's wolf out, Baby Joy, and I'll come back."

I curled up in the feather mattress and the quilt and thought it was easier to be little and get taken care of than to try to grow up big so you could help.

When Mama came back she held me and said it would be all over soon. We would move off the plantation to the townhouse and forget about how much we missed Daddy. And we would start to feel a little all right after a while, I would see.

I stayed in bed all that day.

I wouldn't eat.

I talked to nobody.

I didn't even answer when Miss Vivian came in the room and said I needed a whipping. I just gave her my meanest look.

If Mama was going to go to town, I would just stay so quiet till everybody forgot I was here and they wouldn't even know they left without me. And that way when Daddy showed up again I would open my mouth for the first time in however long it took and tell him Mama was gone for good now and it was all his fault.

And I would never fly with that angel again even if she did come back.

But she couldn't come back because now I knew for sure that there are no angels. Only monsters. I didn't care what Mother Magdalen said.

Mama started sleeping in my bed at night.

So she was with me the night the light fell on us and woke us and we sat up to see was the whole house on fire. There was a light so bright in the room we both raised our arms to cover our eyes. And my angel spoke out of the light, smiling, and said, "I have good news for you, Solace and Joy. I've found your Uncle Sami."

After that, everything changed.

Now when my angel would wrap her wings around me I could feel the tingling and the scratching like I never really noticed it before.

And when she slept beside me on my bed I'd see the rising and the falling of her chest and hear her breathe.

And when she'd move to wake or sit and hold me I'd hear music in her wings like birds make, even little ones too young to sing.

And when we'd fly I'd feel how safe it was because her arms were strong and her back curved under me like a seat.

And then my mama took to pulling shawls on every time that Mr. Shavers came to call. I heard him from my place in the back room, asking her why. I thought it was to hide her hands if he reached for them. But she said, "Sir, I've taken ill."

I heard noise like he'd moved his seat, and Miss Vivian came in big-eyed to tell Mother Magdalen he'd gone down on one knee. We all listened and heard him say he wanted the privilege of taking Mama to town to take care of her.

We heard Mama tell Mr. Shavers that she had Vivian and Magdalen for that, but he kept arguing. And something in his voice made me afraid.

Mother Magdalen said, "Miss Vivian, maybe you should get your husband or your son to chaperone. Hurry."

Mr. Tim and Zion both came running in from the field and they went into the parlor. But Mr. Shavers didn't leave till it was night.

I went in and found Mama asleep in a chair. Zion was picking her up to carry her to her room. And Miss Vivian said, "Careful, now she got that baby."

That night my angel came through my bedroom window. I told her, "Something's really wrong."

And she said, "I've asked your mother to write a letter I can take to her Uncle Sami, asking for help. But she won't."

We didn't fly that night.

I was glad. Cause this way, I was home when the light in the hallway woke me.

I heard sounds. Like whispering. I eased my door open and peeked through the dark. I had tiptoed all the way to the stairs before I was sure.

It was my mama. She had her shawl wrapped around her. But under the black loops of strings you could see the white of her gown and where her belly looked just a little too big.

I went and sat near her under the stained glass and put my hand on the bulge. "Does it hurt?" I said.

She sat staring at the glass with a candle on the floor beside her that flickered. She said, "Only in a way. Inside my heart." Then she said, "When I look at the glass, there's only a woman hung from a tree and burning." She pointed. "Nothing else. How did I ever think there was anything else?"

We stayed there till you could see dark breaking up in the sky behind the glass. Mama stood by it with her candle and ran her hand over the glass and shook her head.

I woke up from the floor and saw her and tried to think what would a grown up do. So I got up and went on tiptoe and reached for her hand but it was raised too high on the glass. Then I got her by her nightgown and said, "You should be in bed, Mama." And when I pulled back her rose quilt and asked her to give me her candle and get in bed she laughed a little but she did it.

I covered her but when I went to kiss her the wax spilled on her hair and I said, "Remember. Mother Magdalen says there's no burning women, hung. And no witches and no monsters." I wasn't sure, but I thought maybe all those were the same thing and that's what Mother Magdalen would have said in my place. I would have to ask her.

I carried Mama's candle with me from the room but I didn't close her door so I wouldn't feel alone and be scared of what I had to do next.

I went down the stairs slow so the candle wouldn't gutter and go out. It took forever to get to the bottom.

I went past Mother Magdalen's back kitchen to the stone hallway. I waited at the doorway there where the stone hallway opened like a mouth caught yawning late in the night. It smelled foul. I called out, "Angel?"

And then I waited.

There was a rustle and a glow like candles getting lit way in there. And then the glow came toward me and took shape. Floated just beyond me.

I said, "Angel, maybe you should tell my daddy Miss Vivian says Mama's having a baby."

And my angel was gone.

That night we were downstairs having supper in the dining room and Mama was telling me again which spoon for stew. I had just spilled on my napkin cause I slurped and Mama said, "Mother Magdalen will never get that stain out. I shouldn't have you using the linen."

And Mother Magdalen called out from the back room so I thought she must have heard and I balled up the napkin so she wouldn't see the spill.

But then we heard a voice calling and Mama's eyes got big and she said, "Boy!"

We were both pushing away from the table when Daddy came through the doorway and said, "Who baby you carrying? Tell me that, Solace." And he came up on Mama like he was going to tear her to pieces with his hands. I cried out cause I was scared. Mama stood and watched him coming.

And then my mama slapped him.

And then he wasn't there anymore.

Where he used to be was my daddy's black wolf. It backed up, snarling, to get away from the tangle of my daddy's clothes catching its hind paws. It crashed up against the table and made the china rattle and some wood break.

Mama backed to the wall, away from the wolf, and it ran.

That night when my angel came to my bed she said we'd better go talk to Uncle Sami.

We flew till the night was cold and the air over the angel's wings was hot. You could smell heavy water and we saw the dark big river, moving. My angel fluttered down to the ground between some trees. She took me off her back and wrapped her wings around me.

She carried me into a big dark hole in the side of a hill.

We went in a long way, but I couldn't see through the thick feathers of her wings in the dark. Maybe I slept a little from the rocking. But then we stopped and her wings floated open around me.

In front of me was a big big man with long rings of dark hair. He stood against a wall of the cave, staring.

My angel said, "Your sister had a child, and you left her. Now here is that child's child. Listen to her."

I was sleepy and a little scared of how big he was. And I couldn't be sure he had heard my angel. But he stared straight at me. And I remembered what I wanted to say. "Uncle Sami? Please come home and help my mother."

My angel's wings closed and it was like I was falling after that, but I woke up in my bed.

No, it wasn't my bed. It was my mama's bed. I was alone in the big rose quilted bed and a fire burned in the fireplace.

I could see my mama and my daddy, too, sitting at the table over by the window. Daddy reached across the table and took my mama by the hand. He said, "Solace, can you forgive me one last time? Can I still come home?"

# CHAPTER EIGHT

### FALL OFF THE WORLD: SISTER, BORN 1752

We had to leave my other daughter, Rose Red, behind at Mr. Dennis's plantation. Rose Red and her young man, Boyfriend, hightailed it to the woods to wander free. You could only hope no evil would befall two young folks out there in love.

But that fake escape saved us from having to tell Rose Red that Mr. Dennis ain't set her free like the rest of us. We all knew why he ain't set free my sweet little Rose Red.

That gal was too comely. From the day Mr. Dennis clapped eyes on her, she set his mouth to watering. All them dark curves swooping up and down my baby from feets to neck, just like mens likes on a woman.

Something's up, so to speak, when mens takes to acting peculiar. We left my beautiful baby girl behind and hoped Mr. Dennis would keel over from old age before him and some posse could catch up with her and Boyfriend in the woods.

And the rest of us set off to where Mr. Dennis had bought for his son Sami Wolf Water some plantation out by a big river.

I had my doubts. My druthers too. I didn't rightly trust that Sami Wolf Water because he was Mr. Dennis's own son and illegal heir. But he had married my other daughter, Rose White, and now I had her happiness to think about. So I came along with them to they new home.

The first days on the road was happy. We rode carts and farm animals Sami Wolf Water shared. Folks was riding their own mule, their own cow, with chickens strapped in a wheelbarrow and a milk goat tied and trotting behind. Children ran and skipped down the road ahead of the caravan, turning cartwheels in the speckled sunlight between the trees.

We had no worries. Because if some patrol was to accost us, Mr. Sami Wolf Water was going to pull out our free papers that Mr. Dennis wrote and signed with his own name.

We'd say, "Look all you want but don't you dare touch. We're free as you all."

Rose White and me rode together in a cart that that no-account scoundrel Bully drove. Me, I'm like Rose Red. I ain't never had no use for Bully. Ever since he was a butt-naked child in the fields, that good-for-nothing lazy rascal would beat people into doing his share of the work, and then he would stuff his face on they share of the food.

But Bully knew just how to kiss up to the boss man.

That's how Bully got his self driving this cart toting Sami's own wife. If you ask me, Sami Wolf Water done turned over everything but the lovemaking to this lying cheating Bully.

Rose White was laying up in here in the back of the cart right now, moaning and groaning with the baby that wanted to be born.

Sami with his big head was riding his horse all up and down along the road through the woods at the head of the caravan, clopping along and talking and "seeing to things," as he put it.

Every now and then he would shout at the poor wight children running alongside, throwing rocks and squatting to poop and throwing that too at the caravan. And Big Man Mr. Sami glared at the scruffy wight farmers and they wives who came to see what the commotion was all about, streaked with dirt till they was blacker than the blackest of us, and frowned up like demons when they realized we wasn't no slave gang in chains, but a caravan of freepeople.

Sami would see that rage building and tell them, "Don't you all dare use those pitchforks and muskets and pistols on my people. Do you see this rifle, here? I'll blast all of you to hell, before I die."

I had already begged him to shut up and get us off the main road through the woods. There was a patrol trailing us since we left Mr. Dennis's plantation. And a man of Sami's race-no matter how light-skinned, and no matter who set him free-didn't have no legal right to a gun.

But Sami ain't wanted to see and hear nothing but how the young gals, all colors and all races, them in the caravan and them staring wide-eyed along the road, would giggle and sigh and flash him a sight of their private parts when him and his horse and his rifle pointing skyward came clip-clopping by.

I'm calling from the cart, "Sami, sir! Mr. Sami Wolf Water! Can I speak to you, sir?"

At last he clip-clopped over to us, cutting his eyes at Rose White, like he wanted to ask why she ain't put a muzzle on her ma'am's mouth.

I whispered, "Mr. Sami, sir, ain't you heard twigs snapping all night and smelled the whiskey on the breeze from that patrol, drinking while they count our heads to figure the money they go'n make stealing us? Sir, they getting all up in the trees to look down and pick out the young gals they going after first."

I growed up hearing about these things. He growed up with his head in a bear skin blocking out the sun.

And I laid up every night on this trek, hugging Rose White and singing her to sleep like she was still a bitty thing. And she would wake through her pain and go on about, "Ma'am, don't you miss our shack with that solid door that shut out the wild animals and the bugs? These mosquitoes has ate me up to get to the baby before we can get where we're going, I swear. And you remember, Ma'am, how them roses outside our wood door would bloom all through the warm weather? And how me and Rose Red would sneak off and go fishing, and Mr. Dennis and Mr. Peter and them would be too scared of Mammy Water putting a hex on them to come after us? Don't you miss everything, the good and the bad?"

I should have said, "Baby, let's you and me turn this cart around and go back, with or without your husband." But I sat up there and lied. "No, Rose White, I don't miss it much. I don't think about nothing but that new baby you're carrying. I think how I'm go'n die free, sitting around rocking my grandchildren. I'm go'n see my little gal living in a big house cooking dainty and eating fine."

She put up a fuss. She was afraid she was dying and wouldn't never do none of them things. "But, Ma'am-"

I just had to wear her out till she would drift off to sleep. And then I would lay up there hankering after my old shack and my old ways while tears flowed.

I'd stare up at the night sky that looked like it would drop on my face and smother me in my sleep, with all them white stars blinking from out the black like eyes, winking like you're stupid. "Don't you know you've come to nowhere, and there's nothing solid around you anymore? You're going to fall off the world in your sleep, and you won't know it till you wake up find yourself floating in the black till you die."

319

I would hug up tight on Rose White, so if I drifted off into nothing, at least I'd take her with me so she wouldn't have to birth her baby alone.

Sometimes I fell asleep thinking I would steal Sami's rifle and put it upside his head and tell him, "Turn this caravan around and head home, and hop to it!"

That day when I got my old skinny back propped between Rose White and the cart sides, jolting that baby right out of her, Sami took off patting his self on the back because he got his mangy bear skin between Rose White and the floor of the cart, with all them gold coins and loose jewels sewed up in the paws poking and prodding my baby's tender skin through the fur.

And then one of the little children running up ahead screamed somewhere under the trees.

Sami Wolf Water kneed his horse and took off. We heard shouts and guns going off.

And then all the ruckus stopped. We waited.

And a hairy-faced man with pale red skin split with spots and scars came from between the bushes and trees, riding a tall wild-eyed horse.

This Hairy Man held a smoking rifle in one hand. And in the other, he got a little boy he just done shot.

The boy's ma'am screamed and leaped off the bull she was riding. Couldn't nobody stop nor grab her. She ran up the dirt road to the head of the caravan and snatched at her dead baby boy.

Her man ran to catch up with her, hollering, "Honey, don't get no closer. You can't help your baby this way! Can't you see he already gone?"

Hairy Man pointed his smoking rifle at the both of them, yelling, "Don't nobody move!"

But the woman done got to the Hairy Man and tried to scramble up the sides of his jittery horse to get at her dangling child. Hairy Man tossed the shot boy on the ground, way out past his ma'am's head, and she reached back to follow the body through the air.

But the Hairy Man grabbed her by the head and got him a handful of little short plaits, all tied down with string.

He snatched her around by all this hair and string and said in her face, "You, woman. Are you the lawbreaker that set that little black pickaninny to trespass and steal wight folks' property? I guess I got to take you on in. The sheriff is go'n want to hear about this."

Her man dived to the ground to pick up the boy. But the rest of us froze in our tracks.

I shoved Rose White's head down below the wall of the cart. "Rose White, don't move nor even breathe loud. Quit that groaning. Bully, hold tight them reins. I got me my paring knife in my hand, and I'll slide it in your ribs if you try to get down off this cart."

But Bully ain't never heard a word I said.

For, just at that time, Sami Wolf Water clopped up behind the Hairy Man, his rifle all limp and hanging at his side, surrounded by the ugliest passel of patrol I ever saw.

Hairy Man said, "You know, you all look to me like a stinking bunch of runaways. I got me a sick sense-" why somebody brag on his sick sense? "-about these things. I can make me a fortune on you all, yes, indeedy."

He yanked on that woman's head while he talked, and her eyes bugged out, staring at her dead boy sagging in her man's arms, her fingers prying at the Hairy Man's hand.

321

Her man wiped at the flowing blood like he could clean up her baby boy for his ma'am's last chance to set eyes on him.

And the Hairy Man set in explaining that we crossed the state line and trespassed and who the devil was go'n answer for us, nothing but a buncha niggers?

Sami Wolf Water got his mouth open and too much shock in his eyes. "These people are all free, I tell you. I have their papers right here."

Hairy Man turned in the saddle and looked him up and down. Then he said, like he was poking fun at the way Sami talked, "You 'have their papers,' boy?" And the Hairy Man and his patrol set to guffawing.

Sami may not be dark as some who just got dragged off the boat in chains like you see in the market in town, but he's pretty toasty, all the same. Maybe he did look a mite strange, up there talking about how he's carrying people's freedom papers.

So Sami said, blushing even darker and talking fast like he was trying to amend his mistake, "I mean, sirs, that I can pay, if you're trying to tell me that the little boy took something he shouldn't have."

Hairy Man took his time hauling out a bit of rope off the horn on his saddle. When Sami hushed, Hairy Man said with his back to his patrol, "Boys, what you catch and what you get for turning them in is your take on this trip."

Sami finally understood and yelled, "Everybody, run for it! Scatter!" while he whipped his rifle up pert and start firing on patrol at close range. His horse skittered and pranced sideways off the road under him.

One thing I always said about Sami. He is good and crazy, but that taste he got for shooting up wight mens surely did come in handy that day. He was picking them off like a boy with a pea-shooter taking aim at a tree.

He was going to someday get us killed for sure. But that day, it was either killed or sold. Folks was off like a shot, ducking and scrambling. One minute, they was there. You blinked. They was gone. Nothing but noise behind, and the woman and man still weeping over they boy.

I jabbed my knife a little in Bully's side and hissed like a snake, "You heard Mr. Sami! Into the woods with this cart!"

He slapped the reins. The cart jumped and Rose White cried out and me, old fool that I am, almost tumbled over the side. But I grabbed the wall of the cart and the knife clattered, falling on the wood.

We plunged between the trees. Bully tucked his big head between his shoulders, and the branches meeting us off the road knocked me flat on my back on top of my aching baby girl, with cuts all upside my face near my eyes.

From there I couldn't feel or think nothing but how my stomach dropped like a stone because the cart hit downhill and we for sure was rattling down into a ravine.

But the horse had a nerve on her and bounced us out and up across some rocks. Next thing, we had come to something almost seemed like a level path.

Off in the distance you could still hear whooping and hollering and shots and screams. I suspected some of our mens had snatched up axes and shovels and pitchforks and ropes of their own and come back after what patrol Sami ain't shot quite dead.

Bully was on the driver's bench panting and staring back where we just got away. I rose a little out the back of the cart to look around and see if we been followed.

Bully looked at me dazed and said, "I gots to get back there, Sister, ma'am. See can I kill me one of them wight mens." And he slid down the side and was gone.

Never mind.

We was in a cane brake or something and Rose White gritted her teeths and got her hands under her belly, like she was pressing the baby back in.

She bit her lip till I worked my finger between the teeths and the skin, cause she drawing blood, and her stomach rose till I could see that, hard as it was working, that baby was coming for sure.

I picked up my knife and stuck it between my teeths. Hauled my old bones over the edge of the cart to sit on the driver's bench. Picked up them reins in my hands, kind of gnarled for this kind of work, but I hung on and slapped the reins for the horse to get up.

I had the idea if patrol seen me driving the cart right in the open this a way, they'd figure I was addle-pated or dangerous or at least not worth they trouble.

I got the cart to where I figured we was in a copse of trees on the edge of somebody's farm, cause I could see fruit trees blooming just past the wild growth. It was getting on gloaming time and I at last climbed in the back to help with the tail end of the birthing.

Rose White had passed out. The baby already came with the cord all wrapped around its little neck. It was curled up in the bear fur, laying still.

So I took and cut away the cord from the baby's neck and took hold the end of the cord to ease the birthing bag out of Rose White's body and bury it, too. Rubbing the baby din't do nothing but flop its little thin limbs and break my heart. *Maybe that baby was too tiny to make it, anyway*, I told myself.

And truth be told, Rose White was still too young for birthing. And no good at all for checking the moon to see when her blood was supposed to come.

But even after I said all that to myself, I hunched down low in the cart and held the baby to my own breast in case it wasn't all the way dead and might just hear my heartbeat and come around.

Started talking to the baby. "Your ma'am go'n miss you something powerful. Don't you want to hang around just a little minute? Get to know your ma'am better? Ain't angels in heaven sweeter than your ma'am here on earth, baby."

But it was gone too far. And at the last I figured I better bury that baby before Rose White came around. *Or should she get one last chance to hold it?*

I slipped it inside her dress right upside her breast and hugged her arms around it.

I had watered the horse and was leading her back to the cart when I heard a snap like someone walking on the twigs had got too close for me to beat him to the cart.

I hauled on the horse, thinking to get near the cart and then take off at a gallop, so they would maybe chase after the nag if not after some old tough woman like me. But when I came in sight of the cart, I could see over the brim it was Sami in there, not one of the patrol.

He had climbed inside and was rousing Rose White, and they was finding together in the blood and the chill from the night coming around that they baby was dead.

He clamped his hand on her mouth when she set in to gasping and wailing. I should have buried that baby when Rose White was still knocked out.

Tough thing about being a mother. Most of the time, your best ain't go'n turn out good as you want it to. And half the time after that, even you can't figure out what you was up to, when you did whatever you done that turned out so wrong.

How could I have been so stupid as to leave that dead baby with my little gal?

It took us days to gather all the folks we could still find. Most of them must have been shot and hauled off for bounty, from what we had to bury, and another bunch of them carried off and sold, when couldn't no more bodies be found. Almost all the animals was gone, probably carried off by the farmers while the ruckus was going on.

Might have been a few of them took to the woods and ain't wanted to be found by nobody. Figured they could get to freedom better without Sami Wolf Water than with him.

Can't say I blamed them.

But my heart went out to Sami and my daughter, in them days after the patrol raid. After the patrol wrecked and slaughtered our caravan, Sami wasn't never again jovial and full of his self.

He had us keep to the woods and walk hushed like runaways do, hiding out and scattering for burrows and banks and caves and hollow tree trunks at the slightest sound. Stealing fruit from orchards and berries off the vine and tubers out the ground when our supplies ran low, instead of walking head held high into the supply stores. Staying away from every town and every no-account tramp along the road, for fear everything was always some kind of trap Sami ain't figured out yet.

Now and again I caught Sami setting up high on his horse with his rifle but got his head slung down between his shoulders like he was scared or shamed or both.

They ain't named the baby before they buried it.

After a while, a few of the ones who run off started sneaking back to join the caravan, talking about how they escaped not just the patrol but after that every two-bit wanderer looking to make him a quick dollar at the next trading post.

They started talking strange about Bully. "You find him," they say, "and you think: 'Somebody big as him? Ain't nobody go'n come after him!' Figure you be safe traveling a little ways with him. But dogged if don't one two nights go by in his company and, next thing you know, the patrol raiding on your little group again."

"Watch out for that Bully," they said.

They fell to talking quick and quiet in little bunches about where was Sami's new plantation from where we was, and how much longer till we get there, and who was too sick and too tired to keep going at this pace.

But who wanted to fall behind and risk what happened to loners?

Everybody wanted to die trying to get somewhere. Some more of them did.

And then the woods gave out.

We came up on a stretch of flat land all cleared of trees and had to take our courage in our hand and form another caravan to go out in the open. Them was mean days.

Sami had to let on all of us wasn't but a bunch of hands off the chain being walked from one plantation to

327

another, and him nothing but the driver, sent to herd us. It hurt his pride something terrible, to lie on us and on his own self that way.

But it was me who counseled him to do it. And, for once, he listened.

I came on him, sitting on his horse and staring at that bald ugly stretch of open road on the spreading plain between us and some strange freedom he done got all up in his head.

I said, "Mr. Sami, baby, can't nothing take away what all you did for these people. But now ain't the time to save us our pride. Time to eat that stale old humble pie, honey. Say what the patrol go'n want to hear, next time we run into any of them."

He said, still studying that road, "Ma'am, I've told you for a year now not to call me sir and Mr. How can you call me those things after what I've done to your daughter, anyway?" And he kneed his horse and started on into the sun and the rocky yellow dirt.

It near on choked him to keep repeating that story, calling all us "Mr. Dennis's niggers," but he stuck to it till we cleared that burning plain and hit some new forest.

It grew up like out of a nightmare.

All us got our head up and looking around at how these woods was thick and dank, air too ripe to breathe good. It was hot and close in there, and got long green things dripping off the scaly tree legs and brushing your face, and then all us slipping into that slime that pass for water in the swamp, till you think the woods they self is alive and coming after you.

The deeper we gone in the swamp and the stank and staring after where the water rippled alongside the path

328

we was cutting, because some living thing slid into it to follow us, the more terror-struck we all got.

And not like you could sleep the terrors off at night.

Because the heat and stank and huge biting bugs never let up. The dark made it so you couldn't tell what strange new thing had lit out after us, or which one of the slushing sounds of the swamp, walking and swimming and crawling after us, was the whisper of the next death in our caravan.

Sami set some mens to take turns keeping watch at night.

But he was low on bullets and powder for his own gun and ain't trusted that to nobody, anyway. So the mens on watch couldn't do nothing but shout and beat the undergrowth to scare off anything raiding and wake us all up to get out of there.

Caught some wild meat to roast and feed folks, who had walked they self all skinny and dry.

My poor Rose White took to walking, too, to ease her aching back and spirit and flush the last of that birthing blood out of her swelled body.

Sami gave her a baby whose ma'am died on the open ground and got buried. The baby needed milk, and we lost all our goats and cows to them scavenging poor farmers that followed the patrol. Sami asked Rose White to nurse the baby that lost its ma'am.

She looked at him and said nothing. But she carried the baby. I didn't know she wasn't nursing it, after all, till days after I thought the stank in this forest had got too thick.

And me, trying to ride as much as I could next to my Rose White, climbed down from the driver's bench on the cart because what Rose White got in her arms worried me.

. I come up on her. The closer I got, the more I said, "No, this can't be."

That baby had turned gray in her arms. She ain't even cared enough to put it down and let somebody bury it.

I reached for her arms, to stop her.

But when she turned full on me, and I seen the wet on the front of her dress, her running milk, and this gray baby ashy and wrinkled, dead with its mouth open for wanting what she got to give, and she wouldn't give it, I just went sick.

I called to Sami, "Sami, you halt this train. Get down off that horse and come get your wife and what be left of this baby."

She stared at Sami while he pulled away the baby, flopping and thin in his hands till you thought it was going to fall apart if he kept on tugging it. I looked away.

The people gathered to see what went wrong now. Next thing I heard was a splash in the muck and the green slime. And folks calling out, "Mr. Sami, it gone? You done throwed it away?"

I turned back to Rose White and told Sami to help me strip that dress off of her, got stiff from the dry milk, and the stank from the baby caught in it. Couldn't wash it in this dead slime.

We got it off her cause she ain't resisted none. Wrapped and tied my old shawl around her hip for a skirt. Waist still boggy from the baby she carried, but getting little and thin from starving and all this endless walking. Sami pulled off his shirt from his back and buttoned it on her and then, on second thought, opened it and tied the ends tight under her big milk breasts, to catch the milk that was already running again. Somebody else baby was crying.

"That cursed milk should have dried up by now, shouldn't it?" he asked me. "I thought milk dries if nothing nurses it."

I said, "Maybe holding that other baby kept it running. It will dry up soon now."

He said, "Help me get her in the cart until we cross the water. She shouldn't look down."

So of course, once I was up and driving Rose White and all the other sick people in my cart, it was me the idiot who looked down.

What Sami ain't wanted her to see was the water was so thick that the dead baby ain't sunk. Its purple head bobbed up out of the black and green muck.

I thought if my cart wheels got stuck right about here and I had to get out and get close to that baby one more time to push on them wheels, I would throw myself in and die.

It was shortly after this that Bully come crashing and sloshing through the mud so thick a man could walk on it, grinning and skinning like no tragedy done struck.

Got a gun on him, too, Sami ain't made him account for.

I come up on Sami late that night tying Rose White to sleep on top of his horse with him, to stay off the ground away from the snakes. I said, "Sami, get rid of this man. You can't trust him. Why he won't tell you who gave him that gun? On account of the patrol gave it to him. Bully is scouting for patrol, and you the only one won't admit it."

Sami turned sober and older in these weeks after the raid. In the dark, somebody's peat fire off in the distance threw light on his face, and little lightning bugs blinked all around his head. Sami said, "Why would the patrol give Bully a gun, ma'am? I know you mean to protect us, but I think we're better off with Bully right now than without him." He hefted his self up on the horse and leaned around my Rose White to say, "Besides, ma'am, he's got a gun now, just like I have. How can I get rid of him without risking everyone's safety?"

"You and the mens sneak up on him when he sleep."

"And kill him? What will everybody think of me if I kill one of the people who left the plantation with me, trusting me? I just don't see what I can do about Bully until more people in the group start feeling he's a danger."

"Sami, you ain't studying on what they feel. You studying on what they get up the nerve to come and say to your face."

"Ma'am, that's the only thing I can go by."

And Bully come stomping and squishing through the dark to say, "Mr. Sami, you go'n sleep, why I don't sit up with mens on watch? Me, I got the only other gun, if patrol come round."

Now that Bully had joined us, it seemed that every few nights some woman or child disappeared in the swamp, with no screaming to mark they passing out the group. Like the Hairy Man and his gang done sold off the people they stole the first time and was now back for more. With Bully back among us, all them cracking, far-off dry sounds of somebody else camping and following had started up again.

I figured it was Bully picking up and carrying off pocket change people to the Hairy Man, who waited nearby in the swamp to take them and sell them off for liquor and bullet money. Just enough to keep his patrol alive, following us, while we died on our feet.

Stirring up them strange slimy things the peoples scavenged to go in the cooking pots, I asked myself why I didn't just take my paring knife and slit Bully's throat while he had his face in a leaf full of food.

Our little group was so lean and ragged and picked off that we didn't look like we could have survived the swamp, by the time we stood at the far side of a rushing little clean creek and Sami drew us up short.

Sami said, "There it is."

All of us was in faded rags running off our body like the sweat that couldn't run, the air was so heavy and wet. Ashy skin and wild hair, cause nobody could get away from the mud and the snakes in the dirty water to wash they self. Couldn't feel the bugs to pull them off no more, everybody was so bit and sore, and had shut they body off from they mind. Didn't feel nothing, not even the meat falling off they bones till they all looked shrunk and shriveled.

It was like the happy, hopeful folks that left Mr. Dennis died on the road. This wasn't nothing but hags and zombies struggling up to Mr. Sami's new place, just pulling they feet out the slush and walking.

Rising up across the dark water of that big river and the clear water of that bubbling creek was a nightmare place like you hide from for fear of haunts, not go to for shelter.

Set way back behind big weeping trees hanging brown and green curling vines that blew and caught in the wind, we saw charred white fingers thick and fat that used to be pillars, but now was broke like claws struggling up out of the ground. They was like something that died but didn't want to stay in the grave. And all around them, a burned walls crumbled just behind, falling away into more green in the swamp and forest beyond.

Sami said, "Looks like our neighbors heard we were coming and torched the place. Word gets around, in the countryside."

Like he lost his mind, Sami started to chuckle.

Then he put his head on the horn of his saddle and slumped with his shoulders shaking. I got down off the driver's bench of my cart and went to him.

My hand ain't touched him before he sat up straight an told me, "Go see to Rose White, please, ma'am. Everyone, at least it's ours, and it's shelter of a kind. Come on."

And our little group straggled across the creek, squinting in the sun that made it through the break in the trees and thinking, *Maybe it wouldn't have been so bad to die on that long road. Maybe it won't be so bad to try to survive here.*

The closer you got to the place, the more the vines and trees reached across over your head and closed together like they was whispering, sighing and laughing light as a breeze because they could shut us in till we missed the chance to turn and run.

These trees had they knees up out of the mud and the water, like they could light out and chase us, follow us into Sami's burned out nightmare house, charred little pieces of wall opening out in welcome.

We stepped on into the blasted place under a waving parasol of leaves and looked up and around, and then down in front of our feet. Vines from the leaping green trees reached across the pillars and the sky and laced a new roof here and there. Patches in the wood and marble floors showed where the fire ain't made it through the wet

334

to burn. Stairs climbed crooked up to nowhere and dropped off to where it wasn't no floor way down below. And it was strange how walls was burnt through the middle and busted at the bottom but roped with vines still holding them up over the green and moving ground, with bits and pieces of chimneys scattered around.

And rising up from everywhere the sound of little creatures skittering and squeaking and calling out, flapping they wings to get away from the smell of the people coming through. Only, you couldn't see them.

Couldn't see nothing but the still, and the shadows, and the light dapped through the leafy green.

We stood on the edge of this crawling pit, and Sami said, "Vandals can't drive us away. Do we need to fear people who won't even come out and face us in an equal fight?" He shouted, "Vandals and cowards!"

He bellowed and turned in his saddle to throw his voice on every side. It bounced off the bits of brick and wood and walls weaved out of vines. "Give my men weapons and face us in a fair fight! Cowards! Cowards, all of you!"

I picked my way over the slippery charred tiles at the entranceway. The slime that crawled over the ash made hard walking.

I reached for Sami in the saddle. Bunch of the mens come around and looked up, talking to him, too. "Mr. Sami, sir, first off, why don't we hunt around see if some food growing on this place? It was a farm, wasn't it? Look for shelter," trying to reason with him.

Somebody muttered, "You keep bellowing like that, you fool, and sure enough somebody be done slid out these shadows and shot your crazy wife clean through the head."

Sami stopped. Looked around, frowning, at his little group. But whoever said it ain't wanted to stand out. Everybody frowned back up at Sami.

I went back and climbed in the cart to hold onto Rose White.

Sami said, "Don't ever call me 'Mr.' any more, any of you. And don't let me hear you calling anyone 'sir.' We're through with all that. You're right. Let's go through here to the other side, where the farmland and Quarters must be. Maybe we can find food and shelter there." Sami clicked his tongue for his horse to go on across.

It shied and ain't wanted to go. The peoples started backing up, too, to go around.

Sami shouted, "Hey! Stop!"

Folks stopped and looked at him.

Sami said, "Everyone, this is *your* house. You are my guests and my friends and my family, here. Go *through* this house. *Not* around it." And he started his horse forward again.

He would pull up on it now and again to keep it from shying, but he still got his back to us, all rigid and tight, like he ain't even got to make sure we still followed him through this blasted house. Because no matter what he said to the contrary, he knew he was still leading us.

At first nobody moved.

So I pulled up on the side of the cart Bully was driving for me again and said, "You! Bully! You heard Sami Wolf Water! If he don't mind this muddy cart tracking all across his floor, then it ain't for you to come along and mind it for him. Drive this old nag through this house and on out back and find us some place to rest."

My voice echoed and rang and flapped on up to the scattered patches of bright sky.

The trek from Mr. Dennis's plantation was long. But the trek through that burned out house seemed longer.

As we followed Sami through the house, them scarred pillars scratching at the moss that draped down to make a ceiling would creak and start to sway when you walked under one. And the floor would buckle and dip like it meant to flip you into the swamp and cover you. And above the groaning and heaving gleamed a coat of running rot that stretched everywhere the shadows hid it from the sun.

You couldn't take but a step at a time.

Me and Rose White clutched the side of the sick cart and watched below where the wheels rolled.

And we watched the raggedy people tiptoe through this burned slime next to us like tiptoeing through the swamp, jumping every time a bat struggled out of a fireplace, sooty and squeaking, to tumble through the air to get away. The people slipped and swung they arms so as not to fall into the ooze all over the floor, crying out every time something scuttled across they feet where they couldn't see but could only feel to walk, leaving little scratchy tickling sticky tracks.

Somebody said, "You all, watch out for snakes."

And just like that, one woman gone down into the liquid dark along the floor screaming, "Snake bite, you all! Help me!"

I was over the side of that cart and onto the floor with my knife before I stopped to think what was I doing.

The floor bucked and rolled under me. The slime that covered it slid away from my feet, and I fell on all fours. Ashes and ooze sucked on my hands. With my knife between my teeths and breathing through my nose, that whole house smelled like rot and fire.

On the floor, the woman or the house moaned. I heard Bully urge on the horse, and Rose White come to herself and called to him, "No! Ma'am out there! Don't leave my ma'am, Bully!"

And I heard other folks slipping and scrambling to come help, and others trying to run and get out of there, calling back, "Evil, you all! The house evil! Get out!"

I crawled, aching, till I bumped into the woman. And then I ran my fingers down her ankle till her hand caught mines and guided it to where you could feel the punctures puffing in and out. Snake that bit her must have been startled and slid away. I ain't felt it nowhere.

The whole time I cut on her and sucked on the bad blood and spit it around me, trying to make a blessed circle like the old folks teach you to do, nothing bothered her nor me again. The few folks who came running leaped back every time I skeeted another mouthful of blood. I started wondering why they was ducking and dodging instead of trying to get inside my blessed circle. I said, "You all, come on in this side the circle. You safe in here."

A voice out the dark, where I see the shapes of people backing away, said, "Ma'am, Miss Sister, that wasn't no snake bit that woman. You gots to get out of here. Drag her, if you got to. That was the house itself that reared up and attacked her. Luring you. Trapping you."

I stopped and sat up to look at her.

But I couldn't. All of a sudden, it was too dark, in the shadows just where she fell.

And other shadows, the people, was steady drawing away, leaving us here.

I stopped sucking on and spitting from this woman's bleeding leg. She started in to shiver. I could feel her under my hand.

Then I could hear her.

She started sobbing and choking in the dark where the shadows fell so thick along the floor I couldn't even see her face from where I was, kneeling at her feets. When I reached to stroke her cheek and say, "Hush. Calm would be better for you," my fingers touched so thick a cold layer like sweat or damp from the swamp and the house that they slid right off her jaw and bounced into the slime on the floor.

Something reached up out of the slime, touched my hand, and wrapped around my wrist quick and tight.

It tugged, like it was going to yank me down.

I hollered. Pulled back. Let loose of the woman.

Some few folks still outside the circle reached in to grab me, saying, "Too late, Miss Sister! You can't help her. The evil in this house got her!" And they hauled me out into the faded sunshine out back behind the ruin.

We sat blinking in the dying light of one sad day, studying what to do next. Go on back in there and try and drag out the dying woman?

We took a peek back into that gathering dark and called out.

No answer.

"She dead," somebody said. "Before you screamed, Miss Sister, I felt it. House took her."

"We'll pray for her when we get settled. Pray for all those lost on the journey here."

Sami called some of the mens to come with him to the abandoned fields that ain't burned. You could hear them out there breaking and snapping something that

339

sounded like stalks. They brought they haul back to the rest of us.

We all sucked on this sweet, wet stuff that ran out the thick strings we chewed on. A woman said, "You all. Ain't it a shame none of the childrens made it here to taste this?" Her and some the others started crying in the dark coming down.

Then we all started spitting out the sweet strings and followed where Sami's voice called that him and his mens done checked the Quarters and it ain't no snakes in them.

These Quarters sat up on stilts that let you know the creeks through this place must flood pretty regular. These stilt shacks was splintered and weather worn, dripping fungus right off the walls and growing it thick and black and green in the corners.

But they all had doors, and a few of them had mats and pallets folks left behind. Some of us scrambled into the Quarters and beat the mats and pallets to shake the vermin out. If you ain't breathed too deep when you first stretched on them, they cushioned your bones.

Only, just like the floor in the big house, some of them shack floors ain't wanted to stay put.

Few folks said, "You get use to it, I reckon," and threw they self down on mats and floors and fungus to get some sleep.

At nightfall, Sami and the mens lit fires in stone circles all around the Quarters, to scare off beasts. They hoped they wasn't drawing the neighbors that burned down the house in the first place.

After Sami and them seen the rest of us settled, they went back to the burnt big house.

In the morning, Sami and Bully told everybody they done went in and found the snakebit woman and hauled her out and buried her decent.

They ain't said where.

And we ain't that stupid. Where you bury something in a place where the ground don't stay put long enough to hold up a shack?

On the way to the field to save some of that cane, somebody said, "We best take care that woman don't turn up like Mr. Sami's grandma'ammy, dancing in somebody else bones." Cause we figured whatever was evil in that house wanted something.

There was no place to go. And Sami wanted the house cleaned out. He said we was going back in there when the sun shined again, even into the corners, and when the shadows stretched, we was going to get out.

But every day, we found good cause to stay out.

Rainy days, and it sure rained a plenty.

We cut and stacked that cane with whatever knife folks got on them or could find rusty in the sheds and hunted around in the swamp, trying to figure what you could eat and what might eat you, and plucked up wild greens that got a stank on them like you was hauling dead bodies to the cooking pot.

And that rain steady falling. Whoever was any good at fishing, the rest of us let them go from the field work and the work Sami wanted in that evil house of his.

He said, "After enough time goes by, let's work up our nerve to go into the big towns along the big river and get wood and tools and to rebuild the place."

Looked like he was going to spend the rest of his life watching and working and planning.

But after what seemed a good long while, Sami Wolf Water recalled he had a wife he ain't set eye nor hand on in a long time. One night when the fire circles burned, and he come creeping up the stair ladder talking about, "Ma'am, have we repaired a cabin of your own for you, yet?"

I said, "Now, ain't that something? Boy done waited till the sun go down and the haunts is prowling to come and tell an old woman to get lost." But I put on a grin, like I was just kidding, so Rose White ain't had to lose that big pretty smile she got all of a sudden, for the first time since the baby died.

It might be good for everybody if them newlyweds at last spend a night together.

We would never get back to normal, though. Like me, carrying a knife everywhere I go, stuck right in the rope around my waist.

Near on normal would just have to do.

I said, "I was just on my way to my shack right now."

I started down the ladder stairs and stopped cause I heard scuffling. I looked and seen shapes of men kicking out our fires.

I screamed, "Sami! The Hairy Man and them!"

Folks flew out they shacks. You could hear the clack of sticks and knives everywhere. Without firelight, I guess the Hairy Man and his posse couldn't see to shoot.

Sami jumped past me down the ladder hollering, "To the house, I tell you! Everyone, to the house!"

And as much as we feared that evil house with its reaching pillars and that sucking ooze, we ran for it now. Scrambled up the steps, pulling each other across the threshold, and ain't paused nor hung back till we was all wedged in tight places. Little nooks up under the stairs.

Corners inside the fireplaces. Burnt holes in the thick walls.

Womens snuggled in and balled up like babies, listening and waiting, cause it sounded like the mens was shouting to each other and hacking at the Hairy Man's gang. You could hear cursing and sharp things hitting flesh and air getting knocked out of big bodies. And all a sudden somebody yelled, "Come on! Let's cut our losses and get, you all!"

It grew quiet in the Quarters.

Then the tramp of strong feet on the walkway behind the house. Bully's voice floated in the dark. "You all, womens? Hey. You all can come on out here. They gone."

Little sounds like some of the womens fixing to creep out of hiding places. I shouted, "Stop! Don't nobody give orders around here but Sami! And you ain't him, Bully! Where Sami, if it's so safe?"

The womens was still.

But there was somebody still creeping. Bully. Looking for me?

I could hear him close to where he heard my voice. His feet went from scuffling where folks laid the slime outside with cane peelings and wild grass to slushing on the floor of the house. Sticky, sneaking sounds.

Him touching things to get his bearings.

All around rose the smell of the house when it got burned and the rot waited to take it over again, abandoned. And all of a sudden, listening for Bully and hiding in the house's blasted belly, I thought I was wrong to take on so about how this house was evil.

Evil was done to it, that was all. Evil stayed like a stench you just had to clean out.

Bully said softly in the dark, "Now, Miss Sister, ma'am, I ain't never knowed what all you got against me. I come sparking your daughter in good faith, all them years ago, and you chased me off. I come here trying to protect the other one, and you trying to tell Mr. Sami I put her in danger. Miss Sister, I think it's time you and me had us a little understanding."

I ain't said a word back till I heard Bully right up on my little piece of wall. Then I pushed out from it and shoved myself hard right into him. I said, "Understand this, Bully."

I could almost see his eyes reflect the starlight that made its way through the chinks in the vine roof. He stared at me the whole time he sank to his knees.

He was still kneeling there, plucking at my knife, but his fingers was getting weak and slippery with the blood, and he couldn't latch on the knife good, on account I had pulled it out his belly as he sank and kept shoving it in his chest while he knelt there, every time he got it worked a little loose. Took me two hands and leaning with all my little weight, cause all them bones is close and tight and strong in a grown man's chest.

If the wall hadn't hid me and pushed me, I couldn't have done it. But now here was Bully, kneeling and coughing blood.

He couldn't talk.

So I said, "You me done talked enough for my lifetime, Bully. I'm go'n let this cooking knife do my talking for me tonight." Only I grunted because keeping that knife in his chest was some hard work

At last, the knife handle slid out of my hands and went with Bully as he sagged to the floor.

I was breathing hard and called out to the womens, "You all stay put. I'm old. I'm go'n go check, see if this traitor done led that Hairy Man's gang in here to find us. You don't come out from wherever you hiding without some sunshine in here, so you see who is in here with you. If somebody comes up to you, kill him like I killed Bully. Don't be scared. This is a good house."

I bent and tried to get my only knife out of Bully. I was still tugging and shoving when I heard Sami call, "Hey! Are the women in here? It's me. Sami. I think we got rid of that gang."

I heard Rose White call to him and run to him, slipping and gasping, in the dark. I heard other womens picking they way across the floor, asking Sami about they mens.

I got my knife worked out of Bully and went to where everybody gathered where the house let out to the shacks and the fields.

Mens walked up to join Sami and the womens, looking back like they might spot some more patrol.

Sami said, "I don't think it's a good idea for us to be sleeping in the shacks, out in the open. Let me show all of you what some of us have found."

Folks had to rekindle the doused fires to make torches. We followed Sami back into the house to a corner behind some stairs.

A metal ring was bolted into a patch of floor. Mens grabbed hold together and hauled the ring up, grunting and swearing because it ain't wanted to come. But at last the ring pulled up a heavy slab door that opened a pit going down out of sight.

A rush of cool air and noises came up like living things was down in there, getting away from our torchlight and seeking the quieter dark.

Mr. Sami said, "It's a wine cellar, everyone. It seems secure. It's lined with stone along most of the walls. Come on. Those who have torches will lead the way. We'll sleep here nights, until we can get the rest of the house built back up around us."

He went down first, the fire strong on his face. Other peoples with fire followed.

Chill and stank, and cold mold on stone walls that Sami said would hold back the mud if it rained and flooded down here.

After all we had done to clear the cane field and hunt the swamp and even beat back the woods from growing close in on the house, we sank down into the dark following little red lights that leapt around in a circle off the few torches.

We huddled together, trying to find niches in the walls for the torches and stones on the floor to hold the fires and keep them burning out of the mud.

Sami said, "It's all right, everyone. I've followed this cellar through, and it leads to a tunnel that gets fresh air. I don't know where it comes from, but there's plenty of fresh air in here. Let's sleep now. We're safe." He came and hugged Rose White on the other side of me.

Sami was as good as his word and fell asleep cramped and sitting up on the earth and ooze with his back shoved against the damp stone wall. Rose White leaned her head on his shoulder.

I sat and listened through the cellar door over our head for the sound of the Hairy Man's gang, coming back.

Somebody got up and found some old bottles covered with dust and spider webs. Somebody else said that was good liquor, the kind folks hides under the ground. So some of the peoples set to drinking. And fell asleep.

I was still wake, drowsing and dreaming off and on about how it felt to stab Bully, when Rose White woke and asked Sami was it morning yet. He got some of the mens up to help him shove the cellar door open.

I crawled out, stiff and hurting. Later, when the folks got to moving stuff they found in the shacks down to the cellar, to make a little village down there, I told Sami about Bully.

Me and Sami gone looking for the body and couldn't find it nowhere.

Sami said, "Ma'am, it's like I thought. There's no way you could've killed that man. But you were right. He was probably with that gang, and made his escape with them. He was the one who relieved me of my watch, so I could be with Rose White, when the men came. Believe me, if Bully comes back, I'll shoot him on sight."

I said, "He ain't coming back. He dead."

Sighs. "Then where's his body, ma'am?"

I said, "The house took it as a peace offering. We made peace together. We're go'n be all right."

And we was.

Living down in that little village every night, cooking around our camp fires and telling stories of the Hairy Man and the way life would now be good to our childrens, because they started getting born, first to Sami and Rose White, and then to more of the new couples breaking off to make they own camp fires.

Hope was Sami and Rose White's baby, the first born in the underground village who lived.

We never did get that house above the cellar rebuilt.

Too many ain't wanted to come out of the ground and risk living where they might be easy to hunt. And why risk it when we had found a place and a way to survive?

After Hope was born and lived, more babies started getting born. Broken hearts and broken families was on the mend.

And Sami took to wandering deeper with his torch through the cellar maze, that tunnel where it ran to earth, close and cold, whenever Rose White told him take the torchlight down off the wall; it was waking a new baby.

He would wander, deeper into wherever the maze took him, and come back to his pallet by morning. Nudging me to move now, let him lay down by his wife and childrens.

All girls. Hope, and Faith. Then Justice and Mercy.

Our group ain't growed but by births. We trusted no strangers and took in nobody new. Soon, the swamp and the cane field and the cellar was our life.

And maybe that was all right. After all, it was freedom of a kind not to have even one of your babies sold from you. Rose White would never know the only life I knew.

The first dozen of my babies was all sold. I never knew the first thing about all of them, like where they went, and how they lived.

But I would know all that about these grandbabies. Whatever kind of freedom this was, it would have to be enough for me.

My time must be coming, at last. When you start thinking like that, about what your life amounts to, you know you're fixing to lay down and start dying quiet.

I started taking to my pallet more careful.

Did it slip my mind to give some kindness that day? Answer some question? Hug one of my grandbabies tight? Tell Rose White she made me proud, and I'm glad I came with her and had the chance to hold and help raise her childrens?

*Better tell her I hope she marry all these little gals to these young boys growing up in our cellar village before they get too shapely for they own good. I won't be around forever, to help guide and advise.*

Already new problems started.

Some of the peoples left our little village and went to town without Sami and his gun to sell the cane, saying they wanted to buy wine when ours got drunk or swap money earned off cane to get clothes, knives, pots, hoes. Or trade honest work for money.

But for all that, whenever they went without Sami and his gun, they never made it back.

Once one of these womens who wanted nothing but a new dress got hauled back past our place on a chain gang, stripped naked and screaming for help.

Her man took off after her, but Sami and the mens chased after him and knocked him down. They hauled him back and got everyone back down into the cellar before the chain drivers broke off and came looking around for where we hid at night.

And then one night, Sami come back through the tunnel, dragging his old bear skin and waving his torch and calling, "People, I've seen the angel!"

I thought sure my time had come, and the spirits had sent me someone to guide me on.

Sami came to Rose White and me and his little gals and dropped on his knees. Peoples crawled up from they mats and drew close to hear Sami.

Sami said, "The angel who saved my wife's life, when we were young, the angel who guards my father's plantation. She came to me again, as she did so long ago when I was lost and wandering in the woods. She came here, where the tunnel opens out into a cave that watches over the town. Do you remember the angel, Rose White? You've seen her, too." He begged, wanting to share this vision.

Rose White nodded, staring into the torchlight like she was scared.

Sami spread his arms, waving the torch wide. "The angel came to me. And in her wings, she carried a child. When the angel opened her wings, the child spoke to me."

"Sami, what did the child in the angel's wings say?"

Sami's face shone wet in the torchlight with tears of joy and sorrow, after all these years. Sami said, "The child hidden in the angel's shining wings told me that we have to go back. People, we have to go back."

Rose White said, "Sami, we're safe here, raising our babies. You don't recall how we suffered on that trek? How I lost my child?" She grabbed her girls sitting wide-eyed around her and started crying with Sami.

Other peoples started talking at once.

"Back to that plantation? To slave for Mr. Dennis?" And spit on the floor.

"Who is Mr. Dennis, Ma'ammy?"

"What does that mean, slave for Mr. Dennis?"

"What is a angel?"

Me, the first one who should want to stay put and get my old bones buried in the earth, I said, "But you all. Rose White. Maybe it's something here us don't understand."

Sami looked over at me and struck his chest with his free hand. "That's just it, ma'am. I don't understand. But I feel it here. Who will come with me?"

Who could stay here without Sami and his gun and him knowing how to sell the cane and yet make it back safe to the village in the cellar?

By the next evening, when me and Rose White and Sami hung around the back of the burnt house instead of going down to safety to the cellar village, trying to figure how to make our way back to the old plantation, folks drifting in from the swamps and the field stopped to listen and comment.

"Going back would mean we'd stop hiding in the cellar," they murmured.

"Stop fearing being out too long in the field, planting and harvesting."

"Stop stealing the clothes off dead bodies floating down the swamp and lynched in the trees, cause we scared to stay in town and buy more with cane money than food."

"We can stop wondering can our childrens carry on like this after we're gone, naked most of the time, wrapped in rags and eating whatever floats or flies by, hiding from getting stole and sold away." This brought murmurs of assent from everyone.

So it came that one day at sundown, we grouped at the back of the burned out mansion. Folks tied knives and hoes on they bodies, slinging babies and water skins on they back. Lingering, because it was hard to leave the place we learned to be safe in.

And all of a sudden, a dark woman was there with us.

It was so quick and quiet, how she came, that some of us screamed that she was a ghost. I know I did.

351

But then my heart about stopped in my throat, and I ran on my stiff old legs to hug her.

It was Rose Red. She hadn't changed. All this time had passed, and she was sprightly as a girl.

She was dressed in a soft skin, had it wrapped around her feets. She had a baby-miracle of miracles!-strapped on her back and sleeping. Rose White put her hands all over her sister like she didn't believe she really was there. She patted her sister's face and shook her head, crying and saying, "Rose Red, you ain't aged one day. Don't you dare look at me! Look at you. You a sight for sore eyes, I swear."

After the hugging and screaming and crying was done, Rose Red looked back through the burnt house and said, "You all, I can't stay. Only, my man knew for the longest where I could find you, and tonight he said I best go to you and say good-bye. That you all wouldn't be here no more. Wish he told me sooner. All this time, I missed you so."

Sami came between us to Rose Red and grabbed hold of her arm, saying, "Your husband knows his way through these swamps? Is that right?"

Rose Red took her arm away, none too gentle. "He knows all the land between here and Solace's plantation. We run it year long, Sami, hunting."

Me, Sami, Rose White, we all looked at each other. The angel had sent us the way home.

# CHAPTER NINE

The people came out of my father's cellar with their own stories. We would walk, and somebody would start a song that was a story.

It was the beginning of fall, and there was mist in the morning. We walked through the gray and the dew drops, and everybody would sing the tail end of each song together, like that was the part of the story they all shared in common.

The sun would rise and send yellow and pink light through the dew. And that song would kind of die and another would rise in its place.

All the songs were stories: of that first trek to my father's land and how we had to live in the caverns. Abut how dark it was, and how we were afraid of what lived in the ruins over our heads and took our dead away in the night.

Of how we couldn't farm for fear of being seen and found out and taken away.

Of the cries of the woman who went alone to the city and got dragged by our ruins on a chain gang.

It scared me how the old folks during the trek back to where they came from changed the life we had always lived into a misery I had never known. Their song stories were killing the life I had been forced to leave behind. At night on the trek, I tried to hear my dreams echo back there in the cellar. I tried to draw them out to me and dream them again.

I missed our cellar. I missed the part of me that lived back there, breathing and blowing through the stone tunnels when it was night and time to sleep.

I felt the cool air always on my skin and felt like it was the world's eyes on me. I'd remember I could never get away into our cavern's darkness and stillness again. It felt like I had lost my real self and the real story of the life we left behind.

The darkness and stillness in our cellar were never only dark and quietly dripping, but were a heartbeat underground.

It was the place where we were safe. Where I knew everybody and couldn't be surprised, like the old ones warned you never to let yourself be taken by surprise out on the swamp. Where little fires could glow on the faces of families that were all really my family, shut away from a world that didn't want us.

The cellar was where love lived and held us all together.

Until we left it for a dream that didn't even make sense.

Walking in the mist and rising sunlight scared me and made me want to go home to the cool dark that smelled like everything in the earth was being born and waiting to grow.

But especially lying down to sleep in that little breeze that ran all over my skin all the time, and never stopped, scared me and made me feel lost.

Our world was broken open. And we were all out here getting lost in a world that hated us, and singing about it. The old people's stories didn't tell it right.

Walking, I knew I was losing myself and everyone else, too.

I had never thought about Ma'ammy until the trek, when she suddenly didn't have time for me. She needed to keep an eye on Justice and Mercy. They were big enough to run around and keep up but not old enough to understand that we could still be in danger.

I wished Ma'ammy would keep an eye on me like she was doing with my two youngest sisters.

Like she had me doing with Grandma'am. Ma'ammy kept mumbling to me that I needed to stay by Grandma'am even after Jim Feather and Father stole off and found her a mule to ride out of the swamp.

Ma'ammy didn't trust Grandma'am on that mule even out on the plain road. She kept saying, "Watch out that Grandma'am don't doze and fall off." It was true that Grandma'am was so bony and tiny we never would have seen her, left lying behind in a dark heap on the road.

So I ended up walking by Grandma'am's mule through the flat plain, thinking of how nervous Father said the open plain made him. His old bald patchy bearskin was draped on the mule as a blanket for Grandma'am. What was left of some old gold coins and all that jewelry it was too dangerous to sell, that my father had sewn in the bear's paws, dangled and clinked while Grandma'am rode. She gripped the fur and pulled out spiky little hairs every time she nodded off and started to slip.

I'd reach over and push her back up straight. She'd slump and doze right away again.

I was afraid Grandma'am was dying. She used to talk about being ready to die, back in our cellar. Maybe nobody used to listen but me.

Now, out of the swamp and on the plain, and once we got to the woods, sometimes for hours walking I would think Grandma'am had already died.

I'd reach over to push her and couldn't feel her breathe.

And then for no reason she'd blink and give a little jump and sit up and say something to me. "Hope, baby, go fetch you old grandma'ammy some water, if Rose Red and them got any in that gourd yonder."

I'd call Faith to go get it. Because Ma'ammy would have pitched a terrible fit if I left Grandma'am even to get her a water gourd.

Faith was none too easy to call away from Aunt Rose Red. Faith thought everything about Aunt Rose Red was the best ever. How she looked as young as us but acted more grown up and in charge than Ma'ammy and Father together.

How she walked with a bounce like she was always ready to leap and run. How she swooped her little girl, Willow, down from off her back and nursed her, doeskin swinging and still keeping step with Uncle Jim Feather. Not like Ma'ammy, who had to stop and sit in the shade like an old woman, to nurse.

Aunt Rose Red didn't fear the woods. Nor the plains. Not even the swamp. She bragged to Faith that all the outdoors was her home. That all she feared was the inside of really big houses.

I got angry when Faith told me that.

We were lying next to Grandma'am and supposed to be asleep. I couldn't sleep for the feel of the wind on my skin, teasing me and scaring me. Faith couldn't sleep because she stayed in a state of excitement these days, Father said.

I guess he meant she thought everything was just so wonderful. Not wonderful one day, after you had been careful and quiet and stayed hidden in the dark until things changed in the world up there where people lived in the sunlight, like we grew up being told.

Wonderful right now. Every minute.

Like something had changed, and our parents hadn't even known it until Aunt Rose Red showed up. Like we were walking into our future with every step we took along this trek. Like that future was perfect to Faith.

Like we hadn't left anything at all of value behind us.

We lay on the dry ground where the dew only rested on the top of the soil until it got burned off again during the day. The ground was hard and felt like it wanted to shove us off.

You didn't sink into its pillows and holes while you slept. This ground didn't slush and talk to you. It didn't want you. You just lay there waiting for the dry open ground to push you up on your feet in the morning.

One night Faith said, "Hope, we'll never live under the ground again." She said it like it was the happiest thought she had, and she wasn't quite ready to believe her good luck.

I started to cry. Grandma'am woke up between us and asked what was wrong.

Faith said, "Hope wants to live under the ground. Aunt Rose Red says that's for dead people."

Grandma'am told me to put my head on those ridges that made her little chest, like when I was little.

I didn't want to do it. But after a while, Grandma'am pulled my head over like a pot and set it on her heart.

I could hear the thump thump inside behind her low old voice going on and on about her shack and her roses that she had from some other woman's garden. She was still explaining how roses open up one piece at a time like smile after smile with red lips and white teeth and even pink gums at the edges, when I fell asleep.

That one night, I didn't think to pull at my old dreams, trapped back there in my father's abandoned caverns. I dreamed about those roses of Grandma'am's.

Smiles grew on stems outside a shack. And Grandma'am stood in the door, smiling too. It made me feel better. I woke up thinking how nice it felt to have a good dream again.

While we walked the next day, I asked Grandma'am to show me any roses. "Grandma'am, where are roses?" I said. "Do you see any?"

She did that little jump of hers on her mule and started looking around. We had entered the woods by now.

Sometimes Father and Uncle Jim Feather argued about whether to walk by day or by night. Father said we'd be too easy to spot in the day. Uncle Jim Feather said we'd be too easy to shoot and kill, lying asleep in the broad daylight. Today, all I could think was how nice it was to be out walking at the same time that Grandma'am said any roses would be wide open and easy to spot.

The woods stretched and dipped and covered us over our heads, even with the frost burning off the leaves and stem tips. The cover overhead felt like we weren't quite so open to the sky and the world. I thought all I needed now to feel almost all right was to see that, in a place like this, those roses grew.

Grandma'am said, "Well now, baby, I don't see nary a rose. But look if it ain't some lovely morning glories climbing on the sunny side of that tree, and it be something looks mighty like flowers sprouting right nigh in that patch of light on the ground. Look yonder, Hope."

Looking for roses gave us something special to talk to each other about every day. We would point out growing things that you couldn't find in the swamp until Grandma'am got so tired she'd slide to the side of the mule before her eyes finished closing. It got so I had to ride on her mule and hold onto her from behind.

And once I was up behind her, holding her warm tiny body, I didn't feel so alone. In the daytime.

I could watch Aunt Rose Red skip like a young girl next to Uncle Jim Feather, their baby tied to her back with that doeskin, and say to myself, "Yes, she is a beauty. I see why Faith wants to be like her. I reckon." And it didn't feel like it cost me too much to see that.

I could look at all the grown ups I'd known to be sour and grouchy all my life, suddenly creeping through these woods smiling like they wondered if it was safe to be happy that they were going to what they called home. And I could say about them, "Maybe where they came from is better for them than the caverns. If they say so."

I even started asking Grandma'am about things like that on our mule, after we finished looking for roses. Grandma'am said, "Hope, baby, where them folks come from ain't better. It's just what they was used to, growing up. So they think they go'n like getting back to it, or whatever be left of it."

Only Father seemed sad any more. Besides me, I mean. Like he had done something that made him ashamed.

Like the time that woman went by our place in chains, and he wouldn't let anybody try to go help her.

And her little girl had to come stay at our family's fire until her own father was ready to take her back.

Father walked ahead of Jim Feather and Rose Red, most of the time. Sometimes he would fall back to keep an eye on stragglers. That meant me and Grandma'am on our mule, mostly. Especially when the mule decided to sit and take a rest.

Grandma'am would slide down off its back. I would hop back just in time to keep from getting bumped off by Grandma'am. And the mule would sit and bray if you yanked at it.

In the woods, if Grandma'am woke up when she hit the ground, she would send me to find flowers to hold in front of the mule's nose and back away saying, "Pretty girl. Come on, mule. Flowers for the pretty, pretty girl." But if the mule sat and Grandma'am fell off and stayed asleep, I would just tweak its ears. That made it move. Smartly, too.

Father would come running and gather up Grandma'am like a bundle of rags and try to straddle her across the mule's back while I rode and reached for her, like a doll.

I used to have grass dolls and even one made from rags. They were passed down to my sisters and finally burned in our family's fire when they were shredded and rotting with bugs.

Grandma'am prayed over them while they burned.

I gathered Grandma'am into my arms on the mule like a shredded grass doll and asked Father, "Sir, do you know what roses look like? Will we live in Grandma'am's shack with the roses?"

Father hung back to talk to me, tapping the mule's flank with a stick and slapping it with his hand now and then so he could look like he wasn't just loafing. He fooled everybody but me. I knew it tore him apart, every minute that he led the people back to where they had come from. He just wanted, sometimes, to get away from the head of the line.

Sometimes it hurt me to think how well I knew my poor father.

It seemed like I spent my whole life following after him, down through the caverns at night when I was supposed to be asleep. I'd rush to leave one of her babies nursing at Ma'ammy, both of them worn out from fussing.

Father would lift the fire out of the niche over our heads, and I would see it moving away from Ma'ammy and my sisters' faces. He would walk further, alone, into the dark tunnels with his torch from off the wall over our sleeping spot.

I would get up and follow after the flickers of light and Father with the feeling all of a sudden that I would be lost in the dark I usually loved so much, if I stayed behind without him.

I would hurry and stop, pressing my back against the wet walls, trying to keep up but stay out of sight, so Father wouldn't hear me and turn and find me and carry me back to the pallets around Ma'ammy and Grandma'am.

He was so sure and strong and brave as he bent into the narrowing tunnels where the caverns led to his cave, always going right into the dark walls that looked closed ahead of him. I would hide behind the juts of the sliding earth and firm stone wall and lean around to watch his bulk stoop and go on. I would fit my feet into the tracks made by his feet or his dragged bearskin.

I would watch my father with my whole heart. I wanted to be with him and have him say everything was okay. I wanted to be like him. I'm the only one of his girls who learned to walk stiff and tall and talk like a rich planter, like Father.

When he had gone as far into the tunnels as he would go for that night, he would set his torch onto a ledge or prop it against the tunnel wall and spread his bearskin to sit and think or stretch out and sleep.

I watched until he was asleep, wishing I could go to him. Then I would turn and feel my way back to Ma'ammy and my sisters, along the dripping stones.

The sounds of the cellar and caverns and tunnels, the slow trickles of water you never quite found and those sad echoes, like people had gotten lost and were always calling out, always stumbling back toward our village, were like Grandma'am's heartbeat to me. Steady, low and always there. Just like my own heart, how it beat hard for how much I loved my father.

I used to think those were the sounds of my dreams that waited in the cellar while I was awake and out in the cane field or the swamp, not thinking about them. And there they were, down where it was cool and safe, waiting and ready to surround me with good feelings when night came and I had to sleep.

My dreams, back there in the caverns, were my life. I used to always come back to them.

Maybe I wouldn't have followed Father into the tunnel if I had been sure he would always come back. If he didn't, then the cavern part of me, the heart of me, couldn't come to me and was going to be forever left behind, beneath the burned ruin. And that part of me, that I was losing now, was my lost life, my lost story of my life. My lost tale.

Grandma'am's heartbeat brought it back as close as it could get, that night she held my head on her chest and told me about her shack and her roses. That was when I decided that, if there was going to be a place for me at this old plantation we had to return to, it would have to be Grandma'am's shack. Maybe there, I could almost be whole again.

I wanted to share that hope with my father, who walked with his head down, ashamed. I tried to share it, when he walked beside me and Grandma'am and the mule.

Usually, Father never talked much about anything with me, more than to just answer my questions. But about the roses, he said, "Yes, Hope. I've seen roses. They're like other flowers except they open up to you." He walked quietly and thought some more. He looked up and smiled. "They're like when the person you love smiles at you for the first time. They give themselves to you." He looked over at me and slapped the mule's flank with a wink. "But you've never been in love, my dear," Father said. "What foolishness this must sound like to you."

In a way, Father was right. I kind of hadn't been in love.

All the other girls from the cellar village carried a flame for at least one of the boys we'd grown up with. Except Mercy. She was still a baby. And me.

What was wrong with me?

Maybe nothing. Maybe it was just that the boys were all thinner and smaller and sillier than my own father.

Father was everybody's leader. Everybody's hero. What did I need to fall in love with some skinny silly little boy for? And beyond need. How could I fall in love with anyone besides my father?

363

He was perfect. And lonely. He needed me. He just didn't know how much.

Which meant all the more I had to be faithful to him and love him and be ready for whenever he finally turned to me.

After he'd explained the roses, Father took no more interest in talking about Grandma'am's shack. Certainly not about whether or not we'd live in it. And once we got deep into the woods, well out of the swamp and past the plain, Father wouldn't let me and Grandma'am fall too far behind on our mule any more. If we did, he'd send Uncle Jim Feather or one of the other men back to walk beside us. And I didn't like that.

Not that Uncle Jim Feather said much of anything. He just walked along beside us on our mule, and you couldn't even hear his feet fall.

When we would camp at night, we lit our fires and slept far from the roads. We sat around our small fires in the woods and the people's stories changed some more. Now the old name of the Hairy Man came back to walk among us, and Father and Grandma'am were the Wily Boy and his mama again, so we could all feel safe.

I had not liked the people's stories on this trek about how some strange plantation was really our home. Now I really hated the people's stories. Like my father wasn't even mine anymore and never had been. He was just the group's leader. I couldn't be proud of that. That took him away from those long walks alone in the tunnel with me. Nobody sang about those, our times alone. Because nobody knew about them but me.

I tried harder to fall asleep remembering the sounds in the cellar. I lay with that pesky breeze on my arms. On my bare feet. I could never be covered enough.

The nights never got dark enough.

When the fires got banked, the stars fell out of the sky onto my closed eyelids, blazing red right through the skin. And I could never think up the cellar and the caverns in it, and the tunnel, long enough to get back the old, good dreams.

The closer we got to where we were going, the harder I worked to dream up Grandma'am's shack. And her roses, though I had yet to spot a real rose and couldn't quite guess what they looked like.

Then one night I woke when Father and Ma'ammy were lovemaking on his spread bearskin, thinking everyone was asleep. I had seen and heard that kind of thing all my life, in snatches of firelight and echoes of throaty sounds.

But this, out in the open and under so much light from all those stars. My mother's skin glowed dark, and she was so open to Father, and he kept sliding into her, like he couldn't get close enough, and how close they wanted to be, alone with each other, made me really wonder about love.

I felt ashamed.

Because I didn't love anyone but Father. And now, watching Ma'ammy and Father in the first black of night, and when the sky was almost breaking into dawn, Aunt Rose Red and Uncle Jim Feather, I could just tell that my kind of love was all wrong.

From that night on, I would kick the mule from my seat behind Grandma'am and make it keep up with Aunt Rose Red and Uncle Jim Feather, walking behind Father.

The first time my mule bobbed up behind them, Uncle Jim Feather jumped and looked at me with his tilted eyes wide. I looked away and ignored him. I still didn't like Aunt Rose Red, either.

But I couldn't get enough of watching people in love.

And I only wanted to be near Father when he wasn't with Ma'ammy. Thinking about them together right now gave me a pain like I hadn't ever felt in my life.

Maybe nothing in my life before had ever really hurt. I used to be happy. Maybe that was the part of me blowing through the caverns that I missed. Or was it hope that I missed?

If I hadn't ever hurt before, maybe I hadn't ever hoped before. Maybe I didn't know how.

I never before wanted anything I didn't already have. That's what hope seemed to be for everybody else. Wanting and then believing in what you wanted.

I didn't believe in anything that began outside our cellar.

The morning dew on the forest floor moss and mulch became morning frost. Now we had to pluck and eat the last of the berries and falling nuts, and forage for neglected tubers on the edge of people's farms, all along our trek, because we would be too cold and weak if we only ate the hot roasted small game around the fires at night. The woods game tasted dry and chewy and too strong. I got full after the first bite of tough game and just wanted berries to get that woodsy taste out of my mouth.

I missed sliding my thumb nail into the shell of something pulled from the swamp, slitting it open from the cooking pot where it tossed in boiling brine, with a puff of fragrant steam in my face and the slick salty insides getting sucked across my tongue. Now I thought that maybe swamp food was like people in love: hard, boiling hot, and slimy, and you can't get close enough.

Flakes of snow started falling at night. We had to sleep huddled even closer to each other and to our fires.

But I stayed away from Father and Ma'ammy so I wouldn't have to hear them making love wrapped in his bearskin, or even see how he looked at her in the firelight and squeezed her close to him. I would wedge myself next to Faith and bring Grandma'am along to lean on my other side.

Faith was usually next to Aunt Rose Red and Uncle Jim Feather and their baby. That suited me just fine.

Willow would giggle and nurse on Aunt Rose Red and slurp on Uncle Jim Feather's fingers when he gave her bits of roasted wild game to try to eat. Aunt Rose Red would play with Willow and smile at her and agree with everything Faith said about how cute she was.

And I would watch Aunt Rose Red and Uncle Jim Feather, past Willow, and wonder what it must be like to have somebody to love who would just be your own, and nobody else's more than yours.

Aunt Rose Red had nothing but smiles around the fire at night, for Uncle Jim Feather, Faith, Willow, and even me, and it was true that she was too beautiful to be real. She had tilted-up dark eyes and a mouth that was thick and all curvy in the middle but tiny and puckery at the sides, and curves and deep places in her cheeks, just like my sisters and Ma'ammy and me. But she had this spark that got lit and glowed in her all the time, like no one I had ever seen before.

When the fire was banked a little for the night, I would curl between Faith and Grandma'am and stare in the sharp kind of light that stars give where it hit Aunt Rose Red through the trees, and wonder why she had the right to be so happy.

367

If I stayed in Grandma'am's shack, would that make me happy, too?

Then the woods grew colder till our bare feet turned bruised purple and blue and cracked from walking on brittle ice, and the trees flowed downhill and spilled out one day onto a cleared field.

And there was a shack with clumps of light snow draped on bright flowers that clung and climbed up its face, wilting and burning from the cold.

Beyond was a field with scattered sharp stalks, dying.

And beyond that were lots of shacks and a giant dirty white house with stones and a few shuttered windows spilling out of it on one side.

We slowed. None of us said anything.

Then all of a sudden Grandma'am jerked awake and cried out, "Rose White! Look! We home again at last, baby!"

Ma'ammy ran with Mercy through the snowed-down grass at our feet, screaming with laughter, toward the shack with the climbing, dying flowers.

People started crying out and running across the field toward the old shacks. Their children looked at each other and started running around just for the fun of it, squealing.

Aunt Rose Red and Uncle Jim Feather followed Ma'ammy to the shack with the dying flowers.

Father just stood in the middle of a snowy patch at the edge of the forest and watched. I sat alone with Grandma'am on our mule, behind him.

I had thought that, when I saw the new place, since I wanted to find my happiness once again here and learn to hope here, it would be something like the cellar. But this big house was whole; it wasn't burned. It wasn't scrubbed with stones and lifted up by tree branches. It didn't open up to your eye with leafy growing things all tangled in it and a part of it.

And these shacks weren't up on stilts, playhouses where children could get away from life and work and snakes on the ground and in the cane fields, almost up in the sky, pretending to fly with the birds. These shacks were flat on the ground and busted open, gaping. They were empty of everything but dust and filth, where dirt floors yawned like dry tongues hanging out.

I looked at Father. He was the only one who seemed to feel like I did. How could I have forgotten how much alike we were?

I was sorry I'd stayed away from him. I wanted to go to him and hold him like I'd seen him hold Ma'ammy by the campfires.

But by the time I slid off the side of the mule, I could hear Grandma'am say, "Hope, baby, lead this mule over to my shack so I can lay down and die easy."

I said, "Grandma'am, you're not dying. You can't die when I just got to your shack," *and it's nothing like I wanted it to be,* I thought. *You have to help me make this turn out all right.*

I ate up my poor father with my eyes as I walked by him, leading the mule.

It was a struggle to get Grandma'am off the mule by myself. I was surprised and relieved when big hands covered mine and lifted Grandma'am past me to the ground.

I looked up and around behind me. It was Father. He didn't look sad anymore. But he wasn't looking at me, either. Grandma'am wasn't steady on her feet, so he carried her inside the shack.

369

Inside was swept and dry. Grandma'am said, "Oh, look how it's been kept up," and Aunt Rose Red said, "Jim Feather and I used to stay here. This was a good home for us, wasn't it, Jim Feather?"

Uncle Jim Feather nodded a little and turned and went out.

Father said, "Shouldn't we go up to the main house and let someone know we're here?"

Ma'ammy sat down in the middle of the floor. "You all go up without me. I'll just stay here a while."

Grandma'am settled down on the floor beside Ma'ammy while Aunt Rose Red started to shake out a straw pallet left in a corner, fussing about how maybe they could get some clean straw in here for a fresh bed before visiting up at the big house. "You and me both will just rest here, baby," Grandma'am said with a lopsided smile at Ma'ammy.

Faith, Justice, and Mercy had their arms spread in the brightest square of light in the shack, where the sunlight fell through the door. They twirled and watched the roof spin over their heads.

Uncle Jim Feather came back in and made his way between them with some kindling in his arms. He and Aunt Rose Red knelt to lay a fire in a spot where stones circled each other and ran right up the wall.

So only Father and I went up to the big house.

As we walked, a few of the people who'd seen to their old shacks-or somebody else's, I suspected-came straggling after us, talking about what a wonder it was to be back home and sniffing like they all had caught cold out here or been crying. Everyone talked at once.

We hadn't gotten quite up to the big house's back door, and Father was still explaining about his sister,

Heaven, who died and left a baby, named Solace, who must be a very grown woman by now, and owner of this place-his niece and my cousin-when a door opened on a pretty house set off by itself with a crowded little garden to one side.

A very young, very tall man came out of this little house. Tall and thin and dark, with short hair in tight curls. Not big and bulky and golden with long ropes of hair, like Father.

So after one quick look, I was through with him.

But I looked back a second time. Because he was staring straight through the whole group of people, right at me.

Father said, "Begging your pardon, son. Isn't this Miss Solace's property?"

The tall young man said, "Yes, sir. Who you all?"

People clustered around behind Father while he explained that he was Miss Solace's uncle, leading what was left of the people back home to her place.

The young man's eyes, already wide open, opened wider. He ran to the back door of the big house and pushed it open and ran inside, shouting, "Miss Solace! Mr. Boy!"

We followed him to where it was dark and yet firelit, inside.

We were all invited to sit by a tall golden woman with her head wrapped in light cloth, whose voice was strong and singing, even though she looked like she might be very old. She hugged Father and wiped her eyes and hugged more of the older people who came around her. She seemed to know all their names and remembered bits and pieces about them, when they were children.

We sat on split logs around a big splintered board Father said was a table. The golden woman started pouring out hot stuff to drink that I could tell was tea, but sweet like cane when you chew it. She told us to call her Mother Magdalen, and she sat down with us to talk to everyone.

They talked a lot. I put my arms on the scratchy wood table thing and rested my head on them, meaning to listen.

When I woke up, there were more people there that I had never seen in my life. The strangers and the people I knew were crying and hugging and slapping each other's backs.

I got up and slipped out of the door to find Grandma'am's shack.

I was halfway across that ugly field with the prickly dead plants that snagged and didn't let you pass, when I realized that somebody was crashing along behind me.

I turned. It was that young man who had let us into the big house.

Now I noticed that he had really good clothes on. Not a rip or tear in sight, and it was the solid shiny shoes on his feet that helped him make all this noise when he walked.

He stopped and smiled. "Hey," he said. "My name Zion. And you?"

I turned again and kept walking. I went into my Grandma'am's shack without another look back behind me.

Grandma'am was stretched out sleeping on Father's bearskin. There was a fire in the stones, just like back up at the big house, and Aunt Rose Red was stuffing nice thick sacks with pine needles and some of that puffy white stuff I'd seen clinging to the stalks in the fields.

Willow was off her mother's back and curled on the doeskin, snoozing like Grandma'am. Aunt Rose Red said, "Jim Feather and some of the men went hunting. If you stay here with your grandma'ammy and Willow, I could go on up to the big house myself and greet Solace and them."

I said, "I'll stay," and sat on the bearskin near Grandma'am. I took her dry thin hand.

She opened her eyes a little in the firelight. "Hope, ain't it? Baby, it be just that good to be back here in my own home. I couldn't ask for nothing more."

Then she closed her eyes and was still again.

I sat with my legs crossed and thought, *So this is it. We gave up the cellar and the swamp for this ugly dry place stuck up above the ground, battered by the wind and that ice they call snow, and we'll have to live with all these strangers. And for what?*

I stared into the fire and couldn't think who I hated more. Aunt Rose Red, for coming along to help lead us out of the swamp? Or Father, for having the idea to bring us back here?

I had never thought that someday I might hate my father. And here it was, all of a sudden.

I hated him. *Why couldn't he have been content in the caverns and the tunnel with what contented me?*

Ma'ammy and my sisters and Father all moved into Grandma'am's shack. I slept with Grandma'am on the bearskin. She never woke up to eat anymore. We had to spoon little sips of stew broth into her mouth while she slept. And Ma'ammy and I had to change and boil rags to catch what little waste her body threw out. In a few weeks, I woke one morning to find Grandma'am dead beside me.

I couldn't be surprised. I couldn't even really be sad.

We buried her next to her shack in the falling snow. Ma'ammy and Father had talked a lot about where to bury her, but finally Ma'ammy insisted that Grandma'am would have wanted to be born again into her roses, clambering up the front of her shack.

We couldn't stay outside long when we buried Grandma'am because some of us still didn't have shoes against the cold. Father and Uncle Jim Feather and Zion and Solace's husband Cousin Boy took turns in the cold shoveling out a hole for Grandma'am to be buried too deeply for wild animals to dig her out.

Then Ma'ammy and Father and Uncle Jim Feather and Aunt Rose Red and I covered over Grandma'am's little body with frozen earth. Mother Magdalen came from the big house and watched in her shawl, standing between Cousin Solace and Cousin Boy.

And Zion. He stood in the snow in his warm clothes and leather shoes and watched.

Me.

He was always at the shack, bringing wood and trying to help fix tools or carve little clog shoes for my sisters. Miss Solace had a rule that nobody was to work in the fields, clearing dead stalks and stones, in the snow and cold.

So everyone spent these winter weeks making doors for their shacks, and clothes from cloth Zion's parents carried from town, and shoes from blocks of wood or heavy leather, and sleeping pallets from sacks full of the stuff that grew here, called cotton, or pine needles combed from the woods. They plugged the cracks in their shacks with mud and dried game meat and cooked stews.

Most people stayed in their own shacks working, and they only visited at midday up at the big house's back room, getting supplies from Mother Magdalen and drinking her real coffee.

But not me.

And not Zion. He would sit in our shack and work on something, talking all the time to Faith or trying to tell riddles and stories that would make Justice laugh.

If they were all up at the big house with Ma'ammy and Father, or pestering Aunt Rose Red and Uncle Jim Feather at their cave shelter out in the woods, trying to learn to hunt, and playing with Willow, then Zion would just sit in the shack with me.

And work. Quietly.

Because I wouldn't talk to him.

I worked, too. I sewed rabbit and squirrel and possum and coon skins together to make a warm bedspread for me and my sisters. Father and Ma'ammy had taken back the bearskin, after Grandma'am died.

We had a big fight over it.

I couldn't stand to think of them together again in that bearskin. And I didn't want to have to live here in this little shack and have to see and hear what they would be doing in it.

I ran into the woods, barefoot in the snow. Everyone knew about it because lots of people had to come look for me.

Uncle Jim Feather was the one who found me freezing on a tree branch. I had climbed it to get my bare feet out of the snow. Uncle Jim Feather motioned me to come down, with his arrows, like he might shoot me.

So I climbed down onto his back, and he carried me to Ma'ammy and Father's shack in disgrace. My father said so. And then he threatened to whip me.

I told him, "You're only talking to impress the people crowded around the shack to see if I am all right and if we have all gone crazy in here together." For Father would never lay a hand on me, and we both knew it. Not to whip me. And not to hug me, either.

And never to ask me if I needed anything from him.

Ma'ammy cried and asked me, with her arms around me, "Why can't you feel better here, Hope, with all your family around you? You loved your grandma'am, and it was her dream to come back home."

Faith started crying with Ma'ammy. That made Justice and Mercy cry. And I started thinking how nice it would be if I could cry, too.

Zion came the next day with clogs he said he had stayed up all night to whittle for me. I handed them to Ma'ammy and said, "They're full of splinters, and I won't wear them."

Truthfully, I had nowhere to go. I wouldn't run away again, or Uncle Jim Feather really might shoot me this time. And I wouldn't go to the big house, nor to Aunt Rose Red and Uncle Jim Feather's cave. So I didn't need Zion's splintery clogs.

He left them, but he came back every day and worked on them until my ma'ammy promised him that they were nice and smooth as silk inside, and he could stop now.

And still he came every day and stayed until suppertime, carving bowls and spoons and dolls for all my sisters and me. And even then, he would stay and eat with us, too, if Ma'ammy remembered to invite him before she started spooning up the stew. Nobody even thought to ask him to leave when they knew they were leaving me alone in the shack with him.

It got so that whenever Zion's mother and father wanted him for anything, the first place they would come was our shack, calling me "Miss Hope" and asking me before anybody else how I was doing.

My parents didn't even stop Zion when he asked me to come dance with him up at the big house.

Folks were celebrating that the snow had stopped and some lawman named Shave Me or something hadn't come calling on Miss Solace for a solid month. It sounded stupid, and I didn't go.

I made Faith wear my clogs and lie and say she had outgrown hers, so I couldn't be expected to go.

Zion came and sat with me in the shack and looked sad. He asked me if I needed him to teach me to dance because my ma'ammy had said maybe that was why I wouldn't go to the celebration. I hadn't ever danced. I was just like my father that way.

I didn't answer Zion. I ignored him, no matter what.

Until he brought me a rose.

It was past the end of winter. I had worked on my fur quilt all that time. My sisters and I had been sleeping under it at night, but during the day I still sewed new skins onto it, if I could scavenge cured bits and pieces Ma'ammy and other women had left over from skinning game.

The sun was out. I had seen it whenever anyone opened the door to go out and join the other people in the field, clearing and singing and laughing, like a cotton field could make anybody happy.

When I got through sewing skins onto my fur quilt that day, I was going to start carving out more stew bowls and supper spoons so I wouldn't ever have to use Zion's. Or if I could get any time alone, I might try again to see if I could learn to carve little dolls for my sisters, so they would never again have to play with the ones Zion carved them. I still couldn't get all those little curves without cutting off their arms or heads.

But no matter what, I wasn't going out into those fields with all that silly singing unless Father came home and made a fool of himself again, yelling at me.

But when the door creaked open, of course it wasn't Father, back for me to show him he couldn't make me do anything, anymore. It was the pest, Zion, calling softly, "Miss Hope? Miss Hope, can I give you something?"

I looked up to tell him of course not and go away.

But there in the little bit of sunlight in the doorway, I could see in Zion's hand a rose.

Not dying like the ones here on Grandma'am's shack when we spilled here out of the woods.

It was deep red and still mostly closed up. But the curly little tender edges were full of color and leaning out, like they wanted to open.

I put down my sharp wooden needle and twine thread to take the rose in my own hand.

And just like that. I started crying.

I didn't know why, and I didn't know how it started. So I couldn't stop it.

Zion sat on the stuffed sack next to me and reached out and put both of his arms around my shoulders. He pulled me to him and tucked my forehead into his neck. My tears ran right down inside his nice shirt.

It seemed like we were there forever before hiccups finally broke up my crying.

Zion got up to get me some fresh water and pinch my nose while I drank it, to stop them. I ended up gagging and spraying him with water because I needed to breathe. He should have been angry. I would have been, if one of my sisters had done that to me. But he wasn't.

He laughed and asked me if I felt better.

If he had asked why I was crying, I never would have told him. But he didn't. So I opened up and told him everything.

I told him about how wonderful the cool dark was under my father's ruined mansion where the burned pillars stood draped with growing moss.

I told him about the echoes in the caverns that were my good dreams waiting for me throughout the day, while I was outside working or playing.

I told him about the salty swamp food that felt tender on your tongue, and about the heavy rains and the howling storms that passed us by with sounds that echoed deep down in our cellar, and how the floors would shift and resettle in deep wet pockets afterwards.

About the campfires scattered along the cellar walls, and how when you ran around the twists and turns of the tunnels, you'd visit at fires where different smells and voices drifted up in the moist dark and welcomed you.

And about how, when I followed my father alone at night, I could hear the quiet drip of the damp off the tunnel walls and feel safe.

I told him how alone I felt, out here where snow fell and everyone could see your house, which was nothing but dead wood standing alone and thin between a field and a forest.

I told him I would never be safe again.

When I was all done telling why I was crying, Zion said, "But Hope. I know a place right here just like what you left back there under the ground."

I frowned at him.

He said, "Well, almost just like that. I been in there with my own ma'am and pap many times. Come on, Miss Hope. You just got to see it for yourself."

He stood and took my hand that didn't have the rose.

We went across the field like that, holding hands and carrying what he called the rose bud, right past all the people working.

Father and Ma'ammy turned to stare. And I saw Father out of the corner of my eye grab Ma'ammy's arm when she would have followed. For the first time ever, I felt all right that they were leaving me so alone.

Zion and I went past the little brick house where he stayed with his parents, and his mother called through the open door, "Well, good morning to you, Miss Hope. How do today, baby?"

"Fine, Miss Vivian," I called. But before I finished with, "And you?" her son had pulled me through the big house's back door.

We went into the back room without even knocking. We were breathing hard from the rush by this time. I pulled back, in the dark and the firelight of the back room.

Cousin Solace was at the table, braiding her daughter Joy's hair. Mother Magdalen was at the fire, stirring something in a pot.

You could smell the fresh sharp scent of vegetables stewing out their juices and a steeping pot of that coffee that all the grownups loved to talk about, tangy and bittersweet, and the full nutty scent of fire-roasted cornbread, which my ma'ammy had taken to frying on the cooking stones for us, too, my sisters loved so to fill up on it.

Zion said, "Morning, Miss Solace. Mother Magdalen. Little Miss Joy. You all, excuse us. I got to show Miss Hope here how it be rooms right here could make her feel right to home. Just like her pappy's place they done left behind. Can I take her to the stone rooms, Miss Solace, ma'am?"

Miss Solace rose, put her daughter down and turned so you could see where a new baby was tied onto her back. "Mother Magdalen, are those rooms unlocked?" she said as Zion took off, tugging me behind him.

From the back room, we came into a dark hallway. From there, Zion pulled me toward a stone hallway, off to one side.

It was as if he had pulled me through the woods and plains and swamps back to the caverns where I'd been born and raised. I stumbled after him, astonished.

Zion said, "You go'n love this, Miss Hope. I just know you will. It sound just like your pap's cellar. I used to lay here at night with my ma'am and pap, and when you talked about that cellar, it was like you was talking about this place."

The stone hallway had risen over us and around us and swallowed us down into its comforting dark where quiet whispers of water on rocks reached us from faraway, unseen. Zion panted, but around all that noise, the further down the dark hallway we went, the cooler and quieter it got, and the more it echoed vanishing sounds of long ago.

He was happy about bringing me here. His happiness was catching.

I couldn't see Zion ahead of me but I felt that he held my hand and pulled me into the deepest belly of the blackness. When we stopped, the silence rushed around us with soft echoes of itself, as if my cellar and tunnel dreams had caught up with us on beating wings.

Or had they been here all along, waiting for me to come and find them, like in the old days, as a child, I came down to the cellar with the setting sun?

Softness touched me. I was all right. I was going to be all right. I threw my arms around Zion's neck and hugged him close.

In the dark, I felt his lips on my cheeks, first one, and then the other, leaving them moist with the kind of kisses I saw grown ups give each other at the campfires.

A circle of firelight came toward us now. Miss Solace with Baby Joy, Mother Magdalen, and even Miss Vivian were all in the doorway of the room Zion had rushed me into. The women carried candles shielded with their free hands, and by the candlelight you could see that the women all smiled.

I said, "Cousin Solace, can I stay in this room? These rooms? And never have to come out but to work in the fields, if you want me to?"

Cousin Solace said, "Why, Hope, darling. Of course you can have these rooms. And you don't have to leave them, ever, if they make you feel secure. I'm sure we can find enough useful work for you to do right in here, honey."

I hugged Zion again. He started in again with those kisses. And Miss Vivian said, "Do this mean you accept my boy, Miss Hope?"

I looked at the women again. Zion held me tighter.

I said, "Accept him?"

Cousin Solace said, "Ever since you came here, dear, Zion's been asking his parents and yours, and even my husband and me, if he can marry you. Do you think, Hope, that you might accept him? I know marriage was my dream when I was-"

But I didn't hear what else she said because I was suddenly thinking what it might feel like to have someone who was my own. I turned to look at Zion.

He kissed me.

On my mouth. Deep. Like he was sliding into me and looking for something in my feelings where no one else could find it.

And I was holding on, and the next thing I could hear was Mother Magdalen voice: "Sometimes, people just need a new beginning."

And hope, I thought, trying out what it was like to kiss Zion back.

It felt good to want something again. To feel what it might be like to look forward, to be held, and to want something that, after all, maybe I could have.

## THE END OF VOLUME THREE